**Book of Yeshua**

Chronicle of Our Spirit vol iii

with annotations

according to Randy

Copyright © 2025 Randy Scannell

All rights reserved. No part of this publication may be produced, distributed, or transmitted in any form or by any means, including photocopy, recording or other electronic or mechanical methods without prior written permission by the publisher, except in the case of brief quotations embedded in critical reviews and certain other noncommercial uses permitted by copyright law. For permission requests, please contact the publisher.

No part of this book may be used or reproduced in any matter for the purpose of training artificial intelligence technologies or systems without consent from the author.

ISBN: 979-8-9937490-1-3

Front cover designed by Randy and produced by AI

Reconstructing Press
Green Bay, Wisconsin

I wish to thank Scott Baron and Kevin Welch who gave me invaluable feedback, Lynn Gerlach of Tamarack Communication who provided helpful review with editorial advice. And ever & always, my loving wife Rose.

Table of Contents

A Word Please	**5**
Our Spirit	**6**
Our Spirit with Yohanan	**8**
Lamentation	**175**
Our Spirit	**246**
Appendix	**249**

- Final note
- First depiction of Yeshua
- First venerable picture of Yeshua
- Rendering of Herod's Temple
- Map

Por favor (an author's plea)   **254**

A Word Please

This book is modeled after the Bible, Gnostic writings, and Dead Sea Scrolls. Beginning with Chapter I, verse numbers have been added to the narrative. If a chapter has notes, each note will correspond with a verse number. The original manuscripts I am modeling this book after do not contain verse numbers or chapters. For the Bible, these features were added over time by three different people. Stephen Langton, around 1200, divided the Bible into the chapters we use today. In 1551, Robert Estienne added verse numbers to the New Testament. Joseph Athias added them to the Old Testament in 1661. Some Gnostic translations do not use verse numbers. Others have had them added.

Though chronologically the third of a projected six volume series, the *Book of Yeshua* is the first book to see the light of print. Conceived thematically as a group, each volume can stand on its own.

Our Spirit

Herein is the New Way
revealed through Holy Breath borne
by children of God
and children of humanity,
voices lost and found in wilderness
to live in Our Spirit.

0 In death our bodies free up our atoms, an offering back to the universe. Yet, while the wastes of sentience persist as stardust in elemental fellowship, the effects our lives had on one another lives on. Just as a person develops and learns and changes throughout their lifetime, so too our beliefs, passed from generation to generation, foster revolutions in our culture. Past lives, as spiritual flames, fire in our minds, and still rove to labor for good and ill among us. Ancestral footprints still impress. Our understanding continues to evolve.

One such spiritual flame is Our Spirit.

Long roamed Our Spirit, unnamed and unpronounced, until Zarathustra proclaimed and promulgated us as Spenta Mainyu, the holy-creative force. The captive Jews in Babylon learned about Spenta Mainyu and recognized Our Spirit as the Breath of God or Holy Breath. It is the Holy Breath upon which the Christian faith rests.

Enchanting air with warmth, Our Spirit rejoices with bonding atoms, sings among swirling gatherings of leaves, glides under feet, settles as a crown on many heads, and seeps into their minds, possessing them. Our Spirit cycles within and outside of our person. The life of Our Spirit fills a long history abounding with many lives in many different times and places. Of the many lives several stand out as exalted and agitating, representative figures. The Book of Yeshua is one chapter in the long and ongoing story of Our Spirit.

Time spins, a gyroscope measured by our minds stretching straight, bending, spiraling in several directions at once, bursting into a mist. The narrative of Yeshua is set in a time when many Gods had already disappeared into temple ruins or metamorphosed into new deities; a time when the great pyramids of Giza already climbed the Egyptian sky for well over 2,000 years–

4,000 since the first Sumerian ziggurat–and most memories had forgotten hundreds of great kingdoms now in ruins buried with age and earth. A time when Gods, some idolized as sky and land and sea, reigned. A time when the mysteries of life were answered, despite or even within the observational & mathematical reasoning of Greek philosophy, as spirits and Gods who possessed rocks and bodies of water, trees and lives, so that healing for most involved magical exorcism or divine intervention. Even numbers danced with spiritual power in many minds of the men who used them.

The homeland of Yeshua belongs to Yahweh, an omnipotent deity. Ruled for a few hundred years by Jewish kings anointed by their God–and therefore each one a Son of God–this strip of land, bordering the Great (Mediterranean) Sea to the west and the Great Rift Valley to the east, served as a land bridge to the magnificent Egyptians in the south and several great empires to the north. A terrain partially conquered by Assyrians, then totally subdued by Babylonians–who destroyed Solomon's Temple–followed by Persians, then Greeks, and, after a brief period of independence, the Romans. With each empire larger than the last, as humanity aged, the capacity to subjugate people prospered. Yahweh, according to his followers, had promised this portion of the world to the twelve tribes of Abraham as their home, a garden overflowing with milk and honey. Prosperity, there as everywhere, did not flow evenly and great disparities in wealth thrived. But for the Jews, a covenant with God is no trifle and sealed, even now, by every male ritually pledging his foreskin.

Yeshua lived during the "Pax Romana" and for many who accepted Roman rule the appellation of "Roman Peace" held much truth. For most of the followers of Yahweh, a people barely at peace with themselves, the Pax Romana meant little. The Romans needed to suppress riots, rebellions, and eventually fought two wars–destroying Herod's Temple during the first one–before pacifying the followers of Yahweh into accepting Roman jurisdiction and paying them tribute.

For two hundred years before Yeshua, three ways, three philosophies rambled, up and down and to and fro on the land covenanted to the tribes of Abraham; each way crystallized in minds like prisms. Sharing much, these differences cut sharp edges. Embodied in flesh they formed into identifiable sects: Sadducees, Pharisees, and Essenes. They quarreled with each other often. The bones of their thoughts carried a bulk of righteous muscle and the fat satisfactions of believing *their* way to be *the* way.

Then the New Way, the zealous and revolutionary way of Our Spirit, stumbled into the fold. We remember when the Holy Breath entered the sweating grunting agony of a body; a mother gave birth to the wail of a child. The Breath of God bided time until the child became a man.

***** ************ *****

Notes: *Zarathustra:* At least 500 years before the birth of Yeshua, Zarathustra–a Persian prophet commonly known from Greek translations into English as Zoroaster–started the religious movement bearing his name. There are 120,000 adherents practicing Zoroastrianism today. *Breath of God/Holy Breath*: The Latin word for breath is *spiritus*. At this point in history, the words "spirit," "ghost," and "soul" in their modern senses had yet to be invented. The words "breath" or "shade" were used to denote a vital essence. *Yeshua*: This is the Aramaic name that, when rendered from Greek into English, becomes "Jesus." Aramaic was the common spoken language of the region. Literate Jews wrote mostly in Aramaic or Hebrew. Other people wrote mostly in Greek or Latin. *Solomon's Temple* was later also known as the First Temple. *Herod's Temple* was later also known as the Second Temple. The Western Wall (or Wailing Wall) is all that's left of them.

Our Spirit with Yohanan

1 Yohanan stepped into Qumran. The distant sun, humbled by winter, rolled through the wet air of dawn, grabbed the grayness of clouds, and smeared the drab color with chilled fingertips on this settlement near the Dead Sea in the Judean Desert. 2 The Essenes lived in reclusive corners of many villages and cities, but in Qumran their exclusive community formed its own, mostly male, ascetic village. 3 Yohanan and his childhood friend, Amos, paced to and fro in the Breath of God. They had left Bethlehem together and roamed about for some time before settling on Qumran.

4 A few years earlier, Yohanan, then full of youth, Caiaphas, a middle-aged priest, and Zechariah, also a priest and the very old father of Yohanan, had argued in a dimly lit room. "Judah and Zadok were damn fools!" [5] The mature voice of Caiaphas filled the whole house. The old head of Zechariah nodded approvingly. "Their rebellion accomplished nothing. All their poor, foolish followers crucified! I can still smell their rotting corpses. For what?" [6] "To kill Romans! To sweep our land free of their defiling feet dancing naked and clear our air of the smoke from their blasphemous sacrifices," the youth shot back. The old head of his father shook with a frown.

7 "You are young, Yohanan. And rash. Consider," Caiaphas cautioned while raising a finger, "your words carefully. [8] The madness of their rebellion risked everything. The remodeling of the Temple is still freshly gleaming. A war brings destruction on all our heads and will no doubt raze the Temple of Herod." [9] "If they were mad, let me be mad," the words of the youth flew as a crazed froth from his mouth. "Let the Temple be battered to a pile of rubble!" The two priests gasped. [10] The youth, with flailing arms, continued, "Judah the Galilean was a great leader, Zadok the Pharisee a great man. Better to die serving God than to live servile under a Roman boot! [11] If the Temple of Herod is ruined in gaining our freedom, then it is ruined. We can always build a third Temple." [12] Two faces, wide with experience, as one looked down at the youth; their lips full of disdain. Old eyes stared at his child as if his son already hung on a cross as a mass of bloody flesh.

13 Caiaphas spoke, his words spilling like a broken string of pearls: "Soon you will be ready to follow the footsteps of your father into the priesthood. We are the bulwark of tradition. [14] Without us, without the Temple of Herod, we crumble as a people like a weak foundation. The wrath of God will be upon us."

15 "The wrath of God is upon us! Are not the Romans a pestilence sent from God?" Yohanan shouted in a whisper as his arms shot out wildly. [16] "Perhaps so," Caiaphas replied, "but if so, that sin does not lie on our shoulders. God has appointed us as priests to lead his people to righteousness." [17] An open space of air filled the room. Caiaphas broke the silence, "Take a little time to consider your life..." [18] The youth scoffed–a sound that vocalized no word, but spoke volumes. Tradition! Time! Time was wasting. [19] Back and forth words flew like stones–smashing into heads or shooting completely past them to fly out the window as angry birds–until the youth stomped out of the room.

20 In the dim light, Caiaphas put his hand on the shoulder of the old man, "I shall speak further with him. He is young. Give him a little space. I will speak with him again." [21] The father nodded, appreciating the efforts of Caiaphas, but rightly worried further words will only buzz like annoying flies to a youth dying for action to serve God and save his country. [22] So began the journey that led Yohanan to refuse the priesthood and leave home. He and his childhood companion wandered until, ushered in with the chill of the season, Qumran opened its arms to them.

23 Yohanan and Amos doffed their clothes. In true Essene fashion, from loincloth to their long robe, they wore nothing but white garments. [24] Unfortunately for Amos, the purity of white can be difficult to maintain for the clumsy and absent minded. Constantly, and always accompanied with a grunt, he washed his tunic and robe. [25] The two settled easily into communal living–mostly. Rising and walking away with full stomachs from a table laid with bowls of dates, olives, apples, and boiled lentils with herbs sitting next to loaves of millet bread and sweet cakes amidst cups of amber wine cut with water, [26] Amos grumbled into the right ear of Yohanan, "We have resided here for a week now and they

serve no meat. No flank of lamb, no side of beef, no fowl or fish ever graced our table or satisfied growls of my hunger!" [27] Yohanan grinned at the beady eyes piercing from the black, bushy, furrowed brows of his friend, "We do not murder animals. I thought you knew that." [28] With rolls of distant thunder in his voice, Amos muttered, "I knew about sacrifices. Slaughtering animals as a prayer to God *is* an abomination. You said nothing about meals!" [29] Yohanan flashed his toothy smile at his friend, patting his back and then putting a comforting arm around his shoulder. Playfully, Amos dug his elbow into the ribs of his friend. [30] Hand in hand they hurried to sit at the feet of their rabbi to learn new prayers, rituals, and deeper understanding of the Essene way.

[31] As volunteers to help teach the children, Amos and Yohanan quietly sat on the floor to the right of Balaam. The rabbi, aged with wisdom, looked over at the young boys sitting in front of him, many of them adopted from outside the community. [32] He put his stubby finger to his lips, hidden in a brown-and-white-streaked beard that hung down to his chest. A swan of silence sailed around the room. [33] "If someone is in need of a robe, do we provide them with a robe?" The sagacious Balaam surveyed his disciples. Zev, a precocious six year old, stood up. Balaam nodded. [34] The boy replied with an enthusiastic affirmative. The younger boys giggled; the older boys perked up. [35] Their teacher smiled. "Do you, your parents, or anyone own the home you live in?" "No!" a chorus of young voices affirmed. [36] Their rabbi smiled, raised his open right hand, and then pointed to his temple with his finger. The children placed their hands over their mouths and grinned at each other. [37] "Do we own our camels, our goats, our animals?" Three older boys stood up. Balaam nodded toward one, and he answered negatively while shaking his head. [38] "Who owns them?" The children stared at him. "No, no one?" Their eyes

looked down. No one stood up.

39 Balaam turned his head to his right. Yohanan, drumming his fingers against his knees as his body gently rocked back and forth from the waist, immediately nodded his head. Balaam nodded back. [40] Yohanan jumped up, "The animals belong to God. We attend to them. They are our responsibility." [41] Balaam turned toward the children. "And what of people? Do we own people as slaves?" "Nooo! Uh-uh. Of course not. No," the boys chimed solemnly, wagging their heads in disbelief and horror. [42] During the response, two boys turned to their classmates while placing a finger to their lips, to no avail. Balaam smiled and reminded his eager students they needed to stand and be called on to answer.

43 "Who remembers what the Sayings of Agur tell us about riches?" "Uhs" slipped from a few minds and out through their throats. The young faces looked at one another or stared into the floor as if digging a hole with their eyes. Silence.

[44] Balaam turned his head to his right. Quickly, Yohanan nodded. Balaam nodded back. [45] "Keep falsehood and lies far from me; give me neither poverty nor riches, but give me only my daily bread." [46] "Yes," Balaam nodded and then commanded, "Let us all repeat it." They repeated it three times. [47] "I want you all to say this verse to yourself every night before you sleep," their rabbi said firmly, emphasizing his command with fire in his eyes, "and repeat it again in the morning when you rise."

48 And so it went for a couple of hours, after which the children left. They still had other lives full of play and chores. [49] Yohanan and Amos stayed until midday, listening to Balaam read and discuss holy scriptures. Then they too had other duties to perform.

50 What their teacher left unquestioned was what every follower of Yahweh, male or female, knew practically from birth. [51] Abraham, the progenitor of twelve tribes, had long ago claimed this strip of land as their own. The Jews

battled long and mightily with the local population. ⁵² When the Pharaoh carried them off and held them in bondage, Moses, the lawgiver, freed them from captivity in Egypt. Yehoshua conquered the promised land, and King David ruled it magnificently as the United Kingdom of Israel. ⁵³ In what seemed a heartbeat, foreign armies made them slaves in their own country. The latest boot on their neck belonged to Rome.

54 What everyone yearned to know was why the face of God turned sideways from his people. What sin holds them in bondage? ⁵⁵ Who will save them? Which is the way of a righteous life?

Notes: 1:1 Yohanan, (translated as John from Hebrew into Greek, then Latin, and finally English), means "God is gracious." **1:2** Amos means "to carry." **1:4** Judah the Galilean and Zadok the Pharisee led a rebellion against the Roman census taken for tax purposes. Judah claimed Messiahship and all too easily stormed Tzipori, the capital city of Galilee. The royal arsenal provided the rebels with more arms than they could wisely wield. Judah proved to be one of several failed messiahs. Rome quickly quashed the uprising and crucified thousands of the insurgents. **1:22** For Yusef Caiaphaas, his journey led to an elevated position. A few years after this conversation, Valerius Gratus, the fourth Prefect governing the Roman province of Judaea, and in accordance with the civil authority's prerogative, appointed Caiaphas as high priest. He held the office for eighteen years. The aged parents of Yohanan died shortly after he left them. **1:31** Balaam means "the ancient of the people." Rabbi means "teacher" or "master." Besides offspring from marriages, a number of Jewish children were adopted by Essene men who practiced celibacy. **1:33** Disciple comes from the Latin *discipulus* which means "student." Some boys from the ages of six to ten received an education. Schooling focused on religion. Writing and especially arithmetic possessed little value while copying and, particularly, memorization were appreciated skills. Other boys worked in apprenticeships. Girls learned housekeeping from their mothers. The literacy rate has been estimated at 3% for an exclusively male Jewish population and 15% overall for everyone within the Roman Empire. In 2023, the literacy rate worldwide reached 90% for men and 82.7% for women. **1:45** Proverbs 30:8, New International Version (NIV). The Proverbs were not enumerated by chapter and verse at this time. In Yeshua's day, they tumbled one after the other on a scroll. Ancient Jewish scholars did recognize that the collection contained internal divisions, one of them being the Sayings of Agur. **1:50** Yahweh means, "I am that I am" or "I will be what I will be" and some also interpret it as "He who brings into existence whatever exists." The history of the Jews is filled with the struggle between the belief that all of existence stems from their God against the constant corrupting influence of polytheism. **1:52** Yehoshua translated from the Greek is Joshua and means "God is deliverance." **1:53** The Assyrian Sargon II conquered the northern Kingdom of Israel. A hundred years later Nebuchadnezzar II conquered Assyria and then the southern Kingdom of Judea, exiling many thousands of Jews to water the rivers of Babylon with their tears. The Babylonians submitted to the Persians, who allowed exiled Jews to return home; the Greeks defeated the Persians. With the support of Rome, the Hasmonaean (House of Maccabees) revolt against the Greeks (House of Seleucids) reestablished Jewish control over their entire homeland as the Kingdom of Judea. Aided by the growing influence of Rome, Herod I, an Edomite whose ancestors converted to Judaism, supplanted the Maccabean king Antigonus II Mattathias. After the kingship of Herod I, Rome, under its first emperor, Augustus, divided the kingdom into districts and decided who ruled, requiring only that they be competent (maintain order and pay their tribute) and loyal to Caesar.

2 Purified from his immersion in ritual washing, Yohanan emerged from his bath. Filling another cistern of collected rainwater like a grain of sand lost in a large jar, Amos finished up his prayers and sat quietly in calm waves of meditation with a smile hidden in his mouth. ² Like every Essene, each morning they muttered their daily confession before ceremoniously cleansing their physical and spiritual pollution to replenish their strength.

3 "I did not realize how busy our days would be," Amos said as he stepped from his ablution. Yohanan nodded. Throwing back his shoulders Amos continued, 4 "I dreamed about the War Scroll last night. 5 Messengers wearing Persian caps with Urim and Thummim-studded diadems charged on magnificent steeds. They wielded spears of righteous fire; their chariots smashed the Infernal Sons. 6 Their evil messengers, armed with smoldering swords, also lay in the dust. Righteousness walked the earth unfettered." 7 Exhilarating pins danced on their skin as Amos paused. Sharp edges of inner light pressed their eyelids down tight. 8 Yohanan sighed, opened his eyes to gaze admiringly at his friend, and with a toothy smile remarked with the sweets of approval, "Truly, you are a Celestial Son."

9 "Do you believe many outside our community are Infernal Sons?" Amos asked as he stepped out of the cistern.

10 "What else can they be?" his earnest friend exclaimed, thrusting his arms out and raising the skin of his forehead into wrinkles. 11 "Some willfully slumber or doggedly persist in corruption or kiss the filthy foot," he sneered, "of the Most Honorable Caesar." 12 He flung his hands up into the air as he spat out the words choking in his throat, "Make blood offerings! Sit at a feast while their neighbor sits in hunger!" 13 Yohanan gathered his fiery breath, "The Light shines at their feet. If they walk away to wander in the shadows, they are lost to evil ways." 14 "Well, yes but..." Amos began. Yohanan interrupted him, mercifully cutting off his troubled thought like a diseased limb. 15 "Some will remain stubborn beasts, but few. Most will be with us on that glorious day. Blind now, they will see. 16 Our families and friends...and no doubt" he added, flashing his toothy smile, "even a Sadducee or two will see wisdom through our light and join us."

17 Amos asked, "Do you think it will happen?

In our lifetime, I mean?" A shrug of the shoulders answered him. [18] A moment dried in the air before Yohanan replied, stretching his arms wide, "I believe so, but if we die before, if our shades whisper through the lips of Death to wander as our reward in the lush gardens of paradise..." [19] Thrusting his right forefinger down, he emphasized, "As Celestial Sons, we *will* return to flesh for the final battle." [20] He added, with the curve of a smile so wide Amos slid into it and could not free himself, "I am sure of it." [21] Setting his jaw in affirmation, Amos nodded before saying, "I will pray for the end time, for our golden age, a new kingdom to come. Come when it will. The will of God be done." [22] Dressed, they clasped hands and walked off with steady steps to join their brethren for breakfast.

Notes: 2:4 Fragments of the War Scroll, the Hebrew Scriptures, a Manual of Discipline (or Community Rule), and a prayer book for the Essene community have been discovered and published as the Dead Sea Scrolls. **2:5** The Hebrew word for angel is "messenger." Urim and Thummim, roughly meaning "cursed" and "faultless," rolled as sacred stones used by priests to divine the will of Yahweh. **2:11** Roman emperors at this time were addressed as Caesar, Most Notable Caesar, or their given name. "King" as a title was despised by Romans who overthrew the tyranny of their monarchy to rule themselves as a republic. As republican Rome prospered, power struggles ensued. Civil war ravaged and tore at them. Julius Caesar lay lifeless with twenty-three stab wounds because his assassins presumed he intended to resume and assume kingship. When Octavian, the maternal nephew and adopted son of Caesar, finally restored order, negotiations with the Roman senate concluded in his acquiring several powerful offices for life. The senate also acknowledged him as Augustus in recognition of his new status. His official title became *Imperator Caesar Divi Filius Augustus*, "Commander Caesar, Venerable Son of Divinity."

---

3 Yohanan left Qumran. [2] When the vacancy of a curator to their affairs offered itself, the position called to him, and the willful restlessness of his pampered youth filled his thoughts and directed his limbs. 3 Yohanan raised himself up as a candidate. Visions of leadership dictated the footloose ways of his breath.

4 Astonishment to all! Yohanan took a novel interest in animals. He examined the teeth of camels and the hooves of goats while scratching them behind their ears. Methods by which they might be made more comfortable and productive became topics of discussion. 5 Walking from dwelling to dwelling, Yohanan listened to concerns such as, "The well could use a bigger pot!" 6 He owned up to suggestions: "On a sunny day you shake as a tree in a storm. Stand still!"

7 On the day of the vote, each contender addressed the gathered electors. Yohanan stepped up to speak first. "I am honored to be here among you." 8 The light morning air turned heavy with his voice. "The Breath of God lives in me. As a dove, the grace of the Holy Breath rests on my shoulders. The secrets of our way sit on my tongue as a stone of fire. 9 To those with a stiff neck and hard head, I speak in parables and offer the riddle. Their foolishness keeps them from learning the eternal mysteries; 10 only we Essenes know true wisdom. We lead simple lives. For us, existence is an exercise in benevolence. 11 Our voices grow in the wilderness." Smooth tones slipped off the tongue of Yohanan and covered his words. "Our bodies stand purified and ready for the Day of Revenge.

12 "I am the son of a priest. That we are as holy as priests is obvious to me. We sit with messengers; we walk with messengers; we rest and rise with divine messengers. 13 We know in the days of Enoch that Shemyaza, the Devil of devils, and the watchers saw and lusted after the loveliness God gave women. Seducing them, the unnatural union produced the Nephilim. 14 Corruption and murder, under the smiles of the watchers, followed the giants wherever they set their foot.

15 "God, with infinite mercy, sent the Holy Breath to whisper into the ear of Enoch, filling him with a dream." Yohanan momentarily shut his eyes to close in on the ecstasy within him. [16] He observed his audience before continuing, "A star, and then many stars fell to the ground. The stars on their knees grazed and fornicated with animals. The cows of this perverse intercourse bore asses, camels, and elephants. [17] Enoch shared his dream from God with Ohya and Hahyah, the ill-begotten sons of Shemyaza, to take the warning of God to their brethren so they may repent and make their way clean.

18 "The Nephilim did not tremble at the dream of Enoch. They raised up their pride, like a strutting peacock, and swaggered in error." The voice of Yohanan stomped like the feet of an army marching across stone pavement. "Arguing among themselves, they warred one against the other. [19] The world degenerated into such wickedness, God sent the rains of His wrath to flood the earth, leaving only Noah and his ark to regenerate His creation. [20] After fallen messengers watched their progeny destroy themselves, God commanded Gabriel to bind and cast the watchers into the valleys for seventy generations. [21] At the end of that time, they shall be judged. God will again arm His messengers. The stiff-necked and hard-headed, and the worshipers of idols shall then know our rule. [22] The days of tribulation shall pass into oblivion. The vision of God will be restored."

23 Yohanan spoke on, describing the community to the community, until he concluded, "I give thanks for immersing me and my good friend," Yohanan pointed to Amos, "into your company. [24] I desire with my every breath to give back what I have been given and lead this community until the imminent Day of Revenge. [25] May God bless you. May you live in the Breath of God."

26 His fellow contender exhorted for as long as the flight of a bird from Qumran to Jerusalem. The dry desert air

filled with a righteous wing soaring with the expectations, the needs, and the rewards of their community. [27] Through air as warm as a lizard on a rock, Balaam ended with a prayer, "God Almighty, your majesty precedes us. Your holiness shines over land and sea from one generation to the next. [28] Grace and truth flow from our Lord like the rush of many waters. Our Lord makes Justice the foundation of the world. [29] We join the messengers in singing praises to God Almighty, whose knowledge we catch a glimmer of in the dawn, the light of understanding stretching from heaven." [30] Yohanan stood as a jar holding a swirling pool of water while his competitor spoke. When the men voted–smooth stones for him, marked stones for his opponent–there was no need to count. When separated into groups, the stones of the winner piled high.

[31] A voiceless raven of despair perched on a rainbow of hope within Yohanan. [32] He knew a mission from God awaited him, but if not to lead the Essenes in Qumran, then what? [33] A voiceless raven shredded his rainbow within him into a conflagration of smoke that clouded his vision, [34] but, like a good Essene, he walked the demon into a pool of peace. The bleeding shards of his ambition he swallowed with difficulty but sincerity. [35] Yet a raw and itchy restlessness festered in him and would not let him be. He paced to and fro in the Breath of God. The Essenes failed to teach him the serenity of calm water. [36] So, he needed to go. Donning their old clothes, Yohanan and a handful of supporters journeyed to find answers in the desert. [37] Our dove left him and circled high above his head. Shemyaza sat on his shoulders and grinned.

[38] For forty glaring days, Yohanan prayed and fasted. For forty restless nights, he walked up and down his dreams. His demons filled the air and buzzed all around him. [39] Sin beat him with fiery sticks of sun. Had he transgressed? Were his ambitions holy or selfish? Did a strutting peacock hang around his

neck so the mouths of all those with eyes to see it, mocked him? Was this his Tzipori? [40] He prayed in the desert like smoldering wreckage. What does Yahweh want of him? [41] As long as his country is a nation of sinners, the face of God will never shine on them. What can he do to free the land of Yahweh from sin? [42] His supporters prayed with him. Amos, his steadfast companion, tended closely to the needs of his friend. [43] At the end of a day of fasting, Amos laid out a small portion of food and drink for Yohanan. At night, he covered him with a blanket.

44 With no answer to the fever of Yohanan in a wilderness blazing with heat or chilled by hidden light, Amos led his friend to the River Jordan. [45] In the fellowship of Andreas, his brother Simon, and one other, they immersed their troubles in flowing water free of the heat of sun and grit of sin. A fresh plunge swooshed around them. [46] Our Spirit swirled and buoyed their limbs and minds. Wet with purification, they sat calmly at the edge of the Jordan.

47 A goatherder, Samuel, clutching his torn and mended robe, watched their ritual bathing. He approached the men fresh from the desert. [48] In conversation, step by step, Yohanan revealed a way of redemption to the goatherder. [49] Samuel bowed before Yohanan. Sin, snorting like a bull with serpents for horns, lay heavy on his shoulders. What could he do? [50] His head banged against Mount Hod Akev. When might he travel to the Temple to offer a sacrifice and absolve his sin? [51] In the fresh waters of the Jordan, Yohanan baptized the contrite sinner and sent him on his way. Samuel reveled in the heady currents of redemption amid the bleating of his goats. [52] Guiding his tribe, the goatherder stepped light as a feather from the graceful wing of our dove. Yohanan the Baptist clasped Our Spirit to his breast and soared.

Notes: 3:13 Shemyaza, also known as Mastema, Satan, and other names, rules the fallen messengers. Watchers were a group of messengers who specifically watched over people. Their closeness led some of them to make inappropriate contact with women. The copulation of wicked watchers with women spawned demon giants called Nephilim. God sends or allows Shemyaza (which means "my name has seen") to tempt mortals. (Mastema means "hostility" or "persecution;" Satan is "accuser" or "adversary.") The story of Job is a Biblical account of one of his missions. **3:39** While Augustus deliberated on the contested will of Herod I (known as Herod the Great after his death), Tzipori, called Sepphoris by the Romans, became the center of a rebellion against Rome led by Judah the Galilean with Zadok the Pharisee. For its failure to snuff out insurrection, smoke from the rubble of Tzipori could be seen by children playing in the narrow dirt streets of Nazareth. **3:45** The Greek name Andreas transliterates into Andrew in English and means "man" or "manly." Simon means "to hear, be heard."

4 They came from hills and lowlands. They came from their shops or ships, from their folds or farms, from their villages or cities. They came. ² Bodies shuffled, heavy with sins on their backs, to a river of atonement. Our Spirit hovered over them, bright as a warm summer sun. ³ Yohanan the Baptist, wrapped in a robe, stood nearly up to his navel in the shimmering Jordan. "Repent," he shouted with his arms opened wide, "the Kingdom of God is nigh. Prepare yourself." ⁴ He pointed at the huddled mass on the shore, "Come! Cast off sin." His pointed finger turned into an inviting wave of his hand. ⁵ "As it is written from the mouth of Isaiah, the words of one wailing in the wilderness,

'Make ready the way of the Lord.
Make his paths straight.
⁶ Every valley will be filled.
Every mountain and hill will be brought low.
The crooked will become straight,
⁷ And the rough ways smooth.
All flesh will see God's salvation.'

[8] Come," once again spreading his arms wide, "receive the blessing from the Breath of God. Let baptism pave your way to salvation." The crowd trembled. [9] "Come!" Yohanan gestured invitingly with a gleam in his eye as bright as the liquid dapples rippling around him, "Redeem yourself in the purifying waters of baptism. [10] The blessing of the Breath of God is yours!"

11 A Pharisee, Sadducee, and Zealot walked a considerable distance as they wound their way to the banks of the Jordan River. [12] On his forehead, the Pharisee, Judah the Scribe, bore the imprint of his tefillin that was now bound around his left arm. [13] He wore a finely twisted, blue linen tunic wrapped with a skillfully woven waistband. A scarlet robe with a tassel in each corner covered him. The four blue tassels were so long he almost tripped over them. [14] Annas, a priest, dressed as all priests dressed: a conical hat, white linen shorts, and a tunic tied in the front by a long, wide sash made of purple, scarlet, blue, and white threads. [15] The priest also bore on his left forefinger a large, gold ring. They both walked in wooden-soled sandals. [16] The Zealot, a poor working man in wool and shod with leather footwear, followed enough respectful paces behind them that their conversation fell far enough before him that he could make no intelligence of it. [17] He sucked on a fig as he journeyed to the Jordan River.

18 Annas listened to his friend with one ear. The words of the high priest charging him to observe the Baptist and report back spun dizzy currents in his head. His attention skipped like stones over the flowing words of Judah the Scribe [19] The priest no longer remembered how his friend got on to the topic of death, but if he wishes to believe that his breath returns like a western wind to his body, there is nothing in the Torah to dispute it. [20] No need to argue. He will hold dear the belief of their ancestors. [21] Now Judah is quoting from the Writings. Fine. They are interesting. The

Torah and the Temple are all that concern him.

22 Oh God! Annas stopped, clasped the bronze amulet hanging down on his chest and waved it around as if the talisman were a net catching the words of Judah out of the air. 23 Noting the reaction of the priest, Judah put his fingers to his mouth, raised them as a pledge, and spat three times. 24 Judah regretted speaking out loud his frustration common to many. Though revealed in hushed tones, he realized that saved no grace. Whether spoken quietly or shouted, words possess a will of their own. 25 When Judah expressed a wish for sovereignty–to be free of the blaspheming Romans–he tread over seditious ground drenched with martyred blood. The priest treated the words as a curse. 26 Spirits inhabit every physical possibility and the very air. Demons salivate for any opportunity to commit mischief or evil.

27 For Annas, if the Romans do not despoil the rich and they allow priestly practices and they do not demand worshiping Caesar, a welcome mat for Roman feet may be rolled out to appease Roman swords at rest in Roman sheaths. 28 Law and order are what matter for the sake of the Temple. The Temple must thrive!

29 The Zealot curiously observed the commotion ahead of him. When Judah and Annas looked back at him, he averted his eyes to the road. 30 Feeling assured they had not been noticed, the two once again walked hand in hand as they resumed their way to the Jordan River. Other than the loose talk about Roman domination, the journey passed pleasingly and quickly enough. 31 The priest felt happy to let his companion fill the road around them with his talk. His lively words paved their way.

32 Reaching the shore, they cleared their throats and the crowd huddled on the bank parted like the Red Sea to allow them to stand in front and witness the work of the Baptist. 33 Squinting their eyes at

Yohanan and his students, the two travelers observed that they appeared to be Pharisees, but the man in the water spoke something like an Essene. 34 Within two breaths, Judah called out, pointing his finger as an iron rod shooting lightning at the wet Baptist. "Who are you to give the benefit of salvation? You are not a priest! How is a man free of sin without sacrifice?" 35 Every syllable of his words scratched as a thorn; every consonant was hurled like a stone. 36 The eyes of Annas, had they the power, would have turned the Baptist into a pillar of salt to dissolve in the waters of the Jordan.

37 Yohanan recognized them as Sadducee and Pharisee by their clothes and bearing. His lips raised a smile while light reflecting off the water whetted as blades in his eyes. 38 "God forgives sins," he replied, pointing to the sky. "With God all things are possible. Who questions God?" 39 Wrists flexed inward and his fingers pointed toward himself. "I am a messenger of God." 40 With a great swing of his right hand, Yohanan proclaimed, "I shall sweep the road of sin and lay down palms for the coming of the Lord."

41 Wiping his nose on his sleeve, the Zealot recognized a kindred breath in Yohanan, but thought him to be as weak as a puddle of water. Forgiving sins would not expunge the hated Romans. 42 All the way to Jordan, the bedraggled man imagined a shadowy, secluded spot to rob the two ahead of him. If not robbery, a crowded road so he could stealthily move up to one of the men, pull out the knife hidden in his sleeve, and slit a heretic throat. 43 Hiding the blade as quickly as he used it, a cry of shock from him draws the crowd closer. As they huddle around the victim, he would slip into and through the throng, allowing him to get away.

44 The way of the Zealot is a walk across burning coals. He seeks for a Messiah to lead their swords. Only Roman blood would wipe the land clean of foreign pollution. 45 Since the

crushed rebellion of Judah the Galilean, their numbers amounted to grains of sand caught in a sandal walking across a dusty road. [46] "Vengeance is mine," says the Lord, but many followers of Yahweh kept their eyes down rather than answer calls for a holy war. Clearly God, for now, held other plans.

[47] Canaanites also came to the river and watched; Yohanan ignored them. The unholy worshipers mattered nothing to him. [48] They stood by and did not engage him, and so he left them to their wonderment and false Gods. The sins of unbelievers lay not within his intentions or power.

[49] A haggard farmer, Micah, surrounded by the students of Yohanan as a curtain, disrobed. Andreas held his clothes. [50] Simon held a sheet and covered the naked man. Already drenched, the sheet clamped around him like a cold fist. [51] Amos led Micah into the water. The farmer shivered with cold and trembled with the slightest tug of the current. [52] Cautious steps waded their way up to the Baptist smiling calmly in the lapping waters of Jordan.

[53] Yohanan took the penitent by the hand and held him steady. "Make your peace with God." Micah shook as he closed his eyes to this world. [54] Yohanan waited. The penitent did not open his eyes. Yohanan waited. [55] "Have you confessed your sins?" The farmer held up his hand, pointing his forefinger and thumb to heaven. Yohanan waited. [56] Micah finally returned to the chilled water and patient ministries of the Baptist. With cupped water in his right hand Yohanan asked, "Do you repent of your sins?" [57] "Yes. I...I do. I do repent of them." As Micah spoke, the chill water Yohanan poured on the head of the penitent ran down the back of his neck and spine.

[58] They walked a few steps deeper into the river. The eyes of Micah widened. Unable to swim, he had never waded so deeply into a river. [59] "Rest yourself," Yohanan calmly whispered as he placed his right hand firmly on the chest of the farmer while

gently laying his left arm across his shoulders, "I have you." Micah smiled weakly. [60] "Your sins are atoned. You are born again. Go and walk easy a Righteous path." [61] Yohanan bent the penitent forward. Before being completely immersed, the sinner, splashing, stood up. [62] "You must be fully submerged. The water is your passage to the Breath of God and redemption." Yohanan calmly whispered. "Embrace salvation. I will pull you up." [63] "Oh, sorry...I...I...sorry," Micah softly stuttered and pinched his eyes closed. Our Spirit whirled around and within the two men standing in the Jordan. [64] The Baptist lifted him up saying, "The Breath of God is with you. Go and tell all you meet the Kingdom of God is nigh and," adding with his smile, "rejoice!"

[65] Gingerly walking out of the river and quickly into the open arms of waiting students, Micah put on his old clothes as a new man. [66] The words of Yohanan still rang in his head, "If you sin again, for redemption, wash and say this prayer three times, [67] 'With this water I wash away the filth of my body. Sin is nothing to me; the glory of God shall light my path. [68] With this water I cast off my demons and purify the breath within me.' Remember..." [69] Yohanan had Micah recite the prayer along with him. After repeating it again, Yohanan felt confident in Micah and released him back into the perils of this world.

Notes: 4:5-7 Luke 3:4-6, World English Bible **4:11** After the death of Herod the Great, a sect of Zealots formed in opposition to Roman hegemony. **4:12/13** Tefillin, leather cases containing scripture, were tied around a man's forehead for morning services. Men wore tassels in compliance with Mosaic law to remind them of the commandments–the longer the tassel, the more devout the wearer. **4:20** Sadducees believed in Sheol which is both the physical grave and, neither a heaven nor hell, an unseen realm of the dead. Priests were not given over much to religious speculations. Their earthly obligations demanded they preserve orthodoxy and make sacrifices, an endless and necessary business to ensure the abundance of God's land and the blessing of Yahweh on his people. **4:21** Pharisees breathed the laws of Moses and studied the Prophets, Writings, Written Torah ("instruction" or "law") and Oral Torah which consisted of laws and interpretation not included in the Written Torah. The Written Torah, or Books of Moses, is also called the Pentateuch, "five scrolls," beginning with Genesis and ending with Deuteronomy. Priests labored over several decades before and after the Babylonian destruction of the Temple to compile and amend the books with their own writing added to make a comprehensive whole. Today's Old Testament generally consists of the Pentateuch, the Prophets, and the Writings. **4:27** Upon the death of Augustus, the Roman senate declared him a God to be worshiped by all within their empire. To sacrifice to one more God was easy for polytheists. Grudgingly, the Romans exempted the worshipers of Yahweh. **4:28** Rebuilt in the third generation after its devastation by Babylon and remodeled to twice its size by Herod the Great, the Temple served as the center of religious rituals and a repository to preserve legal and holy documents. Unlike other religions with many Gods and many temples for each God, only one holy sanctuary existed for the believers in Yahweh. Only at the Temple did priests perform perfunctory rituals with grain or blood offerings of offal to burn and expatiate sins, smile on hand wringing hopes, celebrate a feast, or pray for the well-being of God's chosen people. **4:42** After the failure of Judah the Galilean, zealotry produced a secret society of assassins the Romans called Sicarii, "daggermen." The cloak and dagger tactics of Zealots put the land in a state of fear and trembling. No assurance of safety was afforded a Roman or Roman sympathizer in a congested area or street. Besides murder, Zealots beat, kidnapped, or stole from any they thought to be an enemy of Yahweh. For these crimes the Romans saw little distinction between Zealots and bandits.

---

5 Yitzhak stepped, with a chilled rippling of his flesh, into a gently rolling Jordan. ² "Well, I thought I saw you on the shore, but once again you stood in front of the sun," Yohanan the Baptist quipped. ³ Yitzhak grinned and skimmed the surface of the river with his hand, splashing a wave of water at the words slipping through the toothy smile of his cousin. ⁴ "Are you here to be baptized?" Yohanan asked with a slightly incredulous tone. ⁵ Solemnly, the penitent looked down and nodded. He stepped into the depths of Jordan. Straight and hard, with eyes clenched tightly, he stood by his cousin, who instructed him to confess his sins.

6 Yohanan thought he heard Yitzhak mutter "mother" beneath his breath. His confession finished with a few short breaths, but his penitent face failed to completely erase his troubled spirit. ⁷ The water swaddled him like a womb. He felt finally at home. ⁸ Our Spirit filled and surrounded him. He looked up to a blue sky that opened and embraced the aching deep within him. ⁹ Yitzhak rose from his immersion, dripping with zeal for missionary work. ¹⁰ The brown irises of his eyes riveting the iron of his conviction, he announced to Yohanan, "I have come to be baptized. And much more."

11 Paired with Judah, an early convert of Yohanan and a healer, Yitzhak went forth to preach the Way of Yohanan and the blessing of baptism.

Notes: 5:1 Yitzhak means "he will laugh" and is translated into English as Isaac. **5:2** The mother of Yohanan, Elizabeth, and the mother of Yitzhak, Miryam, were related. Both Elizabeth and her husband, Zachariah, a priest, were well advanced in age when she gave birth to Yohanan. Many considered the child to be a miracle. There is a story that Miryam helped deliver Yohanan. Miryam is an Aramaic variant of Miriam in Hebrew, which is Maria in Latin and Mary in English. Miriam means "rebelliousness."

---

6 The Baptist worked the brisk waters of Jordan with the frenzy of a man walking barefoot across burning sand. Multitudes gathered to hear the Baptist preach. ² Many journeyed into the River

Jordan to be wrapped in the firm embrace of Our Spirit. ³ With the Holy Breath, the Baptist preached the gift of redemption. ⁴ "If you own the joy of two coats, give one to the man who has none. And give him the better of the two. ⁵ If your table is laden with food, share your bounty with the bare table. If someone is without shelter, provide them with refuge. ⁶ To those who are in sickness, comfort and pray for them. Furthermore, I tell you, blessed be the impoverished, for they shall dwell in the kingdom of heaven."

7 All sorts of people traveled far for forgiveness. Those in fine clothes and those in ragged ambled to the lapping waters of the Jordan. ⁸ Tax collectors with clasped hands asked Yohanan, "What shall we do? A gold goat eats our hearts out." ⁹ The Baptist replied, "Collect not a coin more than your allotment." ¹⁰ Soldiers with clasped hands asked him, "What shall we do?" ¹¹ The Baptist exhorted them, "Do not prey on the weak and those who tremble at the strength of your sword arm. Be not an extortionist. Be delighted with your wages."

12 To the wealthy Pharisees and Sadducees desperately heaped on the shore waiting to be baptized, the veins in the neck of Yohanan stood tall and each word shouted from him stung as the sting of a scorpion, "You bed of vipers! You pond scum of frogs. ¹³ You seek to flee from the Wrath of God? To receive grace, you must bear fruits that befit repentance. You must truly grieve over your sin."

14 Toward them, the body of Yohanan stretched straight as a striking snake, "And do not say to me you are the sons of Abraham." ¹⁵ With a splash of water, pointing to himself and then at a crop of rocks on the shoreline, Yohanan exhorted, "For I testify that God may raise these stones as children of Abraham. ¹⁶ Beware, the ax is at the root of the tree. Its blade, sharp with the judgment of God, will cut down any tree that bears rotten fruit, to be pitched into eternal fire." ¹⁷ The Baptist dismissed them with a wave of his

dripping hand. Their heavy steps shambled toward home with the scourge of the scorn of the Baptist on their crooked backs. [18] Yohanan believed no absolution was possible unless the penitent accepted Our Spirit.

Note: 6:8 Mesopotamian kingdoms believed, as most civilized people did at one time, the liver to be the seat of the intellect and emotions. Since Aristotle, most everyone now thought the heart fulfilled those functions.

---

7 As the ministry of the Baptist grew, the number of his followers multiplied, and his closest students increased to nine. Three of them assisted him at the Jordan River while the rest traveled dusty roads to spread the message of the Yohanan. [2] His words reached many who, sore with dry spirits, followed their feet to the muddy banks, where their ears opened to the Baptist preaching redemption. To unburden themselves of sin, many entered the welcoming waters of Jordan to be embraced by the Holy Spirit. [3] Downstream from the Baptist, in an indentation of the Jordan surrounded by willows, Rachel stood with her feet in the river. Using a cup filled with Our Spirit, she quietly baptized a small gathering of women one by one. So she saved an untold number of women.

4 In the cooling shade of a burly mulberry tree, three students sat eating locusts and honey while Yohanan sat and ate in the sun. [5] Our dove swirled around them gently as they ate. Their bodies filling an emptiness, their needs reveled in companionship. [6] Having taken the edge off their hunger, their appetites turned to talk of Herod Antipas and his new marriage.

7 "This marriage is a sin," Yohanan declared. "A wooly ram butts them into a foul intercourse. Their union is a stench polluting our land." [8] Amos agreed, licking his fingers as honey dripped onto his robe. "It is an abomination." [9] Simon swallowed a locust and added, "It is Herod being horrid." [10] Amos asked,

"Why would he marry the wife of his brother? How can the Kingdom of God come to such a land?"

11 "Tomorrow, when I preach to the faithful on the banks, they will know this marriage is an abomination, a plague on our sacred land. I will call on Herod to renounce Herodias and repent his sin," 12 Yohanan said, honey dripping from his lips, "I will not stop until he walks a righteous path." 13 Our Spirit, with the wings of a dove, took to the limbs of the mulberry and looked down on them. 14 Shemyaza, as a smiling peacock, strutted around the tree.

15 Several tomorrows later, a troop of Herod's men appeared along the Jordan. They dispersed the crowd on the shore. 16 The Baptist called with his toothy smile to the soldiers, "Come. Come in and join me. Come be baptized and redeemed by the Holy Breath of God." 17 Amos clenched his fists. The soldiers smiled, showing their teeth, as some surrounded the students while others waited for the Baptist to wade ashore. 18 The waters of the River Jordan turned to dead weights, dragged by his body with each slow step. 19 The Baptist plodded to waiting arms, and walked a long and hard road to Tiberius.

Notes: 7:7 Herod Antipas II divorced Phasaelis, daughter of King Aretas IV of Nabatea, to marry Herodias. Herodias divorced Herod II to marry Herod Antipas. Both Herods were sons of Herod the Great by different mothers. Herodias was the daughter of Aristibulus IV, another son of Herod the Great by yet another wife. Yohanan believed the new marriage to be a violation of Mosaic law. King Aretas considered Herod's divorcing his daughter an insult to his kingdom and attacked with the vengeance of his army. It proved to be a minor contest. Herod escaped the bloody carnage incited by his passionate love match and fled from his defeated army to the protection of Roman arms. **7:19** With Tzipori in disgrace after the rebellion by Judah the Galilean, Herod built a new city to be his capital along the Sea of Gennesaret. (Now called the Sea of Galilee.) Upon its completion, he named the city after Tiberius, the Most Honorable Caesar who succeeded Augustus. Because of the new capital, some now called the Sea of Gennesaret, the Sea of Tiberias.

8 What now? When his rabbi no longer walks this earth, what is a student to do? ² The followers of Yohanan shook like trembling dogs. They pulled their own beards. Their minds spun webs of confusion. Alternately, the cacophony of arguments or unscalable pits of listlessness possessed them. ³ Andreas and Simon returned home to work the Sea of Gennesaret for its bounty. ⁴ A handful of lost and weary men gathered in the desert as if beaten by rods. They paced to and fro within the Breath of God.

5 Yitzhak sheltered himself in the wastes of wilderness, praying and fasting. "God Most High, what is Your will? Precious Lord, make me your instrument!" ⁶ For forty days and forty nights, demons coiled in the sweat of his brow, their venom dripping into his eyes. ⁷ Yohanan had failed. Why? The dry dust of Yahweh gave no answer. ⁸ Yitzhak pondered the plan of God. Where did he fit in it? What did he expect of himself? ⁹ As a relation to Yohanan, he had the best claim to supplant him. Was that what God wanted of him? The mind of Yitzhak burned with the fire of the sun off the desert.

10 *Was it all folly?* Shemyaza suggested with a whisper inside the ear of Yitzhak. Jumping up and down like heat pounding a rock, Shemyaza shouted, *Yes! Yes!* ¹¹ More whispering, *Would it not be better to pursue gold and the succulent fruit of a lover's orchard?* Shemyaza shifted his shape into a gold goat. *Yes! Yes!* ¹² Yitzhak wiped sweat from his brow. Lips of the fallen messenger curled upward in delicious temptation and slipped into a strutting peacock casting a long shadow. ¹³ *"Bow to me and I will introduce you to powerful men. With the right connections a carpenter can advance to architect and do very well. Women will*

open themselves to you. All will know your greatness! Just follow me." [14] The brilliant feathers of the strutting peacock excited his vision. He grew faint.

15 Shemyaza sat on his haunches, the sharp teeth of his reasoning dazzling in the sun. [16] Our Spirit smiled, and Yitzhak saw faces rise up from the sands in waves of heat: faces worn with weariness and beaten down with sin, faces that traveled to the River Jordan, faces Yohanan lifted up. [17] Their words echoed over and over in his head: "A stone is lifted from my shoulders…I am a new man!" [18] Yohanan saved them to prepare for the Army of Light, to lay idolatrous Rome at their feet and return not the Kingdom of Judea, but establish the Kingdom of God. [19] But pollution runs deep. The sins of Israel are greater than Herod or any individual; they fester in the people… the wealthy! [20] Yohanan purified more men from sin more quickly than any priest. Yet, it would take forever to wash every sinful man. [21] And then they would just sin again! This is no way to usher in Sovereignty.

22 Our Spirit danced across the brow of Yitzhak as a cool wind. He breathed deeply. [23] Let there be no more false sacrifices. Let the poor be uplifted! Let the Jews be a community following the New Way. [24] The Holy Breath touched the inner flame of the man feverishly finding his prophecy in the desert; he embraced the fire of Our Spirit. [25] A fervor to save his people devoured him. He will build the Kingdom of God.

26 Staring the devil in the face, Yitzhak held our dove to his breast. No. No pursuit of earthly pleasures for him. [27] A trembling dog quivered momentarily within him. Is this truly what God wanted of him? [28] *"Go home and work in the shop of your father. Help support your family. What greater purpose is there than supporting your family? Go home,"* Shemyaza tempted him while twirling his chin hairs like a dust devil.

29 The faces along the Jordan whispered with their eyes. What were they telling

Yitzhak? What was God showing him? ³⁰ Faces melted into each other and covered the sun. The sun grew larger and larger. ³¹ One part narrowed at one end and shot into his right eye. Another part narrowed at the other end and shot into his left eye. The remaining portion rested on him, setting his head on fire. ³² As he stretched out his arms, his hands turned into burning brands. He opened his mouth and a flame shot out. Consumed with fire, he collapsed.

33 Yitzhak opened his senses to the sulfurous Shemyaza shouting with open hands revealing silver coins glistening like morning dew. *"Look! Come with me! This land, the whole world, will bow to you!"* ³⁴ Yitzhak gazed through the devil and his apparitions as if through a large hole in a wall. He closed his eyes and felt the breath of his cousin within the Holy Breath upon him.

35 His body floated. our dove lifted him up higher and higher while grounding him to a path paved with truth as he understood it. ³⁶ He clearly saw a New Way, one that will harbor the time of swords tempered in the fire of Justice and the waters of Salvation. ³⁷ Shemyaza craftily smiled. Our dove smiled. ³⁸ Glazed over, the vision of Yitzhak thinned to one thought after another. Thoughts piled up like wood in his mind. ³⁹ He possessed Our Spirit. His thoughts blazed with illumination and the fire rocked his body.

40 Reborn, Yitzhak adopted a new name. As if in a dream, he shared his new name and vision with the lost followers of Yohanan gathered in the desert. ⁴¹ As the cousin of Yohanan, they looked toward him, but he resurrected no gleam of salvation in their eyes. No recognition of the shade of Yohanan nor of Our Spirit swirling within the man gesticulating wildly possessed them. ⁴² They were of Yohanan. Doggedly sticking to their martyred rabbi, they left the desert with the ways of the Baptist scrolled into their being. ⁴³ No matter. He believed. The

man of Our Spirit left the inferno of the desert, swirling with the dust of the devil, for home.

Note: 8:1 It may have been that Herod feared spilling the blood of a holy man on his hands. It is very likely Herodias felt displeased and even threatened by a man who considered her a sin that required being put away. There is an oral history or rumor put to paper in the Gospel according to Mark that Herodias and her daughter from her first marriage, Salome, conspired to have Yohanan executed. Realizing her stepfather and uncle admired her, Salome proposed to dance for him if he granted her a favor. In Oscar Wilde's play *Salome*, she performs a dance with seven veils. With the drop of the last veil, Yohanan the Baptist lost his head.

9 He preached to whoever listened and accumulated a small band of students who followed him to the little town of Nazareth sitting on a hill. ^{2} It had been many years since he had run away from home at the age of twelve. He waited on the Sabbath to go straight to the qehalah. ^{3} The eyes of the congregation screwed into him as he paced in front of them with a spring in his step. Finally, he stopped and faced the village residents of his youth. Like flashes of light dancing on water, he spoke as he extended his arms,

^{4} "The Breath of God Almighty

is upon me, because our Lord has anointed me to bring

good tidings to the afflicted.

^{5} "Reborn in the Holy Breath, I am Yeshua!" He then launched into the vision given to him by the grace of Our Spirit. ^{6} His words rode the air clearly as the shining of the sun rounding a sleepy world. Words warm and uplifting like a father raising his newborn high into the air for all to see. ^{7} Words like blue eggs of a starling found by a child and brought home with joy for their marvel to be shared. Words whose portent dangled a cloud of lightning around the heads of the congregation. ^{8} The longer Yeshua spoke, the more ecstasy beamed from his vision, the more his chest swelled with revelation, the more his breath poured out in speech illuminating eternal light.

9 But what is a word? Its significance lives behind two eyes and between two ears. 10 Loudly, the words of Yeshua rang out to hurtle from wall to wall and ear to ear. The ears in the room listened like walls and proved incapable of absorbing his wisdom. 11 The words of Yeshua struck and startled them like a ball, a plaything of a child that bounced off them and around the room wildly, only to escape by bounding away down the road.

12 Astonishment sealed the understanding of the congregation. Turtles, they retreated into tried and true shells of expectations. 13 A few began to whisper, to shriek and cackle to their nodding neighbors. "Yeshua? Who is Yeshua? What is Yitzhak bar Miryam up to?" 14 A man stood up. Through the eyes of a strutting peacock, he surveyed the room as he pointed a finger at Yeshua and asked, "How did he come to all this?"

15 Another stood and looked around and pointed, saying, "Where do such wise words come from?" And another, "Where does the *son* of a carpenter get such wisdom?" 16 And another, "Is this not Yitzhak bar Yusef? Is his mother not Miryam? Are not his brothers Jacob and Yusef, Simon and Judah?" 17 The congregation muttered and stared. His sisters–Adi and Naomi, Sarah and Miryamla–sat in attendance, their gaze sealed to the floor with the rest of his family.

18 The clay of bewilderment, fired in a kiln of judgment, glazed into a vessel to pour out burning oils of scorn. 19 They all knew him. Who did he think he was, another Elijah? 20 As one, they turned the backs of their understanding and sympathy to Yeshua. Amazed ears turned to red faces; his family shrunk into a hole of silence.

21 To the curled lips and hung heads facing him, Yeshua answered in flying spittle, "Who am I? I am the Son of Man!" 22 Raising his finger into the air, "Know you, in the days of Elijah, widows

wept in Israel for three years and six months when heaven turned its face from them. [23] When the lands bore neither fruit nor grain and Elijah sought refuge from the anger of Ahab, not one of them took him in, but only the widow Zarephath in the land of Sidon. [24] You have proven to me: no…no prophet is accepted in his own home. Neither his own family nor good neighbors will honor him."

25 A snake may strike and release its venom with some satisfaction, but the effect does no good for the victim and brings no appreciation or love for the snake. [26] For two days, Yeshua walked up and down in the disbelief of his community. [27] A few beggars heeded him, but great works lay well beyond his grasp on the little hill he called home.

28 The sisters of Yeshua whispered to each other, their words huddling together, "What is he doing? I do not know. What is going on? I do not know. What does he mean, 'I am Yeshua'? I do not know." [29] Yusef and Judah cornered their errant sibling. "Enough!" they shouted. "Why must you be this way?" Judah asked with the roar of a bull. [30] "It is time to put away your foolish ideas," Yusef stated firmly to his younger half-brother, "Yitzak, it is time to settle down." [31] He stared into the eyes of Yusef and responded through his teeth, "My name is Yeshua." Yusef vented a scream and threw his hands into the air. [32] Words choked in the throat of Yeshua. Only his eyes carried his words. [33] They would nail him to the worktable of his stepfather. He brushed past his siblings as if they were a torn curtain.

34 A prophet is useless among unbelievers. Why did he come back? [35] "As a dog returneth to his vomit, so a fool returneth to his folly." He felt the lead weight of the proverb heavy in his mind. [36] Drained. Beaten. Once again, he walked the dirty streets of Nazareth with shoulders slumped and eyes cast to the ground.

37 A few good hours, Yeshua spent in the Essene neighborhood

with his childhood friend, Rafal. As a child, no matter how many times his mother scolded him for doing so, he often stole away to be with his friend in the secluded Essene community of Nazareth. 38 "Come with me," Yeshua beckoned. "There is much that can be accomplished," pointing with his head, "out there." The son of the carpenter knew the answer before his friend spoke it, but he still asked. 39 Rafal smiled and shook his head, "My way is the way of my community; this is where I belong." Pointing with his nose he added, "Out there, there is nothing but blood." 40 Though he knew what his friend would say, Rafal beckoned, "You know your family loves you and you can stay with us." Yeshua grimaced, smiled, and shook his head.

41 The child of humanity felt the Breath of Yahweh, and his sight glazed over. There was a way for him. It was not here. 42 No matter how hard he tried, nothing ever worked for him in Nazareth. The followers Yeshua picked up on his way home disappeared shortly after he spoke in the qehalah. 43 The little village he called home grew smaller and smaller, squeezing him tighter and tighter. Breathing here did not come freely. He gasped for air. 44 "Take care…Yeshua, wolves growl at your door." A short smile flashed across his face, and then they embraced each other for the last time.

45 The next morning, he turned his back to Nazareth. Firm steps walked straight and steadily down the dusty street leading out of town. His mother gazed long after her son until the road swallowed him up like a whale. 46 Yusef stood behind her with his rough hands on her shoulders and gently told her, "We did all we could for him. 47 I taught him a good trade. It will not make him rich, but never would he be a beggar. 48 I did what I could, Miryam." He paused. "We did all we could," Yusef assured her. 49 Miryam put her hand on top of his and around his palm, tenderly hooked her fingers like a gold

clasp. [50] Through stinging waters in the troubled seas of her eyes, Miryam stared down the hard length of the empty road.

Notes: 9:3 Qehalah "to congregate" served as a community center. Rectangular in shape with doors facing Jerusalem, the seats lined up against three walls for the wealthy to sit on. Everyone else sat on the floor. Qehalahs served as hostels for strangers, shelters for the needy, public meeting places, storage for local documents, and a house for religious study and worship. The Greek word meaning "gather together" is synagogue. **9:4** Yeshua is paraphrasing Isaiah 61:1. **9:5** Yeshua means "to deliver" or "rescue." Yeshua was also known by several titles: Son of David and Son of God, Messiah or Christos in Greek which means "the one anointed with oil." All are titles that designate kingship. That is why the genealogy of Yeshua in Matthew and Luke is important. Without a royal lineage, the Jews would laugh at Yeshua for claiming these titles. When the Romans needed to take his claim seriously, the result proved to be unkind to him. Yeshua and the prophet Ezekiel both referred to themselves as the Son of Man. What they meant by it is as clear as a diamond held up to a penetrating light. **9:13** Yitzhak bar Miryam translates to Yitzhak son of Miryam. Jews in this time were identified as the son of the father, Yitzhak bar Yusef. It was well known in some circles that Yusef did not sire Yitzhak. Those friendly to the family accepted that Yusef took Yitzhak as his own. Others were not so generous. Throughout his life, "Yitzhak bar Miryam," hurled from children in the streets and his skeptics, crawled through his ears to nest in his mind. **9:16** Jacob means "supplanter." Translations have supplanted the name Jacob with James, a name derived into English through Vulgar Latin and Old French. The name James did not exist at this time. **9:17** Miryamla means "little" Miryam. **9:22** Yahweh sent Elijah to chastise King Ahab for submitting to the religious influences of his wife, Jezebel, a Phoenician and worshiper of Baal. As a consequence of Ahab's wickedness, Elijah informed the king that God, with the heaving of a heavy, withering sigh, caused the severe drought over his kingdom. Ahab did not take kindly to the admonition, and Elijah needed to hide in Phoenicia. A poor widow took him in. Out of gratitude, when her son died, Elijah raised him from the dead. **9:35** Proverbs 26:11, King James Version (KJV) **9:37** Rafal means "healing God."

10 An old and arthritic finger, the road away from home stretched out long and crooked along the eastern shore of the Sea of Gennesaret. ² Yeshua avoided the towns and walked the back roads or along the beaches, his sandals filling with either dust from trampled paths or the sand the sea pounded between tides of the moon. ³ The grit of his journey gathered between his toes and smudged the soles of his feet.

4 As he strolled along a beach, Yeshua saw two students of Yohanan while three gulls cried above them. Andreas sat with a net in his lap. His brother, Simon–who Yeshua would one day christen as Cephas–came around the boat. ⁵ The child of God walked up to them. "Come, come with me," Yeshua commanded, "and I will make you a fisher of men." ⁶ The brothers recognized Yeshua, but he appeared different from the man in their memory. The swagger of his walk, his calm face and set jaw, the strength of the voice of Yeshua ran down their arms and opened their hands. ⁷ Dropping their nets, they followed the son of a carpenter.

8 Their sandals spun up golden grains of sand under their tread as they approached the boat of old Zebedee. His sons, Jacob and Yohanan, along with his servants fixed nets to begin a day of toil at sea. ⁹ Yeshua caught the eyes of Jacob and Yohanan. "Come, come with me," he firmly called. They looked at Yeshua and saw Andreas and Simon-Cephas behind him. Jumping ship, they fell in line to follow Yeshua down and off the beach. ¹⁰ Their father watched them go. He felt gutted like a fish. Half his life just up and walked away, clouding the dreams of his future. ¹¹ Spit dribbled in his beard as Zebedee shouted after his sons like the creak of a loose board being stepped on. ¹² His boys did not look back. They no longer heard his voice.

Note: 10:4 Cephas means "rock" in Aramaic. In Greek the word for rock is petros, which is rendered as peter in Latin.

11 Yeshua stepped into the bustling fishing village of Kfar Nahum on the northern shore of Galilee. Straight and stridently, he made his way to the qehalah. ² Among those sitting there was Saul, a tradesman who had traveled from market to market. For over thirty years, he offered simple wares used by women in many a kitchen up and down from Galilee to Judea.

3 Less than a week ago, he had returned home weary, laden with coin, and found his bed soiled with sin. His young wife, Sarah, knew her cousin. ⁴ How long had she been unfaithful? Not long, she insisted. Her lengthy and winding explanation lay heavy on him. Every word Sarah spoke rang hollow, as if eaten out from within by parasites. ⁵ What should he do? He was an old fool! Charge them with adultery? Divorce?

6 In the shadows of his mind, he staggered. Why did he still love her? A wooly ram smote him. He was an old fool! ⁷ Saul remembered when he first saw Sarah standing by a gate, welcoming him in. Such a welcome! ⁸ He thought of his children. Tamar, the little princess who sits on his lap and strokes his beard. ⁹ Timothy, the little man following in the merchant steps of his father, selling his sister a wooden bowl. ¹⁰ What about them? His children. His children?

11 Yeshua, within the walls of the qehalah, opened his arms wide. To the startled eyes and ears sitting there, he revealed his vision. ¹² "I am Yeshua, the light of the world, and I shall give you what no eye has seen, what no ear has heard, and no hand has touched. ¹³ The Holy Breath fills the land. Disown," he flung his hand toward the floor, "the demons within you; realize the Kingdom of God around you. Breathe with the Holy Breath of God and take it wherever you go. ¹⁴ If you repent your sins, if you share your bounty, no matter how meager, and

forgive the trespasses of your neighbor, you will live in the light no evil can vanquish. [15] It is through this heavenly light we see the Kingdom of God around us." Yeshua made circles with his hand. [16] "There have been those who lead you that say foolishly, 'Behold, the Sovereignty is in the sky!'" He pointed up with his finger. "If that is so, then the birds of the sky will precede you. [17] If they say to you, 'It is in the sea!'" His finger pointed down. "Then the fish of the sea will precede you. [18] Seek not out, but in. The Sovereignty of God starts within." Yeshua pointed to himself with a finger from each hand. "It waits for you," beating his right fist to his chest three times, "here."

19 "Whoever recognizes himself shall find it, and then you shall know that you are the Sons of the Living Light. [20] Yet, if you do not recognize yourselves, then you are impoverished, and your poverty spreads as contagion, making others poor." [21] Tilting his head to the roof while raising both hands, he proclaimed, "Lift up yourself to God and be recognized." [22] Lowering his hands to chest level with his fingers pointed inwards, he flexed his wrists outward. "Cast off your sins by accepting the Holy Breath, the kindness of sharing and forgiving. [23] It is the Holy Breath will fill you and fulfill the promise within you of the Kingdom of God. [24] Without the Holy Breath, even on the brightest day, you dwell in the dark. With the Holy Breath, the deepest dark shines like the day." [25] Clenching both hands to his stomach, "Let hunger never know another man or woman, or wail within a child." [26] Stretching out his open hands, "Let love fill our eyes when our hands hold the lives of those who wrong us. [27] Let your heart be baptized in the works of giving and compassion. For," raising his finger into the air, "know you, blessed be those pure with the Holy Breath; they shall be with God." [28] As Yeshua spoke, a glow surrounded him. The more Yeshua spoke, the more animated the

glow grew around the room.

29 The vitals of Saul felt gored as if by a snorting bull. A voiceless raven perched on the haunches of a wooly ram in the shadows of his eyes. [30] Saul stood up. The possessed man advanced on Yeshua. "Who are you to speak this way? I know you, Yitzhak of Nazareth! Yitzhak bar..." [31] "Be silent!" Taking a step toward him and with the fire of the Living Light in his eyes, Yeshua commandeered the words of Saul. [32] "Not this time," Yeshua thought. He will stand his ground. [33] Reaching out with his finger, he crossed with an X the chest of the man twisted by demons. "Fiends, come out of him," Yeshua calmly, firmly ordered. [34] The eyes of Saul followed the narrow paths of the penetrating stare of Yeshua and saw his misshapen self reflected large. [35] The eyes of Yeshua softened with Our Spirit carrying a vision of Tamar and Timothy. Saul convulsed as a pain deep within him cried out. [36] The unholy breath of a voiceless raven with a wooly ram in its claws flew from him; a snorting bull tore out from his body.

37 The congregation watched with eyes and mouths open in wonder. They blinked and focused on Yeshua, but their minds did not know what to do. [38] When words tumbled from their tongues, they said to each other, "What just happened?...He moves and teaches with authority...[39] What is the Holy Breath?...

Demons obey him!...What is all this?"

Note: 11:1 Kfar Nahum "Village of Comfort" is translated into Greek as Capernaum. Therefore, the Greek name is used in the Bible and on many maps. The earliest surviving map of the region is a badly damaged floor mosaic in Saint George, an early Byzantine church in Madaba, Jordan.

---

12 Simon-Cephas and Andreas stared blankly at one another, then at Yeshua. He appeared to glow as if sunlight on burnished bronze reflected from him. [2] Yohanan the Baptist, with the agency of Our Spirit manifested in water, purified bodies of sin, but never cast out demons. ³ Simon-Cephas flung the doors of the qehalah wide open for Yeshua. In the street, Simon-Cephas guided Yeshua by the arm to the home of his father-in-law, while Andreas, Jacob, Yohanan, and a small crowd rushed with them like a widening river as more people along their path joined the swelling party.

4 At the house of Asaph, Simon-Cephas ushered Yeshua to the bedside of Anah, his mother-in-law. She lay worn out, a limp rag of fever. ⁵ Yeshua extended his gaze and held out his hand. ⁶ A groan within her looked into the eyes of Yeshua penetrating her with a warm cushion of fire. She took his hand; her hand–rough with work and age–closed a circuit starting from their eyes. ⁷ Anah rose out of bed, leaving her fever in sweat-stained sheets. The raging demon within her consumed by the fire of Yeshua, Anah rose out of bed to serve her family and guests.

8 Word spread like the diving of a hunting hawk. The news leapt from ear to ear in a jumble of conversations as one long breath. ⁹ "A powerful healer is in town…Who is he?…A powerful healer!…What is his name?…No one knows…¹⁰ What did he do?… In qehalah a demon dropped at the snap of his fingers…A demon in qehalah?…Yes, and as the holy man approached the doors, they flew open!…No!…¹¹ Yes, and then he removed the seals from the sight of the blind beggar in the street…Has he left town?…He is at the house of Asaph…¹² Where did he come from?…He walked across the Sea of Gennesaret…¹³ Why is he at the house of Asaph?…The devil held his wife in his burning hands. He raised her from her sick bed…She got out of bed?… Yes. And now she cooks for them…¹⁴ He says the Kingdom of God has come… What are we waiting for? To the house of Asaph!"

15 People wrapped in misery raised themselves into a force. The sick and disabled, inhabited by

grinning evil devils, worked their sore and weary bodies to the door of Asaph. ¹⁶ The sun counted hours as Yeshua attended to the ailing host crying out to him. ¹⁷ The demons hunkered down and trembled. Yeshua showed them no mercy. With firm words from his lips, with sharp gleams from his eye, they knew their master. ¹⁸ The malignant spirits lost that day. Demons–demoralized, cast out, in despair–littered the streets of the "Village of Comfort."

13 As night approached the midnight hour, Yeshua skipped out of the house of Asaph and slipped down the streets of Kfar Nahum to withdraw to a lonely place. ² The stars wheeled, a dazzling chariot to the racing of his heart and mind. ³ He captured their lights and magnified them a million-fold, as he circled his vision in prayer, feeling against his temples the cool air of the deserted night.

4 Yeshua trembled at the events of the day. Before his baptism, purpose had twisted him into knots or found him useless. ⁵ With Yohanan, a firm direction had moved his spirit and limbs. Still, it was as if he were a wine skin half full. ⁶ When his cousin died, Yeshua emptied himself to the dry sands of the hot and cold desert. ⁷ It was then Yahweh made him a vessel of redemption and handed him a torch to illuminate– not as Yohanan, not just a path to forgiveness and charity–but the omnipresence of the Holy Breath of God Almighty. ⁸ The body housing Our Breath is the true temple of Yahweh. ⁹ When enough people work and live and breathe within and as Our Spirit, anything is possible in the land granted by God as flowing with milk and honey for his people. ¹⁰ That was the covenant Yahweh made with Moses, but greed and ignorance broke that bond. Only when it is restored will the people be lifted and the Word of God be fulfilled.

11 As if on a potter's wheel, Yeshua felt himself being shaped as a lump of fine clay. With the guiding hand of Holy Breath, Yeshua trimmed

his thoughts. ¹² As a wine skin, seams of Yeshua bulged about to burst. As a vessel, Yeshua overflowed with grace. ¹³ The Breath of God resonated with him as his image in a mirror. Which one did he see, Our Spirit, Yohanan, or himself? In a mirror, Yeshua embraced all reflections as himself multiplied in magnitude a hundredfold. ¹⁴ No longer *carrying* the torch, Yeshua burned *as* the torch. With eyes shining clearly, his body rocked back and forth with the strength of Our Breath.

15 "Lord… Lord… Lord…" Yeshua blinked and slowly looked up at Simon-Cephas. "Why are you here? We have been searching for you." ¹⁶ The sun burned a sharp edge on the horizon as the sky rolled to embrace the greater light of another day. ¹⁷ "Let us go to the nearby towns and villages," Yeshua told him, "I must preach there also the good news of Sovereignty." ¹⁸ In the qehalahs in and around Kfar Nahum and along the shores of the Sea of Gennesaret, Yeshua taught the New Way, and those who cried out in pain or sorrow he delivered from their suffering.

14 Obadiah came begging. ² In foul rags of flesh covered with tattered cloth, he hobbled over and knelt before Yeshua, pleading, "Make me clean! Make me clean. ³ You need only desire it and I will be free of sin." Yeshua observed the leper with a limp and gently reached out to him. ⁴ The strength of Our Spirit emanated from the touch of his hand as he said, "Yes. I desire it. ⁵ Go, and daily purify yourself with water. Your sins are forgiven. You are clean."

6 The body of Obadiah shivered. The fingers of Our Spirit warmly stroked his rotting flesh. The leper broadcast his ecstasy. ⁷ Yeshua chased him, "Shh! Shh!" The Son of Man admonished him. Yeshua trembled at the wild show of faith. Instead, he instructed Obadiah to go and testify to the priests the power of belief to remit sin. ⁸ The enthusiasm of Obadiah could not be persuaded to rub the message of Yeshua in the faces of priests, nor could it be

contained. He roamed far and wide proclaiming the healing powers of Yeshua. [9] By this trumpeting, when Yeshua stepped into any village, town, or city, a crowd of the curious and bored, the needy desperate for relief, the eager zealots aching for a leader–all mobbed him.

[10] With all these hopes raised and stirring, Yeshua fell under the official eye of suspicion. A healer was one thing; a healer that does not charge for services is up to something. [11] A preacher was always viewed cautiously. Preaching smacked of zealotry and messiahship and rebellion. Only fools wanted rebellion. [12] The government and the religious eye of suspicion followed Yeshua like a man tracking a poisonous serpent in his house. [13] Their cutting glare peered from everywhere. To them every little action by the carpenter was writ large. The nails of their visions hammered into him. [14] Yeshua needed to teach in broad daylight, yet hide his work with shadowy words to blind serpentine eyes following him.

[15] Yeshua and his students, wishing to rest and plot out their course, retreated to the desert. Though they scurried secretly away, the wastes offered them no sanctuary. [16] Many in need found them and filled the desert air with their dire pleas. They would not, they could not, be ignored. [17] Yeshua smiled at their faces, their minds opened to his teaching. He spoke, and together, as grains of sand caught up in a dust devil or water curling into a wave to lap the shore of Galilee, they joined as one sorrow, one grievance. [18] Raising his arms to embrace them, Yeshua saved them and ended with the benison, "You are cast down. Why? [19] Because they," his finger pointed away from them, "tremble at your presence. They know," his finger pointed at them, "you are the chosen of God! [20] They curse you, believing that is a blessing on themselves." Yeshua shook his head. "Not in the eyes of God. [21] Blessed be you persecuted for righteous sake,

for yours is the Kingdom of God."

21 Returning often to Kfar Nahum to preach, Yeshua frequently took his rest at the home of Susanna, a devoted patron. One night, word of his presence quickly spread like the wind of a storm. [22] People filled the house of Susanna inside and out. Yeshua crowded their empty ears with the Holy Spirit and called on them to lift themselves up to the loving grace of God Almighty. [23] "If some ask you, 'From whence have you come?' Answer, 'We were born from the Light, the place where Light has come into being from Him alone.' And always smile generously at those who question you." [24] Yeshua urged them further, "If they ask you, 'Who are you?' Say to them, 'We are the Sons of Light. We are the chosen of the Living Light.' [25] If they ask you, 'What is the sign of your Father in you?' Answer them, 'It is movement with repose.'" [26] The preacher smiled warmly to the swooning approbations of those huddled around him.

27 Under the strain of their elongated arms carrying Tobias, a paralytic, four men hustled down the road to the home of Susanna. [28] Their entry into the house to lay Tobias before Yeshua stood blocked by a throng of bodies. The enthralled listeners packed in the house gave way to no one. [29] Looking in the windows and waving their arms like trees wrestling with a violent wind, they tried to catch the fire in the eyes of the healer to call him outside. [30] The words of Yeshua, filled with the grace of our dove, circled the room and captivated everyone, including himself. [31] Like a hot piece of metal worked furiously by a blacksmith, words from the child of humanity flew as sparks all around the room, his vision blazing inwardly and outwards.

32 The stars shone down as the four men, with Tobias at their feet, squatted against the building and stared up at the celestial bodies to contemplate their options. [33] With a snap of the fingers, they climbed the house and diligently

dismantled its roof, board by board. As they lowered him, the face of Tobias stared at his friends while he held his breath. [34] They eased him down on a mat to the feet of Yeshua as best they could. Yeshua looked up and saw four faces shining in shadows from the glow of inner light. Looking down, he locked eyes with Tobias. [35] Acknowledging the power of their faith, he absolved the man helpless at his feet, "Son, your sins are forgiven."

36 A short scribe with a squeaky voice, following the well-tread path of his mind, whispered to those sitting next to him, "Why does this man blaspheme? Who but God alone can forgive sin?" [37] Yeshua overheard him and asked, "Why do you reason this way? Which is easier, to tell this man, 'Your sins are forgiven' or to say, 'Arise! Take up your mat and walk?'" [38] Raising his finger into the air, "Know you, the Son of Man has authority on earth to forgive sins." [39] Yeshua turned to the cripple and bid him, "Arise. Pick up your bed and go home." Tobias stood. He rolled up his mat and limped out. [40] People moved to clear a path for him as all gaped at what they had witnessed. The companions of Tobias joined him, the corners of their mouths raised to their ears in jubilation. [41] Each patted the back of the other, sauntering into the night until only empty space lingered behind them. [43] In the house of Susanna, many mouths below amazed eyes proclaimed to each other that never had they seen anything like this. [44] They praised God. Our Spirit smiled with the lips of Yeshua.

Note: 14:36 Occasionally, scribes might still work as copyists. Some might be secretaries for priests, but mostly they studied Mosaic laws and holy scriptures. Members of the upper class, their expertise made them writers, lawyers, and teachers of what was correct and what was wayward according to holy writ and custom. Scribes embodied in their profession the spiritual meanings of the way of Yahweh. After the destruction of Herod's Temple, Judaism would transition from the priesthood and Temple worship to Rabbinic Judaism based on tradition, the Torah and Talmud.

15 The seaside once again called Yeshua from the dirty clusters of human habitat and parched desert. Did he know he would be fishing for an emissary? ² White crests of the sea crashed onto the beach. The earth lay beaten into a waste of hot, golden grains to greet worn-out sandals as the multitude sought out Yeshua. They trampled across the sand in small waves, chasing after him and his four emissaries. ³ Retreating to a seaside town, Jacob and Yohanan, taking on the role of bodyguards to Yeshua, held the crowd back. As the multitude pressed their needs bodily upon them, the two brothers pushed and yelled at the mob to stand back; Jacob cursed them. ⁴ Yeshua heard and upbraided Jacob. "Let not the devil take your tongue." From that day on he called the brothers his "benē reghesh," which means "sons of thunder."

5 Levi bar Alphaeus, with long slender fingers, counted his coins. A publican, his days gorged themselves like a glutton with the clink of numbers. Levi wore fine linen and lived well, but scorn and revulsion over his profession hung on him like the filth of a leper. ⁶ Each bit of metal he counted slipped through his fingers like a short, heavy breath; misery piled up in stacks on his table. ⁷ He felt as if his wealth towered above him. It made him dizzy. The towers threatened to topple on him like a Philistine buried under the pillars tumbled by the righteous wrath of Samson.

8 Mechanically, Levi reached into the leather bag he carried strapped to his hip and pulled out more coins, the breaths of more lives to be handled loosely. Was it his own breath slipping away through his greedy fingers? ⁹ Out of his home overlooking the sea, a buzz drew him away from the face of the Most Notable Caesar minted on silver standing tall on his table. ¹⁰ Observing from a window, he lis-

tened and watched Yeshua preach and heal against the rolling sea and clouds. He had heard of a holy man and healer in the area. So this is the man.

11 On a wharf, Yeshua preached once again the good news of the Kingdom of God. "Lift yourselves up to the light of the Lord. [12] Love your brother as you love your own self. Protect him as the pupil of your sight. [13] In the morning, do not be anxious about the evening, nor in the evening about the morning. None should need to worry for the food that they will eat nor for the garments they shall wear. [13] If we all live in the Holy Breath, all will be provided for. Since God gives all, with charity and forgiveness we work the grace of God. When everyone lives in the Holy Breath, then everyone will be provided for, and the Kingdom of God will reign. [14] Know you," He said, as he always did, with his finger in the air, "unless you fast from the feast gathered from the poor, you shall not find the Holy Breath; [15] unless you keep a whole week as Sabbath, you shall not behold the presence of our Lord. [16] I tell you, blessed be those who hunger and thirst for this righteousness, for only they shall be satisfied."

17 As Yeshua spoke, he clasped his fists to his chest, pointed with his finger to his right eye, pointed to the east and the west, tapped his head, [18] motioned with his right hand as if putting food in his mouth, pinched the right shoulder of his garment with his right hand while his left swept down his side as if showing off a new tunic, [19] pointed his finger at the crowd, and ended by tilting his head back while opening his arms upward toward heaven.

20 Those who were sick approached Yeshua. Their cries circled the air like hungry seagulls. [21] He fed them the manna of Our Spirit and cast their demons into the pummel of waves as if they were stones to sink forever into the sea. [22] The crowd divided into two to open a path–led by Jacob and Yohanan–for the shuffling, tired feet holding Yeshua up. He would

rest, but he had miles yet to go.

23 Yeshua entered the small town and passed by the dwelling of Levi. Through the window of the tax collector, the gaze of Yeshua lay like a fresh sea breeze on the man staring him in the face. 24 "Come with me," Yeshua ordered. The searching eyes of Levi settled on the resolve of the preacher. Pushing himself up from the table, the publican rose and followed him. 25 "What is your name?" Yeshua asked. Levi responded, "My life is an abomination and a burden to me." 26 With a nod Yeshua told him, while counting on one hand five emissaries and leading his new convert with the other, "Then come follow me...as Matthew."

Notes: 15:1 Emissary translates as "apostle" in Greek, a language Yeshua would never have used. **15:5** Publican was another name for a tax collector. Many despised them for the common practice of overcharging to make a profitable living. That the taxes collected filled the coffers of Rome only heaped greater censure on their heads. The Hebrews ranked tax collectors with the poor, the unclean, the undesirable. **15:7** Samson, shorn of his power by the keen scissors of Delilah and made a Philistine prisoner, with one burst of righteous might pulled the columns of an arena down on his and Philistine heads. **15:26** Matthew is Matittyahu in Hebrew and means "gift of Yahweh."

---

16 In righteous Chorazin, Annas and Judah the Scribe walked to the marketplace. "Will it be done in time?" Annas asked as he observed the ink-stained fingers and garments of the scribe. 2 "Oh yes, yes," the scribe assured him. I still have some and will have more ink tomorrow. "Are you sure," Annas pressed. 3 "Yes. Yes. I have moved my table to a corner. The children will not interfere with me there. Only a little...well, I have some and will be getting more ink tomorrow." 4 He held the hand of his good acquaintance. "Your Torah will be completed in another two months." 5 The muscles carrying Annas relaxed a little, but he

added, "It is important. I wish to give it as a gift to Herod." ⁶ Judah raised his right hand. An inked stained sleeve slid down his forearm. "Yes. Yes. I know. Do not worry. It will be done."

7 They paused as they entered the market and heard, "Step right up! What is the meaning of the troubling dream tossing your days into devilish stomping nightmares? I divine the truth to put trouble to sleep. ⁸ What is the ailment sickening the root of your life? My touch will drive out your demon." ⁹ The man spoke while waving his hands through the air as if chasing away flies buzzing around his face. ¹⁰ "I am familiar with Elijah the prophet who raised the dead and called forth fire from the sky! Like Honi the Circle Drawer and his grandson Hanan the Hidden, I have called out rain from a parched sky! ¹¹ For a coin loose in your hand, the clucking chicken tucked under your arm, or a loaf of fresh bread, I can cure ailments. ¹² I can reveal your dreams. Step right this way."

13 Annas asked, "Who is that?" Judah replied, "Um…ah…I have forgotten." He frowned. "I will remember his name later, I am sure," he said as he raised and half closed his eyes. ¹⁴ Then looking at Annas he went on, "He calls out prophets and thinks he is another Apollonius of Tyana, but he is not a prophet nor is he Apollonius of Tyana! ¹⁵ Though his magic might heal… fevers… or perhaps leprosy, he is not all he claims to be."

16 At the other end of the marketplace, they noticed another multitude. They joined them and heard Yeshua speak, "A Pharisee in rich garments and a publican went up to pray in the Temple. ¹⁷ The Pharisee raised himself up straight and tall, and prayed, *I thank you Lord that I am not like other men.* ¹⁸ *I am not unjust. I do not extort from any one. I am not an adulterer. I am not like this...publican. I fast twice a week. I give tithes from all I earn.* ¹⁹ The tax collector standing far off to the side could only look down and beat his breast to pray, *I have sinned. Lord have mercy*

on this sinner! [20] Know you, the tax collector returned to his house justified. Everyone who exalts himself will be humbled, but those who humble themselves will be exalted!"

21 The ears given to Yeshua turned as eyes studied the ground or peered at one another. Mumbles filled the air; the multitude began to thin. [22] Yeshua exhorted, "The Kingdom of God is much like the king who arranged a marriage banquet for his daughter. [23] When the great day arrived, he sent his servant to tell his invited guests all was in readiness. The fat oxen and calves slaughtered and prepared lay out on the tables. Come and feast!

24 "The first guest the servant came to said with nettles in his voice, 'Do you not see this field I recently purchased? I must inspect it. Please excuse me.' [25] The next guest said to the servant, 'Do you not see these five new yoke of oxen? I must examine them. Please excuse me.' [26] The next guest told the servant, 'Do you not see my bride? It is impossible for me to come. Please excuse me.' [27] The next guest had to attend to business and the next to his farm. One guest after another filled their lives with excuses.

28 "When the king entered the banquet hall he found it empty. He called his servant and asked, 'Did I not send you to tell my guests the feast is ready?' The servant repeated all the excuses made. [29] The king took to his anger and ordered his servant, 'Go! Go quickly out to the roads and bring the poor, the crippled, the blind and the outcasts to the feast!' [30] After they had been seated, the king saw the hall had not been filled. He called his servant and commanded, 'Go. Go out to the highways and bridges. [31] Bring all you meet so the banquet will be complete, but none of those who were invited shall sit at my table. [32] They shall not make merry of my bounty. They shall not taste of my feast.' So..." Yeshua stopped.

33 Despite our dove circling over the people of Chorazin and their

neighbors, the great majority of them turned from the teaching of Yeshua and chose to show him the heels of their sandals. ³⁴ Yeshua shouted after them, "Woe to Chorazin! If your deeds had been done in Sodom and Gomorrah, you would have sat in sackcloth and poured ashes on your heads." ³⁵ Pointing his finger at those walking away, "When the day of judgment comes, worse it will be for you than those dens of iniquity!"

36 At an earlier time in that city on the northern shore of the Sea of Gennesaret, while under the gaze of suspicious eyes, devout Pharisees and scribes asked with the tossing of stony words, "What is he doing here?" ³⁷ Someone scuffed the air with an ear-splitting shrill, "Look! He receives sinners and breaks bread with them."

38 Yeshua replied with a smile, "If a good shepherd had a hundred sheep and lost one, which of you condemns him for leaving his fold in the wild to chase after the one lost? ³⁹ When he finds his missing sheep, who among you despises him for carrying it home on his shoulder to celebrate with his friends? ⁴⁰ Who denies him his joy of saying to his companions, Look! Rejoice with me! My sheep that was once lost is now found.' ⁴¹ Know you, there will be more joy in the Kingdom of God with the one sinner who repents than over a righteous ninety-nine needing no saving grace. ⁴² The holy messengers will dance and clap their hands over one sinner who repents."

43 Now the eyes of Annas and Judah, with the rest of the crowd, hunted from one face to the other and grumbled low like distant thunder. ⁴⁴ The words of their derision–angry bees from a hive being pillaged by a bear–buzzed all around them. Two turned and with the feet of devils ran off to inform the pointed blade of the authorities. ⁴⁵ Yeshua measured his time and chided, "The Kingdom of God is like a net. ⁴⁶ The net is cast into the sea and catches all manner of fish. When the net is full, it is hauled onto the beach. ⁴⁷ What is good is placed in vessels

and what is bad is cast out to rot and be eaten by scavengers. So it is in the Kingdom of God. ⁴⁸ The good will be blessed and the wicked will be thrown into the fire. They will make moans and weep and grind their teeth." ⁴⁹ On the wings of messengers, Yeshua and his emissaries left the sinful stones constructing Chorazin, never to return.

Notes: 16:4 When copying the Torah, strict procedures commanded the flow of a scribe's ink-stained fingers. Each column of writing must be at least forty-eight, but not more than sixty, lines. Every letter, word, and paragraph required counting. If two letters touched each other, the document lost its potency and was no longer legitimate. Pens must only scratch out a special, black ink, with each word repeated out loud as the pen scrawled it on the page. Every time the tetragram for Yahweh was written, the scribe needed to clean his pen and wash himself from head to foot. (God commanded Moses never to use the name of Yahweh in vain. The commandment developed over time into a priestly taboo of never uttering or writing "Yahweh." Many epithets such as Adoni, "My Lord;" Elohim, "God;" and El-Shaddai, "God Almighty" are substituted for Yahweh. If a scribe needed to write the name of God, it appeared as the tetragram, YVHY. Orthodox Jews continue this practice today.) **16:14** The healer, Apollonius of Tyana, famously lifted the legs of the lame to walk and the eyes of the blind to once again see. He also raised the dead back to the living. Everywhere, demons and messengers wove in and around humans. Spirits, filling the world as abundantly and commonly as stones, possessed humans or whatever they chose, working tirelessly for good or evil or lounged about aloof, uncaring, mischievous. Professional healers roamed from market to market to make a living with their magical powers over demons.

17

One hot Sabbath day in an ornate qehalah, Yeshua stood up for the New Way. "Lift yourselves to the grace of God. ² His kingdom is here. The Sovereignty is beneath your feet. Free yourself of sin and stand in the Kingdom of God. ³ The Sovereignty was proclaimed by Yohanan the Baptist. From Adam until Yohanan, there is none more exalted among those born of women than Yohanan the Baptist." [4] His assertion slapped the ears of his listeners. Murmurs of "What of Moses...Abraham?" circled the room.

5 Ignoring them, Yeshua saw a multitude–faces of the poor and needy at hand embraced by the shade of Yohanan. [6] Opening his arms he joyfully proclaimed, "Everyone who hears my words and follows them will be as wise as a man who builds his home on a rock. [7] Torrents of rain will fall, swirling floods will come, harsh winds will blow and beat the home of the wise man, but it will not fall. It stands tall on the rock he built it on. [8] But those who hear my words and do not carry them will be as foolish as a man who builds his dwelling on sand. [9] And when the rains come, and the floods, and the winds beat against his home, it will fall. Yes, and great will be the fall!"

10 Judah the Scribe stood up and cried out, "You think us a wayward and diseased people, physician, heal yourself!" Yeshua turned to him and answered, "Know you, a man had two sons. [11] To one of them he said, 'Go into the vineyard and do the work for a day in it.' The son shook his head at his father and retorted, 'I will do no such thing.' [12] After his father left him, the son hung his head. Changing his mind, he worked in the field of his father. [13] The man went to his other son and ordered, 'Go into the vineyard and give me the work of a day in it.' His son smiled at him and replied, 'Yes, I will go.' But he did not go.

14 "Which son did as his father wished of him?" An old man from the crowd replied, "The first son." [15] Yeshua fired back at the scribe, "Know you, the harlots and publicans into the Kingdom of God go before you." [16] Drawing nearer to Judah the scribe, Yeshua scolded, "Yohanan came to you with the New Way and you turned your ear away from him. [17] The harlots and tax collectors heard Yohanan, and when you witnessed their faith, you did not repent and open yourself to the Holy Breath. If you go into

Sovereignty at all, you go last!"

18 Upon a Sabbath in a qehalah, Adriel raised his hands and proclaimed his faith in the teachings of Yeshua. The right hand of Adriel, a man with few prospects, hung withered from his wrist. 19 Yeshua told him to hold out his right hand. The eyes of conservative Pharisees unsheathed their daggers and pointed them at Yeshua. 20 Would he break the Sabbath by healing the afflicted? Yeshua threw a question, a rope of hope, into the midst of mulish Pharisees as one trying to save a drowning man. 21 "Is it lawful on the Sabbath to do good or to let harm thrive, to save life or let life die?" None answered him. 22 They stood swaddled in their religious commandment, as old as Moses, that no work be done on this holy day. Their squinting eyes sharply watched in silence.

23 Yeshua grieved at their tradition they carried as stubborn as camels. The rope straightened into a spear he hurled at them in anger. "The Sabbath is for man, not man for the Sabbath." 24 To Adriel he directed, "Stretch out your hand." The man reached out to the Son of God. Yeshua slowly extended his arm and their hands touched. Adriel raised his cured appendage in joy for all to see. 25 "The Kingdom of God is like a treasure hidden in a field. A man wise with Holy Breath knows where the treasure is. He sells all he owns and buys the field." 26 Yeshua looked at the congregated faces and asked, "The breath of grace is endless bounty and mercy. Who here is wise with the Holy Breath?"

27 The offended Pharisees stomped out of the qehalah on the soles of Shemyaza and huddled in their hatred with the Herodians to plot the destruction of Yeshua. 28 "We must stone him." "Yes!" "It will not be easy." "We must destroy him." "Yes!" 29 "His following is more than a few. 30 His words and deeds are the footprints of a frog; they land here, they land there. We stomp after him with our feet like fools! 31 He surrounds himself in a fog; his words bend like reeds." "The man tweaks

our beards!" A Pharisee bit his fist. ³² "His followers are more than a few. He is a healer." Another cried out through his teeth, "We must stone him!" "I know. It will not be easy."

Note: 17:27 Herodians were the men of Herod Antipas II, a son of Herod the Great and tetrarch of Galilee and Perea. Herod the Great ruled as the Roman client king of Judea for forty years. His will, written by his hand with Roman ink on Roman papyrus, carved up his kingdom into four parcels. Three of his sons and his only sister, Salome I, ruled as tetrarchs, ethnarch, and a toparch under the eyes and swords of Rome.

18

The husband of Adah died, leaving Adah with considerable material comforts. ² Two years after his death, a demon took Adah to its bosom. Her abdomen ached and grumbled. She hemorrhaged often, so her children treated her as a pariah. ³ Spending freely on sacrifices and healers provided no sufficient relief. Nothing eased her pain. Nothing cleansed her body. ⁴ Adah felt as if she were a sponge twisted and squeezed dry. Her demon danced in her body, ravaging with glee. ⁵ She lived in the old Phoenician port city of Sidon in Syria. When word of a healer working around Galilee who cared for the poor and sick reached her ear, a rainbow picked her up. Attended by a household slave, she immediately set out to find him.

6 Adah directed her feet toward Tyre, where she heard Yeshua was preaching. ⁷ Near the house of an official in that city, the words of the carpenter flew loudly; "For I tell you, blessed be peacemakers, for they are the sons of God," and he cast out many demons that day. ⁸ When she entered the city gate, Adah discovered Yeshua had already departed. Some thought he had journeyed to Bethsaida. So to Bethsaida her weary feet took her. ⁹ There she heard him preach in an admonishing tone; "Judge not so that you will not be judged. As you judge others, as you take their worth, so will your worth be

taken." [10] He spoke in a strong yet soft, wavy timbre of strange things she did not understand. Then she heard in a friendly, teasing voice, "Why do you see the speck of sawdust in the eye of another and see not the sliver in your own? [11] Oh hypocrite!" Yeshua tutted, "Would you remove the speck of sawdust and leave the splinter in your own eye? Rid yourself of what is in your eye and then help your brother."

[12] The sick gathered close to him, and he cast out their demons, but not her demon. [13] The crowd packed thickly around Yeshua Adah made no headway to him. The cries of suffering from many others drowned out her plea. [14] He retired for the night and she waited on the morning, but when the sun adorned the day in full attire, Yeshua had already skipped out of town. [15] This man moved with the wind. How was she to catch him? [16] After several inquiries, Adah learned Yeshua was well on his way to Sidon. Could she corner him there?

[17] Adah hurried herself home. How she arrived home without running into him she did not know. His path must not be a straight one. [18] As she watched the main gate into town, Adah worried she had been misinformed. Perhaps his feet took him elsewhere. Then a pause of dust settled at the gate. [19] Slowly a crowd moved forward. She darted out to be in front of him, but his "sons of thunder" guarded the lead of Yeshua, blocking Adah from reaching him. [20] They pushed her aside like dirt turned by a plow. [21] Yeshua, his head facing away from her as he spoke to Simon-Cephas, did not notice her. Adah managed to slip into the people tailing along, leaving only a few people between her and Yeshua. [22] Her body pushed forward, and her hand stretched out to grab his tunic. She failed to reach him as others cut in, driving her back. [23] Expelled from the crowd, she fell to her knees and yelled for Yeshua. He rounded a corner as her cry, a wounded bird, flew off to a distant cloud.

Note: 18:2 A woman is unclean during menstruation and for seven days after. Whatever the ailment of Adah, persistent bleeding made her perpetually unclean and untouchable.

19 Back on the shore of the Sea of Gennesaret south of Kfar Nahum, a throng gathered around Yeshua. His words dropped listlessly to the ground. ² It did not matter. In a mad scurry to scoop up the pearls of his wisdom, they trampled over each other. ³ Yeshua stood limply before the demanding multitude, a sail without wind. ⁴ A few touched the hem of his garment and sang praises of redemption. They felt cured! Still, they clamored for more. ⁵ Smiling, his eyes drooping half shut, the Son of Man blessed those congregated before him, a stormy and troubled sea pushing and pulling him. ⁶ Someone tore his tunic. Their needs stung like needles in his face and hands, his feet and knees, impaling his breath on a sharp thorn.

7 Sweat ran down his tired face and gathered in his brows and beard like morning dew across a field. His feet were worn to a nub; his head ached. ⁸ Yeshua nodded to Jacob and Yohanan. They held the faithful at bay while he stepped back from the throng and into the midst of his emissaries. "I am going up the mountain to pray. ⁹ Go to the boat and sail out from shore so none may see me gone," he told Simon-Cephas with a tired voice. The emissary nodded. Yeshua stepped out ahead. ¹⁰ The bodies of the emissaries shielded him as he slipped unnoticed from the trailing flock. Bunched together to confuse the pressing crowd, the emissaries boarded their boat and sailed out a decent distance from shore.

11 The desert is a crucible of wide-open spaces for the lost, a land offering few features to ensure a path, find a way forward. ¹² A place to go to gather up hollowed out needs, set them on fire, and bury them with burning sand. A forlorn spot to be alone. ¹³ Mountains, through ages of quiet conflict, climb with

confidence to a point and tower over surrounding landscapes. 14 Along shelves of rock or among secretive crevices, high solitude proposes heady perspectives and purposes. Reflection takes to the open air, riding clouds to lofty destinations. 15 It was on Mount Sinai that Moses communed with Yahweh and walked down with the Commandments. A mountain raises aspirations to a level of certainty, with full faith in possibilities.

16 Yeshua stepped up Mount Arbel. A spot with shade welcomed him as he sat and leaned back into the aspirations of rock. 17 Clasping his hands, Yeshua prayed. Prayer led to meditation, meditation to relaxation, relaxation to slumber, and slumber to a familiar dream. 18 Once again his body floated naked and drifted toward the midday sun, though night surrounded him. 19 The Breath of God shone as the sun, swirling sometimes with the face of Yohanan, growing larger and greater until the shine of Holy Breath swallowed him whole. 20 Yeshua reached into the fire of the Holy Breath and pulled out a small portion of challah. The piece of bread glowed in his fingers as he put it into his mouth and slowly ate the morsel of leavened light.

21 Like a polished breastplate on parade, his body shone; like rain from a cloud, hair fell from his body. 22 The glowing eyes of Yeshua looked down. He had no genitals. His body flashed brighter and brighter. 23 Gossamer wings grew and billowed from his arms to spread over the entire country once ruled by King David. 24 The dross of flesh with its joys and corruptions, its manifestations to be celebrated or fought over, melted into a radiating glow, an essence of Our Spirit. 25 Pure light, Yeshua suspended on the edge of space between night and day until he awoke.

26 Returning to the shore, Yeshua shouted to his emissaries out on the water. They did not hear him. 27 He stretched and jumped, waving his arms to catch their attention and motioned with his

hands to come ashore and fetch him. [28] Only the waves clapping on the beach responded to him. His students failed to notice him. Yeshua shouted again, but his voice skipped like a stone right past them. [29] As if on a frozen lake or on a sandbar, the child of humanity walked out to the boat floating in indifference. [30] When Yeshua was halfway to the boat, Simon-Cephas spied a body walking on water, pointed and cried out, "See! A haunting shade comes for us!" [31] Shock rocked the ship to a standstill as they all followed the finger of Simon-Cephas. [32] Yeshua heard him and responded, "Be calm! Be strong! [33] It is I, your teacher." He laughed, opening his arms wide, "See the power of faith?" The emissaries marveled.

[34] Simon-Cephas yelled back, "I have faith!" and jumped from the boat. [35] He had taken but one step when the wind stood up in his face and took all the sail out of his faith. [36] His body sank into the water. Unable to swim, he flailed about. Andreas threw his brother a net with a wry grin. [37] He fished Simon-Cephas from the thrashing waves. When Yeshua had told Andreas that he would be a fisher of men, this is not what he had expected. [38] They rowed to Yeshua. When he clambered into the boat, the knees of his emissaries buckled. Like a collapsed building, as one body they fell at his feet and praised him saying, "Surely, you are the Messiah!"

Note: 19:20 Challah is a braided bread often eaten on ceremonial occasions, excluding Passover when eating unleavened bread is required. A small portion of Challah is always set aside as an offering.

---

20 They sailed across the sea to Gerasa, making landfall near a cemetery. When Yeshua stepped from the boat, a half-naked "Man of the Tombs" stepped to greet him from the graves. [2] Wild with many eyes, as if he saw from out the back of his head and all around him, as if his fingers and toes

sprouted eyes, many contrary visions crowded his head; he stared wildly into the steady gaze of Yeshua.

3 The man lived in the cemetery, muttering to one grave and then to another. Putting his ear against the smooth stones, he listened to their whispered secrets. 4 To return him to the land of the living, many people had tried to bind him with many different bonds, but neither familial ties nor chains restrained him. 5 All who wrestled to fetter him met the sorry tidings of failure. His strength overcame any who crossed his path.

6 Voices pulled him. One yanked in one direction, another dragged him differently, another over here, one more this way, still another that way. 7 A man torn apart from the inside, no one knew what to do with him. He knew not what to do with himself.

8 Day and night, night and day, he wandered among the tombs or took to the mountains that heard and cast his wail from one boulder to another. 9 Those same mountains witnessed how he hit and bruised himself with rocks or beat his head with his fists. 10 He lived among the tombs and ate wild fruits or what food kind strangers and kin left for him. 11 His greatest companions were the wind, the graves, and the voices in his head.

12 When the man saw Yeshua, he recognized a light and walked to it. 13 From deep within him, his words amplified across space and reached Yeshua. "What do you want of me, Son of God? 14 Do not torment me. You know me, I think. But what will you do with me?" 15 Yeshua asked him, "What is your name?" The hands of the man pulled at the hair on his head and he replied, "I am Legion, for we are many." 16 "Leave him," Yeshua commanded. Legion made a hollow reply, "Yes, master. But where are we to go? Send us not out to restlessly roam this country."

17 A drove of swine milled on a nearby hill. Yeshua gestured and told his emissaries to bring him the pigs. 18 Inexperienced as swine herders, they chased and hustled

and corralled the pigs to the feet of Yeshua. [19] Simon-Cephas fell more than once on the slope, slippery with their waste. The child of humanity smiled. [20] The pigs put their snouts to the ground, but peered up at their neighbor, the Man of the Tombs. Their snorts rose in the quiet air like a morning mist on water.

21 Yeshua looked at the man and pointed at the swine. Unclean animals were perfectly made for unclean spirits. [21] The eyes of the man concentrated on the multitude of swine. His optic nerve focused on one. With one he saw many. With many he saw one. [22] The demons left him like the frenzy of animals running out of a building on fire. They jumped up and down and danced on the pigs before entering the drove of swine, all 1,998 of them. [23] A pig minding its own business can be herded along with an indifferent grunt; to become the habitation of a demon is an amazement. The alarmed squeal of pigs ripped the sky to shreds.

24 The emissaries attempted to return the pigs to their hill. Instead, the swine stampeded. The emissaries tried to calm them and push them up the hill. Pig after pig ignored them. [25] Pig after pig shoved Simon-Cephas aside, almost trampling him under the grip of hooves propelling a body suddenly burning from the inside out. Yeshua chuckled. [26] The swine made for the sea; cool waters waved welcome. Shouts from the emissaries to stop only hurried them on. The panic of the trapped demons only added to the mayhem of the pigs. [27] The drowsy swine herders resting on the other side of the hill, roused by the commotion, came bounding over the hilltop. They arrived too late. [28] Absorbing the horror before their eyes, a scream opened their mouths as their livelihood dashed headlong into the ravenous maw of the sea. The entire herd drowned not far from the boat newly arrived in Gerasa.

29 Our Spirit looked sorrowfully upon the swine herders. They felt

their loss like a jolt of lightning. ³⁰ Their cries and feet turned and ran to the city and to the countryside to share the shock and grief of their loss. People from all around came to see for themselves the power of Yeshua. ³¹ They witnessed the renowned Man of the Tombs sitting quietly–in his right mind. Is this the same man who beat his head against a mountain? It is. ³² They stared at the Sea of Gennesaret, narrowing their vision to find the bobbing corpses of pigs, but they wore their eyes out in vain.

33 With the assistance of the emissaries, the swine herders had quickly turned into fishermen and retrieved carcasses to minimize their loss as best they could. At least no one drowned while fishing for pigs. ³⁴ The creatures of the sea and the very depths of water consumed much, for only a small portion was harvested from the waves. ³⁵ Perhaps some bloated bodies miraculously wafted to a distant shore. No one could say for sure. People asked, "Did 2,000 swine drown here?" ³⁶ The lonely hill where they often grazed gave witness to the devastation of the drove. No longer did the pigs soil its head or trim the green growth of the hill. ³⁸ The people were almost too afraid to look upon Yeshua. His power terrified them. What is next, a plague of frogs? ³⁹ Will crops be devoured by a plague of locusts? They begged him to leave their country.

40 Everywhere the glare of eyes, underlined with suspicion, trained on Yeshua. He knew by their squint that the glare is often followed with a pointed argument carried at the end of swords handled by local troops. ⁴¹ If the fate of a few pigs startled a country into dismay, little more remained for Yeshua to do. Looking around, the Man of the Tombs, Caleb, begged to go with him. ⁴² Yeshua looked kindly on him. No. That will not do. Caleb needed to stay, even though he wet his scruffy beard with tears to join him.

43 As they got back in their boat, the man attempted to climb in after them. A firm hand stopped him. ⁴⁴ "Go

home," Yeshua ordered, gazing steadily into the eyes of Caleb, "Go home to kin and friends and sing the praises of the day Legion left you by the power of your faith. [45] Leave no stone unturned in proclaiming the joy of the Holy Breath." [46] The Man of the Tombs felt the flames shooting out from suspicious eyes. Still, how could he refuse his savior? [47] With a wave of farewell, he turned to walk the length and breadth of Decapolis, telling every man he met how Yeshua had saved him from Legion.

21 A sea decked with fury. A boat decked with trembling hands. [2] Shortly after they shoved off, an arrogant wind full of its own strength picked up, the kind of gale heaving waves that raise the hairs on the back of a sailor's neck. [3] Yeshua slept in the stern of the boat on a blue cushion, as if he were a baby swinging in a cradle. [4] The emissaries leaned into the fierce blows of wind that blinkered their sight as they rolled into watery fists smashing their boat in anger. [5] The men looked at each other with faces that asked, *how does a man sleep through this?* [6] The waves and wind, as they had done with many a boat with many a man, drew their attention to the prospect of being sent to embrace the sunken chest of deep waters.

7 They turned to each other once again and asked in loud mumbles, "Do we wake him?" Perhaps if they stared long and hard enough at him, their glare would rouse him from sleep. [8] Simon-Cephas studied the prostrate form of Yeshua. A chill came over him as if suddenly staring at a dead body. [9] He rushed over and shook the slumbering shoulder and shouted, "Rabbi! Rabbi! We are afraid."

10 Yeshua woke with consternation flashing from his face. His eyes widened as they registered the fear large in the eyes of Simon-Cephas. Sitting up, Yeshua measured the rough weather with a withering survey. [11] His emissaries cried out, "Rabbi, do you not care if we live or die?...Have mercy and help us!...The boat fills

with water!…Help us!… ¹² We will drown!…Do you not care?… Help us!" One after another, the cries of his undisciplined students beat against him.

13 Yeshua measured his men. "Be still." Their words stopped at the gates of their mouths. "Am I not with you?" Their spines stiffened. ¹⁴ Yeshua cast his eyes over the troubled water. A wave of his hand and boom of his voice saying, "Be still," struck out like lightning. ¹⁵ Shortly after his words calmed his emissaries, the clouds brightened and the sea relaxed. A doting breeze carried them while waves chanted contritely against the boat. ¹⁶ "Oh, you men of little faith," Yeshua retorted, wagging his head before he laid it down and dropped back into the blue cushioned depths of exhaustion.

22 Crossing the Sea of Gennesaret once again, Yeshua landed and walked up the beach. Quickly a large crowd grew, pushing him to the waterline. The brothers Yohanan and Jacob, his "sons of thunder," failed to hold them back. ² Returning to the safety of their boat, Yeshua raised his voice. The people sat or stood attentively like grains of sand. ³ "Know you, a man worked his field, sowing it with seed." Yeshua flung his hand wildly in many directions. ⁴ "Seeds scattered everywhere." The teacher directed his hand and eyes at the multitude so fiercely they bent backwards, saplings in a strong wind.

5 "Some seeds fell on the path." The right hand of Yeshua pointed to the ground, then raised up to sweep down, his hand clasping into a fist. "Sparrows waiting in the trees swooped down and ate them. ⁶ Seeds fell on stony ground." The left hand of Yeshua pointed to the ground. "The plants sprang up…" His left hand turned up and his splayed fingers wiggled. "…but their roots gained no strong foothold. ⁷ The sun rose. Rays scorched the plants." His fingers withered into his palm. "They withered away. ⁸ Seeds fell among thorns." Yeshua raised both hands in front of him. "As the plants grew,

the thorns choked them." He clasped his hands into fists. "The thorns prospered."

9 "Into good soil the rest of the seeds fell." Yeshua raised and opened his arms before slowly lowering them as if embracing the crowd. [10] "Those plants thrived and increased. The grain yielded thirtyfold and sixtyfold and a hundredfold. [11] Lift yourselves to the light of the Lord. All who do the work of the Holy Breath shall be exalted." [12] His right index finger pointed to his ear. "Those who have ears to hear, let them hear."

13 Moving on to Gennesaret, word spread with the wings of a falcon, and the needy gathered for the good news and healing powers of Our Spirit. [14] The sick sought him out or their brethren laid them in the bustle of markets. As Yeshua walked by, they cried out to him or healed themselves by touching the hem of his garment as he passed them.

15 With wide open arms, Yeshua taught to one crowd and then another. "If you inherit the dead, you are yourself dead; Death is your inheritance. [16] The dead inherit nothing. How can the dead inherit anything? [17] If you inherit the Holy Breath of God, you are alive, and Death along with Life are your inheritance. [18] When your death takes you, the Holy Breath revives you and you shall not die. Your inheritance will be eternal life in the Holy Breath."

19 Matthew from the crowd cried out, "Where shall I find the Holy Breath?" Yeshua pointed to his eye, "You shall not find the Holy Breath by searching for it." [20] He then pointed in different directions, "You cannot say, 'See here it is! Look there it is!' [21] The Father has spread it over all the earth, and like seeds in the ground we cannot see it. [22] The realm of God is in your midst. You shall recognize it by living and working the Holy Breath of God within you. With faith, give to those in need and bless those who have transgressed against you. [23] Whoever lives in this world exists as a corpse. Who wishes to be dead among the living? To live like a corpse is to live without grace. [24] You

are unworthy of the Holy Breath. Whoever lives in the Holy Breath lives eternal life."

23 From Decapolis a group sought out Yeshua walking through the market. In the center of the group was a man who stumbled with his speech because he dimly heard anything except his own words tumbling in his head. ² His friends' plaintive pleas to make him whole caught and pleased Yeshua. Taking the man by the hand, he led him from the crowded street. ³ Yeshua put two fingers into each ear, took them out, spat on his fingertips, and placed them on the tongue of the man trembling like a lily anticipating rain. ⁴ Heaving a sigh as big as the wind in a shaking tree, Yeshua looked up to heaven rolling with clouds and from the core of his being said, "Ephphatha!"

5 Immediately the ears of the man opened and he spoke clearly. ⁶ Yeshua commanded the man and his friends to tell no one, but with his newfound voice the man rejoiced and, having passed from the fetters of travail and grief to the expansive bands of joy, told all who he encountered of his cure. ⁷ The more Yeshua tried to stop him, the more fervently he and his friends proclaimed like trumpets blowing at a grand entry the marvel of the Son of God who made the deaf hear and untied a tongue knotted with speech.

8 The reputation of the carpenter as a healer attracted many desperate people. ⁹ Tugging her daughter along, a worshiper of Baal trailed closely behind Yeshua and his emissaries. ¹⁰ The haggard mother cried out, "Mercy! Oh Mercy! Have mercy on me! Son of David! Hear my plea! A demon has taken my daughter from me!" ¹¹ Yeshua kept his back to her. An unbeliever, she was no more to him than a distant braying of an ass refusing to be led down the path home.

12 Ignored, she cried out in shrill shrieks more loudly. Simon-Cephas threw up his arms and spoke to Yeshua, ¹³ "Please, rabbi, make her go away. Her cries stab like thorns in our ears and an endless beating in our

heads like waves crashing into rocks until they crumble." [14] Grinning at the clenched eyes and furrowed brow of Simon-Cephas, his rabbi replied, "My house is the House of David. I tend to my dwelling to make it right." [15] The mother came up beside him and wailed, "Son of David, help me!" Yeshua stared into her pleading eyes as if they were two dead fish rotting on a beach and answered her, [16] "I will not throw pearls to swine, lest they be trampled under their feet. The Son of God," he whispered, "is here to feed the children of Abraham, not to steal bread from their mouths and throw it to scrawny street dogs."

17 He turned to leave her, but her voice caught him up. "Yes, master, yes, but even a mongrel may serve as a good companion and eat the crumbs fallen from the table of the master." [18] Our Spirit as a tongue of fire sparked and danced in the vision of Yeshua. He told her, "Your faith in me is great. Be content, woman, your child is healed." [19] The mother looked at the stricken thing she led by the hand. Instantly she saw the demon leave. A smile overwhelmed her; now her daughter can be married. [20] She sang out, "Blessed be the mother who bore you! Blessed are the breasts that suckled you!" [21] Yeshua turned on her gently and replied, "Better be the blessed who listen to the word of God and store it up all their days."

22 Outside of fertile Gennesaret, Yeshua, to find his rest, sat on the mound, known locally as the "Humped Back" of a trapped demon, under sycamores wafting with wings of messengers. He should have known better. [23] When the whereabouts of Yeshua became known, a few gathered which grew into a crowd and then swelled into a multitude. They shouted to him for a blessing. [24] "Come," Yeshua waved to them, "join me!" None dared. "If you believe in me, come!" A few slowly made their way to him. Then a few more until a fourth of the crowd rode the demon's back with him.

25 Standing, Yeshua blessed them and then addressed the yearning faces looking up to him, "Know you a man of business called three of his servants to his side. 'I must be away for a short time. ²⁶ Here, take this and do my business for me while I am gone.' He gave one servant five talents, three to another, and one to the last. ²⁷ To each he gave according to their abilities. To his face they each thanked him.

28 "Ashur with five talents applied himself. Through steady work he doubled his store of talents. ²⁹ Judah with three talents feared losing them. Secretly he buried them in a secure place. ³⁰ Samuel with one talent, spent it on flute-girls and drink.

31 "When he returned, the master called his three servants to account. Blessed with five talents, Ashur returned ten to his master saying, 'I have traded and invested. Here are your five talents and five more!' ³² The master smiled on his faithful servant and set Ashur in his joy with great praise and rewards. ³³ Blessed with three talents, Judah told his master of his fear and returned what was given to him. The man of business pointed a scolding finger and through tight lips came the displeasure of his words, ³⁴ 'You must sow, that you may reap. You have squandered your opportunity. I am a stern taskmaster. You have always known this.' ³⁵ The three talents he gave back to his servant and told him to neither shirk his duty nor return until his work was done. ³⁶ Blessed with one talent, Samuel did not want to say how he spent it. With lowered eyes he told his master a thief stole the money. ³⁷ The master saw through the lie and narrowed his sight at his servant, 'You have wasted your good to turn a profit. ³⁸ Though I gave you but one talent, your loss is the greatest.' And he cast out Samuel into the road with nothing."

39 When his emissaries were alone with him, scratching their heads, they asked him the meaning of this parable. Yeshua explained with his finger in the air. ⁴⁰ "Know you, the Holy Breath is all around us and in us. ⁴¹

The Breath of God is a strong and willful master. We are all tasked by the Holy Breath to go work the fields and the markets, the land and the sea to increase a hundredfold our bounty and mercy. [42] To fail to work the good in yourself is a sin. To waste it is a loss to yourself and our people."

43 Yeshua taught under the sycamores from early morning to late in the day. Yohanan and Jacob approached their rabbi. [44] Yohanan whispered into the ear of Yeshua, "Do you not see the hour of the day? All this time there has been no rest; no time to eat." Jacob whispered in his other ear, "Send them away now so they can replenish themselves." [45] Yeshua heard an exhaustion fattened on hunger and replied without looking at them, "So, let us all eat." [46] The command grabbed the air in the lungs of Yohanan with a tight fist and pulled it out. [47] When the Emissary Yohanan regained his breath he replied, "All? We have not the means! There is little here and no time to go to market and fetch provisions." [48] Jacob added, "And at what expense! Send them away, rabbi, so they may feed themselves and return nourished."

49 The eyes of Yeshua took in the faces eager to hang on his words. "What provisions have we?" Yohanan told him, "Three loaves and a few fish." [50] Yeshua told the multitude to sit in groups. He then took the basket of bread and the basket of a few fish and held them up. [51] "My bounty is ours and your bounty is ours. Eat your fill and know that grace sustains us more than bread or wine. [52] We are as one body. My hunger is your hunger, and your nourishment is mine and your neighbors." [53] Yeshua took a pinch of bread and ate it. He took a pinch of fish and ate it. [54] Smiling, he instructed his emissaries to pass the baskets from group to group. The fish and the bread proffered their abundance. [55] Each one in each group served his hunger. All were satisfied. For three hours more Yeshua

blessed them with his teaching.

Notes: 23:4 In Aramaic "Ephphatha" means "be opened." **23:18** It is difficult to ascertain the historical accuracy concerning Yeshua curing Gentiles (Goyim in Hebrew). The audience of the Gospels were formerly idol worshipers. The Gospels would have good reasons to include these stories to assure their listeners that in his lifetime, Yeshua cared for them. On the other hand, for a Gentile, a healer was a healer. If someone demonstrated enough faith in his ability, Yeshua may have relented, under circumstance, to their acknowledgement if not of his authority, then his power. **23:26** A talent was equal to fifteen years of wages for a common laborer.

24 Jairus, a leader of the qehalah in Gennesaret and the father of an only child, threw himself at the feet of Yeshua and pleaded, "My daughter is at the door of death. Save her! With your touch, save her." ² Yeshua raised him up and told Jairus to lead him to her. As they walked through the market, a heavy cloud covered the face of Yeshua, his breath sucked out of him like a blow to the stomach; ³ the reach of desperate fingers momentarily grabbed his garment. Yeshua reeled around and demanded, "Who is touching me?"

4 All looked about in confusion. The lines on the face of Jacob illustrated his despair. ⁵ Words from his mouth spoke out in aggrievement, "Oh rabbi, how can you ask? There are many here and they crowd us! Who can say who touched you?" ⁶ With eyes squinted to a focal point of determination, Yeshua sought to find who had touched him. ⁷ He saw a woman tremble and look down as his sharp eyes caught her. ⁸ She fell at his feet in full confession. Prostrated, she laid out her suffering before him like a feast for a king. ⁹ Yeshua took her by the elbow and helped her up, saying, "Go in peace. Your faith has healed you." ¹⁰ Her long, circuitous, and erratic journey had worn her sandals down. Yet, to her home their weary tread carried and lifted her with a flair only those who believe know.

11 They proceeded their walk to the house of Jairus. One of his servants met them on the street. Calmly he walked

up to them and told his master the services of the healer were no longer needed. Judith, his daughter, had died shortly after he left the house. [12] Yeshua heard the servant and, putting his hand on the shoulder of Jarius, told him, "Pay him no mind. [13] Cast your trembling away. If you believe, your daughter will be well. Come. I will show you. Come."

14 They came to the house of Jairus. Yeshua allowed no one to enter with him except the mother and father of the little girl, Simon-Cephas, Jacob, and Yohanan. [15] All who were in the house wailed and wept over the passing of the darling girl, the joy of the household. [16] "Stop this wailing," Yeshua told them, "She does not know death, but lies in sleep." [17] The thunder of his words stunned them into a moment of silence followed by a pounding rain of derisive laughter. Yeshua swept them out of the house.

18 Jairus led Yeshua and his three emissaries to the bedside of his daughter. Taking her warm hand and rubbing it, Yeshua called her three times to wake up by saying, "Talitha cumi," as he inhaled and then exhaled his breath into her mouth. [19] The eyes of Judith opened; she stood out of bed and walked around the room. [20] Amazement hugged her parents as they clasped their daughter to their breasts. Yeshua directed them to feed her and not speak a word of what had happened to anyone.

Notes: 24:18 In Aramaic "Talitha cumi" means "Rise, little girl." **24:19** Judith was twelve years old when Yeshua resuscitated her. She lived four more happy years before dying giving birth to her daughter, Anna.

---

25 A handful of women served Yeshua wherever he traveled: Miryam Magdalene, Susanna, and Joanna. They packed, carried, and set up provisions, prepared and cleaned up after meals, washed and mended clothes, fetched water and wood, made themselves, in an all-round way, useful. [2] In a world muscled over by men,

many women squeezed in and asserted themselves as best they could. Their influence mostly remained, as it had for thousands of years, through personal relationships. ³ For Miryam Magdalene, it should be remembered, temple prostitution as a sacred profession lay in the heavy dust of ancient ruins. Men and women no longer offered themselves under the fertile sanction of the Gods. ⁴ These were modern times and, if she succumbed to the dregs of necessity, the bread Miryam Magdalene earned soaked in the sweat of grunting bodies and writhed with the worms of shame. ⁵ From an early age the Excitement of Death possessed her. When thirteen, Miryam Magdalene started seeking out Yeshua. Seven times demons worked her young body and seven times he took the unclean spirits from her. ⁶ Now, hand and foot, she waited on him or sat at his knees to listen and gaze up, wide-eyed, at her savior.

7 Susanna from Kfar Nahum, an early convert to the Holy Spirit, loved listening to the voice of Yeshua. His words lay like manna she gathered up to nourish her days and sustain her nights. ⁸ Joanna, wife of well-fed Chuza who stood in high regard as the household steward of Herod Antipas, suffered miscarriage after miscarriage. ⁹ When Yeshua made a sign and looked into her eyes, whispering strange and soothing words into her ear, Joanna realized Yeshua as an abbreviation of God. Yeshua touched her womb. Now she nurses a healthy son, Reuben.

10 And so the women served Yeshua and his emissaries, their labors being the only means for them to work their missionary zeal. ¹¹ Daily burdens, heavy with necessity, weighed them down. The joy of our dove lifted them high.

12 The successes of Yeshua in Galilee could not surmount his failures. Galilee would not be a stronghold for the Breath of God. ¹³ Yeshua labored to build a glorious house. Too much old wood rotted from within. He felt a need to work in fresh fields. ¹⁴ But first, just as

twelve tribes composed the Kingdom of Israel, so Yeshua would build the Kingdom of God with twelve close students. [15] They would be his chosen emissaries. He pondered upon his seventy-two students and picked seven more to join Simon-Cephas, Andreas, Yohanan, Jacob, and Matthew. Then he took the women and his twelve emissaries up Mount Tabor.

16 What distinctions divided the chosen seven from their sixty-five brethren? Did their zeal for the Breath of God set them apart? [17] All his students formed a network to sustain Yeshua and his chosen emissaries. Some took to missionary work of spreading the New Way or, like the man of the tombs, the miraculous power of Yeshua. [18] Perhaps the connections of these seven made them too valuable not to elevate. Maybe something about them tickled Yeshua into wanting their company close to him. [19] Only Yeshua knows which particulars of the seven caught, circulated, and resolved in his mind. Only their rabbi could say, though he never did, what singled them out.

20 The first of the chosen, Phillip the Greek, was one of the last to follow Yohanan the Baptist before his arrest. Raised in Phrygia, he journeyed to his religious homeland as soon as he was able. [21] Baptized by Yohanan, Phillip converted to be his student and returned to Greece to spread the joy of baptism to the followers of Yahweh residing in Phrygia. [22] When he heard Herod had executed the Baptist, Philip traveled back to his religious home, a broken vessel in a broken land. [23] Laboring in the fields, he gathered nothing more than the petty wages of a long workday.

24 Though they both knew Yohanan, Philip never met Yeshua until he heard him in the marketplace. The words of Our Spirit worked Philip like a barren field, old soil churned up to reveal a garden of possibilities. [25] He followed the carpenter from place to place, a stray picking up the many crumbs from a man spreading out feast after feast. Yeshua noticed him, took him in, and put

him to work. ²⁶ Faithfully the Greek from Phrygia followed every instruction, every beck and call of his new rabbi. Philip found his future.

27 Before ascending Mount Tabor, Yeshua certainly noticed fortitude in the brows of his new emissaries. ²⁸ Bartholomew, lean and wiry, soft spoken, often pacing pensively to and fro, marveled at the labors of his friend Philip for Yohanan, but did not join him. Not until he met Yeshua did he give himself over to missionary joys and tribulations. ²⁹ Abandoned as a young child, adoptive parents raised Bartholomew for ten years in the joys of their smiles. Their death left him migrating from field to field to survive.

30 Judah Toma, "Judah the Twin," usually called Toma, was another student of Yohanan who found his way to the teaching of Yeshua. ³¹ A trained carpenter, he was a man whose footprints, like many common men, became lost in the trample of many feet. ³² Perhaps Yeshua chose him because of their experiences of working with wood. To take a substance and craft something new from it, maybe that resonated between them and built a bond like no other.

33 Simon as a young child watched his father, a soldier in the misbegotten army of Judah the Galilean, hoisted onto a cross to writhe in agony for days, then hang as rotting meat for scavengers to tear flesh and peck out eyes. ³⁴ As a very young man, Simon joined the Zealots. ³⁵ Unlike many of them, when Yeshua urged his listeners with a wink, "Those who have ears to hear, let them hear;" his message resonated with Simon the Zealot. ³⁶ It was not, however, until Yeshua cured him of a vicious snake bite that he procured Simon the Zealot as a student. ³⁷ Even a blind man knew the affection of Simon the Zealot, who often held the hand or kissed the cheek of his companions.

38 Judah Thaddaeus of soft, hairy hands and stubby fingers first encountered the magical powers of Yeshua at his wedding in Cana. Thaddaeus, being a friend to

Yusef, the brother of Yeshua, invited the entire family of his friend to his wedding. ³⁹ All wobbled, well in their cups, when the jars of wine stood empty, drained of their merriment. Though his mother pulled at his sleeve, Yeshua was not yet prepared to go home. ⁴⁰ He ordered the jars filled with water. Covering them he traced a circle on the lids with his finger. Mumbling a few words, Yeshua removed the covers. ⁴¹ He dipped his cup and drank deeply. "A delicious wine," he declared. ⁴² Judah and the guests quickly filled their cups. Half-inebriated eyes opened wide. The water tasted like an expensive wine! ⁴³ They all continued celebrating until turtle doves and roosters began calling in the morning. ⁴⁴ Many, many years have rolled away since then. For the groom the joy of that party ended a lifetime ago.

45 Jacob bar Alphaeus/Jacob the Just/Jacob the Less was another man leaving a trail of mystery, a spirit of uncertainty. ⁴⁶ Keeping mostly in the background, he appears to be an amalgam or a person of Many personalities.

47 And there was Judah Iscariot, a family man who left his family. And he loved Yeshua more than he loved himself.

48 With twelve in tow and the three women, Yeshua took them up the mountain to instruct them further on his teachings and on how to cast out demons. ⁴⁹ As trained rabbis and healers his emissaries would go forth to sow seed under suspicious eyes. If rough hands tore up his grain, many seeds would still grow beyond their grasp. ⁵⁰ *There will be a harvest of grace*, he thought. *Nothing shall stop it. The Kingdom of God founded in the Holy Breath is at our fingertips.* ⁵¹ Hauling themselves up to a shady and secluded spot, the women made camp.

Notes: 25:3 No Biblical sources directly refer to Miryam Magdalene, Miryam "from Magdala," as a prostitute. In the year of our Lord 591, Pope Gregory the Great was the first to associate Miryam Magdalene with the sinful woman in Luke 7:36-50. The idea she prostituted herself grew in the popular imagination from that time forward. **25:20** Philip is a Greek name meaning "fond of horses." **25:28** Bartholomew means "son of Talmai." **25:30** Toma is Aramaic and translates as Thomas in English. **25:38** Thaddaeus is a nickname meaning "courageous heart." **25:45** Slipping and hiding between the lines in many scrolls, it is difficult to say if Jacob is a composite character or the manuscripts are simply confused. Is he the brother of Matthew? Is he the brother of Yeshua? Is he someone else entirely? **25:47** Iscariot is generally accepted as the Greek rendering of the phrase, "the man from Kerioth," a city thirty miles south of Jerusalem.

---

26 "Know you, to follow me is to show your back to your mother and father, brother and sister, wife and child, even your own life. If your will is weak, you are no student of mine. You must be strong." Judah Iscariot firmly nodded his head. [2] Yeshua held up a coin and dropped it. "Silver and gold are hoarded by the rich. They strut wickedly through this world. The Kingdom of God does not know them." [3] Gazing down at the coin, "What profits a man to gain the whole world if he lets loose his eternal breath to sin?" Looking up at his students, "He will wander lost forever." [4] The right arm of Yeshua thrust out as if throwing something away. "Whoever saves his life in this world will lose it." Reeling his right arm in, he clasped his chest, "but he who denies his life and loses it in my name and the name of the Holy Breath will find eternal salvation." [5] Opening his arms, "Blessed are you, for your ears are open to hearing and your eyes open to seeing. [6] For, know you, many kings and many prophets longed to hear what you hear and heard only the sound of their own voices, their own lost footsteps. They longed to see what you see, but all they know are reflections of false images, of their own shallow faces."

7 After a long day of being nourished by the words of Yeshua like honey on bread, the emissaries sat together during

a pause to replenish and focus their breath. [8] Beaming, Simon the Zealot praised Yeshua, "Twenty-four prophets professed up and down the land of Israel and they have all spoken within you." [9] Yeshua looked at him coolly, "You speak of the dead. Do not ignore the Living One within us." [10] Noticing the downcast look of his emissary, Yeshua patted him on the back, saying, "Forgive me. You have spoken well."

11 Jumping up onto a rock, he yelled, "Yohanan was a man from the wilderness. What do you find in the wilderness?" [12] The emissaries stroked their beards while raising their eyes in thought. [13] "A dust whirling with wind," he answered as they nodded, *Ah, yes*. [14] "Did you think to find such a man soft as silk?" His students shook their heads and scoffed. "Soft men live delicately at court." [15] Yeshua held his right hand next to his face, pinched two fingers and his thumb together, and made a sickly obeisant smile. The emissaries slapped their knees in laughter. The women tittered behind them.

16 "Who do you see in the wilderness?" Yeshua asked and waited. Each emissary froze, hoping not to draw attention toward himself. Yeshua waited. [17] Bartholomew timidly spoke up in a whisper, "A holy man?" Yeshua leaned his ear towards the voice of his student, "A what?" [18] Bartholomew repeated as loudly as he could muster while all ears opened to him, "A holy man." His rabbi pointed at him, nodded, and added, "And another name for a holy man?" [19] Mouths opened to speak, but no answers came out. Their teacher took a breath and exhaled, saying, "A prophet!" The emissaries nodded their heads at one another, *Of course!* [20] Yeshua continued, "Yohanan prepared the way. 'After me,' he informed them, 'another comes to fulfill the Prophecies.' I am that one," he announced, spreading his arms open. [21] "I am the light of the world. Follow me and you will be a flame of light. Never shall you walk in shadows, but shine with the

light of life. [22] You will clap hands with joy and the strength of your faith shall free the sick and crippled. [23] Know you, some of you sitting here will not taste death before you see the Kingdom of God." The smiles of his men were so large they nearly fell off their faces.

[24] Around the crack and flicker of flames, gathered in chatter and gossip, Simon-Cephas asked Yeshua to explain the parable of the sower. [25] Yeshua looked at his students for a knowing face and turned to the heart of the fire with a sigh before studying the earnest, quizzical lines in the face of Simon-Cephas. [26] With a breath of exasperation he began, "You do not understand the parable?" His emissaries slowly shook their heads. "How will you understand any parable?"

[27] Yeshua stared into the faces of his students and launched into the explanation, "A prophet sows the word of the Holy Breath. [28] Those on a well-worn path will never hear the word. The ease of this world swoops down and instantly takes the word from them. [29] Those that reside in rocky ground, when the word is given them, rejoice and raise their hands. Yet the joy is but little. [30] They have no root in themselves. When the word brings troubles and persecutions, they no longer know the word. [31] Those in the thorns hear the word, but temptations and the desires of the world choke it off and the word bears no fruit. [32] Those who are good and faithful, they take the word, nurture and grow with it; the word thrives thirtyfold and sixtyfold and a hundredfold." [33] Yeshua observed the sparks of understanding in the eyes of his emissaries. Simon-Cephas smiled and the arms of satisfaction took and held them all to its breast.

[34] They sat staring into the fire; their visions burned brightly with the flames. [35] After a little time, Simon-Cephas perked his head up and asked, "But rabbi, why speak in parables?" [36] Yeshua replied as much with his eyes as with his words, "To you the Sovereignty is no secret. For those of faith the Holy Breath is no secret. [37] To

the rest of this wicked generation, they will hear but not understand; perceive, but not witness. Consumed by willful ignorance, they are slaves to a vicious snake. ^{38} There is no bounty or forgiveness in them. An ignorant person may learn; those in the throes of willful ignorance are damned to eternal flames of our pity. ^{39} And since we work for Sovereignty under the sharp eyes of suspicion, we must be as secretive as a Zealot while as open as the Baptist."

40 One early morning upon waking to a squabble, Yeshua listened to his emissaries and grinned. "Let us be calm," Bartholomew interjected, his light words blowing in the wind between fiery shouts. ^{41} When their arguments rose in temperature, with angry words elevating frustrated fists and the gentle Bartholomew was pushed aside falling to the ground, Yeshua quickly rose and exhorted, ^{42} "We live by the commandment, 'Thou shalt not kill.'" He stepped in amongst them. ^{43} "Know you, if anger takes to your hands and you strike your brother, that too shall be judged as harshly as murder. ^{44} Be mindful a bull of wrath not swallow you whole or rend limb from limb among you. ^{45} If any two of you make peace with each other, the two shall say to the mountain, 'Move!' and it will move. ^{46} If in each other you possess a little faith, as small as a mustard seed, you can say to this mountain, 'Move from here to there,' and," with a sweep of his arm, "this mountain will move. ^{47} Nothing is impossible with faith. The faith of Moses parted the Red Sea. Your faith will move mountains."

27 Every morning after waking to a glimmer in the opening eye of the sun and the hooping from the long beaks of hoopoes, the men purified themselves with a little water ^{2} and prayed to the supreme Seraphim, the Chief Messenger Seraphiel, assigned to every root of the world, for the courage to follow the path of the New Way. ^{3} Their prayers also offered humble gratitude for each lesson they had

previously received and always ended with their most fevered gratitude to be alive in the Kingdom of God. [4] Meditation to clear their minds in readiness for another day of learning devoured the next hungry hour. [5] The women softly prayed, "Hear Israel, our God is the one and only God. Shouting with all my breath to our unfolding future, Lord your love is greater than wine and unifies us in an infinite present." [6] Their prayers also expressed the same gratefulness as the men and ended, "May the Chief Messenger Michael soon lead the messengers swift with swords of Justice. Let the will of God be done." [7] Instead of meditating, the women prepared breakfast. All broke bread together; the women sat at their rug, the man at theirs.

8 Behind the men, the women sometimes listened to Yeshua. Mostly his teaching hung loosely on their ears as daily tasks occupied their day. [9] Joanna tended the fire and gathered wood for the day in one pouch over her left shoulder while, over her right, a sling carried Reuben behind her. [10] She gave him sticks to play with until he accidentally smacked the side of her head with one. [11] Miryam and Susanna hung up bedding in the morning and laid it back out for everyone at night. When they could, they helped Joanna carry wood or tend to a fussing or smiling Reuben. [12] All three worked to maintain orderliness in the camp, prepare meals, clean dishes, wash and mend clothes, maintain the fire, fetch water, and labored over other sundry tasks, all the while tending to the menial needs of their master and his emissaries.

13 Every night before they lay down, the men prayed, "With the foundation of the Chief Messenger Seraphiel beneath our feet, the truth, rooted in the ground, will spring from the earth." [14] They then prayed for the strength of understanding. The women prayed for blessings. [15] Everyone dozed off to sleep with the wisdom of Yeshua like benisons filling their ears and the fervent wish ringing their minds:

"May the messengers swift with swords come. Let the will of God be done!"

16 "How blessed is the man who does not walk in the counsel of the wicked, nor stand in the path of sinners, nor sit in the seat of scoffers..." Joanna sang near the fire where she knelt kneading dough to bake over an open fire. [17] Miryam and Susanna sat next to her and, wetting the barley flour with one hand, they worked the dough on a flat stone with the other. [18] The three of them sang, "He will be like a tree firmly planted by canals of water, Which yields its fruit in its season And its leaf does not wither And in whatever he does, he prospers."

19 Simon-Cephas walked up behind them and said, "Our thirst is great." Miryam rose, grabbed a large waterskin with her wet hand, and walked to the nearby stream. [20] The Emissary Simon-Cephas watched the bread being baked. "Looks good," he salivated, "Our hunger is also great." Susanna looked up at him, "Soon," she smiled, "it will be ready."

21 The sweat from the brow of Joanna fell on her dough. She stopped and offered him a small, freshly baked cake. The emissary shook his head. "I will wait for the blessing of our rabbi." [22] Miryam returned with the waterskin clutched against her body. Simon-Cephas coolly took it from her and returned to his schooling.

23 On a day when a hot sun stared down from its highest arc, the women drifted to the shade of an oak to relax and play a game. Susanna untied a checkered cloth holding two sets of smooth, round chips of wood, one set etched with a spiraling circle. [24] Spreading out the corners of the cloth, she then took a smooth chip in one hand and a marked one in her other hand. [25] Before she put her hands behind her back, Joanna laughed at her and chided, "You can take the marked chips. I know how much you admire them." [26] Joanna smiled as they set up the pieces on the cloth. Truly she fancied the look and feel of the

marked chips, but she enjoyed moving first even more.

27 Miryam softly sang, "I have compared thee, O my love, to a mare of the chariots of Pharaoh. ²⁸ Thy cheeks are beautiful between the earrings, thy neck between the necklaces. ²⁹ We will make thee earrings of gold with studs of silver. ³⁰ While the king was on his couch, my spikenard gave forth its fragrance. ³¹ A bundle of myrrh is my wellbeloved unto me that rests between my breasts. ³² My beloved is unto me as a cluster of camphire in the vineyards of Engedi. ³³ Behold, thou art fair, my love; behold, thou art fair; thou hast doves' eyes. ³⁴ Behold, thou art fair, O my beloved, and pleasant: also our bed has flowers."

35 A babbling Reuben, nestled in her arms, swayed with her body as they watched Susannah and Joanna play. ³⁶ The Breath of God possessed the women, filling the air around them as they sweated through their toil and play and songs.

Notes: 27:16 & 18 Psalm 1:1 & 1:3, New American Standard Bible (NASB1995) **27:27-34** Song of Solomon 1:9-16 Jubilee Bible 2000 (JUB); spikenard or nard is an expensive oil, amber in color with a slightly sweet, deeply earthy scent used as a perfume and for medicinal purposes, especially as a sedative; Engedi means "Spring of the Wild Goat," and was a place noted for its aromatic plants, vineyards, and where David hid from the deadly jealousy of King Saul.

---

28 After a long day beaten with the stupor of fatigue and the minds of his students wandering off with every passing cloud, Yeshua led his emissaries to the mountain top. ² Like sheepdogs, on one side a strutting peacock with a full fanned tail and on the other our dove herded them along. ³ Raising his arms he told them, "Someday soon the reign of the Holy Breath will open the door to Sovereignty." Turning his body in every direction he told them, "And all this will be yours!" ⁴ They looked to the east and the west, the north and the south as the sun opened up a fresh day, a new world of possibilities. ⁵ "We shall rule with the Breath of God. Our kingdom will be righteous, just, and indomitable," Yeshua said with a firm smile.

6 The next day Yeshua instructed his eager emissaries, "Just as evil messengers serve the serpent Shemyaza, a demon is the servant of an evil messenger. ⁷ When a demon enters someone, they become sick. That is the best opportunity to exorcize the demon. ⁸ The longer an evil servant lives in a person, the more power the demon has over them until they become completely possessed by evil. ⁹ Then they are damned to the greatest sin of all, a vicious serpent of willful ignorance. ¹⁰ Lost to God, the possessed are nearly impossible to save. As a slave to the devil, he will work day and night to empower his evil master.

11 Many different demons roam far and near. ¹² To cast out a demon and restore a person you might or might not know the unholy master that the possessed serve. If you do know, you will more easily deal with them. ¹³ With anger, a snorting bull clouds an eye that stares past you. The arrogant tail of a strutting peacock fans the air as on a cold morning. ¹⁴ There is…is…what is it, Toma!?"

15 Toma sat staring at the ground and shaking his head. When Yeshua called his name, his vision lifted but did not look upon Yeshua as he responded, "I do not believe I can do it. ¹⁶ I cannot heal the sick! Who am I to cast out demons? I am not…holy…not worthy of such power." ¹⁷ Yeshua replied softly, "What is the cure for the infirm or diseased?" ¹⁸ Toma thought as Simon-Cephas answered, "Faith!" Yeshua nodded and asked, "Faith in who?" A smile flashed across the face of Simon-Cephas as he answered, pointing his finger at Yeshua, "You." ¹⁹ Yeshua nodded and added, "And who is my power?"

20 The faces of his emissaries offered uncertainty. Simon-Cephas opened his mouth, but no words answered his teacher. ²¹ Miryam Magdalene, preparing supper with the other women,

but listening to Yeshua, whispered beneath her breath, "The Holy Breath." [22] Watching his emissaries, Yeshua affirmed, "The grace of the Breath of God within and around you," he paused and then spoke on, "as a holy dove, grace lifts you up. You must open yourselves and accept your master and give yourself wholly to Holy Breath full of grace." [23] Looking at his students but settling his sight on Toma, Yeshua asked, "Do you have faith?" Toma looked up at Yeshua as he firmly replied he did. [24] Yeshua told him, "It is not you that heals. It is your love and faith in the Holy Breath that drives out demons." All heads nodded.

25 Yeshua checked the faces of his emissaries for understanding. Satisfied, he continued, "A demon works as a sword of the devil, but sometimes the possessed and the demon work together. Then he is a lost breath. [26] The most common demon trembles like a dog, shivers as if in a thunderstorm. Another, as a vicious snake, strikes our eyes so we do not see the truth. These demons ravage a person and strangle his breath. [27] When casting out their power," Yeshua softly said, "penetrate with your eyes like a dagger into the heart of the demon. Your faith must concentrate to grab it by the throat and wrest it out." [28] Yeshua taught them words to say and signs to make to undermine the strength of a demon and place the possessed within a spell of the Holy Spirit. [29] "Remember, it is important that sinners feel your faith. Draw them in with your gaze, as to the River Jordan for baptism. Without faith, there can be no miracle."

30 His voice elevated in warning, Yeshua told them, "When a demon leaves a man, it seeks rest in waterless places. If the demon finds none, it returns to the house you drew it out of. [31] If the host stumbles and no longer lives in grace, then the demon will call seven unclean messengers. They enter and dwell in the body. [32] If the host still has faith, you may purge him again. If he be of this wicked generation, then pity him, for he

is lost. Cast him off as one of the damned."

33 Pointing to Simon-Cephas, Yeshua called, "Come. Show me how you will dispossess me of a demon. Wrest the sword from a watcher." 34 Simon-Cephas stood and stared steadily into the eyes of Yeshua. Yeshua stared back. His pupils did not open to his student; they penetrated the brown irises of Simon-Cephas, who wavered and wobbled into a spell of dizziness. 35 Yeshua stepped back. Simon-Cephas gathered his wits and gritted his teeth on the bitter fruit of frustration. 36 "Again," Yeshua commanded. Their eyes locked. Yeshua crossed his eyes. Simon-Cephas fell back as if he had stepped on a serpent. 37 Yeshua laughed. "Let us break bread," he grinned while helping his emissary up, "and drink a little wine. An empty stomach is no way to chase out demons!" 38 This impressed his emissaries. Never before had they worked after the supper hour.

39 A morning after a troubled sleep, the emissaries, almost to a man, asked Yeshua through the voice of Toma, "When will the New World come? When will the Kingdom of God open to us?" 40 Yeshua shook his head. Looking at his men he answered, "Doubting Toma, how is it you are not in the kingdom now?" 41 The limbs of Yeshua shook. "Have you been searching for it? Look!" Their rabbi pointed to the sky. "It is here!" He walked over to a rock and lifted up a corner. "Look! It is there!" 42 Opening his arms and swaying to his left and right, "Sovereignty is spread everywhere upon the earth. That which you look for is here, but you do not recognize it. 43 When you are fully of the Holy Breath, when you live within grace, you will stop seeking that which you already have."

44 The men looked at one another. A troubled Simon-Cephas fished for a better answer. "But people will seek a sign. What shall we tell those who ask us for a sign?" 45 Yeshua responded with a full chest, "If a sign is asked of you, tell them an evil and unregenerate people seek for a sign, but no sign will be given

them save the prophet Jonah. ⁴⁶ After three days and three nights in the belly of the great beast, Jonah emerged as a sign to the people of Nineveh. So will the Son of Man be a sign to a new generation."

47 On a sunny day Yeshua pointed to his emissaries and then to the sun as he exclaimed, "You are the lamp of this world! ⁴⁸ A hill does not hide the town built on it. A person does not light a lamp to place it under a bowl. The lamp is placed on a stand to shine for everyone. ⁴⁹ For nothing is hidden when it is placed in light; nothing is secret save it is hidden for it to be revealed. In this way you must be a light shining for others that they may see your good works and glorify the Holy Breath. ⁵⁰ So you are. So you must preach to the multitudes."

29 Their work on the mountain almost accomplished, Yeshua took Simon-Cephas by the hand and led him with Jacob and Yohanan to an elevated height. ² Our Spirit rose following closely after them. A strutting peacock pranced ahead of them. ³ Reaching a good height of solitude, Yeshua stood with the sun behind him while the three emissaries sat at his feet. ⁴ The long fingers of Yeshua stroked his beard and he spoke, "Soon we must pick up our workload and leave this place. Two of you must go one way," he flipped his wrist with two fingers pointing to his right, "and two another," he pointed to his left, "but I shall go south," he said, pointing with his fore finger. ⁵ This amazed his emissaries. "But why?" asked Yohanan. "Rabbi, you have many students here," he implored as he stretched out his arm and finger as a needle pointing north. ⁶ "They are scattered, but they are many, and the many will increase as the lilies of the field."

7 Speaking as if in a dream, Yeshua told them that on his right, Moses always walked with him; on his left, Elijah. ⁸ "At one time Moses, with the Commandments in hand, led the way to the Promised Land. With some struggling the country

prospered into the realm of David, the Kingdom of Israel. [9] Through the righteous displeasure of Yahweh, the kingdom broke in two. In the north Elijah taught the ways of God. It is said that Elijah will return and then the Son of Man will fulfill his prophecy. [10] Yohanan was Elijah. The Son of Man stands here," he affirmed with his fingers pointing to himself. [11] "All the more reason to stay north," Jacob declared, emphasizing with a pointed finger. "This is where Elijah spoke of the Kingdom of God."

12 Yeshua shook his head, "God is everywhere." Once a city would have sufficed as a center, a lamp to illuminate his teaching, but which city accepts him? [13] His mission, Yeshua explained with some bitterness, always took to his feet. His words scattered like seeds too often falling on barren ground or nettles or stony turf. [14] Yet, even the fruitful soil never encompassed a city or even a village. It is time to till different soil. The seeds he plants in the south will be in new...in fresh soil. [15] The eyes of his emissaries squinted at him, "Fresh soil?" The Son of Man smiled as he told them the south will be different. They will see.

16 Looking down at the three emissaries sitting at his feet, Yeshua asked, "Why did Moses wander in the desert for forty years? Was he lost?" [17] Their faces turned to blank slates. "No? People raised as slaves make poor soldiers. [18] Moses needed to wait for the children born in freedom to grow into conquering heroes." They nodded their heads in unison like a three-headed man. [19] "Suffer the children," Yeshua advised, "and forbid them not to come unto me, for they are of the Living Light."

20 "And Herod fears you are Yohanan the Baptist, resurrected. He has his blade sharp and at the ready," Simon-Cephas added to the reasoning of Yeshua. [21] Yeshua continued, "This is necessary to fulfill the prophecies." [22] With a smile he asserted that the Samaritans would open their arms to him. And Judea he held up to the light as the most

delightful prize. ²³ He wondered if they knew the reason. Each man searched the face of the others. Suddenly the dream of Yeshua shone from the eyes of Simon-Cephas, and he answered, "Jerusalem." ²⁴ The vision of Yeshua cut like diamonds into his emissary. "And why?" More quickly Simon-Cephas responded, "Passover." ²⁵ They walked down and joined the others. Our Spirit lingered behind them as a strutting peacock led them back down to those who waited looking up at them.

Notes: 29:9 The United Kingdom of Israel divided itself into Israel in the north and Judea in the south. The rebellion of ten northern tribes to the rule of Rehoboam, the Grandson of David, caused the kingdom to split over religion and taxes. Judea takes its name from Judah, one of the twelve tribes of Abraham. Judah is also the root of Judaism and Jew, and a popular male name handed to us, from the Greek spelling, as Judas. Israel means "Wrestled with God." When Jacob, the son of Abraham, wrestled with a messenger, the messenger called him Israel. **29:22** It was in the district of Samaria that the Baptist worked the waters of the Jordan.

---

30 The women broke camp. Joanna and Susanna gathered up the supplies. Miryam Magdalene put out the fire. ² She started to help gather odds and ends, but drifted from her tasks, as she often did, to stand off to the side of the men and hear their conversations. ³ Around their rabbi, the twelve gathered. Destinations were plotted out in the roads of their minds. ⁴ The idea of Matthew becoming treasurer raised its head, but Matthew quickly distanced himself from the proposition, as if threatened by a serpent. He wanted nothing to do with handling money. It settled on Judah Iscariot to handle the purse. ⁵ Two by two they would go, as if disembarking from the great ark of Noah to repopulate the world. Phillip teamed up with Bartholomew; Toma and Simon the Zealot; Matthew and Andreas; Judah Thaddeaus and Jacob the Just; the rest remained with Yeshua to assist him. Upon the call of their rabbi, they would meet again in Jerusalem during Passover–this year or the next.

6 All in readiness, Yeshua spoke to his emissaries, "Be strong. Be prepared. If you are given much, much will be required of you. If men expect much of you, they will demand that much more. [7] The servant who knows the will of the master but is not prepared or does not act as needed will be beaten severely." He grinned. "Those servants who do not, but should know, will be given a little beating. [8] The Holy Breath is a demanding and relentless taskmaster. But," pointing his finger into the air, "know you, do not worry about your body: what you will wear, what you will eat, what you shall drink. Our holy mission is more than clothes, more than food. [9] Do you not see the birds of the air? They do not sow. They do not reap. They do not gather into barns. Yet God Almighty tends to them. You are more important than the birds! [10] See you the lilies of the field. They do not toil. They do not spin. Know you, even all the glory of Solomon compares not to the beauty and majesty of one lily. [11] If the Father clothes the grass of the field, the grass that grows today and is burned in the oven tomorrow, will he not clothe you too?" Yeshua paused and smiled reassuringly, "Who by restless worrying can add one cubit to his span of life?"

12 He paused to search their faces and then went on, "We make no blood offerings. The Temple is our body. If you should pollute your temple, you may purify your body with three days of washing and fasting." [13] Pinching the skin on his right hand he went on, "When flesh settles in dust," the rabbi pointed at his emissaries, "when death dreams it owns you," the words shot from him straight through his emissaries, "when we shed our mortal robe," Yeshua dropped his robe to his feet, "when I am a shade…" Everyone gasped; Simon-Cephas, Judah Iscariot, and Simon the Zealot put their

hands to their mouths. "...in three days I will return to my body and," in one motion he picked up his robe, wrapped it around his shoulders, and lifted his arms and face, "rise to the gates of paradise!"

14 The smile of Yeshua shone on them before he earnestly continued, "If you are troubled, pray and I will be with you. Prayer is the path that leads to sure ground and strong footing. [15] If the people throng to you, open your arms to them. They have been harried and preyed upon as sheep without a shepherd. [16] Do not go from house to house, but when a home receives you, stay there until you leave the town. In that home say, 'Peace be with you.' And when your mission is finished, when you have taught all you can teach and healed all you can heal, and it is time to move on down the road, be sure the last message you leave them with is, 'Be strong, the Holy Breath is with you.'

17 "Know you," Yeshua said pointing his finger into the air, "the reign of Sovereignty is nigh. Lift yourselves up to the grace of the Holy Breath. To be my emissary is to be exalted. One day we shall sit in splendor. Six of you shall sit on my right and six on my left. [18] But now you must toil. Unfold yourselves like light from a morning sky and your words will be pearls of water to baptize the transgressor and uplift the poor. The harvest is full. Reap in plenty."

19 Yeshua considered his emissaries with a steady gaze, his fingertips tapping the side of his leg. They were good men. Were they ready? [20] He could do no more. If he taught them until the mountain crumbled to a nub, he could do no more. It was time. How would they do without him? His fingers drummed the side of his leg.

21 "I have taught you much; before you go, you have ears. Who do people say is the Son of Man?" [22] Phillip replied, "Some say Yohanan the Baptist." Toma replied, "Some say Elijah." [23] Yeshua nodded and asked, "And you? Who do you say is the Son of Man?" Simon-Cephas stepped forward and said, "You are the true prophet of the living

God, the Son of David, the Anointed One." Yeshua beamed in his reply, ²⁴ "Simon bar Jonah, a blessing on you! This is not revealed through flesh and blood, but by the Holy Breath of God."

25 Pointing to Simon-Cephas, Yeshua stated clearly, "Know you, today and tomorrow you are my rock; you are Cephas. ²⁶ Upon Cephas I will build my congregation and though Satan opens his gate, no devastation shall prevail against it. To you I give the keys to the heavenly realm. Whatever you hold on earth will be held in the kingdom. Whatever you let loose on earth will be let loose in the kingdom." ²⁷ Yeshua paused and opened his arms to all of them. Raising his finger in the air, "I am the Anointed One." Placing his finger before his lips, "Be sure you tell no one." ²⁸ He paused and suggested, "Let us pray." They shut their eyes and their rabbi led them in prayer.

29 Beams of sun steadily filled the air around them. They breathed it in and out. The women burdened with their bundles and the men with their missions, they all, soaring with the lift of graceful wings of our dove, stepped off Mount Tabor to walk on air filled with heavenly clouds.

31 Yeshua struck out for Salim in Samaria under an autumn shine with clouds bold as the first steps of a new day. Cephas led the way, entering the town the day before the others to prepare for the arrival of Yeshua. ² The reputation of the "Son of God" preceded Cephas. When the emissary set the streets abuzz with the coming of Yeshua, the walls rebounded with a dull thud as if the name were made of mud. ³ As the finer citizens gathered about him, Cephas felt the grabbing and pushing of hands. ⁴ With frowns on every face, the body of Cephas landed ignominiously outside the city gates.

5 Shedding the dust of Salim to gather the dust of the road, Cephas found Yeshua sitting with the other three emissaries and the women by a crossroad under a sycamore where slowly each

leaf danced with a lazy breeze. ⁶ At the news of the salutation Cephas received from Salim, the eyes of his "sons of thunder" burned like shooting stars. "Rabbi, shall we call fire down upon them?" ⁷ Yohanan pleaded. "Let us burn them to the ground!" Jacob shouted, flexing his eyebrows as his spittle landed in his beard.

8 Yeshua marveled at them and shook his head. Looking down one road he asked, "What lies that way?" ⁹ The search for an answer circled in the minds of the men and then appealed from one blank emissary face to another. They shrugged their shoulders. ¹⁰ Joanna, with Reuben swaying on her hip, pointed with her head, "That?" The men nodded. "That way leads to Sychar." ¹¹ Off they went. The road to Jerusalem was going to be a long and winding one.

Note: 31:10 Sychar was known as Shechem in ancient Biblical times. Today it is called Nablus.

---

32 Stops along the road attracted Yeshua. In one qehalah after another he proclaimed parable on parable, some old, some new. ² "Who has a friend he may go to at midnight and say, 'Give me a loaf of bread. An old companion has unexpectedly come to me from a long journey and I have nothing to give him.' ³ If the friend shuts his door," Yeshua flipped his wrist as if slamming a door and then wagged his finger, "and says, 'Do not bother me; it is late and I am in bed,' you have no friend. ⁴ But if your friend rises from bed and gives of his bounty not one but two loaves," he lifted his arms, bringing them in to clutch his hands to his chest before extending them with open hands, "then you have a friend indeed. ⁵ So it is," he pointed up, "with the Holy Breath. Ask and it will be given to you. Seek," Yeshua brought his hand to his eyebrow as if scanning a horizon and then, with a sweeping gesture, pointed his finger at the crowd, "and you shall find. ⁶ Knock," he rapped the air with his fist and flung it forward as if a door swung open, "and the door will be opened to you. [7] If you live in the Holy Breath, the Holy Breath will be like a good friend to you," he affirmed with a smile as wide as a road.

8 Yeshua continued with a blessing from the Holy Spirit, "Whoever among you becomes childlike to learn anew shall know the Sovereignty, and you shall be more exalted than the Baptist. [9] Know you, blessed be the meek, for the earth is theirs to inherit. [10] Blessed be the merciful, for their sins shall be absolved. [11] Those who do the work of the Holy Breath shall be exalted."

12 If Yeshua did not stop at a town or village, people came to him. [13] While he taught in the countryside, a servant of Martha and Miryam tracked him down. The sisters and their brother had long stood by Yeshua as followers and patrons. [14] The servant delivered his message: Yeshua must come right away—their brother lay ill in his bed. [15] Yeshua thought of him, a devoted follower of the New Way, but felt the blindness seeking the light, the hands reaching for forgiveness, the ears eager to be tuned with the bounty and mercy of those around him. Their needs demanded much from him. [16] He asked the servant to describe the illness and then told him he would come before the belly of the moon was full. [17] He must remain here awhile; the sick and needy at his feet also needed him. The servant observed all around him, returned home, and reported all he had heard and seen.

18 The next day, when teaching in the countryside from early morning to late in the day, Judah Iscariot approached Yeshua and whispered in his ear, "The hour is late. [19] All this time there has been no rest. It is well past the hour to eat. Send them away so they may fend for themselves." [20] Yeshua looked out at the intent eyes focused on him. "We shall share what we have. Bring it to me." [21] Shaking his head, Judah dutifully brought two baskets and stood by Jacob and Yohanan; both

smiled on him. One basket contained three loaves and one held a few fish." [22] Yeshua told everyone to sit in groups. He then took the baskets, held them up, blessed their contents, and announced, "We have little, but what little we have… here, replenish yourselves." [23] Yeshua encouraged all to share what each possessed as one community, one being. [24] Smiling, he instructed his emissaries to pass the baskets from group to group. All hunger satiated, Yeshua taught for three more hours. [25] The emissaries gathered up the baskets and discovered, to the wide-eyed, open-mouthed surprise of Judah with the grins of Jacob and Yohanan upon him, the baskets contained more food than what they had started with.

26 The servant of Martha and Miryam once again found Yeshua and begged him; he must come now. A demon throttled their brother by the throat. [27] The strength of the demon mastered his strength. The life of the man waned to a thin breath. [28] Yeshua pointed to the throng around him. They would not let him go no matter how much he wished to depart. [29] Tomorrow. He promised his feet would take to the road for Bethany early the next day.

30 Even so, on the way he stopped and taught. Too many stood eager to hear the New Way of the Holy Spirit. [31] "You have learned 'An eye for an eye; a tooth for a tooth,' but," Yeshua raised his finger in the air, "know you, if you are struck on the cheek, turn the other cheek. [32] If your coat is taken from you, give also your shirt. If a ruffian forces you to go a mile, walk with him two miles. Refuse not the beggar nor a borrower, but give freely. [33] You have been taught to love your neighbor, but you let loose a sharp-toothed wolf on your enemy. Know you, you should love your enemy also. [34] Love and pray for those who straddle the yoke around your neck. For in this you will be as God Almighty who sends rain on the just and the unjust. [35] The sun shines on all, good and evil. If you love

only those who love you, how are you any different from your enemy or a Goy? ³⁶ Love your enemies and with grace you will rise above all others."

37 A Zealot wiped his nose on his worn-out robe. ³⁸ This was the second time he had listened to the preacher from Nazareth. ³⁹ *No. This will not do.* He turned the back of his sandals to Yeshua.

40 When he arrived in Bethany, Martha and Miryam went out to meet Yeshua. "Rabbi, what took you? Why did you not come sooner? ⁴¹ Eleazar died four days ago. Had you come sooner my brother would be alive," Martha choked through tears and fell into bitter weeping. ⁴² Yeshua told her, "Your brother will rise again." Miryam nodded her head and affirmed, "Yes. ⁴³ He will rise again on the last day. The day of resurrection." She fell and clasped the knees of Yeshua, sobbing for the loss of her brother. ⁴⁴ Their grief rolled as a storm on a sea tossing every boat in its path. Yeshua wept. The emissaries and women wept.

45 He told them, "Show me where he lies." The sisters took him to a cave with a stone rolled in front of it. ⁴⁶ Yeshua ordered his men, "Roll back the stone." ⁴⁷ Martha stepped forward, "Rabbi, he has lain in his grave for too long. His body...the stench..." Yeshua told her, "Did I not say he will rise again?" ⁴⁸ He pointed with his finger, "Roll away the stone." His emissaries, with considerable effort, did as he commanded.

49 "Eleazar," Yeshua called, "Come. Come out." ⁵⁰ All focused their eyes into the darkness of the tomb. All breathing slowed to a hushed cushion of air. Every thought leaned its body toward the grave. ⁵¹ Eleazar stepped forward. His feet and hands bound with strips of cloth and his face covered with a fine linen, he groped about. ⁵² "Remove his death clothes and set him free," Yeshua ordered, adding as he looked upon the sisters of Eleazar, "Blessed are those who mourn, for they will be comforted."

53 Yeshua stayed with them for two days. Hearing Eleazar had

risen from his grave, the curious and demon-possessed appeared on the first night. [54] Yeshua commended the life of Holy Breath to the curious. To the sick he worked the devil furiously out of their lives.

55 On the night before he left, a larger crowd of supplicants gathered at the door. Yeshua lay in a dream. [56] Judah tapped him and whispered loudly of the needy waiting on him. Heaving a sigh as tall as Mount Sinai, Yeshua remained still. Judah waited and then tapped Yeshua again. [57] The son of the carpenter grunted, "I am bone weary. They must go away." [58] His emissary offered to help him up. Yeshua shook him off. "Would they drain the well dry? I must rest! They must...wait." [59] Judah whispered sharply, "They need you. They need you!" The Son of Man shouted into the face of Judah, "Enough!" and shut his eyes.

60 When Yeshua awoke, Miryam opened a jar of nard. She poured the oil on the feet of Yeshua. The oil felt cool and slick. [61] Yeshua and everyone else watched as she washed his weary feet. Using her brown hair as a cloth, her long fingers rubbed her tresses gently and firmly over his ankles, his soles, between his toes. [62] Miryam began to stroke his calf and shin. Yeshua smiled but stopped her at his knees.

63 Many kin and friends of Martha and Miryam ran to witness the good news of Eleazar. Some clapped their hands with the joy of his resurrection. Others took to their heels to testify against Yeshua to the high priest, Caiaphas. [64] Before they left the home of Eleazar, Our Spirit possessed both Yeshua and Judah. They spoke kindly, each asking the other for forgiveness.

Note: 32:13 The first time Yeshua stayed with Martha and Miryam, Martha diligently served them. Miryam loitered around Yeshua, captivated by his teaching. Martha appealed to Yeshua to put Miryam in her place, the kitchen. Yeshua upbraided Martha. Miryam learning at his feet *was* in her rightful place. **32:** Goy is the singular of Goyim. Goyim is the Hebrew word for "nations," which translates from the Latin as Gentiles. In time Goyim and Gentiles came to mean anyone who was not Jewish. **32:41** Eleazar means "whom God helps" and translates from the Greek into English as Lazarus.

33 Yeshua dreamed of the Baptist. Not for the first time, and whenever he dreamed of Yohanan, the dream always was much the same. ² It begins in the dusty cell of the hilltop fortress of Machaerus. The lines on the face of his cousin, as if drawn with a faulty calamus, stun Yeshua. ³ Amos steps from the shadows to visit his friend and rabbi. The voice of Yohanan rings as clearly as when he spoke by the River Jordan.

4 "Yes. I have been interrogated. The wicked Herod with the vain-glorious harlot at his side sat on their nefarious thrones. I stood before them, and I stood my ground. ⁵ I called her a whore for sleeping with her brother-in-law. What virtuous woman does such a thing? How could she degrade herself and take Herod with her? ⁶ Herod trembled. I dismissed him as an abomination before God.

7 "Their marriage is a curse that will murder the first born in every house! Their bed stinks as a disease spreading Godlessness! ⁸ Because of them a moral famine devastates the land. The dry furrows of the field grow only the seed of unclean messengers. Demons dance and sing for joy. ⁹ No good can come from their union, their sham marriage. I called upon them to repent their evil ways."

10 His words at first spilled out desperately from his lips as if, had he not spoken them quickly, they would disappear and be forever lost. ¹¹ Taking a breath, Yohanan continued in measured meters, "It was strange to watch their faces." He mused, "Implacable. Like statues. ¹² But their eyes. In their eyes I saw the whip of my words beating them. ¹³ The miscreant slaves to their lusts! They knew. They knew."

14 The voice of Yohanan faded and wandered within himself. Then he became aware of the faces of Amos and Yeshua. [15] They tried to put on a confidence as sure as the flowing waters of the Jordan, but that is not what Yohanan saw. Grinning his toothy smile and with a short laugh, he washed away lines of concern on their faces. "It is in the hands of God," [16] Yohanan assured them. "I do not tremble at any fate in the hands of God Almighty." Clasping their shoulders, he looked into their eyes, "Will the sinners repent?" [17] He paused as the memory of his trial flooded his mind. "The eyes of Herodias turned cold like a fish. But Herod... Herod I think saw his error."

18 The three men prayed. Two desperate men left the Baptist with blessings from Our Spirit. [19] Nothing more could be done for Yohanan. His admonition to his captors was a confession and a death sentence.

20 The severed, dripping head of Yohanan appeared large. He looked down upon his cousin and dropped into the hands of Amos, who hurried away with his prize. [21] The body of the Baptist turned into a flying scroll to stalk despoilers and demons of false oaths. No prison held Yohanan. [22] His ghost took to the sky, a raging unstoppable wind. Death did not stop his spirit from being a power in the world. Our dove soared with the grace of his breath. [23] Yeshua woke from his dream; the words of Yohanan singing in his ears and the sun shining into his blinking eyes.

33:2 The calamus, a reed pen with a hollow inside, made in Southern France, was exported the length and breadth of the Roman Empire.

34

Yeshua stepped up to preach, "Know you, the Holy Breath is like a king who settled his account with a servant. The servant owed his master a thousand talents," he stretched out his open hand, "but lacked the means to pay it." [2] Yeshua quickly retrieved his stretched arm, clutching his hand into a fist as if snatching air. "The king ordered the servant, his wife, his children, and all his possessions to be sold to make good his debt. 3 The servant fell to his knees, kissed the foot of his master, and begged, 'Lord, show me mercy! If you bless me with your patience, I will repay my entire debt.' 4 His master pitied him." With his palms open in front of him, Yeshua bent his elbows to raise his hands. "To raise him up, the lord forgave his servant his debt and set him free.

5 "The servant went out from the king and ran into Judah, who owed him a hundred denarii. The servant grabbed Judah by the throat," Yeshua clutched his throat and snarled, then dipped his voice in boiling waters of anger, "and demanded payment." 6 Yeshua changed his voice to the tenor of a beggar with his hand out. "The debtor fell to his knees, kissed the foot of the servant, and begged the servant for patience. 7 If given a little time, he would make good the money he owed. The servant lifted up his chin while lowering his eyes and sent the man to prison until the debt be paid.

8 "The people who witnessed the mercy of the king and the righteous cruelty of the servant, with their distress in their hands pulling their hair, reported to the king the cold-blooded actions of his servant. 9 The king summoned him." Yeshua motioned with his finger to come and said, his voice a beating stick, "'Ungrateful man! I forgave you your debt. Should not you have taken my mercy and carried it with you? Should not you have shown your debtor mercy?' 10 The master turned his servant over to his jailors until the debt owed him be paid."

11 The voice of Yeshua softened and went on in a matter-of-fact tone. "Know you, it is right for you to be forgiven your transgressions and to forgive the transgressions against you." 12 Yeshua finished with the look and voice of one who observes people in a careless hurry, obliviously walking over gold coins under their feet. 13

"If you live not in the breath of forgiving and sharing, you shall never know the Kingdom of God." Pointing upward with his finger, "You see light from the sky." [14] Pointing his finger at the crowd, "You see nothing. Compared to everlasting light shining with the Holy Breath, every other light is lost in shadows."

15 He noticed stares of suspicion. Seeing a mother nursing her toddler, Yeshua pointed to the child and proclaimed loudly, "Those who enter the Living Light are like little children shown the way by the light of the Holy Breath." [16] He paused. Matthew, who stood among the crowd, asked, "Are we then to be as little children?" [17] Yeshua answered, "Yes! The wonder of a child should be yours. So as the children of light, so should man be of the light. [18] I shall choose you and you," his words hammering out his intentions, he pointed to one child and then another, "one from a thousand and two from ten thousand. They shall stand, becoming a single body."

19 Yeshua, aware that suspicion followed his every word and gesture, raised his voice. "Just as two should be made as one, the inside the same as the outside and the outside the same as the inside." [20] Make the above and the below as one; establish the male with the female as a single being so that the man will not act masculine and the woman not behave as feminine." [21] A woman carrying a basket of fish stopped and listened with her mouth open like a fish. One head turned to another. [22] "When you establish eyes in the place of an eye and a hand in the place of a hand and a foot in the place of a foot and an image in the place of an image, then shall you enter the Kingdom of God." [23] Stretching his hands to embrace the crowd, Yeshua shouted, "Blessed are the reviled and persecuted! [24] If you believe in me and someone leads any of you to sin, better for him a great stone be placed around his neck and he be thrown into the sea! [25] You who follow me and are persecuted by men who utter falsehoods and mutter

unspeakable evil against you, rejoice!" The outstretched hands of Yeshua rose up over his head, "For your reward is great! ²⁶ Be glad, for heaven waits on you!" With his last words his right hand lowered and his finger swept the crowd pointing at one person after another.

27 Yeshua stepped down and walked off to leave the market. Before he escaped, elders from the qehalah approached him. They told him of a slave prostrated with sickness and near death. ²⁸ Marcus, a centurion and the owner of the slave, paced to and fro in fretful fires of trepidation. He had witnessed broken limbs set like new or successfully amputated, surgery to mend wounds or, once, to clear a cloudy eye, and twice trepanning. ²⁹ For ailments, he had used potions like Rosemary for an upset stomach; for relief, he had used poultices such as fish brine for rheumatism. All were accompanied with prayers, sacred music, and holy ornaments. ³⁰ Yet neither any advancements in medicine nor the power of sacrifices and magic had healed his beloved slave and ended his torment.

31 As a Roman he did not feel comfortable asking a Jewish healer to save his slave. So, he asked the elders to beseech Yeshua. ³² The elders hoped the Son of Man, since Marcus looked kindly on them and built for them their qehalah, would accept their petition to save a sick slave. ³³ Yeshua stiffened. The elders pulled their beards and implored. The child of humanity nodded, and they led him toward the home of Marcus.

34 Before they arrived, a servant of the centurion caught them and gave Yeshua a message from his master. "Lord, my roof is not worthy of your presence. Do not trouble yourself to come further. I am unworthy of meeting you. ³⁵ If you but say the word, my slave will be healed. I am a man accustomed to authority. To my soldiers I say, 'Go here,' or 'Go there,' and they go as I direct them. ³⁶ To my servants I say, 'Do this,' and the deed is done. I know

if you but say the word, my servant will be healed." Yeshua marveled at the words of the centurion. ³⁷ He stopped and told the wake of people now pooled around him, "Know you, I have found no such faith in all our land." ³⁸ To the servant of the centurion he responded, "Return home. It is done." And so it was.

39 The next day at a gathering Yeshua said, "For those who stand with me, love one another as your own self; protect each other as the pupil of your eye. ⁴⁰ It is your eye that is the lamp of your body." Yeshua put his hands by his eyes with fingers pointing out. "If your vision is sound," he stretched out his arms, "your body will be filled with a shining light." ⁴¹ He brought his fingers to his chest. "But if your vision is not sound," his hands dropped limp to the sides of his body, "your body will be empty of light, a cave deep in the earth, a grave full of bones. ⁴² You must take care, or the breath within you will be lost and you will be lost forever with it. ⁴³ If your whole body is full of light, you will be wholly bright as a lamp giving its rays to shine on others and will lead them to grace. Sharing and forgiving is the Living Light, the eternal light. ⁴⁴ The sky and earth are rolled up in the presence of the sacred light. If you live within the Living Light, you will never taste fear nor see death."

45 "Give us a sign of Sovereignty!" "Yes!" "A sign!" loudly filled the air from the crowd. ⁴⁶ Yeshua wagged his finger and swatted away their words as if they were flies buzzing around a great feast. ⁴⁷ "You scrutinize the sky," he chastened, pointing up, "you study the earth," pointing down, "yet you fail to see who is facing you!" Opening his arms wide, "How is it you do not recognize the present time? ⁴⁸ The Sovereignty is like a woman who puts a little leaven in her dough and makes many great loaves from it. ⁴⁹ The Sovereignty is like a woman carrying a jar full of grain down a road far from home. While she walks, the bottom of the jar cracks open. ⁵⁰ The woman does not know the jar has broken open or

that the grain streams out behind her in a long tail. Only when she gets home and sets the jar down does she see the jar is empty. The grain is all gone." [51] Yeshua looked around him. Noticing the eyes of suspicion upon him, he quickly added, "Whoever has ears, let him hear."

[52] Yeshua walked quickly away, passing a house where two blind men had been listening. They cried out, "Son of God! Son of David, have mercy on us!" Yeshua entered the doorway of their home and the blind men stood up to greet him. [53] "Do you believe," Yeshua asked, "I can remove the demon from your eyes?" "Yes!" They both shouted as they drew near him. [54] "Because you believe," Yeshua told them as he touched their eyes, "let it be done." The men regained their sight.

[55] "Be sure you tell no one of this," Yeshua commanded and left them. Unable to lie still as water in a bowl, the joy of the men leaped up the next day. [56] They rushed out, spilling all over the district to tell all they met about the miracle worker from Nazareth.

[57] When Yeshua left their dwelling, a man, Bazeus, made dumb by a demon throttling his tongue, approached him. [58] Bystanders watched as Bazeus gestured his plea. Yeshua understood and cast his demon from him. Bazeus spoke. [59] The amazed crowd declared, "Never have we seen anything like this!"

[60] A scribe pointing a finger at Yeshua retorted, "This magician is possessed and casts out demons by the power of the Prince of Demons!" The crowd regarded the healer from the corners of their eyes. [61] Yeshua rebuffed the accusation with a laugh and retorted, "How can Shemyaza cast out Shemyaza? [62] A house divided against itself cannot stand. A kingdom divided against itself cannot stand. [63] If Shemyaza has risen up against himself, the kingdom of Shemyaza cannot stand and is coming to an end!"

Notes: 34:5 One denarius was equal to one day of wages for a common laborer. **34:28** A centurion originally commanded a unit of a hundred men. Army reforms changed this to a unit of ten contubernium, "tent groups," totaling eighty men.

35 Two priests began cleaning the spattered and spilled blood from the Court of the Priests as Caiaphas washed his hands and long, hairy forearms in the Molten Sea. Blood from sacrifices had splattered heavily up to his elbows and stubbornly stained his skin red. ² After a long day of animals offering up their lives to atone for sins or bless hopeful prayers, Caiaphas finished scrubbing up. Annas waited on him.

3 Finally, fit for more social duties, they walked to the Nicanor Gate to the jingle of golden bells dangling at the bottom of the blue robe of the high priest. ⁴ "This cannot wait?" Caiaphas asked with the fatigue of a day spent slaughtering, burning offal, flinging blood on the altar, and praying. Annas shook his head and said, "They are not just reporting; they need new orders from you." ⁵ Before they passed through the gate, a man pulled his goat to the high priest. He had come late. It was unpreventable. Apologizing, groveling, he pleaded with Caiaphas to make his offering and cleanse him of sin.

6 The High Priest Caiaphas paused. The man looked as pitiable as his sacrifice. ⁷ The sun of tomorrow quietly called to Caiaphas with all the ache in his bones. He opened his mouth to tell the man to come back in the morning, but the face of the penitent told Caiaphas a story not to be ignored or put off. ⁸ Our Spirit gleamed in the eye of Caiaphas. A long sigh slipped through the lips of the high priest, "Come," he commanded Annas and the man. ⁹ "But..." Annas started to say. "They can wait a little longer," the high priest told him firmly. "Come. Assist me."

10 Annas stifled a grunt and, as if stung with a lash, followed after Caiaphas. Usually, Aaron helped the high priest with sacrificial duties. ¹¹ Early this morning when

he had arrived at the Temple and stripped for Levites to check his body, the religious servants had observed a small rash on the back of his right arm. [12] Sent home with a salve, Aaron would return to the Temple and undergo rites of purification when the rash no longer polluted his body. Only then might he resume his priestly tasks. [13] The priest that replaced him to aid Caiaphas had already left. With a backward glance thrown like a javelin, Annas, hurrying to catch up to the high priest, glared at the penitent and his goat.

14 To and fro, Manaen and Azareel paced the courtyard of the high priest many, many times before they finally stood before Caiaphas. [15] Azareel spoke, "It is impossible. Whenever we try to plant an informer, the Nazarene is wise to us. It is as if he knows us before he sees us. [16] The few who he admitted to be students, he sends off to speak of the Breath of God. No one has been able to get near to him. He keeps only a few emissaries close at hand." "Emissaries?" "That's what he calls them."

17 Annas asked sharply, "And disruption? Are you able to turn the crowds into mobs against him?" Azareel cautiously replied, "He has a way with people. We can turn some against him, others do so on their own, but...he has a way about him." [18] Manaen spoke, "His eyes are like two fiery stones." [19] Azareel cleared his throat and continued, "We run for the guard. And he leaves town before they can seize him." Manaen added, "But then he teaches in the fields." "And he works wonders..." Azareel started to say, but Annas cut him off with, "What has he been saying?" in a tone that squeezed perspiration from the two informants.

20 They started to answer; the High Priest Caiaphas raised his hand. Silence fell over them like leaves falling from a tree in the middle of a quiet night. [21] He looked at Annas. Annas turned to the men and asked, "Where is he now?" Manaen replied, "He has many feet! Look," the informer

pointed with his head where his eyes focused, "There he is!" Pointing his finger, "Now he is over there! Now..." Annas frowned. Azareel interjected, "Samaria. Mostly, he is in Samaria these days."

22 Annas asked the high priest, "What is to be done?" The High Priest Caiaphas stroked his long, black beard for a few moments and thought, *This carpenter believes he has a special, a personal connection with God. Blasphemer!* 23 Caiaphas shook his head as the danger presented by this man circled in his head. The weary eyes of the high priest settled on Annas and replied, "We will need to devise another path, but for now...more of the same."
24 Manaen and Azareel smiled and looked toward the high priest. He pointed to Annas, who stood by the courtyard gate with a small bag of coins in his hand. 25 They left Caiaphas to the jingling of bells as he paced to and fro in his courtyard.

Notes: 35:1 The Temple contained three courtyards. The innermost courtyard, the Court of the Priests, accommodated a slaughterhouse, ten bronze lavers to rinse meat and offal, a basin for priests to wash up called the Molten Sea, which rested on twelve bulls facing outward–three in each direction–and an altar of gold to burn offal and cereals as sacrifices. The next two courtyards were innovations by Herod the Great. The Court of Israelites served as an observation area for men to watch priests make their sacrifices. Women witnessed their offerings from the Court of Women, larger than the men's courtyard but behind it. **35:3** In addition to the four garments of all priests, the high priest wore a blue, sleeveless robe open at the sides with a bottom fringe of thirty-six pomegranate ornaments and bells. For some ceremonies he also donned an ephod: a blue, purple, scarlet, and gold apron opened and tied in the front with shoulder straps on which a breastplate fastened. The breastplate stored the stones Urim and Thummim in its inner pouch. On its front, three rows of four gemstones represented the twelve tribes of Israel. To top it off, below the rim of the high priest's hat and tied to his forehead with a blue thread, a gold plate affirmed, "Holiness unto YHWH." **35:10** The Levi, one of the twelve tribes of Israel, carried out religious functions and recruited men for the priesthood. Religious duties required priests and their assistants to maintain a highly regulated level of purity. Their conduct needed to be without sin. Any injury, disease, or deformity to their body prohibited them from performing religious tasks. For them to touch a sick, dying, or dead person soiled them and required acts of purification before resuming their services. Scribes were also Levites, but performative religious regulations did not touch them. Levites who performed religious duties tended to be Sadducees, while scribes tended to be Pharisees.

36

"Know you," Yeshua said with his finger pointed in the air as he often did, wavering slightly near his temple, "the Kingdom of God is like a man who rose early to hire workers for his vineyard, the lush grapes ripe for hard working hands. ² At dawn four laborers agreed to work for a denarius and entered his field to begin earning their wages. A few hours later the man noticed idle hands seeking work in the marketplace. He hired them to labor in his fields. ³ After a few more hours the man found more workers and sent them," Yeshua plucked at the air, "to pick his grapes from their vines. And again after a few more hours he employed more field hands. ⁴ Near the end of the day the man entered the market and saw the restless feet of men standing around. He asked them why they did not work. They answered that there was no one to hire them. Engaging their labor, he sent them into a world abundant with grapes.

5 "The day ended, and the man told his steward to call the laborers, beginning with the last and going up to the first, so they may collect their wages. Those who had worked only an hour received a denarius each. ⁶ When those hired first witnessed men who had labored only an hour walk away clutching a denarius, their eyes grew as large as a full, golden moon. ⁷ When their turn to be paid came, their

outstretched palms received only a denarius each. Their feet stomped and their mouths grumbled to the landowner," [8] Yeshua said in a high-pitched voice as he stamped his foot, "'Why do those who worked one hour receive the same pay as we who sweated all day in the blister of sun? We worked longer.'" [9] Stomping his foot again, Yeshua continued in a high-pitched voice. "'We worked harder. Why are our wages not greater?'

10 The man replied in a firm voice, 'What wrong have I done you? You agreed to work for a denarius, did you not? Take what you have earned. It is yours. [11] Why do you begrudge my generosity to those who worked one hour? Am I not lord of what I own? May I not do as I choose to do? [12] All who labor for me shall receive my bounty.'" Yeshua paused, probed the pairs of eyes around him focusing on the vision his words carried, and finished, "So it is in the Kingdom of God; the first will be as the last and the last will be as the first."

13 Yeshua and Cephas dined with an official who was a Pharisee. The host smiled pleasantly while many around the table warily watched the Nazarene. [14] Yeshua recognized a servant of the Pharisee moving in pain from swelling in his arms and legs. Not long ago he had cured the man. Calling the servant to him, Yeshua asked him, "What ails you now?" [15] His master spoke up for him with a cold eye on Yeshua, "You healed him on a Sabbath. Now he is cursed."

16 Yeshua scoffed. Placing his hand on the shoulder of the servant, he asked, "Do you believe?" The gaze of the servant locked into the eyes of Yeshua. [17] "Yes," he affirmed. "Then go in peace." Yeshua moved his hand from the shoulder to press against the breast of the man and then flung his hand toward the ground as if throwing something down. [18] "You are free of sin." The servant smiled and painlessly continued to serve them. [19] Turning on the Pharisee and his

guests, Yeshua asked, "Does or does not the law permit healing the sick on the Sabbath?" No one spoke, but their eyes flashed with fury over breaking the Sabbath. [20] Yeshua questioned all in the room, "Who among you, if into a well an ox or a son fell, would not save them even on the Sabbath?" [21] Their tongues formed no answer, but their eyes danced with visions of cutting Yeshua down.

[22] Undaunted and noting where each guest chose his seat at the table, Yeshua asked, "At a marriage feast, do you take a seat of honor?" [23] Looking around at each face, Yeshua continued, "Now, what if a man of greater standing than you arrives? You must give up your place to this man when your host approaches you and tells you to move. [24] Shame pours on your head, and you drag yourself to the lowest seat. Know you, it is better to take the lowest seat immediately. [25] When your host sees you, he may say to you, 'I beseech you, friend, go up higher!' Then all at the table will know your eminence and honor you. [26] Anyone who honors himself will be humbled, and he who humbles himself will be honored." [27] One guest stared into the air, trying to remember where he had heard such words before. A few who knew well the Proverbs of Solomon sharpened their attention on Yeshua or clucked their tongues.

[28] Looking at his host he said, "You have kindly invited me to dine with you; let me return the favor." Yeshua grinned. The host coldly smiled. [29] "When inviting guests to a feast, do not invite your kin or your friends or rich and important people, for they will invite you to their feast, and you will be repaid only in kind on this earth. [30] It is far better for you to invite the beggars in the market, the crippled, and the blind. Then you will be repaid for your generosity with blessings in the Kingdom of God."

[31] The next day Yeshua came upon a crowd in front of the home of Elizabeth, a patron. In the middle of these gathered witnesses, scribes argued

with Yohanan and Cephas. 32 Yeshua watched as tempers flared back and forth. He approached. The crowd turned to him as he asked, "What is the matter here?" 33 Tavi stepped forward and answered, "My son is possessed of an evil spirit." He clenched his fist, "It seizes him and throws him to the ground. My boy gnashes his teeth and foams from his mouth. 34 The demon turns his body rigid like a staff. I asked your men to cast the demon out," he shook his fists and then went limp, "but they failed to do it."

35 Yeshua looked the father in the eye, "Bring him to me." As the boy came near, the devil thrashed him and threw him down. Groaning, he foamed at his mouth like water rushing against rocks. His body stiffened. 36 "How long," Yeshua asked Tavi, "has this been going on?" The father answered, "Since childhood the demon has thrown him into water and into fire. Have pity on us, healer. Show us your mercy!" 37 "All is possible if you believe," Yeshua assured him. The father cried, "I believe!"

38 "Destroy my unbelief," a scribe yelled out. Yeshua noticed that the crowd had grown. 39 "Deaf and dumb demon, come out! And never enter this vessel again." The demon within the boy cried out, convulsed in its bed of sin, and fled. 40 The youth dropped down by the feet of Yeshua. "He is dead!" cried the scribe. Yeshua ignored him. Taking the boy by the hand, the healer raised him up to walk away with his father.

41 Snug within the home of Elizabeth, Yohanan and Cephas took Yeshua aside privately. "Why," they asked him with troubled brows, "could we not cast out the demon?" 42 Yeshua put his right hand on the left shoulder of one and his left hand on the right shoulder of the other as he quietly said, "This was a beast of Shemyaza, a bat. 43 They require more prayer. With more prayer you can cast out the beast of the unclean messenger."

Note: 36:27 The Book of Proverbs is a compilation of various collections (Solomon, Agur, King Lemuel, and others). All are Wisdom Literature. Yeshua puts his own spin on a proverb. "Do not brag about yourself in front of a king or stand in the spot that belongs to notable people, because it is better to be told, 'Come up here,' than to be put down in front of a prince whom your eyes have seen." Proverbs 25:6-7, Names of God Bible. (NOG)

37 Outside the qehalah, the mother of Yeshua, his brother Jacob, and his youngest sister Miryamla waited for him. Jacob paced and muttered under his breath or sat by his mother and spoke to her. Miryamla stood or sat by her mother and held her hand. Their mother sat still and quiet. ² Finally, Jacob called out for his brother. Yeshua continued to speak. Jacob called again. ³ Inside the qehalah, a man told Yeshua, "Your mother is outside. Your brother is calling for you. Do you not hear him?" ⁴ Yeshua replied with a sweep of his hand, "In here. Here is my family. Those who hear the word and do the will of the Holy Breath are my mother and father, my brother and sister."

5 Yeshua continued to teach, "A man had two sons. Judah, the youngest, said to his father, 'Father, give me the share of property that is mine.' ⁶ The old man took an account of his living and divided it fairly between his two sons. Before long, Judah gathered his share of prosperity from his father and left to live in a distant country. ⁷ There, like grains of sand, his wealth slipped loosely through his fingers." Yeshua thrust out his hand with fingers splayed and moved his eyes as if following sand sliding through them.

8 "A famine turned its desolate face to that country and took the land in its fist." He cupped his hand and lowered it from his forehead to his chin to draw out his face and then shot it forward in a fist. ⁹ "Judah had nothing for himself and, feeling the bite of want," stretching out an open hand and clenching into a fist, "gave himself over to a rich man who put him in his fields to feed swine."

He dropped and waved his hand by his knees as if sweeping swine. [10] "Gladly would Judah have filled his belly," his hand clutched at his stomach, "with the feed of the pigs, for his rich master provided him with little. [11] Before long, Judah scolded himself, *I waste here with hunger. How many servants of my father have plenty of bread to eat and even more than to eat!?* [12] *I will go to him and say, 'I am a fallen and unworthy son. My sins against you and heaven rain down as ashes upon my head.'* [13] *I will clasp his knees. I will beg: take me in as a hired servant, and let me work for you!*

14 "And so Judah took up his shame," Yeshua grabbed at his heart with one hand, then extended his other arm and hand in a gesture of going away, "and left that country and returned home. [15] As he came near the house of his father, his father saw him and ran up to him and embraced him and kissed him. [16] Judah fell, clasped the knees of his father and cried, 'My sins against heaven and you are a stone on my back. I am no longer worthy to be called your son.' [17] His father raised him up and called to his servant to bring the finest robe and put it on his son; put also the ring from the little chest on his finger and bring shoes for his feet. [18] 'Then go kill the fatted calf. We will eat and drink and make merry!" Yeshua raised his hand as if holding a cup. [19] "'For my son was dead, but is alive again! My son was lost and now is found!' [17] And so it was done and they rejoiced.

20 "Returning home from the fields, the elder son heard music and laughter. He called a servant over to him and asked for the meaning of all this merriment. [21] The servant told him that his brother has returned; his father killed the fatted calf and is celebrating the return of his youngest son alive and well. [22] The news raised the anger of the eldest son. He bit his fist and refused to enter the house and join them.

23 "When his father knew of this, he came out and plied him with kind words that his eldest son join them. Shaking his head, the eldest gave

voice to his wound, 'What have I done wrong? [24] Have I not served you these many years? Have I not followed your every command?'" [25] Yeshua stomped his foot as he continued, "'Yet, never have you killed the fatted calf for me to make merry with my friends! [26] But my brother, who squandered your wealth on harlots, dares return home, and you pour for him the best wine and kill for him the fatted calf!' [27] The father said to his eldest, 'Son, is what is mine not also yours? [28] Are you not always here with me? It is fit we cheer the return of Judah. Your brother, my son, was dead and now is alive; he was lost and is found!' [29] So the father," the carpenter paused and looked at the congregation, "raised his son." Yeshua finished as he looked out the window, "Let all who have ears, hear."

30 As he left the qehalah, his mother rose to greet him. He turned away. She called him and Yeshua turned back to stand before her. [31] "Come home," she pleaded. He searched into the depths of her eyes and shook his head. "Do not trouble yourself. [32] Or me. I am doing what I must do." "We need you. I..." "I am who I am. What I am, you have done much to make me." [33] "Yeshua..." He cut his mother off, "You have no faith in me?" Miryam could not hide the turbulence of trouble in her eyes. [34] His future, reflected from her, appeared bloody and short. "You have no faith in me," he spat out bitterly.

35 Turning away from his mother, Yeshua walked with his brother to a nearby sycamore. Under the chiming of leaves, the arguments of Jacob dragged his brother to reason, [36] but with each argument Yeshua slipped through his grasp. "If you have no thought for yourself, have you considered what the Romans might do to us?" His brother beseeched with open arms and hands. [37] "Yes." Jacob lifted his agitated head toward the clouds above them. Yeshua proudly said, "Have you..." pointing at the chest of his brother and then his own, "...considered what I will do to the

Romans?" ³⁸ "God Almighty!" "Yes. Exactly. God Almighty." Yeshua placed his palm on the chest of Jacob. "Have faith." ³⁹ Yeshua turned and walked a few steps before turning back and pointing his finger at his brother. "Live in the Holy Breath…and have faith."

40 Walking back to his mother and sister, Yeshua faced Miryamla. Like brackish water, her worry washed over his face and troubled him. But only for a moment. ⁴¹ Yeshua smiled and slid his finger down her nose as he had done often to tease Miryamla. As a child, when upset, she pouted in a corner until his antics cheered her. ⁴² She found nothing within her capable of responding to his foolishness now. With trembling lips she turned from him. ⁴³ Then turned back as tears quickly routed her eyes. But she could not face him. She put her hands to her face.

44 Yeshua turned from her to his mother. Their eyes met like two waves crashing against each other in a storm. The watery eyes of Miryam studied his face and pleaded with him to come back to her. ⁴⁵ She had raised him with songs of how beautiful he was in this troubled world and what a blessing he was to her. ⁴⁶ The troubles he now traveled crumpled her peace of mind. She pulled at him with all her might to come home.

47 The hour grew late. The irises of Yeshua glazed into a distant stare past his mother. He turned and walked away with his emissaries and the women. ⁴⁸ Miryamla took the hand of her mother. A quick look passed between them, saying all that needed saying. The mother hugged her child before her daughter ran after her brother. ⁴⁹ Catching up to Yeshua, Miryamla tugged at his sleeve and they exchanged smiles. Then she helped the women with their load.

38
After a long day of teaching, Yeshua turned to leave the qehalah. He turned back and firmly said, "Know you, I am not here to bury the prophets. The law will not be abolished by me. The law will be fulfilled through me. ² For not till

heaven and earth pass away will one line, one word be taken from the law!" ³ He turned to leave but turned back again. "Not until all by saving grace is accomplished. Unless your works exceed that of the scribes and Pharisees, you will never enter the Kingdom of God."

4 When Yeshua walked through the market, a scribe and a Pharisee ran to him and proclaimed, "We know your truth." ⁵ Yeshua sounded the depths of their eyes and recognized their deceit. They would sit at his feet as students while coins from the high priest jingled in their purse. ⁶ Turning to the emissaries and women with him, the child of humanity announced, "Some will come in my name, but they will be wolves clothed as sheep." ⁷ Looking at the scribe and Pharisee he said with scorn, "Not all who call my name shall enter the kingdom of heaven, but those who practice sharing whatever they have and forgiving all transgressions made against them."

8 Turning to those gathered in the market, "You are the salt of the earth. What happens if salt loses its flavor? ⁹ It cannot be restored. It is thrown onto the road for everyone, soldiers and priests, to trample and grind into the ground. ¹⁰ As long as you are with the Holy Breath, you will never be lost."

11 That night privately, Yeshua quietly told his emissaries, "If called upon, we have been taught it is wrong to testify falsely. Know you, it is wrong to testify at all. ¹² When you speak before a magistrate, simply say, 'Yes' or 'No.' Say no more. It will do you no good and lead you down an evil path," he paused with a sigh, "for they have no understanding."

13 The next day, like bees in a garden, a crowd clustered around Yeshua. Sunlight wrapped around him and the scent of a fresh wind filled the air. He spoke first of the Son of Man and then in parables. ¹⁴ Nadov stepped close to Yeshua and asked, "What must I do to enter into the everlasting life in the Kingdom of God?" Yeshua looked the

young man up and down, "Know you the Commandments?" [15] Nadov, as if being tested by his rabbi, nodded his head as he recited the Commandments of Moses stiffly and firmly, the final one with enthusiasm. "I have practiced them all my days." [16] "Very good!" Yeshua smiled, "Practiced and followed, I should expect." The face of Nadov turned into a question mark.

17 Yeshua patted him on the back and put his hand on the shoulder of the youth. "Never mind. Now add this, be unto others as you would have them be unto you." [18] Nadov recited the words in his head as his lips silently spoke them. Then he said them zealously to Yeshua. The young man smiled. [19] Yeshua smiled back and asked, "Do you believe that?" Nadov readily agreed it would be a just way to live. [20] Still smiling, Yeshua asked, "If I gave you a coin, would you give a coin to me?" Nadov firmly replied with an affirmative. [21] Yeshua pinched and pulled the fine garment of Nadov. "Then give all you have to the poor." The face of Nadov registered the hit slowly. [22] Yeshua pressed the necessity of poverty. "Sell all you own. Give your wealth to the poor and come follow me. Your bounty will be increased tenfold in the Sovereignty." [23] The body of Nadov sank into itself. Silently he turned and broke away.

24 Yeshua watched him as he spoke to everyone around him. "It is impossible for a rich man to enter heaven." [25] His words filled the air with sharp corners and the sigh of a body settling into death. They listened to him with open mouths as they fastened their eyes on him. [26] "It is easier for a camel to pass through the eye of a needle, than for a rich man to pass through the gates of paradise."

27 Judas Iscariot asked, "Then who can be saved?" Yeshua looked all around him. "With man, who can say? With God all is possible. [28] Whoever gives up his wife and child, his mother and father, his brothers and sisters, his livelihood and possessions to walk with me

will be rewarded a hundredfold in the new kingdom." ²⁹ Cephas spoke up, "Rabbi, we have given all. And followed you faithfully." ³⁰ Yeshua smiled, "And so those who are now first will be last, and those who have been last will be first."

31 Zacchaeus, a short man with a long beard, came upon the crowd surrounding Yeshua. Unable to get close, he climbed a nearby sycamore tree to see and hear the child of humanity. ³² When Yeshua finished speaking, he walked beneath the sycamore. Zacchaeus, like ripe fruit, fell to the ground in front of him. Amazed, Yeshua quickly gathered himself together to assist the strange, fallen fruit. ³³ "I wished to see and hear you," Zacchaeus informed the rabbi, brushing himself off. Yeshua took him by his arm and walked with him, saying, "I will spend this night under your roof." Zacchaeus smiled.

34 A Pharisee cried out with pointed words that shot an arrow of disgust down his pointed finger, "This is a damn publican! Slime under a rock! How can you spend the night in his house?" ³⁵ The mouth of Yeshua opened, but it was Zacchaeus who spoke, "Rabbi, you judge. I provide the poor with half of my goods. ³⁶ If it is shown to me I have defrauded anyone, I pay him back fourfold. Does this make me a sinner?" ³⁷ Yeshua shook his head, then to the Pharisee he warmly stated, "Tonight I will dwell in the house of Zacchaeus for we are all offspring of Abraham. ³⁸ The Son of Man is here to find and reclaim the lost and the dispossessed who seek the grace of the Breath of God."

Note 38:35 The tax collector need not pay a tithe. (Tithe means one tenth in Hebrew.) The law requires producers of agricultural products to pay yearly one tenth of their goods to be distributed among the Levites and the poor. Zacchaeus not only pays the tithe; he pays much more than a tenth of his income.

39 Out of the night a voice, followed by a face, emerged to sit at a campfire surrounded by Yeshua and the emissaries. The women huddled around their own fire, hushed their quiet laughter to strain their ears and, like the men, listened to the words of the stranger. ² Nourished with greetings, a handful of figs to eat, and water with a little vinegar to drink, the man stood up and began in a deep voice, "I am Levi, I bring word of Emissary Matthew and the Emissary Andreas, grievous sinners, called by Yeshua to live in the Holy Breath, send their warmest blessing to their rabbi and brethren in the service of the Holy Breath. ³ I tell you, Matthew began his mission the way timid toes, sticking out of sandals too small for feet, anticipate the scrapes and stubs of this world. Andreas helped him step firmly." ⁴ Levi, a young man fully flickering in the firelight, rose up carefully so as not to singe his right foot in the fire, wiggled his toes and then stomped the ground. ⁵ The movement almost cost him his balance, but he managed to stay erect and continued, "With his greater knowledge, Andreas led the way.

6 So the two emissaries spread the teaching of Yeshua," he said, pointing with his open hand. ⁷ "Not long after residing in Iturea, the Emissary Andreas fell sick." Now the young man reporting on the mission of Andreas and Matthew, put the back of his wrist to his forehead and wobbled his knees. ⁸ "The two emissaries took refuge in the home of our sister in Yeshua, Sheera, and her husband Judah. Matthew wished to attend to Andreas. ⁹ Feeble in body but with a strong voice, Andreas urged Matthew to go." Levi waved the back of his hand, flickering with light and shadows from the fire. "'Go forth, to teach and to heal.'

10 "To the marketplace Matthew went, a place where he knew our rabbi often taught and healed the sick. After taking a few deep breaths, he spoke of the Holy Breath and the parable of the sower. ¹¹ Your emissary started strong; a crowd

gathered. The confidence of Matthew grew as their ears turned and opened to him. [12] And then it all went wrong." Around the fire, eyebrows raised. Levi continued, "The congregated eyes...suddenly they felt to Matthew like a knife being sharpened–and he was the whetstone. [13] Startled, he faltered. A small trip led to more stumbles as he went along, and some of the crowd drifted like boats lost in a storm, a few one way, others another." [14] Many around the fire shook their heads. The man raised his voice, "Matthew spoke louder," then lowered his voice, "but they strayed off to attend to their business. [15] With the few who stayed, Matthew gathered himself up and went on, and the Living Light did shine in their faces. [16] He felt as if given the keys to a kingdom, as if he flew with the graceful wings of our dove." Levi put out his hand as if receiving the keys to a kingdom and then clutched it to his chest.

17 Then he hid the lower half of his face within the crook of his elbow as if ashamed. "A leper stepped up and pleaded with Matthew to heal her. [18] His eye could not catch her eye, for her eye wandered. He reached out," Levi stretched out his hand, "to touch her but," Levi clutched back his outstretched hand, "she shrunk back. [19] The emissary called on her faith. She said she believed in the grace of the Breath of God. [20] Matthew told her her faith purified her of her devil and she was devil-free and also clean and should go and sing praises to the Holy Breath. The leper recoiled as if Matthew were the leper. [21] As if set on fire, she shrieked and screeched more sharply, cursing him, for Matthew had not cured her." Mouths around both fires gasped and a few muttered, "Oh no." [22] "The emissary assured her her faith is the power that cures. The leper screamed all the louder and a crowd began to murmur against him. [23] Swiftly Matthew moved to the nearest seller, who sold fruits. He bought a melon. Leaving his change and the market, Matthew hid himself

within the home of Abby." ²⁴ Levi raised both hands above his head as if holding a melon; then he thrust them downward. "The emissary smashed the melon against the house before he entered.

25 "Inside Matthew put his face to the wall. No sackcloth contained his grief. A voiceless raven smothered his breath." ²⁶ Heads around the fire lowered. Eyes stared into the ground or the flames which danced with the cracks and steady roar of burning wood. ²⁷ "Matthew felt his faith slipping through his trembling fingers. His incompetence shook him to his core. ²⁸ He spared himself nothing. The emissary thought he failed his rabbi and betrayed his master. ²⁹ Like a child abandoned at a garbage heap, he stumbled about. All his strength lay in ruins." Some bodies around the fire swayed with agitation. ³⁰ "Doubt bit and tore Matthew with sharp teeth. Mortification grew the way a sudden storm catches a fisherman, tossing and relentlessly battering his boat until he sinks beneath the waves.

31 "Wet with sweat, Andreas rose from his bed." Levi crouched and spread his arms in front of him with his palms up and then stood up. ³² "Andreas could not help but notice his fellow emissary beating his chest with his fists. Matthew confessed his failure to him. ³³ A great laugh burst out of Andreas. Patting the back of Matthew, he snorted and shared his own failures. ³⁴ As an emissary, he counseled, be prepared for hardships and missteps. Pride must be emptied from their pouches of expectations. ³⁵ The road they walk is narrow but opens wide. Their long path bears galling, yet also sweet fruit along the way. ³⁶ Yeshua chose Matthew. That told Andreas all he needed to know. ³⁷ Matthew was still a child of light and possessed the Holy Breath. He must continue the work of their rabbi." ³⁸ Bodies around the fires straightened with beaming faces. Levi went on.

39 "The words of the Emissary Andreas lifted his brother up to be caught by the Holy

Breath. Matthew felt forgiven and blessed. [40] Then Andreas insisted Matthew must return to the market and preach again. Matthew stepped back as if hit by a stone, but Andreas calmly insisted. He would also be there. Matthew protested." [41] The young man paused. His grin danced in the firelight, "Andreas assured him he was well enough." The men around the fire chortled.

42 "The Emissary Matthew fasted and prayed long into the night. He put doubt in a jar, sealed it, dug a pit and buried the spirit far from the door. [43] With prayer came meditation on the teachings of Yeshua." He tilted his head up and opened his arms as if receiving a blessing from on high. [44] "Remembering how his teacher healed the sick, Matthew felt the firm hand of his rabbi on his shoulder.

45 "The next day Matthew stepped resolutely into the center of the market. As he neared the square, Andreas trailed behind him and joined the people as they congregated around Emissary Matthew. [46] A flame of fire possessed his tongue. He does not remember what all he imparted, but he knew from the faces surrounding him that his words filled their ears with glad tidings, their eyes with the light of the saving grace. [47] Before Matthew left the market, two cripples approached him. Their faces filled with heavy wings of despair; their eyes gleamed like broken glass, yet, shades of hope reached out as they grabbed the sleeve of Matthew. [48] By the touch of the Emissary Matthew, using the name of Yeshua through the Holy Breath, the cripples threw down their crutches and sang praises of Yeshua, the Son of God, as they walked around the market." Rings of applauding hands and full-throated voices rose warmly around the fires.

49 "So the Emissary Matthew told Sheera, who told Adin of Ashdod, who told Yuval of Shechem, who told me, Levi, son of Simon of Cyrene." [50] Levi put his hand to his chest and smiled, "who tells you." Heads nodded,

faces smiled at one another, and shimmers of laughter teased the leaping flames. ⁵¹ After breakfast, Judah put a coin in the palm of Levi while Miryam provisioned him with a handful of biscuits and another of dates. ⁵² Yeshua spoke to the stranger who had come from the shadows of the night. A man this youthful and gifted with story-telling must be put to good use. Our Spirit smiled.

Note 39:52 Though reading and writing skills were at an all-time high, the vast majority, certainly carpenters and fishermen and even many of the rich, never received a formal education. They learned and communicated by word of mouth, not by letters. No doubt this message was embellished from mouth to mouth, particularly in the words of Levi. Yeshua may well have been aware of this circumstance, but nonetheless considered that elaborations added rather than detracted from the message. For both the educated and uneducated, truth need not be tied to accuracy. What mattered was the core veracity and entertainment of a story. In those days it was commonly accepted that a myth might be just as or even more truthful than a fact.

40 Jericho, long noted as a resort for the rich as well as for its production of date wine, perfumes, bitumen, and a balsam balm to remedy headaches and eye ailments, attracted the attention of Yeshua. Within the sturdy walls of Jericho, yet outside its qehalah, he preached the way of the Holy Breath in courtyards and the market. ² Once, after teaching under the umbrellas of a small stand of oleanders, the miracle worker ended with a parable. ³ "Know you, you should love your neighbor as yourself." Judah Iscariot spoke up from among the crowd and asked, "And who is my neighbor?"

4 Yeshua smiled, nodded, and answered, "A man named Rafael, while traveling from Jericho to Jerusalem was waylaid by robbers. They beat him," the fist of Yeshua struck the air, "and robbed him," his hand opened and closed, "and left him for dead," his

fingers pointed to the ground by his feet. ⁵ "A priest also traveled from Jericho to Jerusalem. He noticed the man on the side of the road and," Yeshua moved three steps to his right away from the spot he had pointed to, "crossed the road to pass him by. ⁶ A Levite, also traveling from Jericho to Jerusalem, saw," Yeshua moved back to the spot of the body, "the helpless man. He too," Yeshua moved three steps to his left, "crossed the road to pass him by.

7 "A Samaritan traveling from Jerusalem to Jericho noticed Rafael. His compassion led his feet across the road to assist the beaten man." Yeshua moved back to the spot of the body. ⁸ Gesturing with his hands as if comforting a victim, he went on, "Wine and oil the Samaritan poured on the wounds and bound them up. ⁹ The Samaritan set Rafael on his donkey and led the beast to an inn where he nursed him. After providing the innkeeper with two denarii to care for Rafael, the Samaritan told him, 'If you spend more on his health, I will repay you when I return this way.'"

10 With his hands on his hips, Yeshua asked, "Now which of these–the priest, the Levite, or the Samaritan–proved to be a good neighbor to Rafael, the man beaten and robbed and left for dead?" ¹¹ No one answered. Yeshua waited. A scribe admitted, "The Samaritan." ¹² Yeshua nodded and smiled, "Go accordingly and show the Breath of Bounty and Mercy within you."

13 A Pharisee stood up and demanded, "Why are you here? The laws and teachings of Moses are all we need!" ¹⁴ Another man stood and said with begging tones, "Rabbi, I drift in a stormy sea of sinners. I am a runt in a fold surrounded by wolves." His voice faltered, "I fear I will be lost."

15 Looking at the Pharisee and pointing to the other man, Yeshua replied, "To a woman who has ten silver coins and loses one, do you censure her for lighting a lamp and sweeping the house clean until she has found it? ¹⁶ Who chides her for calling her neighbors to

rejoice with her now that she clasps her lost coin in her hand? ¹⁷ Know you," he pointed to the Pharisee, "there will be more joy in the Kingdom of God with the one sinner who repents than over a righteous nine who need no saving grace. ¹⁸ The messengers will dance and clap their hands over the sinner who repents, over one who has been lost but now is found."

19 Looking at the other man and pointing to the Pharisee, Yeshua replied, "The Kingdom of God can be compared to a man who sowed good seed in his field. ²⁰ That night while he and his servants slept, his enemy stole into his field and," flicking his wrist, "sowed weeds among the wheat. ²¹ When the plants grew and bore grain," raising his right hand level with his shoulder, "the weeds grew and flourished with them." He raised his left hand level with his shoulder. ²² "His servants came to him and asked, 'Master, did you not sow good seed? How is it,'" both hands spread out in front of him, "'your field is full of weeds?'

23 "The man replied, 'My enemy has done this.' The servants asked, 'Do you wish us to go and gather them?' Their master replied, 'No. ²⁴ In rooting up the weeds, you will root up wheat with them. Let them both grow together until the harvest. ²⁵ At harvest time tell the reapers to gather the weeds first. Let them bind and bundle them," his hands appeared to be holding out a batch of weeds, "to be thrown into the fire," he flicked his wrists. ²⁶ "Then let the wheat be gathered and stored in my barn.' ²⁷ Know you," he firmly stated, pointing a finger and taking a step forward, "none may stand in the way of heavenly light. All who embrace it walk within the Kingdom of God. ²⁸ Lift up yourself to God Almighty. He who does the work of sharing and forgiveness shall be exalted." ²⁹ Observing the eyes of the crowd, weighing possibilities and suspicions, Yeshua added, "Let those who have ears, hear."

Note: 40:7 Most Jews considered Samaritans to be religious deviants. Allowed to stay behind during the Babylonian exile, many interbred with foreigners and assimilated portions of Gentile practices into their worship of Yahweh.

41 The next day, Ishmael, a Pharisee, invited Yeshua and Judah Iscariot to dine with him. At the appointed hour, he gestured for Yeshua to sit on his right and Judah on his left. ² Yeshua sat down with a smile beaming toward his host. Ishmael opened his eyes widely and then narrowed them before speaking, "You sit at table, but you have not washed your hands."

3 Licking his lips in anticipation, Yeshua retorted, "You Pharisees and scribes wash the outside of your cups and plates, you walk in fine robes and sit in the best seats in the qehalah, but inside you are filthy with rapacity and flies of corruption." ⁴ Yeshua paused as the chatter around him turned to dust and ears opened to his words. "Hypocrites! We are made as one inside and outside. If first you purify the inside, the outside will also be clean." ⁵ Steadily, firmly Yeshua went on, "You tithe to the law, but stumble blind down streets of charity. You exercise the law, but walk not in ways of mercy. ⁶ Justice is a heavy bundle you bind on the backs of the poor. Never is it applied to yourselves. ⁷ You raise monuments to the prophets with righteous pillars, but you are the sons of the murderers of the prophets," he chastened, raising an admonishing hand.

8 "When Yohanan walked among you, your ears were deaf, your hands bathed in his blood. Wash them! They will not come clean. ⁹ God sends you prophets. You make martyrs of them. ¹⁰ And you scribes,"–the scribes sitting at the table jumped at the vehemence Yeshua laid on the name of their profession– "bend the laws to your purposes. The key to knowledge you hide in your pockets as if the laws were made only for you. ¹¹ I pity you Pharisees and scribes. You are whitewashed

tombs bright in the sun, but inside a corpse rots. Woe waits on you!"

12 The other guests fumed over their cups and bowls. One quietly asked his neighbor, "Who is Yohanan?" His neighbor shrugged. 13 Ishmael lowered his head in thought. He nodded and calmly responded, "Yes. I see what you mean." 14 Pointing with his eyes at the hands of Yeshua he quietly added, "Still, your hands are dirty." 15 A mallet hung in the air. All eyes watched Yeshua. Judah fretted with his fingers; his eyes darted around the room. 16 A smirk spread across the face of Yeshua and the hanging hammer struck his belly with laughter. One laugh ushered another. Mirth carried the room away until all sat satiated. 17 Yeshua called for a bowl of water, dipped his fingers, and wiped them on his robe. The meal was served and all, both clean and unclean, ate ravenously from the common bowls and plates set out for them.

18 Later that night when Yeshua sat with his emissaries, the feet of Judah Iscariot paced as his mind hoofed from thought to thought. Words spilled in spurts from his lips, "How could you...Why...?" 19 Yeshua stared calmly at the limbs shaking with agitated thoughts. 20 Finally, thoughts formed coherently for Judah to blurt out, "We were his guests! How could you insult him so?"

21 Yeshua softly answered, "Beware the leaven of the scribes and Pharisees, their bread rises with hypocrisy. Is it not just to say it is so?" 22 With affirmation from the nodding heads of his emissaries, Yeshua continued, "I speak without trembling. 23 Nothing can be shielded or concealed, but must be made known; everything that is hidden will be revealed. Secrets will be out. 24 What we speak at night is what we should say in broad daylight. Whatever we whisper should also be shouted from the highest rooftops."

25 Beating his chest, Yeshua continued, "I have no fear. What is the worst that can be done? 26 Those who would kill my

body cannot kill my eternal breath. Only God, who can kill bodies and damn shades to eternal perdition, is to be feared. [27] God knows the number of hairs on your head," he said, ruffling the hair on the head of Judah with his hand. "What can you hide from God?" [28] Yeshua paused as if for an answer. Yohanan, Jacob, Cephas, and Judah looked away from the piercing gaze of Yeshua and at one another. They knew not what to say. [29] "Whoever is ashamed of me, who would hide my words or cast them to be carried away by winds, is ashamed of the Son of Man." [30] Yeshua stopped and looked keenly at his emissaries, settling lastly on Judah. "Whoever blasphemes against the Son of Man will be forgiven, but woe to those who blaspheme against the Breath of God."

31 Reading the faces of his emissaries like a scribe reading the Torah, Yeshua assured them, "You will stand before judges and kings. [32] Be strong. Fear not what you are to say. The Holy Breath will speak through you. [33] The Living Light of the Holy Breath will guide you. Do not tremble. You will not be left speechless when your time comes."

34 "Rabbi," Yohanan informed him, "while you dined at the home of Ishmael, we came upon a man who cast out demons in your name. [35] We," he pointed to Jacob and himself, "chased him away." Jacob added, "We told him never to speak magic in your name again!" [36] Yeshua shook his head, "Do not oppose any who do good works in my name. If he works in my name, he cannot later trample it in the dust. [37] Any who are not against us," he paused, peering into their eyes, "are for us. Any who gives you bread or fills your cup with wine in my name will be rewarded in the Kingdom of God."

42
On a Sabbath, Yeshua led his group of emissaries and women through a kamut field. Hunger hunted them down and gnawed on their insides. [2] They picked a few heads of grain, soaked them in their mouths, and ate

them to satisfy the wolves of their stomachs. 3 When a Pharisee witnessed this, he cried out to Yeshua, "Look you! You are breaking the Sabbath! You turn the holy day into a sacrilege!"

4 Yeshua replied, "Know you, was it a sacrilege for David and his men to satisfy their hunger by entering the House of God to eat the consecrated bread meant only for the priests? 5 Does not the Law allow priests in the Temple to work the day, yet remain innocent of sacrilege? Men are greater than the Temple. 6 An admonishment already sits in judgment upon you, 'I need mercy, not sacrifices'! That is the truth you should bear. 7 You condemn the innocent because you still have not learned the Son of Man is greater than the Sabbath."

8 Stepping into the marketplace a man approached Yeshua. "Son of God, compel my brother to divide the inheritance of our father with me." 9 Yeshua stepped back, "Man, who am I? What made you think I am a judge over inheritances? 10 Covetousness is the business of a gold goat. This demon divides a house and is worn like a heavy chain around the neck. 11 Know you, your life is not measured," Yeshua grabbed and tugged the tunic of the man before letting go with a grand open handed gesture, "by your possessions.

12 "Have you not heard of the rich man whose land grew an abundant crop, a crop so large he had nowhere to store it? He decided to build new barns large enough to hold the bounty of his land. 13 With wealth laid away, he rejoiced and made merry for many years in comfort. Over his joy God said to him," Yeshua whispered, "'I shall come in the night and you will no longer tread this earth.' 14 I ask you now," raising his voice earnestly, "what of his bounty? To whom will it go? 15 The treasure of God is sharing and forgiveness, the Holy Breath, a tongue of fire illuminating with everlasting light. 16 What good," with a sweep of his hand, "are the riches of this

world when you have not," bending his elbows, Yeshua raised both hands with fingers, as incredulous digits, wide open, "laid up riches to God?"

17 Near the outskirts of the city, Linus gazed out his window at the hills less than a mile away from him. They appeared to be rolling distantly in a country far away. 18 The captain of the guard, Atticus, ushered into the room Jael, the Pharisee whose religious vehemence upbraided Yeshua for breaking the Sabbath. 19 "Yes," Linus asked after a moment of silence. The hills still drew his attention out the window.

20 "I want to report a crime," Jael blurted out. "Oh," Linus responded with his back still to him. Jael waited and then said, "He is breaking the Sabbath! He is in the market! A fox in our henhouse!" 21 Linus replied with the weariness of a long day, a long week, a long two-and a-half years, "That is no concern of mine. 22 Whoever he is, you have gone to the wrong authorities. Go to your priest! This is not a Roman matter."

23 Out of the mouth of Jael words tumbled like one stone falling into another, the two tumbling into more rocks, cascading into a landslide of sound, "But…but I was told to report here. 24 The Nazarene cannot, he must not be allowed to blaspheme the Sabbath! It is…" 25 Linus held up his hand. The centurion saw the purple lupine on the hills. He inhaled deeply as if he took in their spicy fragrance. 26 "Ah," he finally said, "The carpenter is paying us a visit, is he?" Linus turned to face Jael. The informer nodded his head.

27 "Arrest the fox," Linus commanded as he looked wearily at the letters on his desk, "and send in Sebastian." Atticus nodded and stopped. "On what charge," he asked matter-of-factly. 28 "Civil disturbance," the administrator said as he shifted his eyes to Atticus who raised an eyebrow. 29 "Look at him," Linus said nodding to Jael, "Does he not look disturbed?"

30 Atticus showed Jael the door, but halted in the doorway when he heard Linus clear his throat. Shutting the door

on the heels of Jael, Atticus turned to Linus. ³¹ "March loudly and march slowly," Linus told him. "Loud and slow," Atticus asked with squinted eyes and cocked head. ³² "Yes, loud and slow," the centurion sharply commanded. The captain jumped to his order.

33 Linus stared into space as he thought, *By the time you get to the market, the fox will be gone. Let the carpenter be the headache of someone else.* ³⁴ He turned and stepped toward the world outside his window. *What quarrelsome people; willful as a whip!* ³⁵ *There are enough Gods for everyone. Why this ceaseless venomous bickering over a God?* ³⁶ Gazing out his window as if peering into a dream, Linus released a heavy sigh toward the hills that lay like beguiling hips; the purple lupine stood straight and tall.

Notes: 42:2 To pick grain is to work; to work is to break the Sabbath. **42:6** Yeshua is paraphrasing, "For I desired mercy, and not sacrifice; and the knowledge of God more than burnt offerings." Hosea 6.6, King James Version (KJV) **42:22** Religion often flared into incendiary incidents between the worshipers of Yahweh and the Romans. Shortly after he arrived in Caesarea, Pilatus ordered standards be placed during the middle of the night in the most public places in Jerusalem. Eyes woke to the staring face of Augustus. The Jews considered this a sacrilege and provocation. Surrounding his home, they protested for five straight days. An exasperated Pilatus ordered his soldiers to draw their swords in a show of force. The protestors did not relent. Gladly they would welcome death before accepting blasphemy. Caesar liked quiet provinces. A riot threatened the streets of Jerusalem. Pilatus removed the standards. **42:27** Linus, a centurion who worked his way up the ranks as opposed to being a wealthy Roman elected or appointed by the senate, did not know how to write and could only read a little. He required an educated Greek slave for a secretary.

43

"Why are we doing this?" With a trembling rasp in his voice, Judah Iscariot asked Cephas as they stretched out large palm leaves across the road leading to the main gate of Jerusalem. "You know he must have a grand entry into Jerusalem! It is prophesied that..." [2] Shaking his head, Judah said, "No," and with jittery hands adjusted the overlapping palms he laid across the road. "Why must we come to Jerusalem *now*?" [3] Cephas stepped back to survey their work before answering, "Oh, well, it is Passover… and Jerusalem was always the final destination."

[4] The emissary Yeshua considered his rock, eyed the length of the road and said, "They should be coming soon." Judah looked up and waved to a group milling around the gate waiting to line the road. His eyes noticed twins, but his head rolled with worry. [5] "But why *this* Passover? We are not ready. We are hardly strong enough…" Cephas interjected, "Our strength is in our faith. [6] Be strong. Believe. That is all. Just believe. Who are we to question our rabbi!?" [7] Judah looked at him blankly as he threw down the last palm across the road. His voice shook like a loose leaf, "We have converted many, but not so many, not near enough to stand up to Caiaphas, much less to Rome." [8] Cephas shrugged and stated flatly, "This is what he wants." Pointing excitedly down the road he shouted, "Here they come!"

[9] Yeshua gingerly swayed and bounced on the back of a hesitant donkey. Jacob and Yohanan walked on each side to guide the animal. After they passed Judah and Cephas, the two fell in behind Yeshua. [10] The other emissaries, called back from their ministries, and the women of Yeshua stood with the crowd they had helped gather to greet the Messiah. [11] The multitude along the road shouted over and over, "Hosanna! Blessed are you who come in the name of God." The emissaries and his women in the crowd also fell behind as Yeshua passed them. [12] Judah Iscariot shivered, "Must they yell so loud?" Yeshua heard him and turned to face the worried eyes of his emissary. [13] With a smile, Yeshua boasted, "If they were

mute," sweeping his right arm at the people announcing his arrival and then thrusting his hand forward, "the stones would shout it out!"

14 The Temple stood prominently at the highest point in Jerusalem. On the evening of the day of the grand entry of Yeshua into Jerusalem, the child of humanity encamped beyond the walls of the city on the Mount of Olives across from the Temple. 15 The numerous pilgrims, many with coin to spare, easily filled Jerusalem to celebrate Passover. The radiance of the Temple served as a beacon for Jews everywhere to worship in the holy city. 16 The next day and every day after, Yeshua, with a coterie of emissaries and his women, taught in the Court of Nations. The rest of his emissaries, each accompanied by a few students, spread the good news in the streets and marketplaces of Jerusalem. 17 They eagerly sought converts among the gathered Jews of the diaspora. The women divided into two groups–some going with Yeshua, others attending the camp.

18 Stephen came from Damascus to celebrate the holy holiday. As a merchant of moderate means, he traveled to Jerusalem with a modicum of comfort. 19 The voice of Yeshua caught his attention. He could not make out his words, but the fire within Yeshua reached out and touched a flame within the pilgrim, pulling him to a corner of the court near porticos full of shadows. 20 What he heard with his ears opened the scope of his vision as he listened to the Breath of God resonating in the voice of Yeshua.

21 "Attended by messengers, the Son of Man will come to sit here on a throne of glory. All the nations shall gather at his feet. 22 As a shepherd divides the sheep from the goats, the Son of Man will say to his fold of sheep, 'Come. Sit at my right side.' The goats he sets on his left. 23 To those on the right he will open his arms and say, 'You may enter the Sovereignty; your breath is one with the Holy Breath. 24 For when I thirsted, you filled a cup for me to drink; when I hungered,

you fed me; when I stood naked, you gave me garments to wear; 25 when I wandered as a stranger, you opened your home to me; when I languished in prison, you came to me; when I lay sick, you attended me.'"

26 With his body and face expressing surprise, Yeshua exclaimed, "And the virtuous will say, 'We do not remember! 27 When were you hungry and thirsty that we gave you food and drink? When were you in want, that we provided clothes and shelter for you? When were you ill or imprisoned that we comforted you? 28 From his throne the Son of Man will tell them," Yeshua intoned in a rabbi voice: calm, kind, firm, "Know you, when you tended to the poorest of the poor, the weakest and most hapless among us, you tended to me. 29 Know you, for they and I are of one breath," he paused and looked them in their eyes, "the Breath of God. And your mercy and charity rose as offerings to the King."

30 Lacing his words with sternness, he continued, "Then the Son of Man will point to those on his left and damn the sinners to enter the cursed gates of perdition. 31 You who dream you lift yourselves up, but you prostrate yourselves and lay as the foundation of the temple of Shemyaza, go to the devil. 32 When I thirsted and hungered, you offered me dust. When I wandered as a stranger and stood naked, you clothed me with scorn. 33 When I was sick, you turned your back on me. When I wasted in prison. you sealed the door shut.

34 "The damned will protest." Yeshua wrapped his next words with exaggerated indignation. "'When did *we* offer you dust to slake your thirst and hunger? 35 When did *we* sneer at your nakedness or treat you as an alien? When did we shun you when you lay sick or in prison?' 36 The Son of Man will answer them sternly, 'Know you, when you treated the poor so savagely, the stranger so callously, you treated me with contempt and derision.' 37 So the virtuous will enter eternal life and the righteous wicked, the

spirits of willful ignorance, enter eternal damnation."

38 The sight of Yeshua dazzled, and his words swirled in the head of Stephen, words flying brightly as our dove. 39 The body of the pilgrim trembled with Our Spirit. The New Way flashed in his mind just as a glistening fish hauled onto golden sands dazzles with light. 40 Judah Iscariot watched the ecstasy of Stephen, observed the puzzlement of a few, and noticed two others slink off towards the Temple. All the while, "king" and "throne" circled like vultures in his head.

Notes: 43:3 Three festivals obligated Jews to make pilgrimages to Jerusalem. Passover celebrates Yahweh freeing Jews from Pharaoh's bondage by sending several plagues and finally avenging messengers. Unleavened bread is eaten to commemorate Moses and the Hebrew slaves preparing quickly to leave Egypt. Pentecost celebrates the grain harvest and commemorates when God gave the Torah to Moses on Mount Sinai. Tabernacle celebrates the fruit harvest and the period when the freed Egyptian slaves wandered in the desert for forty years. Tabernacles are makeshift shelters farmers lived in during the harvest and the shelters the freed slaves made in the desert. **43:11** "Hosanna! Blessed are you who come in the name of God" was a common greeting welcoming pilgrims to Jerusalem. **43:16** Surrounding the entire Temple complex, the Court of Nations, another modern innovation by Herod the Great, offered an expanse for Temple business. This courtyard, often referred to in later times as the Court of Gentiles, lay open to all as long as they respected the sanctity of the Temple. Only the faithful entered the Temple proper.

---

44 Under a portico in the Court of Nations, Dimitri, at his table, made ready for another day of exchanging foreign currency for shekels, the only coin accepted by the priests for offering sacrifices. 2 A northwest breeze shifted, wafting into his nostrils and mouth the stench of nervous animal excrement and urine consorting with burnt offal and blood

from Temple sacrifices. ³ The odor did not bother him much. For Dimitri, the smell filled him with the scent of money. ⁴ Neither cheap nor exorbitant, Dimitri considered himself fair and sound in his fees. Nor did he, as other moneychangers did, charge extra to collect the Temple tax the priests required of the faithful. ⁵ Many who knew modest means sought him out. Dimitri worked a good living and provided well for his family.

6 The crowds first caught his attention. Sometimes they overflowed and someone knocked into his table. ⁷ Then Dimitri started paying attention to the man who came early and preached, drawing the crowds to him. Often the man stood by the pillar not far from him, and Dimitri heard words and phrases, ⁸ "Son...the poor...Breath full of kindness and...Yohanan...know you... camel... the poor..."–over chattering of caged birds, bleating sheep, baaing goats, and people conversing or bartering over the purchase of animals to slaughter for the blessing of Yahweh, until a customer would rap on his table to get his attention. ⁹ That man, standing as strong as the pillar next to him, was a marvel. So instead of going to his table the next day, he joined a small crowd to listen. ¹⁰ The gathered multitude always attracted more women than men and the number of listeners always seemed to dwindle as the day spun its wheel of changing light.

11 "Know you, I am come to set the world on fire! Oh, would that its kindling already glowed. Are you ready for a baptism of fire?" ¹² Some eyes sparkled; some searched the eyes of their neighbors; Dimitri stared straight ahead in wonder. "Are you prepared to drink from the cup that I drink? ¹³ I am one with the Holy Breath." Yeshua made circling motions with his hand, "Together our lives will be accomplished.

14 "You are mistaken if you believe I am here to spread peace on earth. Know you that I divide the wheat from the chaff. ¹⁵ The righteous shall

walk with me though their brothers are cast aside. Within the home, I divide three against two and two against three. [16] The son will contest against the father and father against the son, mother against daughter and daughter against mother, mother-in-law against daughter-in-law and daughter-in-law will fight with her mother-in-law. [17] For some know salvation and some do not. Some embrace the Holy Breath and some do not.

[18] "You are wise..."– the loud baaing of a sheep interrupted him–"when you see a cloud in the west rising and say, 'Here comes rain,' and so it comes. [19] You are wise when..."–the sheep interrupted him again–"the wind from the north blows and you say, 'Here comes heat to scorch us today,' and so it comes to pass. [20] How can you be so..."–the bleating of a sheep interrupted him once more–"wise in understanding the sky and earth, but fail to understand, and be mute?" [21] With a smile he pointed toward the sheep. "As mute as these sheep should be..."–the crowd laughed. "When it comes to the present time, the righteous must stand and be heard." [22] Many listeners nodded as they considered his words. Bumping into the shoulder of Stephen, Dimitri returned to his table scratching his head.

[23] On the Mount of Olives, with night falling, Yeshua gathered with his emissaries. Those who had scattered throughout the streets and markets of Jerusalem, preaching and collecting gifts, turned over their few coins to Judah who put them in his light purse. [24] Other gifts of breads or fruits, some fresh, some old, were handed over to the women. [25] The emissaries asked those they converted or cured only that they live in saving grace and spread the New Way to everyone they know. [26] But some, elated with gratitude, felt obligated to make an offering. And so, with the added assistance of patrons, the mission of Yeshua was provisioned.

[27] Yeshua filled his mind with the timorous tread of the words of his emissaries through the air

as they discussed their day. ²⁸ When they had first arrived in Jerusalem, the multitude gathered and listened with eager ears. As days passed the crowds rose and ebbed. ²⁹ Huddled around the food and wine the women laid out for them, the men sat munching and slurping restlessly. ³⁰ Miryam Magdalene hovered nearby. Cephas waved her away with his free hand; she moved off a little. ³¹ Yeshua absorbed the fidgety cloud emanating from the spirit of his men like a fog filled with a sailor's worries.

32 Chewing on a mouthful of bread Cephas asked, "Will the faithful be few? How many must we save?" ³³ The child of humanity stroked his beard and answered, "The gate that is wide is the easy way, but the wide gate leads to destruction. ³⁴ To enter the narrow gate is harder, but the narrow gate leads to eternal light." Yeshua dipped a piece of bread in olive oil before consuming it with satisfaction on his face.

45 The next day as they walked to Jerusalem, leaving two of the women behind to tend to camp, Judah Iscariot peered into the eyes of his rabbi, let loose the trembling dog running wildly within him, "You work a field filled with serpents. ² What you gathered at first was promising, but is..." he looked down, "less now." Looking up with eyes soft with supplication, Judah asked, "Let us...should we not find another field to work?" ³ The eyes of Judah glassed over as he continued, "We are surrounded by vipers. Do you not see them?" His voice quavered, "They slither all around us." Then earnestly, "We are in danger." ⁴ Yeshua spoke to his emissaries raising his finger into the air, "Know you, for one who speaks against the Son of Man... they...in my name they will fornicate and destroy their children. ⁵ Yet, any slander or sin against the Son of Man can be redeemed; but do not speak against the Holy Breath! ⁶ Whoever works against grace, whoever joins the messengers of Shemyaza will not be forgiven now or in any age to come."

7 Yeshua stopped to speak. His emissaries gathered around him with the women behind them. "Your breath within you, stand it before me. Show yourselves. 8 Seeds sown on good ground will be fruitful and multiply. Seeds sown on rock will be scavenged by birds. 9 A good tree will flower and bear good fruit. You will know a bad tree by the awful fruit dropping from it. As we know the character of the tree by its fruit, so it is with men. 10 For the good man, the goodness that he shares from his life lives on after him. For the bad man, the evil he propagates in his life lives on after him. Which judgment will you have made against you?"

11 Yeshua shivered. Cephas placed a cloak over the shoulders of Yeshua to warm him against the early morning chill. 12 "Know you, he who clothes me is my friend. He who is not with me, works against me. He who does not work to gather with me, scatters."

13 Yeshua paused and said, fixing his eyes on the eyes of Judah Iscariot, "A fox will travel far, but has a hole. A bird flies from tree to tree, but has a nest. 14 Not I. The Son of Man has wandered with no home to lay his head. Here I am. Here I will stay. 15 It is here God Almighty calls me." Yeshua looked around at his emissaries as he said, "Be strong." Focusing on Judah he added, "Besides, it is Passover, is it not?"

16 As they walked further on in the quiet dawn, the women walked several feet behind the men. Cephas stared at Miryam Magdalene and the chill of the morning settled into his bones. 17 He hissed close to the ear of Yeshua, "Let the women depart from us." A strutting peacock spoke through his mouth, "This is the work of men." 18 Yeshua coldly looked at his emissary and warmly replied, "By my word, every woman who believes will be made male. Every male who believes shall enter into the Living Light. 19 Is it not also written, 'So God created in his own image, in the image of God he created male and female.' 20 Male and female are one. All who live in the Holy Breath of

God shall dwell in Sovereignty."

21 They walked a while in silence. Yeshua quickened his pace and they all hurried to keep up with him. ²² Suddenly he stopped, pointed his eyes with daggers of irritation at Cephas, and said, "How is it you do not know what I am doing? ²³ Know you, it is the children that shall build the Kingdom of God. And who, Cephas, who holds the hand of the child?

45:19 Yeshua is paraphrasing "So God created mankind in his own image, in the image of God he created them; male and female he created them." Genesis 1:27 New International Version (NIV)

---

46 After entering Jerusalem through the eastern side of the Huldah Gates, Yeshua greeted with blessings the students waiting for him. ² Yeshua, Cephas, Jacob, Yohanan, Judah, and his women headed for the Temple after seeing off the other emissaries and students, who scattered throughout the city to preach in and of Our Spirit. ³ Yeshua and those attending him walked back out of the Huldah Gates and over to the Shushan Gate on the east side of the city, leading directly to the Temple. ⁴ At the gate, Stephen waited with the twins, Ezra and Asher, two of the first converts from Jerusalem. The child of humanity greeted them with blessings before the enlarged party entered the Court of Nations.

5 Dimitri sat idly and patiently at his table while Yeshua positioned himself at his spot, with Jacob and Yohanan standing nearby, one on each side, slightly behind him. ⁶ The rest roamed about the court, conversing with people and deftly leading them toward Yeshua. When he saw his students drawing near, their rabbi began to engage the crowd and speak to them, pulling them in closer to him. ⁷ Judah stood ready to collect any friendly donations or offerings. By

mid-morning the Court of Nations bustled with activity. ⁸ Dimitri, having observed the routine of the carpenter for days, moved his table a little nearer from its usual spot so he might hear the words of Yeshua more clearly.

9 "We are one with saving grace." Yeshua held up a finger from his left hand in the air. "Grace is one with God." He held up a finger from his right hand in the air and then locked the two fingers together. "We seek the light." ¹⁰ His right hand extended out and up. "Yet how many of you wax dull with gall and sleep in the belly of a gold goat? Both night and day the bones and breath in your body hoards gold. ¹¹ It intoxicates and drives you mad. You believe you live in rich houses, but you, full of lead and iron, live as captives in dirty hovels."

12 A Pharisee laughed. Yeshua pointed at him and exhorted the crowd, "You laugh! It is the laughter of madness ¹³ You are numb and blind to the death you dwell in. Your understanding is drunk on a red wine pressed on the backs of the poor. ¹⁴ Your possessions corrupt you; a gold goat owns you." As Yeshua castigated them, more and more faces pinched with anger. ¹⁵ "Your head is fastened to wealth. Riches, the baubles of this world, burn as a fire. ¹⁶ That fire dazzles your eyes and so you," his right finger pointed and scanned the crowd, "serve it as it consumes," his left hand clenched into a fist, "your eternal breath. ¹⁷ The smoke of that fire changes you into an impurity. Your breath turns to smoke." He raised his right hand as if his fingers were tails of smoke. ¹⁸ "You choke the air. You char and smother the good fruit sweet with bounty and mercy. ¹⁹ Yet the Holy Breath is impervious to you. The good fruit will be washed with good works while you rot as ashes for fat, golden worms."

20 The Pharisee, Hillel, shouted at Yeshua, "I pay my tithes! The poor swarm as locusts. Would you impoverish me?" ²¹ Yeshua smiled, "I would enrich you in the Kingdom of God! You live in

the body, you should live in the Holy Breath."²² Judah the Scribe screamed out, "We follow the laws of Moses!" Yeshua retorted, "You do not move within the breath of Moses. The law without the Breath of God is a dead letter." ²³ Hillel asked Yeshua, "You treat all as one. A beggar is no different than a king with you, ²⁴ but what of the Most Notable Caesar?" Hillel picked a coin from his pocket and held it high, "Should we pay taxes to Caesar?" ²⁵ The coin caught the glint of treason as it flashed with the light of the sun. Yeshua winked at the trap, ²⁶ "Look at your coin; does it not bear a face on it?" Hillel replied that it did. "And whose face is it?" Hillel replied, "The face of Caesar." ²⁷ "Then," Yeshua told him with a smile, "the coin belongs to him. Return to Caesar the property of Caesar, and the rightful property of God you must return to God." ²⁸ This made a fine distinction to some, but it would hang in Roman ears as sophistry. Had not the Senate declared Caesar a God?

²⁹ Judah the scribe cried out from his righteous beard, "What authority have you to speak on these things? Who are you? Show us a sign and prove your authority over us!" ³⁰ Yeshua pointed to the Temple and made an answer to him, "Destroy the Temple, and I will raise it up again in three days. For..." ³¹ Judah interrupted Yeshua with a shrill laugh filled with thorns of derision, "For twenty-four years Herod the Great labored to reconstruct the Temple, ³² and it took another twenty-two after him to finish it. You say, if the Temple is destroyed–God forbid–in three days you will raise it up?" ³³ The burning oils of his laughter overflowed into the crowd who lit up with his scorn. Yeshua could only blankly stare as his words drowned in their shrieks and fell into the dust of their derision. ³⁴ The spell broke. No word from Yeshua held them. The spirit within him sweated and grunted. ³⁵ The crowd returned to their affairs. The students and women began to spread out over the courtyard to begin conversations to attract a

new crowd for the child of humanity to show the saving grace of our dove.

36 Standing close by, Dimitri laconically commented to no one in particular, "Tough day." A little laugh escaped him as he thought of the assertion about rebuilding the Temple. [37] Yeshua heard him, rushed to his table, and tipped it over. Coins spilled like wine from a broken cask. [38] He then knocked over the nearby stands of hens and owls sold for the augury of their entrails. Many birds escaped their cages. Seven hens perched themselves on top of the portico to watch the turmoil below. [39] "Sacrilege is all you know! You plunder the poor! Is forgiveness only for the rich and powerful? [40] Does God answer only their prayers? Away with you all!" Yeshua shouted at the moneychangers and vendors.

41 Many pilgrims who had turned away turned back and gathered at the commotion while a few ran for the Temple guards. [42] Yohanan and Jacob stepped forward, in front of Yeshua. The crowd began to close on them. His students rushed to the head of the crowd, adding more bodies between Yeshua and the mob. [43] The women formed the outer shield while Jacob and Yohanan led Yeshua through a side gate. In the narrow street they rushed like a river flooding down to the Huldah Gate. [44] Yeshua commanded all who were with him to remain silent on all that had happened. Jacob looked around and asked, "Where is Judah? Has anyone seen Judah?" [45] During the cleansing of moneychangers from the Court of Nations, discerning eyes saw Judah stridently walking toward the Temple.

47 Matthew, Andreas, and Judah casually inspected the room. [2] Matthew and Andreas had recently arrived. Having wandered far in spreading the teachings of Yeshua, they found the journey back arduous. It took longer than expected to rendezvous with their rabbi and brethren in Jerusalem for Passover. [3] They converted a merchant and joined his caravan in hopes of expediting their trek back home,

but the winding way of his business–and his refractory camels–dragged on their progress. ⁴ So, after an exchange of farewells and blessings, they left their traveling companions and made as straight a line as possible for Jerusalem. This time, Matthew took sick.

5 They arrived in time to partake in the final days of the holiday. Yeshua decided to decamp from the Mount of Olives to celebrate the rest of Passover in Jerusalem. ⁶ Andreas, Matthew, and Judah were dispatched to town to find suitable accommodations–no easy task, as Jerusalem overflowed with pilgrims. Only the disreputable quarter near the Dung Gate had any available rooms. ⁷ Yeshua instructed them to seek out a man carrying a water jug; he would assist them. They did, he did, and the room opened to their inspection. ⁸ Nodding their heads, they agreed the room was satisfactory. Judah opened the purse in his keeping.

9 The women came and laid out two woven mats, a large one for the men and a smaller one off to the side for themselves. ¹⁰ They placed dishes full of cut-up cucumbers and apricots, almonds, olives, and olive oil along with loaves of unleavened bread and a few bottles of sour wine in the center of them. ¹¹ Cups circled the food like sentinels. Candles on plates stood flickering on the mats and around the room. ¹² The men arrived. All, as customary before entering a dwelling, removed and set their sandals aside to wash their feet. ¹³ Cephas, hanging on the shoulder of Judah, smiled and chimed in his ear, "So you made it back?" Judah stared at his feet as he replied quietly, "Yes. I have had a narrow escape."

14 After the men and women gathered around their separate tables, Yeshua and Miryamla lit the candles. All chanted in song, ¹⁵ "The Breath of God, the Holy Breath is with us; the Kingdom of God is here for the will of God Almighty to be done. As the power of God is in heaven, so let the power of God reign on earth. ¹⁶ Provide us with our portion of communal bread today and

tomorrow. ¹⁷ Let others forgive us our offenses made against them as we forgive them their offenses made against us. ¹⁸ Let our feet not stray onto a wayward path. We live to complete ourselves in the power and glory of the Breath of God, the Holy Breath. Selah."

19 The meal absorbed their attention. Little was spoken above the smacking of lips and licking of fingers. ²⁰ In the middle of the meal, Yeshua saw with eyes of the future, all those around him. The hour was nigh: *Are they strong enough?* ²¹ He studied them. Yeshua pondered further what had been cornered in his mind since fleeing the Temple. ²² Time pressed against him, a foot weighing on his neck. His breathing quickened: *Could this be their last supper together?* ²³ Clearing his throat he spoke loudly as he held up a loaf of unleavened bread, "There will be times when my body does not walk with you or sit beside you, when my voice will linger as if from a room far away." ²⁴ His words stopped them cold. Anyone with food or the cheap wine in their mouths, could not swallow it. Anyone reaching for food, froze as a statue.

25 Yeshua broke off stiff pieces of unleavened bread used to celebrate Passover and passed them to his emissaries. Rising he gave pieces of bread to the women at their table. The last piece he held up for all to see, saying, ²⁶ "Whenever you break bread, remember me as if my body were here with you." Yeshua ate the bread and everyone ate the portion he had shared with them. ²⁷ Taking his cup, Yeshua filled it full and held it up for all to see. "When you drink, drink in remembrance of me as if I sat here in flesh and blood." ²⁸ He sipped from it and passed it around for his emissaries to drink from his cup. Then he passed his cup over to the women. ²⁹ "We are our own sacrifices. Together as one, our breath as one in the Holy Breath; when we are apart, yet we are together."

30 Everyone continued eating and drinking. The lips of those who had attended Yeshua at the

Temple yesterday trembled at their thoughts. [31] By the end of the meal, Judah and Cephas sat quietly arguing under the eyes of Yeshua, who heard the low voice of Judah plead, "We should return to Galilee." [32] Cephas looked to Yeshua and asked, "Rabbi, are you worried about what happened at the Temple?" [33] Yeshua gazed past Cephas and responded, "Yes." He paused for a deep breath. "I have been betrayed." [34] Everyone stopped. Each man looked from Yeshua to each other with piercing eyes. All but one declared, "Not I!" [35] Judah rose, left the bag of coins in his charge on the floor, steadily walked to the door, put on his sandals, and left the room.

[36] The eyes of the emissaries filled with cold fires of disbelief. The empty space of Judah held them in suspense like men hanging from crosses. [37] Grimly Yeshua asked, "Have we swords?" Simon the Zealot replied, "A few." Yeshua nodded and Simon left to fetch them. [38] To faces like fishermen caught in a sudden storm, Yeshua assured them, "Do not despair. God is with us. The messengers stand at the ready. We are not abandoned." [39] The women huddled together. Cephas spoke a few words, shaking with faith and defiance. [40] Yeshua nodded his head but added quietly in his ear, "Have no fear of Caiaphas, but if the net of Rome is cast, you and all of you must not be caught in it." [41] Yeshua looked with soft eyes at the worried women as they gathered around him and the faint quiver on his lips slipped into a reassuring smile. "Let us pray," he said.

48

Gethsemane is a quiet grove, Yeshua discovered, at the foot of the Mount of Olives. With many secluded areas, it attracted other men besides Yeshua. [2] Each night, paying no heed to others, he retired to his favored place of solitude for meditation and prayer. [3] Tonight, he took Cephas, Jacob, and Yohanan with him all carrying concealed swords so awkwardly, it was a miracle they did not cut or stab themselves or each other. ⁴ When they reached Gethsemane, they chanced upon Stephen wearing only a linen cloth. He stood nearby as the emissaries set up watch and Yeshua, weary in limb and mind, entered deeper into the wood, found his soft spot, and leaned against a rock.

5 Breathing deeply, he considered his day. Yeshua grunted. He had had better days. ⁶ What moved him to snort like a bull? Was it hope hanging as ripe fruit always just beyond his reach, or the constant maw of the serpent opening wider and wider to devour him? ⁷ Well aware that his actions placed him in the position of a blind man walking along the edge of a cliff, what should be his next step? ⁸ The wind ran with the question coolly across his brow. He felt the presence of his cousin. ⁹ Would his fate be similar to that of the Baptist? Will this be his time? He felt the beating wings of messengers. Are they far away? ¹⁰ How well will his emissaries carry on? Will many sown seeds of saving grace take root and flourish? Are they ready? Are they enough? ¹¹ Yeshua breathed deeply. His mind squinted at the limited prospects sprawling before him. What should he do?

12 A noise lurking in the night intruded. Yeshua opened his eyes. A lost wind in the leaves? Or...? ¹³ He got up and cautiously made his way to his three emissaries. Seeing no sign of Stephen, Yeshua found Jacob, Yohanan, and Cephas asleep! ¹⁴ Swords lay on the ground! Picking one up he slapped the flanks of his emissaries with the broad side of the blade. ¹⁵ "Can you not stay awake? For me!?" Cephas rubbed his eyes and yawned out words, "We yearn to be strong, but our flesh is weak." ¹⁶ Yeshua commanded, "I need you to stay awake!" They firmly nodded. He left them to find more strength.

17 Had it been wise to bring them? Was he asking too much? Perhaps. Perhaps he expected too much. ¹⁸ A few swords against the Temple guards, against Rome! He grinned at his panic. It is not the swords of fishermen that will open the

gates of heaven on earth. [19] Swords in the hands of fishermen! What was he thinking? Did the slaves Moses led from Egypt wield swords? Ridiculous. [20] The Egyptian slaves did not free themselves. The messengers of God smote the enemies of Israel. And it was the children of the slaves who conquered the Promised Land. [21] It will be the youth of this generation who will own it again. Their parents! Slaves of Rome! He will lead their young to the Kingdom of God.

22 Unaware that the faint grinning fan of a strutting peacock flared before his eyes, Yeshua cleared his mind and thought of paradise on this earth. What a wonder he worked to bring into this world! [23] Is now the time? It must be. What more can he do? His time ran down a steep hill. [24] What are his next steps? Is there a way out of this? He needs more time. Does he need more time? [25] Should hours or days or years concern him? He felt the Breath of God fill his lungs. With grace, Our Spirit rose within and beyond his fate. [26] The thoughts of Yeshua crashed into bloody waves waiting for him. Thinking of his cousin, he shuddered. [27] Taking a deep breath he believed: *The Breath of God and I breathe as one.*

28 Our dove perched near him. Suddenly the knife of a thought stabbed him. "Send the messengers!" Yeshua prayed, "send your messengers soon. [29] Send them now! Too much sweat and blood has been given to establish the Kingdom of God. It must not be in vain!" [30] Yeshua stepped up to his prophecy. Never had he felt more assured of the presence of Yohanan, Isaiah, and Moses. They secured him as a rope pulling a drowning man from grasping waters. [31] Messengers. He needed the messengers. Yeshua prayed, "Please Lord. Let messengers with swords swiftly come. [32] I work Your will. Let your will be done." Yeshua looked up and, through a net of tangled olive branches, saw the face of the sun reflecting from a full moon.

33 Why were so many of his countrymen blind to what he was up

to? He leaned against the smooth surface of a rock. ³⁴ Again, a shaking of terrible possibilities startled his thoughts. Again, weary emissaries lost themselves to the draining demands of rest. Eyes blurred with slumber stared up at him. ³⁵ Thorns of frustration turned to petals. Smiling kindly, Yeshua softly encouraged them to pray for greater strength and left them to find it.

36 *We all need more strength. Judgment casts its eye on us. Will we stand tall or fall as dry chaff?* ³⁷ *It is Passover. Now is the time for messengers to swing avenging swords to free us. We are enslaved in our own land by the foot of Rome. Wearing the sandals of our sins, they press their hard heels on our necks.* ³⁸ *The messengers must come soon or I am lost. Have I misjudged my moment?* ³⁹ *Perhaps I should have waited another year. What will it take to join my people as one? They blindly trample Sovereignty under their feet!*

40 Yeshua felt light-headed. Everywhere he looked his prospects appeared dismal. ⁴¹ Shemyaza in a flash whispered in his ear, "It is never too late! Put aside this cup of poison. Not a throne but a cross waits for you. ⁴² Turn away. Save yourself!" Shrugging off temptation, Yeshua faintly grinned at himself.

43 As the Son of God he breathed deeply and swayed gently with the cool night air. The moment is the moment. ⁴⁴ To beg is a sorry errand. The will of Yeshua no longer belonged to himself. Offering his life, Yeshua submitted to the will encompassing a world. ⁴⁵ Uncertain whether poison or wine was his lot, with both hands Yeshua grabbed the cup staring at him and drank deeply.

46 This time a distinct disturbance brought him to his emissaries. Stephen stood by the emissaries. Jacob, Cephas, and Yohanan absurdly pointed their swords in the air. ⁴⁷ Yeshua gently but firmly ordered them to put down their weapons, saying, "Turn your swords into plowshares." First Cephas, then the rest, threw their swords to

the ground. ⁴⁸ Several well-armed temple guards and slaves, led by Judah, stared through the torch-lit air. At first the armed guards of Yeshua surprised them. ⁴⁹ Recovering from their astonishment they gritted their teeth. When the emissaries dropped their weapons, the temple guards slackened their jaws. ⁵⁰ Stephen stepped up to his rabbi and quietly told him he knew a way to escape. He pleaded into the eyes of Yeshua, but the eyes of the rabbi stared past his student. ⁵¹ Judah stepped forward. The air hung heavy. Yeshua walked toward his former emissary.

52 Judah kissed his cheek. It appeared as if they whispered, Yeshua into the ear of Judah and Judah into the ear of Yeshua. ⁵³ For a moment they embraced one another the way a hungry lioness seizes her prey. Judah stepped aside. Three of the guards surrounded and bound Yeshua. ⁵⁴ Stephen picked up a dropped sword and cut through the air, slicing the cheek of a slave from his ear to his jaw. The sword, too much to manage, dropped from his trembling hand. ⁵⁵ As the posse grabbed Stephen, he pulled away, leaving them with his garment as his feet took him deep into the naked night; with him scurried Yohanan, Jacob, and Cephas.

Notes: 48:47 Yeshua is paraphrasing, "...they shall beat their swords into plowshares and their spears into pruning hooks;" from Isaiah 2:4, New Revised Standard Version updated edition (NRSVue).

49 They brought him to Caiaphas. No one knew if his arrest would be a source of unrest. ² The high priest wanted to resolve this quickly in order to efficiently cut out any possible demonstrations or rioting by foolish adherents of...this rabble-rouser. ³ The end of the holy festival should not be marred by further disturbances. The high priest called only the most prominent members of the Great Sanhedrin to his house and arranged for a trial. ⁴ He saw no need to risk a public prosecution in the Hall of Hewn Stone. If all went as planned, the carpenter would be led outside Jerusalem, executed, and buried to greet the sun rounding the horizon.

5 Inside, torches flickered on the tired, grumbling faces of the scribes and priests of this remnant Sanhedrin. Witnesses stared through bleary eyes at the magnificent rooms of the high priest as they all settled into the belly of the night. [6] Captivated, every eye observed the accused. Annas stepped forward and addressed the attending Sanhedrin, [7] "This man broke the Sabbath and committed blasphemy." Capital offenses! A pile of Jerusalem stones thirsted for his blood.

8 Manaen and Azareel stumbled forward. Azareel raised his hand and stated, "I lift my right hand to heaven and may God damn me if my words are false." Manaen also took the oath. [9] Annas told them to identify themselves, and then speak on what they witnessed concerning the accused and his behavior on the Sabbath. Their testimony mired the accused with guilt. [10] Annas then turned to the prisoner. He took the oath: "I lift my right hand to heaven and my left hand to heaven. May God damn me if my words are false." [11] The importance of this trial weighed a little heavily on Annas. He cleared his throat and asked, "You are Yitzhak bar Yusef of Nazareth? [12] Also known as Yitzhak bar Miryam," Annas slyly said with a smirk on his lips and in his eyes. The judges of the accused raised their eyebrows. [13] "Yet you call yourself Yeshua, yes?" The accused stared kindly at him and replied, "As you say." [14] Annas set his face and asked, "Is the testimony of Manaen and Azareel true?" "No," he replied. Annas stared at him, "No? Then what have you to say?"

15 He caught his tongue from slipping. *Every day is holy, and there is no blasphemy in living in Holy Breath.* [16] He remained silent. The air spun a cocoon of echoing stillness around them. Annas asked again and waited. Again nothing. [17] The accused stared

at the floor. Annas looked to the Sanhedrin, threw out his arms and shrugged his shoulders. [18] The Sanhedrin mumbled in their beards. Was the accused too afraid to speak? Was he possessed by some demon?

19 Yohanan of the Sanhedrin examined Azareel and Manaen. "Did he eat any of the wheat that was picked?" Azareel hesitated, "No, but he defended his students picking the wheat on the Sabbath." [20] Gamaliel made further inquiries. The answers of the witnesses tumbled at cross purposes. Rumors multiplied over facts. Their testimony turned from bright as day to evidence shady as the hour it was given. [21] Gamaliel opened his mouth to examine the prisoner, but given the testimony against him had tumbled into dust, given the enigma of the man before him, given the late hour, Gamaliel asked nothing of the accused.

22 Annas motioned for Dimitri to step forward. "Do you acknowledge the wrath of God if you speak falsely?" The money changer knew that his table in the Court of Nations stood in peril if he did not cooperate. Dimitri answered with a distinct affirmative. [23] "Your sight will be struck from your eyes." "Yes." Your voice will lose its tongue?" "Yes." "Sores will cover your body." "Yes." [24] Annas studied the judges to see if they accepted the unorthodox presence of Dimitri, but the torchlight did not extend to their faces hidden in shadows. [25] Hearing no objections to the testimony of a Goy, the priest continued his prosecution.

26 Pointing to the prisoner, Annas asked, "Did this man start a riot in the Court of Nations?" Dimitri scratched his cheek as he answered, "He pushed me and knocked over my table." [27] As Dimitri answered Annas gazed toward the gathered judges. Turning back towards the witness he asked, "What else did he do?" [28] A wave of tiredness passed over Dimitri causing his head to droop which hollowed out the volume of his answer, "He knocked over other tables and

cages...of birds." [29] Annas stepped close to his face and shouted, "I did not hear you!" With eyes popped open and his head snapping back firmly, Dimitri loudly repeated his words. [30] Annas smiled as he rounded to the conclusion of his inquiry, "And why did he do this?" The eyes of Dimitri squinted as he searched his tired memory. [31] His brow relaxed as he recalled, "He said forgiveness is also for the poor. He thinks we money changers cheat the poor, but I do not. I do not!"

32 Annas waited, then asked, "Were those all his words?" Dimitri squinted his eyes. "Did he say he wanted to destroy the Temple?" [33] Stillness bound the Sanhedrin as they listened for his answer. Dimitri yawned as he nodded his head and replied, "Oh, yes. He said that first, before he knocked everything over." [34] The judges gasped. Annas stepped back. No one from the Sanhedrin asked anything of Dimitri.

35 Annas turned to the accused. "Why do you wish to destroy the Temple?" Silence. "Is that not what you proclaimed you would do?" More silence. [36] Annas turned to the Sanhedrin as he asked, "Are you here to tear down the Temple?" After a pause the priest exclaimed, "And rebuild it in three days!" [37] The judges, as one body, laughed. The mirth in their eyes shifted to study the accused for his answer. [38] The prisoner stared holes into the shadows on the floor. He gave them nothing. [39] Annas scowled at his victim, turned to the selected Sanhedrin and raised his hands. Looking at Caiaphas, he asked him with an anxious face, *Now what?*

40 The high priest, still in his ceremonial vestments from performing Passover services, stepped forward. The twelve gems on his breastplate winked with the fire of midnight torches. [41] Caiaphas, Shemyaza shining in his eyes, confronted the man who had yanked and ripped the beard of the priesthood. "Why so silent now? You talk high and mighty in the Court of Nations. [42] What demon is holding your

tongue?" Silence. "You will establish a new kingdom with you as a prophet-king–is that not your plan?" Silence. 43 Turning to the judges, "This man will destroy us! He claims to be a Messiah. But it is not just Goyim; to him we are sinners who must be expunged for a..." he snarled, "New Way."

44 Glaring at the accused, the high priest gleefully stated, "Oh yes, I know all about you. Our eyes were upon your cousin. They have been upon you for a long time." 45 Caiaphas pointed to himself repeatedly as he fervently spoke," You think you are better than I. But do not I risk death on the Day of Atonement? 46 Only I enter the Holy of Holies to face God. If the Lord is angry with his people, it is I who face his punishment. 47 It is I who step beyond the curtain of the Holy of Holies willing to bear the sins of Israel and face the wrath of God." 48 More silence. Caiaphas inhaled deeply before raking the prisoner with his last question as if his words were hot coals," Who are you?" 49 Another pause hung over the accused like a bird of prey. "A carpenter," slithered out of the mouth of Caiaphas followed by, "Yeshua bar Miryam."

50 Turning back to the judges the high priest sharply accused, pointing a finger at the offender, "He claims he will be the ruler of a new Kingdom of God." 51 A carpet of laughter, rich as the rug they had gathered on, rolled through the handpicked Sanhedrin. Caiaphas turned back and glared at the accused, "Is that not so?" Silence. 52 "This man has provoked and degraded the priesthood since his days in Galilee. Now every day his words fill the Court of Nations with foolish tales and blasphemy. 53 Why will you not speak to us? You think we are a pollution. Go on, tell us, you will pull the Temple down on our heads!" 54 The accused stared at the ground, but his eyes filled with pity for Caiaphas. He lifted his gaze to meet the fiery stare of the high priest but acted as if deaf and dumb.

55 The High Priest Caiaphas could do no

more. He ripped his robe and exclaimed, "What more do we need?" The weary members of the Sanhedrin turned to one another and deliberated. [56] A scribe whispered loudly, "An unbeliever testifying in the house of the high priest!" Arguments echoed heatedly in the dim halls of the high priest. [57] Caiaphas waited. And waited. Finally, a decision. The Sanhedrin faced the accused and Caiaphas. [58] Gamaliel threw his hands in the air and asked, "Where is the blasphemy?" The scribes mumbled amongst themselves. Another spoke up, "Are we to condemn a man during the holy week?" [59] Gamaliel voiced the decision of the majority, "He may be dangerous, certainly misguided. Yet, 'The Lord preserves the simple.' How can one stone in Jerusalem be lifted to right a 'riot' of one person in the Court of Nations?" [60] He paused for a breath, "Whip him. It would be a sin for us to execute this man." [61] Priests desperately raised their voices vociferously for a vote of death to no effect. Their day had passed and the judgment of the Sanhedrin allowed the high priest to administer up to forty lashes according to his wisdom. [62] Caiaphas listened grimly and then turned from them. His wisdom took another turn.

[63] The stars still stared wide awake in a night sky preparing to fade into a brisk dawn as the Sanhedrin and witnesses left the house of the high priest. [64] Gamaliel spoke through a mouth gaping with weariness to a priest walking next to him, "What was Caiaphas thinking?" The priest opened his mouth to argue, but only yawned. [65] Another voice carried in the air: "What an extraordinary night!" as soles of sandals dragged their owners to their homes.

Notes: 49:3 The Great Sanhedrin was a judicial body composed of priests and scribes that convened to hear cases on the north side of the Temple in the Hall of Hewn Stones. The name of the hall distinguishes it from the uncut stone used for structures inside the Temple. Hewn stone is prohibited by scripture to be used for ritual purposes. **49:45** The Temple, the sanctuary of Yahweh, contained an inner sanctum, the Holy of Holies, separated from the rest of the Temple by a plush curtain. The Holy of Holies once stored the Ark of the Covenant and other relics. On the Day of Atonement the high priest dutifully stepped behind the curtain to offer himself as a scapegoat for the sins of Israel and face the possible wrath of Yahweh. If God chose to exercise retribution, priests firmly stood ready at the other end of a rope tied snugly around the waist of the high priest to drag him under the curtain and retrieve his stricken body. **49:59** The quote, "The Lord preserves the simple." is from Psalm 116:6. **English Standard Version 49:61** Forty lashes were a common punishment for criminals and slaves. When administered, however, only thirty-nine were applied. Prevalent wisdom believed forty or more risked killing the person. Coincidentally, the Romans also often applied forty lashes as a punishment. They had a saying, "Forty minus one."

50

The high priest stroked his beard. "What shall be done?" Annas asked, "Forty…" Caiaphas scowled at him and shook his head. 2 A public flogging during Passover would be blasphemy. To wait risked the dangers of intrigue and rioting from the supporters of this…rabble rouser. 3 What was the Sanhedrin thinking?! Caiaphas fumed in a growl he could not contain. Yeshua smiled to himself. 4 The high priest circled him like a starving wolf. Only the jangle of the bells on his robe occupied the night in the flickering firelight of the room. Then Caiaphas stopped. 5 He spoke of his captive through a grim smile, "At daybreak, take him to Pilatus." Startled, Annas asked, "What shall I tell the Roman?" "Nothing," Caiaphas replied with lips curled in disdain, "I will speak with Pilatus." 6 Annas peered into the shadows. The high priest, after a slight nod to the captain, turned from Annas and retired for a short rest.

7 The guards played the remaining time for sport. Blindfolding their captive, a guard spat on him. They then removed

the blindfold and asked him to divine whose spittle marked him. [8] He answered them with silence. "Some prophet," they scoffed, and repeated the same amusement again and again until they grew bored. [9] Wiping him down with his robe, the guards assured him he would enjoy the next game much better. [10] Their low laughter echoed in the hall. Flames flickered on their smiles reflecting the grin of Shemyaza. [11] Blindfolding him again, someone slapped his face. When they asked him who had hit him, [12] Yeshua, beaming with Our Spirit, offered them his other cheek. [13] The dull pupils of the guards stared into his eyes. Without skipping a beat they accepted his offer. Taking turns, their slaps came harder and harder.

14 When their diversion became tiring, a guard ended it with a fist to his chest. The prisoner lay gasping for breath. [15] Yuval, conspicuous among his fellow guards for his jovial nature, picked the gasping body up from the floor and set him on a stool. [16] "By the prophets," Yuval exclaimed with admiration, slapping him on the back, "you are a tough one!"

17 In the courtyard of the high priest a small warming fire flickered against the faces of Temple guards. The sun, almost up for a new day, stretched unseen just beyond the horizon. [18] Upon hearing of his arrest, Miryamla, Miryam Magdalene, and Joanna checked out the likely places for Yeshua to have been taken. When they learned the house of the high priest held him, [19] they took to the cold shadows for a long night near the residence. On the night side of dawn they hung around the courtyard gate. [20] The stare of a guard who noticed their furtive figures drew the icy, attentive gaze of his companions. A guard called out, "What are you doing there? Come here! Who are you?"

21 Miryam Magdalene stepped forward. "What are you doing here?" the guard demanded. She meekly answered, "You have arrested someone." [22] With suspicion grasping the hilt of his sword, he

pointedly asked, "What is that to you?" Followed quickly by, "Do you know him?" [23] She answered softly, "I have heard him preach." The guard laughed, "I do not think you will hear him preach again." The fire lit up the smiles of the other guards. [24] She asked, "Then the charge is serious?" A guard snorted, "We followed orders and arrested him. We know nothing of charges. [25] He has spent the night a prisoner in the hall of the High Priest Caiaphas–I do not think they are drinking together." The guards laughed, a scrape of iron against stone.

26 Seeing that the phantoms in the night were women, they turned their backs to them and faced the welcoming wave of fingers of fire. Miryam Magdalene stepped back out of the courtyard and the women moved off to a safer distance. [27] Joanna returned to the emissaries in hiding to tell them what she knew. Miryamla and Miryam Magdalene watched for Yeshua intent on following him wherever he went.

51
"And who is this?" Linus asked. "Yeshua bar Yusef of Nazareth," Judah, the captain of the Temple guard, answered. "And why is he here?" [2] Unsure, the captain paused. He expected the high priest to be here. His words stumbled as he reported about a riot at the Temple the other day. [3] Linus, recently promoted to administer Jerusalem, clasped his hands together. The panicked tongue of the captain spilled out that the man is a troublemaker." [4] The left eyebrow of Linus rose with impatience. Well, he was ordered to bring the prisoner here. Linus looked to Pontius Pilatus who looked wearily back. [5] Pilatus had traveled to Jerusalem to observe the festivities with a vigilant eye. Knowing how Jewish insurrectionists liked to use this festival to begin their rebellions, he would not be caught flat-footed. [6] Linus stepped toward the captain. "This is a religious matter. It does not concern us. Why bring him here?"

7 The captain of the Temple guard opened his

mouth but, unable to put two words together, empty air from his throat filled the room. Pilatus cleared his throat. Linus stepped back to him. [8] With the nudge of a question, Pilatus quietly spoke to Linus, "Did he not say," nodding slightly with his head in the direction of the prisoner, "That is from Nazareth?" [9] Linus nodded, thought for a moment as he studied the face of Pilatus, and responded, "Ah, Herod!" A little smile grew in affirmation and then disappeared like a ship lost at sea. [10] Linus stepped toward the captain and ordered, "Since he is a Nazarene, take him to the Tetrarch of Galilee and...Perea." [11] The captain hesitated. Linus stared at him. He turned and they escorted the captive to Herod.

12 The captain of the guard paced a short line back and forth as he and his men waited in the courtyard of the palatial house Herod Antipas II resided in to celebrate Passover. Finally, Herod came out. [13] The captain informed him of what he knew. Herod had overheard gossip when dining one night with the high priest about the miracle worker from Galilee preaching in the Court of Nations. [14] He did not expect to see the troublemaker standing in his courtyard. Grunting, Herod girded his resolve and squinted at the prisoner. [15] With the sun in his eyes, he stepped close to the captive to inspect him. A beaten rag of a man. He smelled of sweat and urine. Herod stepped back. Is he...no. [16] This was not the Baptist. Then he paused. Or was he? Covering his nose and mouth he stepped closer to the accused. The face seemed different, but the eyes! [17] Wild in their ability to penetrate like a javelin while staring distantly past him, those eyes seemed all too familiar. Eyes that have followed him through his days and watched him in his dreams.

18 Herod stepped back and asked, "Are you Yohanan, the Prophet of the Jordan River?" The prisoner studied the eyes examining him, eyes starkly clouded with trembling and worry. [19] Though bound, Yeshua felt the breath of Yohanan

and Our Spirit swirling freely around him. "No," he softly replied in a half-truth. [20] Herod stroked his beard. He looked up at Herodias watching them from the balcony. If she thought Yohanan stood in their courtyard, it would be hard for her...and him. [21] Yohanan or not, his hands refused to be the bloody instruments against any prophet again. Fooled into killing one holy man, he would not be fooled a second time.

22 With a decision in his mind clear as the voice of his beloved queen, Herod told him, "I do not know your fate, but it has nothing to do with me." [23] Sweeping his fingers against each other, the tetrarch dusted his hands of all responsibility. [24] Stepping away he told the captain with a wave of his wrist, "Take him back to Pilatus." [25] Herod pinched his eyes at the prisoner. "If he offended in Judea, let him be judged in Judea." [26] He brushed the air surrounding the carpenter away with the back of his hand as he commanded, "Take him. Take him back to Pilatus." [27] Herod gave his servant instructions and returned to his adoring wife, waiting for him high in curiosity. The captain of the guard sighed, and the little group marched away. [28] Between the house of Herod and the Praetorium, Miryam Magdalene walked a little with Yeshua, until his guards pushed her aside.

29 In the courtyard of the Praetorium the clinking of bells worn by the high priest circled the captive until Pilatus and Linus appeared. [30] To Pilatus the servant of Herod bowed and spoke, "My master bids me to speak in his name; I, Herod, servant of God, Tetrarch of Galilee and Perea, send glad greetings to the Roman prefect of Judea, Samaria, and Idumea, [31] in the wise and just hand of the Most Notable Caesar, beloved by all people, judicious ruler of men; as the sun sets and the sun rises may prosperity and well-being find him and you." [32] After another bow he delivered a curt message, "I send you my gratitude for considering my prerogative, but by your leave the prisoner committed no

offense in Galilee or Perea for which I may judge him. [33] I return this man and surrender him to your authority and wisdom." [34] The servant ended with a bow saying, "So says Herod, servant of God, Tetrarch of Galilee and Perea. [35] May we rejoice in the good will of Caesar and the blessing of God be upon us." Then he stood off to the side to witness the proceedings and report back to Herod.

[36] Pilatus and Linus turned to Caiaphas. The high priest turned his face to the Roman prefect and thrust out his arm to point his accusing finger, "He is a Sicarii." [37] That straightened up the irritated prefect. "He claims to be the Son of God and seeks to overthrow the authority of Rome. " [38] Pilatus raised his eyebrows at Linus; Linus turned to the man under suspicion, now barely able to stand. [39] "Is this so? Are you the King of the Jews?" The captive kept his eyes pinned to the floor and said nothing. [40] Caiaphas continued, "He is a rabble rouser. He intends to destroy the Temple and defeat Rome." [41] The eyes of Pilatus widened with astonishment and his long finger pointed at the prisoner as he asked the high priest, "*That* is raising an army?" [42] The high priest firmly responded, "Yes. With an army sent from God he will conquer Rome and build a new kingdom of Israelites."

43 Words came to his mouth, but Pilatus paused, then, "Army…" Caiaphas nodded and replied, "Yes." [44] With a heavy breath Pilatus could only say, "Well..." He turned to Linus to say something but stopped as if struck by a thunderbolt. [45] Pilatus thought little of a Jewish army or their God. Yet, to ignore this might prove a dangerous game. The next time he sacrificed to Augustus, would the smoke of his offering blow back into his face? [46] Caiaphas noticed the thoughts spinning in the eyes of Pilatus and pressed on, "Is not Augustus a God? What would he think about this man calling on an army from our God? [47] What would the Most Notable Caesar think?" The High Priest Caiaphas paused, a cat crouched to pounce. With a vigorous thrust of

words he continued, "He started a riot. His followers are armed. [48] They attacked a party in the garden of Gethsemane. How long before a foolish mob also takes up arms in senseless rebellion?"

49 Pilatus gave Linus a look. Clearly no need existed to bring Tiberius into this business. Linus turned to the prisoner, "What have you to say?" The room closed in on an answer. [50] Dizzy with pain, hunger, exhaustion, the accused replied, "I was born to be a witness to the truth." He waved his arms, "All who know the truth hear my words." [51] The eyebrows of Pilatus raised themselves and an exclamation shot from Linus, "The truth!" Both Romans smirked. "What truth do you speak?" [52] Silence. "Is it true you are king of the Jews?" A moment of stillness flew around the room like the distant echo of a hollow cry. Yeshua answered, "It is you who say I am." [53] The face of Pilatus metamorphosed to stone. He turned and, with a glance at Linus, walked out of the hall. [54] "Crucify him," Linus commanded. A slave scribbled on a document. From Caiapahas a sigh took to the bright air.

55 They took him to Brutus. Brutus sized up his victim. As a professional, the Roman observed right off, by the eyes of the prisoner, that someone had already brutalized the captive. [56] Two soldiers stripped him. They ushered him to a stump on which his chest rested as they tied his hands to an iron ring. Brutus grabbed the flagrum. [57] The handle of the scourge knew his grip well. The sound of the tails made a dull slapping thud as it bruised and ripped flesh. [58] Each stroke upbraided Yeshua as a failure. Each lash cut his ambition. The hand wielding the flagrum demonstrated the folly of conspiring against Rome. [59] Each tail of the whip was fastened with bits of bone or metal. The sharp and tearing talons of the scourge worked its bloody commentary on his back.

60 Each stroke beat the Living Light inside him. At first, Our Spirit flew resiliently within Yeshua. Each fresh cut

stripped grace of meaning and filled him with gasps of despair. ⁶¹ His spirit withered. His body panted for breath. Flesh torn, nerves shrieked at stroke after lacerating stroke. ⁶² Again and again the smack of the tails slashed and cut him. He screamed. He cried out to God.

63 Satisfied with his work, Brutus returned the flagrum to its place and left. Now the added stench of blood marked the prisoner as damned. ⁶⁴ They untied him, threw him his clothes, sat him down, anointed him with filthy water, crowned him with thorns. It is not every day a mere soldier stands this close to royalty. ⁶⁵ Brutus returned with a crossbeam. "Enough," he said. The soldiers busied themselves with the preparations for a crucifixion.

Notes: 51:4 After Herod the Great's death, his son, Herod Archelaus, ruled as the ethnarch of Judea, Samaria, and Idumea from his seat in Jerusalem until Augustus removed the bumble of his incompetence. Many Roman prefects then administered his districts from the coastal city built by Herod the Great, Caesarea Maritima. The fifth Roman to put his hand to managing this portion of land thrashing for freedom like a fish caught in a net was Pontius Pilatus. **51:29** Praetorium is the Roman camp of a general. Here it refers to the palace Pilatus resided in when in Jerusalem. The interrogation by Pilatus took place in the courtyard because the high priest refused to enter the palace. To enter the residence of a Gentile during Passover would have polluted the high priest. Caiaphas would then be unable to perform Passover rites. **51:54** Caiaphas, after the emissaries came out of hiding and began proselytizing, interrogated Cephas and Yohanan concerning their healing of a cripple in the name of Yeshua. Finding them to be uneducated and the healing of the cripple too well known to repudiate, the high priest released them with a warning to stop working exorcisms in the name of Yeshua. What became of Caiaphas after that is not known. **51:56** Before crucifixion, the condemned were flogged.

52 The walk to Golgotha was a long mile. From the Praetorium to the little hill of Golgotha beside the road to the Hulda Gate the condemned carried the coarse crossbeam used to hang them. ² A night without rest, a day with beatings and little to eat or drink, he stumbled to his execution. The wind led the way carrying the cry of a strutting peacock. ³ Failure in the shape of a crossbeam bore him down. Not even his faith could carry the rough plank to the little hill used for executions. ⁴ He fell to the ground. A Roman beat him. As a lump of flesh he pushed himself into the ground. Futility did not stop the whip. ⁵ Simon of Cyrene stood behind the jeering spectators along the road. The sight of a fallen and beaten Yeshua hit him as a bolt of lightning. ⁶ His muscles reacted more quickly than any considered thought. He jumped forward. A Roman noticed him, pointed with his whip, and shouted at him. ⁷ Simon looked at the Roman, pointed his finger at himself trying to appear astonished. The Roman nodded and pointed to the crossbeam. ⁸ A third Roman stayed the hand with the angry whip. Killing the condemned on his way to execution was unprofessional and bad business. ⁹ Simon stumbled away from the crowd. He took up the crossbeam and they continued their death march.

10 On Golgotha, posts, standing out against a stark sky, waited to rejoin their crossbeams. ¹¹ A pole was pulled out and laid on the ground, soldiers nailed the crossbeam to it. After reading the titulus, "Iesus Nazarenus Rex Iudaeorum," it was nailed to the cross ¹² Stripped, the condemned was offered myrrh with wine. After one sip, he pushed the cup away. Avenging messengers stood a whisper away. ¹³ Stretching him on the cross, the soldiers strung his arms with ropes. They hammered nails between the bones at the top of his wrists into the crossbeam to add to his pain. ¹⁴ A soldier also drove a nail into the side of each foot, just under the ankle bone, to a side of the pole. ¹⁵ Each

blow of the hammer struck clearly in blood the wound of his failure. With a heave, they raised him up to drop the post back with a thud into its hole. [16] He rested the back of his head against the post until the pain from his crown of thorns pushed into his skull, forcing him to hang his head, which thrust his body forward, making it more difficult to stay erect.

17 Earlier, unable to find any of his emissaries, the Temple guards stood at the city gates with their palms resting on the hilts of their swords. [18] Unaware of what had recently transpired, several unsuspecting students showed themselves. Pointing fingers led the guards who grabbed them to be roughly handed over to the Romans. [19] All but two of the captured trembled and denied being his followers. Ezra and Asher did not realize until too late that their faith in Yeshua marked them for execution as fellow zealots.

20 Marked as bandits, their backs flogged, their bleeding shoulders carried rough crossbeams as their feet led the way to Golgotha. Stripped, they drank myrrh with wine. [21] Ropes fastened their arms to hang from their crosses, one on each side of their messiah Their titulus declared them to be Sicarii, though they had never held a dagger or hurt anyone. [22] Using their arms for leverage, they raised themselves up, pinching and pushing against the splintered posts with feet and legs to keep their bodies erect.

23 Word spread: The Temple destroyer was to hang from a cross. Singly, two by two, or in small parties, Sadducees and Pharisees with a few Zealots blending in trailed like a snake out of Jerusalem to gather at Golgotha and witness his death. [24] The bored and the ragged poor from Jerusalem straggled with them. Susanna nearly joined the other women at the cross, but the emissaries insisted she best serve Yeshua by staying and attending to them. [25] Miryamla, Miryam Magdalene, and Joanna with Reuben strapped to her back stood near the cross

of Yeshua. ²⁶ Averting their eyes so as not to witness his nakedness, the women wept and wailed as a low wind in the dry heat of a desert when the sun sets behind a distant blaze of clouds on the horizon.

27 With a wagging finger pointing to the sky, Judah the Scribe smiled through his words, "You who would destroy the Temple and build it again in three days, how is it you cannot save yourself?" ²⁸ Spreading his arms and searching the air, a priest chimed in, "Yes, where are the messengers?" Another spectator cried out, "You who looked down on us, how do you see us now?" ²⁹ Judah stepped up, "Come down from the cross! Come, you who saved so many. Come down and we will believe in you." ³⁰ The scribe tapped his foot. Squinting his eyes up into the face riddled with blood, Judah the Scribe wagged his finger, "No? Well," shrugging his shoulders, "I guess we must wait for another messiah." ³¹ The two hanging beside him cried out to him to save them. When he told them to be strong they cursed their pain, cursed themselves, cursed the day his words had filled their heads. ³² They hurled every curse they knew at him like excrement, like stones. Before long only groans issued from their throats as the need to stay erect sapped all their strength.

33 When the post heavily drops into place, the jolt to the body often results in dislocating the shoulders. The arms must help to keep the body elevated. With dislocated shoulders this becomes difficult and painful. ³⁴ If the sides of the feet are nailed to the post below the ankles, the body uses the nails as supports to stand erect, to breathe more easily until convulsing muscles finally collapse. ³⁵ The body slumps with its own weight and, while fighting for air from deep within, the heart rapidly beats as if it would burst. ³⁶ If strength returns to the legs, a back whipped raw scrapes along the rough post when feet, using the iron nails as fulcrums, push the body back up. ³⁷ Using the nails for support the body stands erect to breathe

more easily until muscles convulse and collapse... [38] A body fixed to a cross flails, a fish out of water with a foot on its tailfin. Over and over the body thrashes for hours. The very strong might struggle for several sleepless days.

39 The crowd watched every muscle tremor; listened to every whimper, grunt, or cry. Their excitement searched condemned faces and followed bodies chafing down and up the bloody wood again and again. [40] Time crawled slowly. A gawker swatted a fly. The pace of this entertainment requires patience. [41] Chatter and gossip filled the slack, tedious moments. Wits snapped jeers like derisive whips to amuse the rest of the crowd.

42 The aged and infirm mother of Ezra and Asher, hearing of their fate, rushed to Golgotha and pushed through the crowd. Her wail filled every ear and chest. [43] The old widow fell weeping at the feet of her only sons. A Roman stood up to push her away, but her screams ebbed into sobs. [44] He turned back and crouched down with the rest of the soldiers examining the garments of the dying men. [45] Through their trials, some of the clothing became too foul and ragged to be of any value. For the rest, dice waited patiently to rattle in a leather cup and then roll out a winner for a lucky soldier.

46 From a parched throat a voice hoarsely rasped, "I thirst. I am thirsty." Miryamla approached the Roman soldiers busy with gambling dreams. [47] She pleaded to give her brother a drink. Two stared at her; one laughed. [48] Another soldier gazed into the tearful concern of a sister pleading for her brother. [49] To the surprise and then the heckles of his comrades— he took a sponge, sopped it in a bowl of vinegar, stuck it to a hyssop, and held it to cracked lips.

50 It was near the third hour of the day when the Roman soldiers had hung them from their crosses. The sixth hour of the day witnessed a sky growing gray with bruised clouds. [51] His vision blurred, Yeshua hung his head. Open mouths and eyes wide

with expectations surrounded him. Suddenly the Living Light swirled sharply in his eyes: [52] He could have saved them, the damn fools! Staring at Judah the Scribe he shouted at the top of his lungs, "You know not what you do!" Out of breath he slid down the post. [53] On his way up Our Spirit rose within him. Yeshua barked out, "Lord, forgive them. Forgive them. I forgive you." the grace of salvation poured out of him, weaving among the spectators on Golgotha. [54] Yeshua cast his eyes at Asher and Ezra grasping and sliding on their crosses, at the spectators enlivened with their suffering, at the soldiers dutifully waiting for their deaths. [55] As flies buzzed in his face or crawled on his bloody skin, Yeshua exclaimed, "Their understanding...they know not what they do...Lord, forgive them. I...forgive you." [56] His voice reached out to each one of them. Our dove swirled among the onlookers seeking a breast to nest in.

[57] Those who heard him clearly failed to comprehend his words echoing in their ears. *Forgive me? He forgives me?* [58] Their eyebrows raised. The corners of their mouths turned from sneers and taunts to pondering vacancies. Faces searched each other for meaning. [59] Like pythons their thoughts tightened around his words. They asked each other, "Forgive us?" "What?" "A condemned man...forgives us. Absurd!" [60] Asher and Ezra scoffed through their agony. One soldier looked at him and thought, *Are we crucifying a madman?* Another turned away with a short, incredulous snort and spat. [61] Judah the Scribe opened his mind and then pinched it to a sliver of light. A proverb jumped out at him and he turned it over and over considering it as he stroked his beard.

[62] Suddenly silence held them in the hollow of hands closed together. An eerie space overwhelmed the jeers and curses and gossip of men. [63] They continued to look at one another, at the ground or at the gray sky. Some tapped their toes or drummed their fingers

against their thighs. ⁶⁴ Silence unfolded, broken only by the low sobbing of women, groans from a hanging man, a hooded crow calling, it seemed, to each one of them.

65 Yeshua caught the eye of his sister; he motioned to the bent and weeping mother of the twins, "She is your mother. Take..." He started to slide down the post, caught himself and scraped himself back up. ⁶⁶ Words failing him, he stared with pointed determination through his pain. Through her tears Miryamla understood and nodded.

67 For six hours three bodies struggled to be upright on their crosses. Their minds given over to death; their bodies refused to die. ⁶⁸ Children made faces or played among the scattered bones as the damned slid down and up their posts to the enjoyment of the crowd that thinned and grew and thinned, a snake fat from swallowing a victim and then slimming out after digesting its meal. ⁶⁹ Of the strangers watching, only the Roman soldiers and a few squatting on their haunches, provisioned with a little wine in skins and some bread, stayed from beginning to end.

70 Through pain squeezing his body like a sponge, what thoughts occupied Yeshua while nailed to a cross? ⁷¹ Did the jibes of a careless crowd oohing and aahing capture his attention? Were weeping women circling in his skull? ⁷² Did the toothy smile of his righteous cousin lift him up? Perhaps pigs tumbling into the sea stampeded his thoughts? ⁷³ A blur of thousands of hands clutching at him with pins of need in their voices? ⁷⁴ Did the curious faces of his emissaries on Mount Tabor raise up to him once more? ⁷⁵ The tickling hair of Miryam washing his feet? Echoes of joyful singing and shouted praises? ⁷⁶ Did the troubled eyes of his mother curse or forgive him? Perhaps, they loved him as only the eyes of a mother can. ⁷⁷ Perhaps he prayed. Maybe he emptied himself of thoughts, shutting them all off in a vain attempt to block out pain? ⁷⁸ Would it only add to his torment if he remembered the promise

of a new kingdom, the strangled hopes of his expectations?

79 The Zealot scrutinized the crucified with squinted clarity. Nothing here. [80] He wiped his nose on his sleeve, turned, and left disappointment hanging on a cross. [81] His expectations satisfied, certainty carried him a long way to knowing only bloody blades would free his country. [82] No miracle worker, preaching, forgiving, giving it all away, could be the Messiah, his Messiah. [83] The Zealot snorted at the idea of the wealthy giving all their riches to him. He stopped short. If he is given their wealth, doesn't that make him a rich man? What is he to do? Give it back? [84] He snorted a laugh. Then his teeth clenched at the thought of forgiving anyone for kissing the defiled ground Roman sandals walk on. No. Only the point of a sword will do.

85 No promise fulfilled. Not a messenger in sight. Yeshua bled his last drop of hope. [86] "My God!" he cried out. "My God, why have you abandoned me?" With a shuddering scream his muscles gave out. His body slumped too weak to rise. [87] Tilting his head back to gulp for air, he smacked the post driving the thorns into his skull. His head bowed. The ground stared into his blank eyes.

88 Possessed with Our Spirit during his life, our dove, perched on the post of his cross, breathed in Yeshua and breathed out Yeshua. Our Spirit grew greater with each breath. [89] The three women stood close to his cross cupping their hands to cover the soft tissue of their eyes turned into water burning with salt. [90] For the mortals who loved Yeshua, a shroud clouded their vision. With his death the world diminished.

91 Not long after the ninth hour, a priest, Malachi, approached the Roman soldiers. It was time to begin to prepare for the Sabbath. For the execution to go on during the holy day would be a sacrilege. [92] The soldier who had pressed vinegar to dry lips picked up a hammer. With each crack of the heavy hammer shrieks gutted the air. [93]

The femurs of two bitter men smashed, their bodies sagged and suffocated. The spectators enjoyed their last writhing gasps for life. [94] Turning toward Jerusalem, even though preparations for the Sabbath weighed on them, yet they mumbled displeasures at the sudden end of their sport. [95] The old woman, aging a hundred years in a few short hours, groaned and collapsed at the feet of her sons. Miryamla went and held her. They wept together.

96 When asked why he did not break *his* bones, the soldier scoffed and declared *he* was already dead. Malachi, ill at ease, pressed for greater certainty. [97] The soldier reassured him. Still the priest expressed his apprehension. The soldier brushed him off. The priest persisted. [98] The soldier threw the hammer to the ground, picked up a spear, and pierced the quiet chest. No blood poured out of the wound. The Roman stared coldly into the eyes of Malachi; the priest bowed his head.

99 Joanna nursed the fussing Reuben. Miryam Magdalene helped the old mother and Miryamla to their feet. Soldiers took down the executed. [100] Besides the clothes, dice determined who won the nails used for their crucifixion. The winner happily pocketed them for their prized healing powers. [101] Golgotha was named after the weathered skulls and gnawed bones of the executed littering the hill, but the fresh corpses could not remain there. [102] Malachi informed the soldiers that to leave the dead exposed during the Sabbath would be a pollution of the holy day. He asked their permission to take possession and dispose of the bodies.

103 Roman eyes took in Malachi, the soldiers weighed their options. A gruff laugh and wave of the hand assented to the wishes of the priest. [104] In quick time the guards, with the crossbeams and their gathered goods, marched back to the Praetorium. [105] Temple slaves carried the broken and bloody remains as Malachi led the way to a nearby grave. [106] Joanna, Miryam Magdalene, and the mother of Ezra and

Asher, with the assistance of Miryamla, followed at a distance. Our Spirit trailed the women walking slowly away from Golgotha.

Notes: 52:1 The word for skull in Aramaic is golgotha; in Latin, calvaria. **52:1l** The titulus declares the reason for the execution. "Iesus Nazarenus Rex Iudaeorum." is "Yeshua the Nazarene King of the Jews." **52:12** Myrrh with wine is a sedative. Once Yeshua realized the wine was drugged, he apparently wished to remain as clear headed as possible. **52:50** For most Jews, the first hour of the day began with the sunrise. For those under the influence of Rome, however, the first hour of the day began after midnight. It is likely Yeshua was nailed to a cross around 9 am under a fair sky. **52:61** "If your enemy is hungry, give him food! If he is thirsty, give him something to drink! This will make him feel ashamed of himself, and God will reward you." Proverbs 25:21-22, Living Bible (TLB) **52:86** Yeshua's last words in Aramaic were, "Eli! Eli lema sabachthani?" Judah the Scribe misunderstood them and said, "Listen! He calls for Elijah to come down and save him!" When Elijah left this earth, it is written he was taken to heaven in a chariot of fire.

Lamentation

1 Sky of sackcloth
sky filled with ash
falls in harsh gray rain
covering my eyes and tongue
with dust of what was

Clear skies
yet they remain ashen
Rise   burning world
wasted with sun
    blot out my eyes
My light gone
My light failed
Sky fills with ashes
Sky of ashes buries me

Fury of smothered fire
scars earth
My wail reaches out
   a voice lost in noise
My cry scrapes as nails
across face of fields
Their furrows   barren of seed
    flood with bitter streams

I seek a way back to days
spilled like water from trembling hands
days beyond human touch
Where is flesh that walked with me
Where is laughter that raised me up

2 Anger grinds teeth
Fingers dig into palms
I wrestle with a shade
Eyes sear into sharp shards
Vision blurs   Thoughts blur
Flesh and bones lay in their grave

Flesh and bones lay in their grave
Rage curls as a pillow
to lay my head on
Rage slithers across floors
   a furtive viper at night
Rage coils around my chest
tighter and tighter then swiftly
rage strikes and strikes and bites
Its venom is my blood
My teeth grind in anger

3 Loss caught and hauled me
in strong and coarse netting
I struggle   I bruise   I fight
to breathe in stifling stillness
Grabbed in a rough fist
I am laid out and cut
open with a long swipe

of serrated purposelessness
My guts fished out to be
dumped in a land of plenty
I breathe nothing   Nothing
No breath now can contain me

4 Life is hidden from me
My delights fill with shades
Voices hollow out as echoes
Gray clouds fill my eyes

Warm breeze full of tomorrow
languishes in my fields
No foot falls along my path
to welcome with joy
My strength cut off
I lay weary and worthless

A breath from death passes
   music without sound
   being without presence
   life without living

5 We are without shelter
Storms threaten us
We wander without refuge
Sun in fit of heat
scorches even our shadows
Rain beats on our heads
Where are we to go
What are we to do

We build tabernacles
to make lamentations
Our tambourines beat slowly
Low voices stir lower depths
wild with light within shadows
swirling with shades within splendor
Our strings pull on waves
reaching in while stretching out
Our laments   fists

full of dry sand
    sing out only to be
blown back into our eyes
Our lives translate into moans
We are lost   We are lost
All our time spent wailing
    fills our moans   rocks beating
against each other   against us

Devastation greets our eyes
Our tabernacles collapse
Wherever we turn we find ruin
Homes that still stand high
    All is desolate
People go to market
    All is desolate
Shepherds tend their flocks
    All is desolate
Potters spin their wheels
    All is desolate
Farmers sow their fields
    All is desolate
Mothers suckle their children
    All is desolation

6 We bury our grief
Our grief resurrects itself
to lay with us   sit with us   walk with us
Wherever we go
our groans fill our sails
driven in trackless circles

7 I call my child   I hear only wind
rustle in cedars   I reach out
to embrace my child   No body presses
against mine   I lay out food
    My child does not sit at table
    Everything tastes like sawdust
I sing a lullaby   An empty pillow
smothers my song   I call my child
No one answers

8 Shadow   you that shone
brighter than brightest day
where is sweet substance
you followed like a child
happy to skip alongside as if
holding hands with a loving parent

Wherever light showed its face
you two were inseparable
You ran laughing ahead
or fell behind to adoringly follow

You and I are two shades
   lost   without substance
   disconnected from our beloved
Only sackcloth and ashes
offer me comfort
Grief lifts up hope as smoke
stinging my eyes

9 We arid creatures know this
   loveless eyes
stare up at us
   flesh we touch
feels nothing back to us
   we witness motion
locked in stillness

After three days
our vision whips
with what cannot be seen
   yet it is all we see

Death lives in our image
We rise with Death
We walk beside Death
Daily we lie by Death

b
Perversions of death

from nameless dimensions
    we come forth
    a fish struggling in a net
We love light but know
we swim out of our depth
to reach luminous essence
Our lips press breathless kisses
Our words of pleasure
crawl as flies in our mouths
We sweat and grunt
in worm beds of want
    until too weak to breathe
    nameless dimensions take us

c
We exist   a fetish of thoughts
hanging onto tails of whirlwinds
Our minds flash with lightning
gathered in circuitous spirals
caving into ruins   We live
as grains dissolving in water

d
We rule backs of seas
We thrive over hills and valleys
Seas and earth are a house
built by death for death
We enter   we wander   we leave
    playthings in pulseless hands

e
A breath of grief possesses me
I am a chick whose mother
takes food from my mouth
Air is sucked out of me
Grief drinks my blood
I lay down in ashes
Cover myself with ashes
Tears venomous with loss
water my ashes to grow
roses   beautiful roses
as red as pooled blood

f
We are a dry day
when storm stepped up
and thrusts of wild currents of sky
danced in green clouds of trees
with leaves lifted as receptacles
    no rain came   no rain

10 Our dove swirls
around and within me
"You are forgiven"

11 Fed on bread of life
sweet and hefty   we fill ourselves
When bread of life crumbles   bounty
offers crumbs   for even crumbs
are the bread of life

12 The way of tongues of fire
    flames buffeted by shadows
fills us with kindling made
of all we dearly possess
Consumed by Living Light
    I am shattered by death
Yet   Our Breath gathers me
in a warm and dizzy embrace
With every lazy breeze or fierce blast
    every shadow or ember of light
I am broken but whole
    alive and dying

---

53 What are emissaries to do when their rabbi is dead? After their experiences with Yeshua, their former lives felt foreign to them. [2] The sun shone at its zenith. They huddled in a room as a body of troubled water. [3] Simon the Zealot sat staring past his right fist as he repeatedly opened and closed it. Yohanan paced

back and forth. Toma gazed into space while either rampaging or rummaging deep within himself. [4] Jacob stood by the door as if expecting it to burst open at any moment. Matthew sat with others, immersed in prayer and meditation. [5] The women gathered among themselves. Miryam and the mother of the twins held each other in mourning. [6] Mouths closed as sepulchers for words. Grief oppressed their vision. Their misery matched that of their ancestors, exiled on the banks of the overflowing rivers of Babylon. Their Jerusalem lay in ruins. [7] All this Cephas observed in the room that served as a refuge from a breath of violence and as a prison locking them in lamentation. [8] Something felt strange. His eyes settled on Miryam Magdalene. She sat in an exceptional stillness all her own.

[9] A breath of air sucked out of him; Cephas gasped for another breath–it did not come to him. A fish out of water, he was drowning on dry land. [10] An attempt to scream died within him. He lacked the wind to cry out. Another attempt–another gasp of empty air–his cry strangled in his throat. [11] A dust storm raged in the eyes of Cephas fastened on Miryam Magdalene. Wailing inwardly, he stared at her.

12 Marching over to the woman who simply sat there quietly, Cephas absorbed her silence and sharply shook it to life, saying, "You were close to him. You spent many hours with him. [13] 'Let him who is without sin cast the first stone,' our rabbi cried out and saved you. [14] How is it you are calm? How is it you do not mourn? Perhaps he imparted some great wisdom to you that raises you above us?" The coiled snake in the words of Cephas raised its head. [15] "Tell us," he commanded. His words hung in the air waiting. When she failed to immediately answer him, his pent up venom shouted out in one syllable, "Speak!"

16 Her lips trembled, troubled waves under stormy skies. Calming herself, she looked up and replied, "I mourn." She hesitated. "And I

have mourned." [17] She collected a fire deep within her. "But I am warmed and lifted by the presence of the Holy Breath. [18] Yeshua told me...did he not say, 'those who have ears, let them hear? And those who seek shall find?' So have we not heard?" Miryam observed their faces to find a glimmer of acceptance. [19] "He taught us our body is our temple. His death ripped the Temple curtain asunder revealing the Living Light does not reside in the Holy of Holies, but ourselves." [20] Looking at those looking at her, she added earnestly, "We can feel the breath of Yeshua within the Holy Breath.

[21] "He told me we are all one, all of nature. All creatures exist with and in one another. [22] We thrive and are resolved in ourselves and in the heart of each other and every tree, every stone, every cup of air. We are one body with the Holy Breath of God. [23] We hold all that is holy and all that is sinful. We are products of glory and sin, and sowers of glory and sin. And all glory and sin are as one."

[24] Miryam paused. Her body straightened as she told them, "When I followed him to the house of Herod, he saw me. His steps stumbled in great pain, yet the wings of our dove lifted him up. [25] The guards allowed me to give him a handful of almonds and grapes. He smiled at me the way only he smiled–like a full sail on a summer day with every wave a step carrying your beloved joyfully home. [26] After the guards took him back to Pilatus–I waited–and waited–such a long time.

[27] When I saw him again he wore a crown of thorns; a beam bore him down. He stumbled, beaten beyond hunger and thirst. [28] I searched for his eyes, but I could not see them. He turned his head from me. He kept his face from me." [29] She paused, staring blankly for a moment. She stared at Cephas and then turned from him. Her eyes found other eyes taking her in. [30] She continued, "I asked a guard what was happening. He told me to come to Golgotha and see." [31] She looked at Joanna and Miryamla, "And so we

did." Her eyes sparkled like broken glass catching flickering flames.

32 "Last night he came to me," Miryam solemnly revealed. "Yeshua appeared covered in blood, the crown of thorns mangled in his hair and flesh. 33 He told me the Holy Breath needed him to offer himself as a sacrifice. 34 In his mortal form he digested all the puffed glory and greed and bleeding resentments and coldness we smother on each other in this world. Only in sacrifice can sin be expunged. 35 Our rabbi, by offering himself, showed us how his sacrifice will lead us away from sin and into Sovereignty. 36 'There was always going to be blood on the path,' he said. It needed to be *his* blood." 37 Miryam cast her gaze around the room. "We just have to believe. 38 Yeshua hung from the cross to show us how to sacrifice our sins so we may live in the heavenly kingdom here on earth."

39 Miryam gasped a breath full of tears and went on, "Yeshua told me he walked the stony way to Sheol and back. The dross of his shade, the flesh and bones of ambition, he left in Sheol. 40 They always belonged to the devil. That is what his sacrifice taught him. 41 That was the purpose of his death. It freed him! It freed us! 42 The Kingdom of Saving Grace is not just around us. It is in us! Don't you feel it?

43 "Then in a brilliant flash he stood by me as a new man. No sign of wounds showed on his body. 44 His crown of thorns turned to gold with gems that radiated as stars. In his death he shed the fetters of oblivion. 45 He said all this in his soothing voice that grew stronger and stronger–as when he healed the sick, the crippled, the blind. Oh how he shone alive with light! 46 Yeshua rose above me and spread his arms. They became great wings. He rose higher and higher. 47 His body and wings grew larger and greater until their span covered land and sea from Galilee to Judea. 48 He hovered for a moment, growing greater and greater. His breath with the Holy Breath covered the whole world. He smiled, and his smile

lit up every land and every sea."

49 Miryam raised herself to her feet and faced her brethren, "Now I am one with Yeshua...and Yohanan...in heavenly light. And so can we all. [50] Do not be wasted with weeping. Be resolute." Miryam stared straight into the hard eyes of Cephas. [51] "I grieve." She looked around the room at everyone. "We all mourn. But we all have work to do. His grace–the grace of our dove–is with us and I am comforted."

[52] Everyone drew near her as water thirsting for a field to nourish, to be one with a thriving and abundant growth of golden possibilities. Andreas and Cephas exchanged sharp and weary glances. [53] Cephas cuttingly chided, "Who are you to speak thus? I do not believe our rabbi spoke to you in this way. I do not understand you. Your words are waters thick with silt. Who can see what they mean? He never spoke to us in this way." [54] Cephas turned away from her and his left arm swept from his body to take in his fellow emissaries. Cephas spoke to them, "Are we to turn around and show our backs to the words he taught us? It is up to us to fulfill his promise. [55] I will not listen to her strange ideas." Cephas threw up his arms, waved her off with the back of his hand, and walked away from her.

[56] Miryam Magdalene sat down quietly as a candle in a corner. For those with eyes to see, Our Spirit–a tongue of fire glowing within her–radiated brightly above her head.

54 Stephen haunted the streets of Jerusalem. Ever since his conversion to the New Way, he had abandoned his business in Damascus. [2] The laborers wandered off to seek other work to provide for their families. His brother sold off all the merchandise. The men of the grove missed him. [3] Ever since the death of Yeshua, his zeal to proselytize exceeded the boundaries of his life. All who encountered his presence tried, but miserably failed to fly from him.

4 In the qehalah of Freedmen–Jews from Alexandria, Asia, Cilicia, and Cyrene–he castigated them for worshiping at the Temple. [5] "You turn your backs to the Holy Breath," Stephen upbraided them. "It would be better for you to use the Temple as a latrine than a house of worship!" [6] Having raised their indignation, they ran to the High Priest Jonathon and the Great Sanhedrin to report his blasphemy which devastated the fields of their thoughts like ravenous locusts. [7] On a day brilliant with early light, a Freedman pointed Stephen out to three Temple guards. Promptly arrested, [8] the zealous devotee of Yeshua spent the next six days crammed with many others in a squalid prison. On the seventh day, Stephen stood in the long rectangular Hall of Hewn Stones.

9 Both entrances, one at the east and the other at the west end of the hall, opened to the Court of Nations to the south and the Court of Israelites to the north. [10] The smooth, white marble walls stood two stories tall, the north and south walls each with four high windows. [11] The windows on the north wall opened to the Court of Israelites. The smoke and stench from burnt offal trailed in to let the Great Sanhedrin know that sacrifices carried the presence of God into their midst. [12] The south windows were more conducive to sunlight, but odors along with the bustle from the Court of Nations sometimes found their way in to abuse those at work in the hall. [13] All within, should they choose, gazed up to an arched roof where birds sometimes perched in the timbers. [14] Reddish umber marble benches ascended the northern wall in three rows and stretched out from the ends like two short arms creating a half circle. [15] The beige marble floor contained the outline of a bronze colored circle that, though they did not touch, with a little imagination appeared to be held by the benches reaching out into the hall.

16 While the Great Sanhedrin sat, the high priest stood commandingly by the right end of

the benches. Witnesses fidgeted across from him by the left end. The accused found their feet in the center of the circle. [17] So Stephen stood and faced his judges. All listened to the recent successor of Caiaphas, the short and wiry Jonathon, relate in his high pitched voice the vulgar proposition of Stephen. [18] The high priest then beckoned Tobias of Cyrene–the Freedman who had fingered Stephen out on the street–to step forward, swear an oath, and testify. [19] Shaking, with arms flying in many directions like a ship falling apart in a raging storm, Tobias testified to the veracity of the accusation. Two others followed suit. [20] The Sanhedrin steadily looked upon the stout figure of the accused and waited. Jonathon asked, after Stephen swore his oath, "What have you to say?"

21 Much. He had much to say. "Fathers, brothers, hear my words!" Stephen started down a long peroration reminding them–as if they needed reminding–of Abram living in Ur when God appeared to him and told him he must leave for a foreign land. [22] "God spoke to him in this way: 'For four hundred years your descendants will be strangers in a country not their own, and they will be enslaved and mistreated. But I will punish the nation they serve as slaves...'" [23] Stephen continued on and on how Abraham made a covenant with God passed on through the circumcision of Yitzhak, the son of Abraham. [24] As Yitzhak was circumcised, so was his son, Jacob. After expounding on Jacob, a lengthy narration followed on the life of his son, Joseph. [25] Eventually, Stephen caught up to Moses. At this point the accused dwelt much time in the desert–for it was in the desert where the tabernacle first housed God. Not until Solomon did God reside in the Temple. [26] This was an error. How could God Almighty, maker of heaven and earth and all things fruitful, reside only in a house made by hands?

27 More than a few judges asked themselves, *Well, was not the tabernacle made by hands?* [28]

What difference does it make if the House of God is transitory or a permanent and proper Temple?

29 Stephen eyed the Great Sanhedrin closely. When he first spoke they nodded approvingly or, like a blank scroll, stared straight at him. 30 Now he thought their lips tightened into grim lines and their eyes sharpened themselves on him. 31 A snorting bull entered his breath and he shouted, "Prophets through Moses gave you the laws, but the laws," he sneered, "crumble as dust in your hands. 32 Your hearts turn away from the Breath of God! You murderers of prophets of old!" His rage suddenly turned sorrowful. "And now you betrayed Yeshua, the bearer of the Holy Breath." 33 With bitter tears and snorting like a bull, Stephen charged again. "What a stiff necked tribe you are! Your ears and hearts uncircumcised!" 34 He paused and, with glaring eyes, finished matter-of-factly, with a tinge of pity, "Your breath is empty of the Breath of God."

35 Whether they had sharpened their eyes on him earlier or not, the Sanhedrin certainly attacked him with their eyes now. A judgment of guilt quickly came to pass. 36 The sentence of death practically knocked over the cries of "Guilty!" The high priest ordered the sentence be carried out immediately.

37 Four Temple guards escorted Stephen from the Hall of Hewn Stones, through the Dung Gate, and lined him up against the city wall. 38 A guard took his robe–they would gamble for it later–and stepped off to join another a good twenty paces away. 39 As they had marched through the streets like a snowball rolling downhill, more and more people followed the condemned man. A good crowd stood ready to either watch or participate in the execution. 40 Many stones lay about to be gathered. Though stoning was not a common occurrence, a few stained with dried blood could be found. 41 Tobias of Cyrene tossed a stone a few inches up into the air and caught it again and

again–a measure of nervousness. ⁴² All the men who chose to throw stones, first took off their robes to free their arms for accuracy. ⁴³ A young man named Saul volunteered to watch over their clothing. The executioners stood ready.

44 "Though you are a sinner, yet we love you as our brother," the high priest said as an attending priest handed him a stone. ⁴⁵ He held the stone up high and pronounced, "Let our brother Stephen be accorded a decent death, and may he find peace." ⁴⁶ So saying, Jonathon threw the stone to the ground. All eyes turned from the stone to the condemned.

47 Before the stones sought him out, Stephen quickly shouted, "Forgive them! Lord, forgive them." ⁴⁸ He said something else as he pointed with his finger to the sky, but many did not hear him. The stones spoke louder than any words. ⁴⁹ The first volley battered his raised arms; a couple knocked him in the chest; one made it through his shield of hands and smashed his mouth; one hit the side of his head.

50 Backed into the wall, with his breath knocked out of him, his knees buckled to the ground. The second volley laid him groaning on the ground. ⁵¹ The crowd closed in. Thud after thud of stone hitting flesh, still the righteous arms hurled more projectiles of their justice. ⁵² His skull crushed, Stephen lay in a puddle of blood, the first martyred student since the crucifixion of Yeshua.

Notes 54:22 Acts of the Apostles 7:6,7 New International Version. (NIV) **54:46** When walking through a crowded Court of Nations, the High Priest Jonathon gasped out his life–his throat slashed by an assassin's blade. Antonius Felix paid to have him killed. Jonathan influenced the selection of Felix as procurator of Judea, was unhappy with how he was governing, and threatened to report him to Rome.

55

Herodias paced the floor in front of her husband. ² Her imagination ran wild, as if she witnessed the third Most Notable Caesar, Gaius Julius

Caesar Germanicus–known by his nickname, Caligula, "little boots,"– holding out his hand. ³ Caligula had just succeeded Tiberius. Poor sick Tiberius. In his last years he found popularity with his people and the Senate denied him. Rumor even circulated that Caligula had smothered him with a pillow. ⁴ Now the third Most Notable Caesar shouldered the responsibilities of the Roman Empire to great applause. ⁵ This happened before a fever shook him, before the simmering great power of his position boiled to a froth of abuse within four short years, before his praetorian guards, escorting him to the theater, turned from protectors to assassins. ⁶ Herodias thought of Caligula holding out his hand to his good friend, her brother, Herod Agrippa. She hoped the generosity of Caesar would also extend to her and Herod.

7 Herodias stopped pacing and turned to her husband. "If my profligate brother can be king, you too should be king!" ⁸ Her words danced dizzily in little circles.

"Well," he replied, looking at her through the soft lens of his eyes, "I do not have his connections." ⁹ "I have them!" "Well, I realize the two of you, since childhood, lived in Rome to be raised in the household of Caesar. ¹⁰ But the time Agrippa spent in Rome far exceeds your own." "Oh, I still know people!" "Those you knew best are dead." ¹¹ Herodias raised her finger. "I am familiar with his sister…" Her husband stared at her with a self-possessed blankness. "…She may be useful." ¹² Herod set his eyes to the wall behind her and took a deep breath. "Even so." ¹³ His gaze turned to her once more. "Agrippa knows many and has chummed with Caligula in dissolution." ¹⁴ "What do you mean?" "His drinking and whoring and going into debt." "That was with Druses and Claudius." ¹⁵ He considered pursuing his argument. "Well…he has known Caligula for a long time."

16 Herod felt *her* stare. Almost he did not bother responding to the first words of his wife. A smile and a walk out of

the room could have sufficed. [17] They both had had a full bellyache of court intrigue when living in the household of Herod the Great. Political machinations never suited them very well. [18] Yet, Herodias blazed with ambition for her husband. He saw by her face, nothing would thwart her determination. [19] Herod softly sighed. "Still, we should exercise our abilities to receive what we deserve, yes?" [20] The smiles on their faces lit up like torches leading them home in the middle of the night, and they embraced.

21 The soft sandals of Herodias shuffled back and forth across the marble beneath her as she waited for her husband to return with news of his meeting with Caesar. [22] The journey to Rome had been uneventful–the roads familiar, the sea manageable. [23] Knowing that Caesar, through his informants, knew why they sought an audience with him long before they arrived in Rome, their warm reception by Caligula raised their hopes.

24 The days spent in Rome, attending banquets and circulating among great families of powerful senators and imperial relatives, passed both quickly and slowly. [25] Finally, the hour for an audience with Caesar arrived. Herod left his wife with the rock solid reasons of his request circling in his head. [26] With each stride to and fro in her room, Herodias dreamed about the possibilities of slightly greater wealth and considerably more prestige. [27] The purchase of a gold ring with a large carnelian stone set in it would celebrate her new position. Perhaps another jet ring for a finger on her other hand to ward off troubling spirits might also be in order. [28] Of course, this will mean more work for Herod. Now everyone will see his strength. And much can be delegated. [29] The eyes of Herodias clouded with visions of more magnificent receptions wherever they went or the brighter deference and respect visitors to their court must demonstrate. [30] The thoughts of Herodias kept her moving, but occasionally she

paused to stare blankly out a window while fiddling with her bronze necklace with her right hand.

31 Well she knew that her husband did not walk with the firmest step. Would he stumble here? Would he fail? 32 And yet, they always supported the power and prestige of the priesthood, strayed not into foolish beliefs of an afterlife or the meddling of zealous messengers. 33 Always they kept the festivals and the sabbath. Never did they shirk the expense of a healthy sacrifice.

34 Herod was a good man. Certainly, her husband laid up "wisdom for the upright" and served as "a shield to them that walk in integrity." 35 He guarded "the paths of just judgement." 36 God had put them through many trials and they may have complained some like Job. 37 Like Job Herod had "gird up (his) loins like a man" and they accepted the might of Yahweh. Begged his forgiveness.

38 Truly now, God Almighty will provide for them twice as much just as he did for Job. 39 Herodias hummed as she sang in her head, "God Almighty is my shepherd; I shall not want. 40 He maketh me to lie down in green pastures; he leadeth me beside still waters. 41 Yea, though I walk through the valley of the shadow of death, I will fear no evil: for thou art with me; thy rod and thy staff, they comfort me. 42 Thou preparest a table before me in the presence of mine enemies; thou hast anointed my head with oil; my cup runneth over. 43 Surely, goodness and lovingkindness shall follow me all the days of my life; and I will dwell in the house of God for the length of the days." 44 Herodias smiled. Yea, truly Caesar shall reward them for they always upheld the power of Rome.

45 When Herod entered her room, one look at him stole her breath away. "Caligula greeted me kindly," he said in a low tone. 46 "But before he allowed me to speak, his finger motioned for someone in the back of the room to come forward. I had not noticed him until then." 47 Herodias stared at him with

anticipation. "It was Agrippa." Herod smiled wryly. "Imagine my surprise. [48] I thought, how lovely! He traveled all this way to give me support. Why on earth did he not come with us?

[49] "Caesar asked him what news he brought with him. Well, what news, Herodias! The first word out of his mouth, 'Sedition.'" [50] Her hands thrust up and over her mouth and she bent at the waist. The word punched her in the gut. [51] Herod nodded his head and placed a hand on her shoulder as he recounted, "'Sedition brought him to Rome.'" He paused in his own disbelief. [52] Gathering himself he continued, "'He claimed that I–who if guilty of anything, it is that I did not help him enough–am plotting to assist the Parthians in overthrowing Caesar. I stockpiled enough weapons in Tiberias to arm 70,000 men. [53] Your brother, my nephew, said, 'Herod Antipas, the tetrarch of Galilee and Perea, my dear Caesar, is a traitor.'"

[54] A little cry, a young bird flying from its nest attacked by a serpent, escaped Herodias. She pinched her eyes, but a few tears burst through and down her cheeks. [55] "Your brother, my nephew, went on and on, but I saw Caesar needed to hear no more. My mouth barely worked when he turned to me. [56] I managed to explain I armed myself to wreak my vengeance against the Nabatean. Caesar rightly considered this, but it mattered not. Nothing did. [57] 'Sedition' filled the air. Caligula needed to hear nothing more." Herodias gasped. Herod snorted, "I thought my ears betrayed me!"

[58] Our Spirit encircled the couple, alone in a city of a million people. With strong hands Herod clasped the upper arms of Herodias. [59] "I am exiled, Herodias." His own bitter tears erupted from his eyes and covered his face. He choked out, "Within a week I must leave Rome for Lugdunum." [60] Her husband collapsed into her arms, his head resting on her shoulder, his wet face snuggled into her neck. [61] "Exiled. I am exiled," sputtered out from his

lips. Herodias clasped his shoulder with one hand while the other cradled the back of his head.

62 He recovered enough of himself to stand back, and they looked at each other through a glass of tears. "There is more. 63 Agrippa..." Herod paused to gather his strength. "Well, we partly succeeded." He chortled. "Galilee and Perea are part of a kingdom...just not mine." 64 Herodias stared at him with eyes as wide as an empty cup. Her husband nodded his head. "Yes. He handed them to Agrippa!" 65 Wife and husband tenderly held each other and gasped at the thunderbolt blasting their lives.

66 When walking on the dock to board the ship taking him on the first leg of his exile to the city of Arelate on the south coast of Gallia–the second leg consisted of riding on the well paved Via Agrippa to Lugdunum–perhaps Herod bumped into Pontius Pilatus. 67 Tiberius had recalled him to face charges of corruption. Underlying the charges stood his suppression of Samaritans on Mount Gerizim. 68 Another local had stirred up unrest. Complaints followed his handling of the rowdy factions–Philistines, the orthodox Jews, and the Jews who lived with a foot in each of those worlds–constantly at odds with one another.

69 By the time Pilatus returned to Rome, Tiberias had metamorphosed into a Roman God. The mortal Caligula stood in his place. 70 Perhaps the new Caesar, in celebrating the inaugural of his reign, granted Pilatus the choice of either being executed or committing suicide. 71 Perhaps he merely fined him. Or perhaps Caligula allowed him to slip into retirement and obscurity.

72 Herod Antipas squinted his eyes and surveyed the city. The necessity of wrapping up some of their affairs had separated him from Herodias. 73 Where was she? He searched for her. Where was she? 74 For Herodias need not follow him into exile. Would she leave him, at the last moment, to stay in Rome or return home? 75 Her prodigal brother, now behaving re-

sponsibly since becoming a king, would no doubt provide for her. ⁷⁶ Since his sentence of exile, the thoughts of Herod roiled like boiling water. They jumped inchoately, taking him to alien shores of wild winds and rain. ⁷⁷ The tide called. Soon the boat needed to cast off. The fingers of Herod drummed the sides of his legs. If she abandoned him, he would throw himself into the deepest part of the sea.

78 Herod focused on the road she must come down. Heaving a sigh, he saw her. Quickly Herodias joined him to walk by his side. ⁷⁹ Back home prohibitions kept them from holding each other in public, but this was Rome. They embraced ⁸⁰ Oracles of sun shone down on the city and glistened in receptacles of waves. Herod and Herodias, hand in hand, boarded the ship taking them to the shore and the road that will lead them to their new home.

Notes: **55:6** Tiberias imprisoned Agrippa for saying he wished Tiberias would hurry up and die so Caligula may rule. The new Caesar, upon freeing him, made him king of Auranitis, Batanea, Gaulanitis, Paneas, Trachonitis, and Chalcis. **55:34-43** There are paraphrases or quotes from the Darby Translation (DARBY) Proverbs 2:7,8; Job 40:7; Psalms 23:1-4. **55:56** Aretas IV, his official title: "*Aretas, King of the Nabataeans, Friend of his People.*" **55:59** Lugdunum in Gallia (now Lyon, France) comes from the Latinization of Gaulish *Lugudunon* which means either Hill (possibly fortress) of Lugus (a Celtic God) or Hill/Fortress of the Hero/Warrior. It was the largest city west of Rome. **55:74** After the assassination of Caligula, Herod Agrippa played a significant role in the ascension of Claudius. The fifth Most Notable Caesar rewarded him with new territories making his kingdom as vast as Herod the Great's. His reign–as wise as imaginable in a contentious land–benefited both Jews and Gentiles. A painful and mysterious illness consumed his last days. Some considered it a judgment from Yahweh, others poisoning.

56

Saul of Tarsus, the Pharisee who held the cloaks of the executioners stoning Stephen the Martyr, paced himself at a good and steady trot on his way to the qehalah in Damascus. 2 Warmed with his commission to root out the pestilence of this heretical gang, the sneer of the high priest towards the Nazarenes spurred him on. The trust placed in him did not burden or weigh him down, but lifted Saul high. 3 His mind filled with righteous stones, the stones piled as a staircase to God, each step laid out with a Nazarene body.

4 As he neared Damascus, the stairs disassembled and the stones stared at Saul with the eyes of Stephen. 5 The martyred voice, thrown like a rock, lingered and echoed, "I forgive you." Projectile after projectile, "I forgive you. Lord forgive them." 6 Saul did not see Our Spirit flashing in the splattered blood of Stephen, but a sliver of light pried its way into his mind. The road to Damascus stretched out clearly, yet the way seemed less defined to Saul. 7 He remembered, before the stones took Stephen, the student of Yeshua pointed and cried out, "There he is! The Son of God risen!" 8 Saul followed the condemned finger and saw a blur of light in the sky. On the road to Damascus a blur of light pulsated wherever he looked.

9 Saul spurred himself forward. Before he reached the city gate, a great beam of light as strong as three suns knocked Saul and threw him down. 10 The light shone with the resurrected Yeshua brighter than day. Saul pinched his eyes closed and groaned. 11 The vision of Our Spirit sparked a sliver of light into a flame, and the flame ignited a conflagration on the graceful wings of our dove smothering his strutting peacock and sharp-toothed wolf. 12 Prostrated, Saul answered the call of Yeshua, his Savior, by throwing down his bloody sword and donning the rich robe woven with everlasting light.

13 For three days the eyes of Saul saw only Yeshua within a pulsing

light. When he recovered his worldly senses, Saul embodied the New Way. [14] He approached the Nazarenes of Damascus with contrition. Carefully they examined his conversion and then baptized him.

15 Yasgur opened his door to the friend of a friend. Saul entered with ease the influential halls of the well-to-do. [16] In the garden of Yasgur, Saul appreciated the small gathering of family, friends, and slaves collected for him. "In the name of Yeshua," Saul raising and lowering himself on his toes started, "I greet you. [17] His life, the life of a Son of God, and resurrection show us a new way to live. [18] There is a Light within the light," Saul gestured in the air around him, "a Power within all power," he said while shaking his fist, "and that greater Light, that most awesome Power lives in Yeshua. [19] As that Power he rose from the dead. As that Light he shines a path for us to live in the Power beyond all power. For we too can rise from the dead to live eternal life!" His audience gasped.

20 Saul spoke about the sacrifices of Yeshua. Yasgur jumped up and interrupted him, "If I turn my other cheek, evil will run rampant. Who will stop bad people from doing bad acts?" [21] The new student answered, "When Yeshua rises again–and that will be soon–evil shall face his judgment. [22] What we must do is prepare for his second coming by following his path."

23 Saul spoke on for a while until a trembling slave of Yasgur interrupted him, "If my master gives away all he owns, what happens to me, to all of us?" He pointed to the other slaves, [24] "We would rather serve our master, for he is good to us. To work for…who knows… and who knows what we will be compelled to do or how well we will be treated?" [25] Looking toward Yasgur, "Please master. What happens to us? What will happen to us?" [26] Saul thought and answered, "The Everlasting Light is your eternal master. In Yeshua you shall live forever. Nothing in this life

matters. 27 You are here. You are gone. See to it you save the breath of your eternal shade."

28 Saul continued to speak, but before long the wife of Yasgur, Deborah, sitting heavily on a bench, drifted off in her thoughts. 29 Certainly she would think less of her husband if he did not stand up against injustice. He is a good man! 30 Why does *this* man want to corrupt him? What would she do if Yasgur did not stand up for what is right? He acts for the family.

31 Certainly no desire possessed her to part with her slaves, silks, and the few pieces of jewelry she owned. 32 Yasgur provided well for her and their children. He worked hard to rise above poverty! 33 And the Temple! The thought of going to Temple thrilled Deborah: 34 the hustle and bustle of slaves, the fuss over dressing and preparing for the trip; the camels and donkeys jingling with bells and laden with wares or people; 35 the ride in a basket on a camel, she on one side, Yasgur on the other, sharing dates and millet bread and red wine: the conversations with her husband over the grunting sweat of animals: the dust rising from the road as if she flew high in the sky above the clouds; 36 stops along the journey to visit her family or at caravansaries, making friends and listening to stories. 37 If they no longer made pilgrimages to the Temple, when else would she see them? How dull life would be!

38 She remembered how every time they neared Jerusalem, tears welled in her eyes gleaming with the gold ornaments and white marble of the Temple that shone brighter and brighter as the caravan drew closer. 39 In the Court of Nations the odor of soiled straw, sheep, goats, and cattle; the bleating, snorts and chewing, and in their cages the chatter of birds; 40 people everywhere talking, holding hands, going in every direction; 41 changing money; selecting a sacrifice; lugging it to the Temple; 42 and in the Court of Women, as everywhere, gossip, 43 the clay of the world mixed with shells and potshards of lives to

mortar the stones of society together and build a home; [44] the roof providing space to wash laundry and where everybody congregates or sleeps in fine weather; [45] the net catching everyone up and pulling them close; the only wisdom within her grasp.

46 Give up the Temple? How else is she to make the world right? What other way can she satisfy God? [47] How can she, how can anybody be their own Temple? [48] Oh, that death would not claim her! A shade of the living. But to give all away... [49] Out of respect for her husband, she stopped a tutting of her tongue in the back of her throat. [50] If her shade amounted to no more than a wisp, she would weep for her lost comforts. [51] Deborah, silent as a summer cloud, stared into the face of Saul with a cold vacancy.

52 Yasgur closed the door behind Saul. He shook his head. His thoughts aligned with the thoughts of his wife. [53] To live an everlasting life sounds great–but... No longer did he recognize Saul as a familiar in his circle. [54] No doubt if he had been tempted, his first Nazarene service would have horrified and gagged him–eating the body and drinking the blood of Yeshua the king! [55] In seeking out his peers of some wealth and influence, Saul repeatedly beat his Nazarene head against a wall of unreceptive ears. [56] Before long, doors no longer opened to him. In public well-dressed people avoided him as best they could or shunned him.

57 Hanna grew fat in discontent. A widow, she lived under the shadows of sheol. Trembling and rage possessed her. [58] As master of her household, she had never whipped her Britanian slaves. A flogging gave her no satisfaction. [59] When Melissa failed to straighten and adjust her hair just right–and no matter how well done it rarely coiffed just right– or any chore was performed contrary to her contrary whims, [60] Hanna slapped with a stinging hand, beat with fists, or kicked her slave. [61] When Balbus cooked with too much or not enough spices, served her meals

too hot or too cold, when his shopping or cleaning the kitchen failed to meet her fussy expectations, [62] Hanna slapped with a stinging hand, beat with fists, or kicked her slave.

63 Their misery within her welled and raised a two headed monster. [64] One momentarily smiled. The surface of troubled waters below her thoughts briefly smoothed over. [65] The other face scowled. The wretchedness of her slaves stirred deeper currents inside her.

66 Hanna heard Saul in the marketplace and invited him to her home. Gazing into the pool of his vision she noticed flickers of a familiar shape. [67] When Saul met Hanna, he saw through her cruelty, swirling as a storm in her brown irises.

68 Our Spirit kindled a tongue of fire in the mouth of Saul. His words warmed and gently inspired, opening her spirit to possibilities she never knew existed. [69] With his teaching our dove circled and then flew into her. Hanna gasped and clung to a wing of joy. She accepted baptism.

70 The conversion carried both of them to jubilation. Their breaths mingled and refreshed as a cool summer breeze. A New Way unfolded for both of them. [71] For Hanna, mercy doubled as a well of serenity and kindness that drowned the demon tormenting her. Melissa and Balbus gladly bathed in her caresses and sang hosannas with her. [72] The power to heal, to change lives–going forward, it was as if the sandals of Saul never touched the earth. The short man grew in stature.

73 After working three years with the Nazarenes in Damascus, Saul returned to Jerusalem. [74] Cephas accepted the contrite hammer of the high priest with a firm embrace and a leery eye. [75] As a student, the emissaries thought it best to send Saul off on a mission to Cyprus under the guardianship of Barnabas.

Notes: 56:2 First known as Nazarenes, the followers of Yeshua were derisively called Christians in Antioch by a caustic wit. It seems the followers of Saul, later Paulus, adopted it as

a badge of honor. It is unclear if the emissaries accepted it.
56:34 Pilgrims, merchants, and other travelers often joined caravans to travel in some measure of safety.

57

Barnabas spoke outside the qehala in the Cypriot city of Paphos. Chloe listened. ² Each word from the student opened like a stepping-stone leading her to a well that had always been right in front of her. Thirsty as she was, she never saw it. ³ The vision of Barnabas–a drink of sweet, fresh water the likes of which she had never tasted before–filled her dreamy head with new possibilities. Excited waves of understanding moistened the dry skin of her thoughts. ⁴ The voice of Barnabas rose and fell in soothing tones. She felt the warm fingers of Our Spirit gently gliding up and down her body. Her parents, sentinels standing on each side of Chloe, noticed her sway in a shiver of ecstasy. ⁵ *Soteria fortify me*, her mother thought. *Interesting*, her father thought.

6 All the way home, the agitation in her mother grew as in a kettle of water over roaring flames. The thoughts of her father whistled with the wind. ⁷ Leading them, he saw with eyes in the back of his head the agitation that would soon visit him. ⁸ Chloe walked on water, a cloud of precocious joy absorbing her. Feeling beyond this world, she paid little heed to her parents.

9 Back home, a familiar argument ensued with a burst of frustration. "What nonsense," her mother exclaimed and then thrust her hands straight up. ¹⁰ There were times, like now, he thought his wife a personification of distemper. He girded his loins with kindness. ¹¹ The husband touched her arm and gently replied, "Now. Now." ¹² Then he went on more firmly, "Words are harmless. They are food on a table. Take what you like and leave the rest." ¹³ She simmered with an inner fire: "Words can be the work of demons. Evil may come from them!" ¹⁴ He, inclined to Greek inquiry, calmly replied, "Words follow ideas. Ideas live for reflection.

It is what you do that matters."

15 His wife jumped. "So if someone calls on an evil breath…" she paused to spit on two fingers, raised them along with her eyes towards heaven, and pleaded, "Soteria, protect us!" 16 leveling her eyes at her husband she finished the butt of her amazement, "That is nothing?" Placing her hands on her hips, she waited on his reply. 17 Like a pool of still water he responded, "It is not the calling, but the answering that matters. 18 It is what the demon does that is of any consequence. If the demon answers and a person suffers," he thrust his finger into the air to add emphasis, "then the caller is responsible." 19 She stared at him with the sharp blankness only a loving wife can make. 20 His sophistry left her nearly speechless, but after a strangled moment she blurted out, "Nonsense!"

21 Feeling a moment of relief, the mother of Chloe shifted to what truly concerned her. "She cannot go back there. 22 There is no reason for her to go back. There is much to do here." The husband gave his wife a small smile of acknowledgement. 23 "Weaving. There is much to weave. And she still works her threads too loosely. Her basket stitch has more holes in it than a sieve!" 24 He chuckled good naturedly. She ignored him and pressed on. 25 "When she finishes weaving, plenty, there is plenty of spinning to do!" 26 Her mother acknowledged, "Chloe may be getting better at that." Then sharply returned to form, "But still a little clumsy." 27 He rolled his eyes, but it could not be said whether he rolled them at his wife or at his daughter.

28 "Well now…" Before he could say more, his wife continued to whirl the wheel on which she fashioned her argument like a lump of clay, 29 "She can also start going to the market. Someday Chloe will run her own household." 30 She raised her hands and head toward the ceiling, imploring Hestia–the Goddess attending the home fire for cooking and warmth as well as the needs and wellbeing of a

family–to smile upon her daughter. [31] Focusing her eyes once again on her husband she went on, "It is time Chloe learned how to manage a little kitchen money and take charge of a slave. It is time for her to accept her responsibilities."

[32] She seemed satisfied with her crafted vase of concerns, when suddenly she added a glaze: "And the way she coiffes her hair!" [33] Always he accepted criticism except when administered in personal attacks. Gently he admonished, "Now. Now." [34] She continued with some exuberance, "What a mess. Let her spend more time and care on her appearance."

[35] Nodding his head, he neither acknowledged further nor refuted any particular point in her argument. His wife and daughter must work out their own lives together. [36] Knowing his daughter, Chloe would work her will. If she wished to pursue the Christians, she would find a way to do so. [37] He habitually encouraged the strong will of their only child–something his wife chided him for. [38] Chloe may err for a while, but he trusted his daughter to always come around to a sound decision and appropriate behavior. [39] Sensing the healthy impression her argument had made and accepting that he would not interfere with her motherly administration of Chloe, her face glowed with the satisfaction of a bird finding a worm. [40] Remembering the fond intellectual relationship between father and daughter, a worried dagger pointed from her eyes. [41] "You spoil her!" She huffed and left the room. And there, as so often, their argument ended.

Notes: 57:1 Paphos is a city in Cyprus where Barnabas and Saul spent much of their time. Barnabas, a Greek name, means "son of encouragement." Chloe is a Greek name meaning "blooming" or "fertility." **57:5** Soteria was a Greek Goddess or spirit of safe keeping to preserve or deliver from harm. **57:14** Beginning in Melitus, an Ionian Island halfway between the Greek mainland and Cyprus, Greek philosophy and a rational method of investigation had been circulating for over 500 years by this time.

58

"I am not going!" Chloe raised her voice to emphasize the finality of her words. Her mother had come to her room to fetch her in order to celebrate the Ploiaphesia Festival. ² Of course, being a Christian now, nothing could persuade Chloe to even be a spectator. ³ Her mother covered her face with her hands and then reached out and shook them at her daughter. She often prayed and sacrificed to Isis and Chloe had been initiated into the worship of the Goddess. ⁴ Neither one understood the other. So, they argued. Exhausted, the older adult left the room, muttering, "Oh, that girl…"

5 Within the burst of an exasperated voice, she sent her husband up to talk to their only child. ⁶ When he walked through the doorway, Chloe burst out, "Oh father, please do not make me go!" She pleaded on and on as a river flooding over its banks. ⁷ With dewy eyes she clasped and held his hand to her damp cheek as her reasons filled his ears until his mind nearly burst. ⁸ Stroking the hair on her head, he softly whispered, "Of course. Of course."

9 He left his daughter and rejoined his wife pacing by the door. She expected to scold her husband. ¹⁰ He looked into the brown eyes of his wife and said with the assurance of a smooth tongue, "She worships a God who demands strict obedience." She rolled her eyes. ¹¹ "Her God commands that only He be worshipped." That raised her eyebrows. ¹² Lowering his voice he said confidentially, "Yahweh is a very jealous God." She sucked in a breath of air and tilted backwards. ¹³ "Best His ire be not roused." That resonated from her painted toenails to her lavishly darkened lashes. ¹⁴ "Why must she worship such a God?" The eyes of her husband answered with a helpless blankness and gave his shoulders a little shrug. ¹⁵ "Soteria, protect us," she petitioned the air as they hurried out the door.

16 Left alone to her thoughts, dry eyed, Chloe remembered the blare of trumpets and plucking of harps hanging onto the thud of drums echoing off the walls of many homes. [17] The soft, slightly sweet, woody scent of burning libanos wound through the air like smokey rope around revelers, spectators, and residents along the parade streets.

18 The Sacred Ship of Isis rode the swaying shoulders of four men and four women. Behind them walked a rugged and skilled sailor. [19] After the sailor, devotees carried a winged statue of Isis with her protecting pinions opened wide. The marching men and women dressed in various costumes or elegant garments. [20] Some men girded a belt round their midsection and carried spears as soldiers; others wore boots and cloaks of a hunter, while some carried the staff of a shepherd or nets of fishermen. [21] Men dressed as women sashayed and women paraded with garlands in their anointed hair. A budding poet–boldly and then hoarsely–recited over and over his poem written for the occasion. [22] An old man led an ape that stared blankly, a blue bonnet on its head. A few hardy men carried a tame bear sitting on a stool. [23] An ass with golden wings glued to its back followed behind the swaying hips of a young man. That and more–an ecstatic carnival of humanity– followed behind the ship.

24 In front of the boat those recently initiated as worshipers of Isis wore white. Chloe remembered, along with other women, marching and flinging colorful petals and sweet scented herbs they each carried in their aprons. [25] Ahead of them the musicians strained to play as loudly as possible. Their bodies swayed or projected with the rhythm or bang of their instruments. [26] All more or less steadily paced themselves after the priests and priestesses swinging censors and praying either for the safe voyage of sailors or that Isis grant everyone smooth sailing through this rocky and troubled life. [27] The procession marched from the Temple of Isis down to the port.

28 At the edge of land and water, with the boat safely launched onto The Sea, the priest and priestess chanted: [29] "Oh Queen of Gods! All-powerful providence! Under many names You reign in many lands: Astarte, Artemis, Leto, Hera, Aphrodite, Demeter, and more;

[30] You created starry heaven and earth, shaped with mountains and fields, seas and rivers; good harvests from land and water come from You;

[31] You calm storm-blown waves of winter for prosperous trade; Benefactor not only of wealth,

[32] we pray and You deliver us from the sweat, the aches, and tremors of sickness;

[33] we pray and You grant our hearts, sleepless and tormented, the desire of our love;

[34] we pray and You fill a womb with life;

[35] Bountiful Savior, just as You brought Osiris back to life, You renew us from endless shades of Death; with You we walk in eternal light;

[36] Omnipotent Isis, Mother of the Gods, the One of all Goddesses, You revel in purity;

[37] we rejoice in You; we beseech your blessing; we thrive in your generosity."

38 Chloe imagined how priests and priestesses, along with temple servants, upon the first step of the rising sun, roused themselves to ritually bathe and wear white linen, purifying themselves for the festive day. [39] The priests sacrificed a roaring bull. The offal and blood stored in vases, the meat was prepared for the communal meal–where Our Spirit reveled–back at the temple after the ceremony. [40] With long fingers, a priestess examined fruit and vegetables for blemishes. Only flawless produce, with the sacrificial portions of the bull, would be loaded onto the boat.

41 Within the Temple, a priestess–as one did every day–offered the Goddess a wine libation while singing a hymn. She then dressed the life-size statue of Isis. [42] Removing the skirt of Isis, the priestess clasped a fresh purple one embroidered with gold thread.

The gold bracelets around the right wrist and left ankle were replaced. [43] Lastly, the priestess carefully took off the necklace and laid a new one of silver, holding a lapis lazuli gem, to rest between the bare, life-giving breasts of the Goddess.

44 Some temple servants assisted with preparations for the day. Others attended to the daily tasks of sweeping and washing the temple. [45] Like every God concerning their own temple, Isis insisted that her abode on earth be spotlessly clean. [46] Uncleanliness meant impurity, and impurity was the home and workshop of malicious spirits. Demons lurked everywhere, ever vigilant for opportunities to work their will.

47 The mind of Chloe drifted like incense to a lovely image of Adamantia. They were childhood friends who, three years ago, had both joined the religion of Isis. [48] A sly smile slipped onto her face as Chloe recalled her initiation, beginning with eleven days of abstinence. No meat. No wine. No touching herself. [49] She barely got by each day on bread and drinking water mixed with honey. At biting pangs of hunger and frustration, she recited, [50] "Oh many-shaped Isis, beautiful and sacred, almighty and savior, grant me strength, lift me up to your grace and bounty."

51 *How Adamantia suffered. Poor girl almost starved. She looked as thin as a little finger–except, of course, her big butt!* [52] *How I remember playing astragaloi and ostrakinda. So cute how Adamantia sucked her lower lip in as she concentrated on beating me. She was always more adept at ephedrismos too.*

53 On the eleventh day, Chloe stood outside the Temple and watched as an old priest quietly prayed. Pouring a libation to Isis with one hand, the priest rubbed a holy ointment on the top of his head while chanting quietly under his breath. [54] When he beckoned with two fingers, Chloe climbed the Temple steps. Placing his wrinkled hands lightly on her shoulders, the white-haired priest assured himself of her abstinence.

55 He then heard her confession. Chloe told him how several times she had lied to her mother and how sometimes she felt so angry with her that she slaps a slave. The priest forgave her and laid a blessing on her relationship with her mother.

56 *I did not think too much about Adamantia clinging to me all the time. Playing with my hair.* 57 *But when she tried to kiss me and grab my crotch! By Isis! I had to laugh. We were no longer children.* 58 *I needed a man. Emilios. I needed Emilios.*

59 Leading Chloe into the temple, the priest brought her to a small room with a high ceiling and one window near the top of an inner wall. Here she spent the night. 60 Chloe heard strange noises and ghostly echoes filled with imagination. Occasionally, flashes of light startled or cast peculiar shadows. 61 Myrrh penetrated her nose, swaddled her tongue with a bitter balsamic touched with sweetness, and swirled in her head. 62 Her meditations on Isis opened her eyes to visions of the Goddess. With arms and wings spread wide, Isis stepped forward and hugged her. 63 Chloe shivered in the warm embrace. She felt like a loaf of bread fresh out of an oven. Tears, lava from a volcano, flowed freely in the night.

64 *Emilios! Tan and strong Emilios! My brave captain! It is he who walks behind the Sacred Ship of Isis.* 65 *Oh how I trembled when he took the ship out, a short distance, but still. And what if he lost his balance emptying the offerings into The Sea?* 66 *Oh, how Adamantia laughed at me. I knew it a foolish sin to doubt the protection of Isis. And never did I doubt his skill as a sailor.* 67 *Yet I could not stop trembling until he stepped once more upon solid ground.*

68 A temple servant gently nudged her awake, handed her a goblet containing water mixed with a little vinegar, and led her to a toilet. When finished, Chloe was brought to a spacious nave with a small altar and couch. 69 There, with eyes wide open, she witnessed a

simulated wedding between a priestess and priest, Isis and her brother Osiris. After the marriage they laid on the couch, grunting and moaning in sacred consummation.

70 *Night after night of wearing a mask of wooly sweat mixed with ground oyster shells, honey, and placenta;* [71] *each morning I buffed my nails to shine like the sun, brushed bright red ochre on my cheeks and layered it on my lips, my eyes highlighted with soot powder.* [72] *I engaged him in interesting and coy conversations. Walking in front of him, I would sway my hips and then suddenly turn and stop for him to bump into me. My eyes beckoned as pools for him to plunge into.* [73] *With a trembling lower lip and kisses waiting in the corners, I smiled at Emilios. He stared right through me to gaze on Adamantia.*

74 Chloe laid perfectly still in a coffin as a temple servant shut the lid. Time passed. The darkness. The closeness. The silence. The silence. [75] Some people panic, but Chloe followed instructions and remained quiet. Low moans of grief began to fill the room. [76] A gong sounded, followed by the name of her mother. A woman shrieked loudly in mourning. [77] The gong once again hollowed out the air, followed by the name of her father. The loud wailing of a man pulled tears to her eyes. [78] Slowly it all drifted away. Silence. Silence. Dead silence. Just when she opened her mouth to scream, a knock rapped the coffin lid. [79] Chloe chanted, "Oh great Goddess, Lady of earth and heaven, come to me, lead me to the light." [80] The lid opened and the priestess sang, "I am Isis. I own magic. With potent words I join dismembered bones. I heal the sick. [81] Come from the dust and shadows of Death. Come with me. Come back to the light." Chloe rose from the coffin.

82 *Ridiculous! What made her think I would consider such an offer? Was it a trick? Or did Adamantia think me a foolish girl? Was she that desperate?* [83] *That if I gave myself to her, she*

would give me Emilios. I pined for him. Food lost all its flavor. My mind pinched with despair. [84] *But if Emilios was going to choose Adamantia over me, that was that. I plied all my charms.* [85] *I offered, I do not know how many sacrifices and prayers to Isis. Begging her forgiveness. Imploring for her intervention to bring me the love of Emilios.* [86] *Nothing more to be done. And certainly not her mad scheme! My father sharpened my reasoning faculties. They were not completely broken. I knew futility when I saw it.*

87 Reborn, Chloe followed Isis to a birthday feast laid out with plenty of wine and meat. She dug in, slurping and smacking her lips as she stuffed great empty jars of her appetite. [88] Between gulping the most delicious leg of lamb she had ever eaten–a little chewy but delicious–and quaffing the most full-bodied wine she had ever drunk–though it was of average vintage–a laugh burst from deep within her. [89] Everyone at the table rejoiced in the company of each other. They felt Isis smiling down upon them.

90 Initiation finished, Chloe ran home. She felt transported there in the blink of an eye! Chloe hugged her father. She hugged her mother. [91] She hugged the household slaves. (The one she tended to slap instinctively stepped back as Chloe rushed toward her. She breathed a sigh of relief when Chloe hugged her.) [92] Reveling in Isis, Chloe did not know what to do with herself. So she spun around and around until she fell laughing onto the floor. [93] Her flesh felt metamorphosed into warm swaths of sunlight. Chloe marveled with sparkling eyes as if the world had just been created.

94 *You took many lovers, Portia...Despoina, and gossip says every female slave in your household, no matter how young or old, gratifies your lust.* [95] *Still, you fulfilled the expectations of your family. You married my Emilios and wasted no time in bearing him a child. I heard you are pregnant again. And he is...happy.*

Note: 58:1 The Ploiaphesia, Greek for shipping, was better known from its Latin name, the Navigium Isidis, Voyage of Isis. This festival, held on the fifth of every March, celebrated the opening of the sailing season. **58:3** For thousands of years Isis was worshiped in Egypt. At first a minor deity, she none-the-less featured prominently in the Osiris legend, where she resurrects her slain brother and husband. As the mother of Horus, who was identified with the Pharaoh, the Egyptians considered Isis the divine mother of the Pharaoh. At first only important in healing spells and funerary rites, during the New Kingdom she became a prominent figure, integrating many traits of the predominant Goddess Hathor. After Alexander the Great conquered Egypt, the powers of Isis increased as her worship spread all over the Ancient World. **58:17** Libanos is now known as frankincense. Labanos means "white" which is the color of the sap drawn from some Boswellia trees. Frankincense derives from Old French, *franc* which means "true" or "noble" and *encens*, "that which is burnt." **58:28** The Mediterranean Sea was called either "The Sea," or "The Great Sea" by most people. **58:47** Adamantia, a Greek name, means "adamant" or "unbreakable." **58:52** Astragaloi is played by tossing animal bones, usually goat or sheep, in the air to be caught or land in a certain way. Ostrakinda is a game where a line is drawn, and players pitch potsherds or stones to see who can toss them closest to the line. To play ephedrismos, two players compete to knock down an upright stone with a ball. The loser carries the winner on her back by making a stirrup with her hand. The winner bends her knee and puts her shin into the stirrup to ride the loser's back. The game ends when the loser, blindfolded and carrying the winner, finds the knocked over stone with her free hand. **58:58** Emilios, from Latin *aemulus,* means "rival."

59 "We must open the New Way to all!" Saul, back in Jerusalem, passionately pummeled the air with the mallets of his words. ² Cephas nodded, "Yes. Of course. All are welcome to join us. But our rabbi never turned his back on his people." ³ "Nor do I," Saul rejoined with his body shaking like a tree in a storm. "I strive day and night for

our people." ⁴ He caught his breath and continued, "I preach to all, but our people are difficult. The Goyim more readily open their ears to me. People…"

5 "People! People!" Jacob impatiently cut in. Like a torrent from a flooding river, he continued, "We are the tribes of Abraham who made a covenant with God–a covenant Moses tabulated into law. ⁶ If Goyim join us and retain their idolatrous manners, we turn our backs on the laws; we renounce our covenant with God. We," spittle flew with his words, "will have polluted and lost our way. ⁷ My brother, the Messiah who suffered, also showed us the Sovereignty around us. He did not renounce Moses! We must carry on his mission. ⁸ All *are* welcome–all who accept the teaching of my brother and follow the laws of Moses!"

9 "How many who follow the laws of Moses," Saul argued with the malicious smile of the high priest hanging over him, "accept the Living Light, the New Way?" ¹⁰ He looked around at the faces staring at him before going on, "Yeshua sealed the covenant and fulfilled the law. ¹¹ Many Goyim are with us as Christians. Is not the Holy Breath of God equal to the Law?" Again he paused and studied the faces around him.

12 Saul continued, "These Christians are not familiar with the laws of Moses. It is a hardship to adopt foreign practices. ¹³ To ask a grown man to undergo circumcision is to ask…much…too much. Many who would sit and break bread with us will turn away. ¹⁴ How many of our people turn to us? They are a stubborn seed refusing to take root in our fertile soil. ¹⁵ For every brother, I convert twenty, thirty to be Christians! These people are ripe fruit waiting to be laid on our table."

16 "Yes," Jacob replied doggedly, piercing the vision of Saul with his eyes. For him the hole in the argument of Saul was as great as the bowed legs Saul stood on. ¹⁷ Stretching out his arms and gesturing with the index finger of his right hand, he continued, "Our table." Then he opened his hand

that swept wide as if showing off food spread before him, [18] "The table laid out with sustenance of the covenant of God and laws of Moses. Without our table we eat off the floor like dogs." [19] Again Jacob pointed his finger and thrust it down like a nail being driven into a board, "Here is where my brother intended to build the Kingdom of God, in Jerusalem. [20] We will all reside in the House of David." Sweeping his hand and pointing up, "It is impossible to do otherwise." [21] Bringing his hands to his chest, "We are who we are. Goyim will only pollute us."

22 Seven women sat conversing on a rug. They had stood in the main room watching the emissaries argue. [23] When their whispered commentary aroused glaring stares from a few men, they retired to a side room. [24] "Should we open the Holy Breath of God to Goyim?" Rachel asked. Susanna and Miryam Magdalene shook their heads. [25] Joanna answered, "How are we to give up our ways? Are we to break our covenant? To accept a Goy as a Jew is to become a Goy. Either they become Jews or we become Goyim.

26 Miryamla asked, "Did not my brother cure Goyim? The slave of a centurion for one..." [27] "Yes," Miryam Magdalene interjected, "the centurion had faith in the power of Yeshua. He believed in the power of the Holy Breath through Yeshua as a healer. [28] He did not have faith in our faith. Yeshua saved the slave with the grace of God because his master supported the qehalah. A favor for a favor. That is all." [29] Joanna spoke, "Why bring up a Roman soldier? We have nothing to do with Romans."

30 "What about the Canaanite woman?" Rachel asked. "She believed Yeshua to be the Son of God." Joanna replied. "Yes. And with her daughter cured, she disappeared. [31] We never saw her again. She believed like the centurion. They flattered Yeshua into..." [32] The shocked eyes of the sister of Yeshua hardened as two fists. Feeling them, Joanna shifted her words, "...he certainly deserved

their praise!" [33] Susanna picked up the thread of thought that Joanna left unfinished, "It is no use. Goyim will never be with us."

34 Miryamla stated slowly, "They both showed deep faith in my brother. Yet, they did not join us." Joanna nodded and added, "Perhaps if Yeshua were living…" [35] Stillness stopped all tongues. Then Miryam Magdalene flatly stated, "They will not risk the wrath of the authorities for our sakes. They cannot be trusted." [36] "Remember Jezebel," Joanna said, "She led Ahab and through him, all of Israel astray." All the women nodded their heads. [37] "These 'Christians' will pollute us," she warned. "And how can they be in the Kingdom of God if they refuse to honor the covenant between God and Abraham?"

38 The conference of emissaries ended; the women rolled up the rugs; the men clasped hands. [39] Saul mustered the strength to do no more than bow his head. Off he went with Barnabas to convert Jews and non-Jews alike to the New Way. [40] But the conversion of Goyim mattered not unless they followed Judaic dietary laws and males offered their foreskins as pledges in a covenant with Yahweh.

Notes: 59:1 Experiencing difficulties in Cyprus, Saul traveled to several cities in the East over several years toiling tirelessly to share the word of Yeshua. The hardships Saul faced led him to a unique perspective that changed the focus of his mission to Gentiles. Now the emissaries called him back to Jerusalem to explain his actions to them. **59:36** Jezebel, a Phoenician princess, married Ahab, King of Israel, and influenced her husband to impose her worship of Baal and Asherah on his people.

60 Away Saul went. Still making little headway among his people, he once again ministered more and more to Goyim. [2] Saving mostly women at first, for these converts tended to bring their household–children and slaves and sometimes even their husbands–into the Nazarene community

with them. ³ The ministry of Saul, far from Jerusalem, grew. Encouraged, Saul beamed more and more with his own light. ⁴ He adopted a Roman name, Paulus: meaning "small" or "humble."

5 Barnabas mirrored more and more the work of his companion. Working shoulder to shoulder, Paulus pulled him, like metal to a magnet, into the sphere of his influence. ⁶ With Barnabas standing off to his side, Paulus stood as tall as his short stature allowed and spoke as if his mouth were a burning building from which his words fled. ⁷ "We gather in the love and grace of God in the home of our sister Deacon Chloe," he began, nodding toward her as she smiled and bowed her head.

8 Taking a deep breath, Paulus exhaled. With the next breath he began, "If you obey the laws of Moses, you will stand in the grace of God. ⁹ If you do not follow the laws of Moses, but believe in Christ, you will stand in the grace of Christ, which is also the grace of God. ¹⁰ It is through our belief in Christ that we are baptized with salvation. ¹¹ When we live in the grace of Christ it is not necessary to be slaves to the law. But whether we live in the grace of Christ or follow the law, the circumcised and uncircumcised are all blessed by God." ¹² All held Paulus in high esteem. The listless sails of their ears gladly caught the thrust of his words.

13 "This is the hidden wisdom Christ revealed to me when he chose me as his emissary, not when he walked through the trials of this life but when he showed himself to me from heaven. ¹⁴ It is important, therefore, that we maintain our belief and not stray into temptations. I am here because I have heard of troubles among you." ¹⁵ Some cast their eyes down. Others lifted their eyes and thinly smiled. ¹⁶ "Our flesh is weak." They felt their own skin as Paulus pinched and pulled the skin on the back of his hand. "We must not give in to the temptations of our bodies. Procreation is folly when the Second Coming of our master is

imminent." [17] Paulus bemoaned, "The thorn of my flesh torments me." Soothingly he added, "The knowledge Christ is returning for me comforts me. [18] Why give yourselves over to the urgency of your members when your flesh is about to die so you may enter into heaven? Pray and live a virtuous life!" [19] Paulus, with his hands open in front of him, closed them into fists and clasped them to his chest. "Prepare for Yeshua coming back for us. [20] Why would you bring a child into this life when this life is going to end, when you should be intent on making ready for the next life, the life-everlasting?" [21] A few jumped up. Those behind them either craned their necks to see Paulus or, bowing their heads, closed their eyes to open their hearing.

[22] "Our sins died with Christ on the cross. We therefore live in grace and do not need the law. His grace purifies us for eternal life." A few more stood up. Those standing raised their hands as their bodies swayed. [23] "If we fall from grace, we may confess our sins. With an act of contrition we again live in salvation. [24] The grace of Christ, however, is not a license to sin again. Desires of our flesh are corruption leading to iniquity." [25] Paulus paused, then filled his voice with exasperation as he said, "You are newly created by the crucifixion of Christ and his resurrection. [26] Why let sin back into your bodies?" Some nodded their heads. Some of those standing murmured, "Amen."

[27] From deep within him Paulus vigorously encouraged, "Do not let your members lead you to wickedness. Use your flesh as righteous instruments of prayer. [28] We must fast from lust. Lust is the feast of the devil. [29] Love one another in the breath of God our Father." Stung by his words, the eyes of some listeners clouded with tears. [30] In a tone both pleading and commanding, he continued, "If you must give in to your flesh, do so within the law as husband and wife." [31] The voice of Paulus hardened into a fist, "Do not succumb to vile acts. Do not be an

abomination in the eyes of our Father."

32 A few stared inwardly with daggers. A soft wing of our dove attempted to shield them. 33 "If you love with your flesh, your body belongs to another. The body of a woman belongs to a man. The body of a man belongs to a woman. 34 As believers always remember, your body is not yours, but Christ's. By giving our bodies to God, we give ourselves over to everlasting life. 35 The more we live in this world, the more we need the law. It is better, though, to revel in the grace of Christ and live, not in the law, but within the love of God our Father." 36 While they listened to Paulus, their minds swirled as his arms curved in half circles in front of him. They felt the beating air of his hands curled into shaking fists whenever he emphasized his words.

37 "When we give ourselves over to God, we live in the body of Christ. Just as a body has many parts, so we have our differences. 38 Some of us are gifted as teachers, some as healers, some as administrators, others as speakers in tongues, and some as helpers. 39 No matter our gifts, we all live in the same body of Christ and, as one body, when someone suffers, so we all suffer; and when someone is elated, so we all rejoice." 40 "Amen," someone shouted, "Amen!" Paulus smiled as he continued, "This is what it means to love in the body of Christ.

41 With Our Spirit Paulus rocked onto his toes, "If I speak in the tongues of men or if I speak in the tongues of messengers, but not a fiber of me exists in love, I am nothing more than a vanity making noise like the clangor of a gong or a clashing cymbal. 42 If I possess powers of prophecy, if I comprehend the mysteries and claim all knowledge, and if I am consumed with faith that if I say to mountains, 'Move!' and the mountains move, but not a fiber of my being exists in love, I am nothing. 43 If I give away all I own to open the gates of paradise, but I am without love, I enter heaven as an empty shell.

44 "Love does not beat its chest and boast nor does it claw with jealousy. Love is not peevish nor insists on its own way; nor is love rude or struts in willful arrogance. Love is not irritable or resentful. 45 Love does not rejoice at mistakes, but rejoices in forbearance and forgiveness. Love is always patient and tender. 46 Love bears all things, believes all things, aspires to all things, endures all things." 47 Everyone not already standing stood up. All held their hands up. A swoon gently swept the room as many clasped their eyes with bliss. 48 Bodies swayed or, bouncing on knees, bobbed up and down. Our Spirit soared around the room breathing in each ear.

49 "Prophecies pass away; speaking in tongues ends in silence; knowledge fades into yesterday's gossip. For our knowledge is a vanity and changes, and our prophecies are vanities and imperfect. 50 Only love lasts forever. The only truth is love. It is only love that makes us whole. 51 When I was a child, I thought and spoke and walked as a child. When I grew into a man, I reasoned and spoke and walked as a man. 52 We are children of God, but in the body of Christ we are fully grown and we see more clearly. Our vanities slough off and we understand more completely." 53 His words elicited many amens. The room metamorphosed into a celestial garden. 54 "Our faith receives the body of Christ; our dreams open to life everlasting; for life everlasting to not live in love is to be forever buried alive. 55 So dwell in faith, dreams, and love; but of these three the greatest dwelling is love." 56 A chorus of amens filled the room. People clasped hands. Neighbor turned to neighbor and kissed cheeks.

57 Paulus quickly wrapped up his sermon, "Christ came down from heaven. He chose me to bring the good news to you. 58 Keep my words with you. Make ready. He will rise again and we will shine in his light. We will breathe the everlasting breath. 59 I call upon you to live in the Love of Christ. Accept the body

of Christ; His love is life everlasting. Leave the sins of this world behind. Ready yourself for His second coming and live forever in His love." [60] The congregation moved closer to Paulus. Some clapped their hands.

61 "Let us give thanks to Deacon Chloe for her hospitality and leadership. May the blessing of God our Father keep you until the Second Coming of Christ Jesus and we dwell forever in heaven. Amen." [62] The words of their apostle echoed in their ears like an ocean in a seashell. His vision beamed into them a great ray of light, warming them like a delicious wine. [63] They gathered around Paulus. Everyone blessed everyone else. A kiss of peace pressed cheek after cheek.

64 Paulus traveled greatly throughout the Roman world. By dictating to a scribe writing in Greek, he stayed in touch with his congregations. His mission flourished, starting a sect within a sect. [65] Did Cephas appreciate the hard work of Paulus or come to think of the preacher to Goyim as a wolf lurking under the wool of sheep? Did Cephas regret admitting Saul into the fold? [66] The tug of war over the body of Yeshua had begun. Whose Messiah was he? [67] With the foundation of the Christian church our dove traveled greatly with growing wings. [68] Yet Our Spirit mourned the portions of that masonry made of stones corrupt with prohibitions cemented with the prejudices of Paulus.

Notes: 60:3 In the beginning Barnabas stood firmly behind the emissaries. When Cephas paid Saul a visit in Antioch, he refused to eat with Christians not following Jewish laws. Saul argued with Cephas. Barnabas sided with Cephas, causing Saul, for a time, to conform to the will of Cephas. **60:41-56** In part, this paraphrases 13:1-13 from Paul's first letter to the Corinthians.

61 "Damn him!" "What was he thinking?" "He is fortunate he was not torn limb from limb." [2] "Him! They are screaming for our blood!" [3]

"What are we to do?" "Damn him!"

4 The emissaries had called Saul (they did not recognize him as Paulus) to Jerusalem to once again account for his mission among Goyim. 5 Before going to see the emissaries, he took his traveling companion, Trophimus the Ephesian, to see the Temple. 6 They loitered in the Court of Nations. He showed off the different animals for sale and explained the integral part the money changers played in making sacrifices. Paulus haggled over the price of a pigeon.

7 With the bird in hand, Paulus told his companion, "Come. Let us go to the Court of the Israelites. From there we can watch the sacrifice of our bird." 8 Dimitri, who eyed Paulus suspiciously when he first noticed him, overheard their conversation and thought, *Oh no. No!* 9 Judah of Gedor also heard Paulus. The words slapped him, buckling his knees and seizing his tongue. 10 He stood as a statue, staring after them. With great effort Judah waved his hands and yelled. 11 His mouth made only an anguished noise. People nearby stared at Judah. He pointed. They followed his finger, but saw nothing in the crowd that warranted the strangled speech in his throat.

12 Judah found his legs and ran in time to see the two take their first steps onto the Court of Israelites. "No," he screamed, followed by a shrill cry. 13 The knee-length red tunic and shoes of Trophimus easily marked him as a well-to-do Goy. 14 Men in the Court of Israelites and women from their court screamed and cried out. The sky ripped in two. 15 Bodies rushed the blasphemers from everywhere. Fists took to the air landing on the faces and bodies of Paulus and the terrified Trophimus. 16 The two were clawed and pushed around, as if tossed about by a cat intent on playing with their lives before killing them.

17 Trophimus screamed. It sounded as if he were torn in two. No one noticed. With a racing heart, the pigeon escaped from Paulus and flew away. 18 The two blasphemers, flailing

their arms, backed themselves into a corner for some protection. [19] Temple guards rushed in. The fury of fists refused to relent. Worshipers turned into a furious mob determined on vengeance. [20] With the strength of Samson the guards pushed back while two of them escorted the two desecrating men away. The mob shifted and blocked them. [21] In a booming voice that splashed cold water on angry faces, the captain of the guard shouted, "Stop! Stop! No bloodshed! You are desecrating the Temple!" [22] A furious voice shouted back with words accompanied with projectiles of spittle, "The Temple is already defiled! Give them to us!" [23] The captain retorted, his words a flurry of fists, "Would *you* defile the Temple?" With eyes flashing like daggers pointed at one and then another he challenged them, "Would you? Would You?" [24] Drawing himself up tall, he commanded, "No bloodshed! There will be no bloodshed in the Court of Israel. [25] We shall take the blasphemers to the high priest. Justice will be done by the high priest." [26] With that, the mob melted into a crowd easily dispersed. [27] Bloodied and bruised, their tunics torn and robes missing, the two were roughly handed over to the priestly authorities by the Temple guards. [28] Paulus and Trophimus happily entered prison thankful to be alive.

29 Like an arrow through a heart word echoed from ear to ear that the blasphemers were Christians. [30] The emissaries trembled at the perilous position Paulus had placed them in. Many knew that Nazarenes and Christians walked in the same sandals. [31] The emissaries gathered to decide how to handle the wrath of their countrymen, their neighbors, their families. [32] "It is too dangerous to stay here," Cephus bitterly admitted. Thinking the same thought, others sadly nodded. [33] "Where shall we go?" Andreas asked. The question weighed everyone down. [34] Jacob the brother of Yeshua spoke with authority, "We must all go separate

ways. The further away, for now, the better."

35 The Emissary Toma spoke up hopefully, "Perhaps we can just hide in Jerusalem again. This will pass. [36] We faced swords pointed at our chests before and we did not run." [37] Jacob and other emissaries shook their heads. "This is different," Jacob responded. "We are well known now. [38] And desecrating the Temple…" Words escaped him. He could only shake his head once more.

39 "Well, where shall we go," Toma asked. "There are communities of our fellow countrymen that might receive us well," Cephas informed them, [40] "I shall go to Rome, that den of lions. He," pointing to Jacob the brother of Yeshua, "will return to Galilee. [41] From there he can see how well it fares here. When all is well he will let us know it is safe to return." Considering the rest of them he asked, "Where do you wish to go?"

42 "I will go to Phrygia." "I thought I would go to Phrygia!" "It makes more sense for me to go." "Wait, I want to go to Phrygia." "What!?" [43] Words bundled with frustration and fired with anger wrapped the emissaries in a cloud full of lightning. They agreed only on bickering. Tension tightened their hands into fists. [44] Cephas spoke up in thunder until everyone held the silence he demanded. [45] Eyeing them calmly he said, "Let us discuss destinations." He paused. "From them Jacob and I shall choose the ten best places." Another pause. [46] "You will cast lots for them." With authority full in his throat, he finished, "And you go where the Almighty wills you to go." Nodding heads put the plan in action.

Notes: 61:10 The emissaries recalled Saul to Jerusalem to answer for his teachings three times by some accounts. On his last trip, he asked Trophimus the Ephesian to accompany him. Honored, did Trophimus know what he was in for? The mere presence of a Gentile in the Court of the Israelites polluted the Temple. For seven days the House of God and the businesses in the Court of Nations ceased to function while priests performed rituals with blood and water to purify the Temple. Almost beaten to death, Paulus narrowly escaped a judgment to be stoned. Only by claiming his Roman citizenship and asserting his right to a Roman trial was he saved from priestly justice. For two years, he awaited trial in Caesarea before being passed on to Rome, where no great hurry stirred the authorities to try him. What happened to poor Trophimus the Ephesian is unknown. Like Yeshua metaphorically ripping the Temple curtain and separating himself from Sadducee Judaism, the sacrilege of Paulus completed the schism between Christians and Nazarenes. **61:38** When the emissaries decided to spread the New Way to the far corners of the world, Toma, according to one Christian tradition, balked at his lot and refused to go. That night, Yeshua appeared to him and told Toma that he need not doubt the wisdom of his rabbi. He must go to India. Toma refused and pleaded to be sent anywhere but there. The next day, the Emissary Toma went to the market. At high noon, Abbanes, a merchant serving King Gundaphorus of Suren–an Indo-Parthian kingdom–happened to be there also. Yeshua entered the market, approached the merchant, and asked him if he needed a carpenter. Abbanes replied he did. Pointing to Toma, Yeshua claimed he owned a slave skilled in carpentry to sell. They agreed to terms with a bill of sale written and exchanged for coins. Yeshua called Toma over, and Abbanes asked him if this man was his master. Toma replied yes, he was. The emissary found himself bound for India, where his missionary work elevated him to be declared the patron saint of that country in 1972.

62 Bartholomew stretched his old legs. Slipping out of Jerusalem in the dead of night under a sliver of moonlight with the Emissary Judah Thaddaeus, Bartholomew parted company with him at a fork in the road. He then trudged on the back of the day, sustaining himself with figs, almonds, and a little dry white wine sweetened a bit with raisins and cut with water. [2] On and on Bartholomew walked at a steady pace until evening. At a home friendly to Nazarenes, he slept soundly until dawn scrubbed light over the earth and lifted his revived eyelids.

3 He traveled on until he reached Damascus. Over the next few weeks, he joined three different caravans. 4 Though Bartholomew regaled many along the way with tales of his rabbi or spoke in parables or exhorted whoever would listen to the New Way of Our Spirit, he found no companion to sleep by his side. He ate alone. 5 With the last caravan, he passed through the gates of his allotted destination, Vartkesavan in Armenia. 6 Inside the city, Bartholomew set out to find the home of Tov, a merchant who had fallen under the influence of Yeshua during Passover.

7 For most of the past hundred years, Armenia had been ripped into three parts. 8 The Parthians grabbed and clawed from the east, the Romans tore from the west, while the Armenians tightly clutched what remained of their volcanic mountains, high plateaus, and deep river valleys. 9 Several years before the birth of Herod the Great, Tigranes the Great had carried off thousands of Jews to Armenia during the expansion of his kingdom. A great body of Hebrews gathered in Vartkesavan. 10 When Bartholomew entered the city, the power struggle between Rome and Parthia over Armenia had already flared again into armed conflict. 11 The Roman-Parthian War eventually ended in a stalemate that placed a Parthian, approved by Rome, on the Armenian throne. Thus sat Tiridates I.

12 The news of the sacrilegious defiling of the Temple preceded the emissary. He received a cool reception, even from Tov, 13 until his honesty convinced the followers of Yahweh that he too abhorred the conduct of Paulus, the apostate and leader of false Nazarenes. 14 Goyim held no interest for him. He had come to convert those who knew Moses and the law. 15 They would be glad to hear the Good News of the New Way. 16 Walking

around him with suspicious eyes, the community finally accepted his word but shrugged off his teaching.

17 Bartholomew possessed a way with women and managed several converts among them. Widows especially favored him. 18 The Nazarene community he created with the assistance of Tov consisted mostly of the women and a handful of slaves and poor men. 19 In the market square, he often spoke more to the air than to any person bustling about.

20 Bartholomew sighed whenever he thought of Yeshua or his fellow emissaries. Still, he fortified himself with Our Spirit and labored on until one day he discovered the King of Armenia had heard of him. 21 Summoned to the presence of Tiridates, Bartholomew traveled to the foot of Mount Ararat, turned east, and proceeded to Artaxata. 22 Through the whole journey he worried about what to tell the King of Armenia. His experiences with Goyim filled a very small pouch–with a hole in it.

23 The king proved to be attentive. Tiridates listened with the ears of a cat following a mouse behind a curtain. 24 Bartholomew mentioned not the vision of his Messiah for a new Holy Land. 25 Instead, he spoke simply, steadily building to an ecstasy of a righteous life fulfilled with the power of the Holy Spirit. 26 As a Zoroastrian priest, the king discovered a kindred, though alien, spirit. 27 No matter. When in Rome, receiving his crown from the great Caesar Nero, he had learned about the proscription of Christians. 28 As a nod to Rome he thought it a good policy to mark the followers of Yeshua as enemies of his state. After all, how many could there be in Armenia? 29 The audience with Tiridates finished, the king passed a startled Bartholomew to the hands of Polymius, a city official, to carry out a death sentence.

30 Not many in Armenia were skilled in the Phrygian method of execution. The ever-efficient Polymius quickly dragooned a Greek physician, who had worked in

the Roman army. [31] Stripped and his entire body completely shaved, the condemned drank the wine mixed with opium offered to him. This would dull his pain and prolong his endurance. [32] Bartholomew softly told the two guards, Polymius, and the physician that he forgave them before they strapped him tightly to a table. [33] Did the Emissary Bartholomew distract himself with reminiscences of days around a fire with his brethren and Yeshua? Did he sigh over his last goodbyes with them? [34] Stretched out taut, his body sank into itself. "I forgive you," he softly said again.

35 Polymius nodded. The physician, using a small, sharp knife, cut the heel of Bartholomew along the outside of his foot. The body of the emissary screamed and struggled to be free of its restraints. [36] The blade continued to his little toe, around and under the nail, then between each toe until back to the heel. [37] Slowly, meticulously pulling with his fingers and sawing with a longer blade, he skinned the sole of the foot along with each toe. [38] Finished, he held it up like a bloody footprint to the cold stare of Polymius who, with the smallest smile the human face is capable of expressing, acknowledged his approval.

39 One down. Another to go.

40 "I forgive you," mewed out among the shouts to God, grinding teeth, and gasping breath of Bartholomew. [41] The bottoms of the feet exposed and dripping with blood, the physician shook, stopped to calm himself, pulled out the toenails, and flayed the tops of the feet. [42] The body of the old man shivered as he shrieked and groaned. A cry forced its way out through his clenched jaw.

43 The knife then sliced from the outside of the leg to the inside above the knee, then three straight slashes down to the ankle: one cutting over the knee and one sliding down on each side of the leg. [44] Slowly, meticulously pulling with his fingers, he sawed each strip off and held the dripping skin up to Polymius.

45 One done. Another to go.

46 Polymius coldly watched the old body of Bartholomew struggle to breathe. He judged the end was near. 47 Pity. He eagerly anticipated the flaying of genitals, but had other ideas for the final cut.

48 Polymius ordered the physician to strip the head beginning with the top, go down, and finish with the face. 49 His head flayed, Bartholomew gasped out a final forgiveness. 50 The physician quietly sobbed while he patiently and delicately skinned the lined flesh off a quivering face. 51 Polymius nodded to a guard who showed Bartholomew a mirror. 52 The emissary shut his eyes. Polymius ordered his eyelids be sliced off. 53 Bartholomew stared at the bloody mass with two eyes. A shudder rippled through his quivering body. 54 The mirror was taken back. Polymius observed his victim. Care must be taken with delicate matters like this.

55 A rattle gripped the throat of Bartholomew. The physician put his bloody hands to his face. 56 Knowing it was over, the ever-efficient Polymius, who prepared for this moment, directed everyone with his eyes and pointing nose. 57 A guard stepped to the head of the table where he grabbed the ears of Bartholomew and stretched his neck. 58 The other guard, Astyages, drew his sword. With one hew he severed the body of Bartholomew from this life. 59 That evening, the physician drank himself into a stupor. Late at night, Astyages tossed and turned, "I forgive you," echoing through his dreams.

63

There he is! Waving his hands as if chasing flies from his supper, the Emissary Cephas thought after rounding a corner in the market on the Aventine Hill,[2] He had dealt with Simon before. In fact, the problem of Simon preaching falsely had set the wind in the sail of Cephas to come to Rome. [3] Shaking his staff and yelling, Cephas chased away the crowd gathered around the man now known as Simon Magus. [4] Before the astonished mouth of Simon uttered a word, Cephas admonished him, "Simon! What are you doing?"

5 Simon opened his mouth to reply, but Cephas filled it with his words, "This is not the teaching of Yeshua! This is not the New Way! 6 The way of our Holy Breath is open, not secretive and mysterious. What you say is wrong. Wrong! 7 When I told you to repent and find forgiveness, this is not what I meant. Stop what you are doing. 8 You lead the faithful down a wayward path that leads off a cliff. You must stop!" 9 Cephas stared at him hard, "How much are you charging?" Simon drew back as if struck by the staff of Cephas. 10 Noticing the reaction of Simon with surprise, the emissary firmly, calmly insisted, "You must stop what you are saying. Just stop."

11 Simon Magus fixed his hazel gaze at the agitated Rock of Yeshua. "Brother Cephas, you should not trouble yourself. I have changed. 12 After you left Samaria, I fasted and prayed for thirty days. I remembered all the words you shared about the grace of the holy dove. 13 And its wings raised me up!" As if a distant light were growing to a glow, Simon told the emissary, "14 One night while meditating on the Holy Breath of God, I forgave myself. Yeshua came to me and covered me in splendor. He told me what to do, what to say. 15 I wandered from place to place until I found myself in Rome. Here I have dedicated myself to the message my Savior gave me."

16 "If you had a vision of Yeshua, why do your words go against his teaching?" Cephas demanded. "This is not his way! 17 If you seek the truth, listen to us who led you to him. Follow us." Cephas pointed to himself. "What we say holds the words of Yeshua. 18 With our guidance, you can teach among us. You can be a pillar that establishes the throne of Yeshua on this earth."

19 "Do you think Yeshua cares about all of..." The head of Simon tilted and circled with his eyes staring at all around him. The head and eyes of Cephas also circled around until the vision of

the two men locked onto each other again, "...this?" he asked, snapping his fingers. [20] "Yeshua does not care for this world. He will never return." Leaning in closely Simon exalted, "He never left." [21] Thrusting his finger violently through the air, Simon pointed outward, "He is there!" Then pointing to his chest, "He is here! [22] Yeshua came to me so he may shine through me. The way of the inner light is all," he clasped his fists to his chest, "that matters."

[23] They spoke further, but every word between them slipped away like a sly fish from a net. [24] "I must teach what I know to be true," Simon Magus airily pronounced and walked away from Cephas. [25] The Rock of the Messiah stared after him with an open mouth, observed the plain clothes Simon wore, recognized the ecstasy and firmness of his voice, and sighed. Changed, but still so wrong! [26] If a ship cannot be righted, then all in its path or carried in its wake must be cleared away and steered to safe harbor. [27] Saul, too, resided in Rome under house arrest, teaching to Christians. Hah! No need to see him, Cephas snorted to himself. [28] Besides polluting the Temple, this "Paulus" did little to stop the malicious rumor going around that he had denied knowing Yeshua! In the courtyard of Caiaphas! Three times! And to a female servant! [29] No, Cephas thought, Saul can be avoided like a plague. I'll leave him to his rumor-mongering Goyim.

[30] Cephas accustomed himself to Rome. Soon he occupied a space in the marketplace near the Jewish quarter. [31] "Listen to me! I am the rock of my master, the Messiah, come to open the gates of heaven on earth." [32] Pointing to a bystander, "Do you wish to live in heaven on earth?" [33] The man not paying much attention to Cephas, but feeling the wings of his words and the eyes of many people upon him, looked at Cephas and then around at those close to him before pointing to himself. "Yes," Cephas shouted, thrusting his finger further forward. [34] The man quickly considered it,

gingerly nodded, and then loudly exclaimed as he opened his arms to Cephas, "Oh, why not?" He stepped into the crowd as they laughed and applauded.

35 "Good! All you have to do," throwing his arms open to the people gathered around him, "all we all have to do is to live in the breath of Yeshua, who lives in the Holy Breath of God, the breath of bounty and forgiveness." 36 Cephas spoke on and, by the time he finished, a respectable number of people remained around him. 37 He then explained the necessary dietary restrictions and that men must be circumcised. 38 The man Cephas had hailed shouted that he would find heaven on earth somewhere else. Right then and there it occurred to him to go visit a brothel. 39 The crowd laughed and, following their feet, pursued their own business. 40 "You run now, but you will return!" The emissary hurled his words after them. 41 He knew this to be true. Sometimes someone did seek him out to live in the Holy Spirit.

42 In a Jewish home Cephas viewed the congregation with weary eyes. Clearing his throat, he began, 43 "We must have faith. But what is faith? A warm glow inside..." He clasped his hands in fists to his chest. 44 "or words we merely utter?" His right hand opened and the fingers spread out as wings to fly from his chin and mouth. 45 "Our faith works like an ox. If we say we will plant seeds, but do not plant them, our faith carries no saving grace."

46 The congregation looked at the emissary thoughtfully with open mouths. 47 The Rock! The Emissary who had walked and talked with their Master! 48 No doubt the rumors of his betrayal purposefully cast a net to pull him down. 49 For many, however, an original emissary–and of such high esteem–still dazzled their senses.

50 "To possess the Holy Breath of God is to work the Holy Breath of God. What use is it for anyone to live in heavenly light and not share the kindness welling within themselves? 51 We embody our Holy Breath.

Let your light shine so others may see your works; let them witness your good deeds that they may join you. [52] Saving grace is a river. We are the canal from the river to the fields. [53] To stop the flow of the river is to strangle the life of the field, the life of the holy dove. We will live in a barren land. [54] To hold forgiveness and sharing inside is to deny the existence of our breath within the Breath of God. To shutter heavenly light is to withhold the most precious part of yourself. [55] You murder our existence." Cephas paused for effect, observing his listeners.

[56] Encouraged, the smile within him stoked a fire in his spirit that lovingly warmed his eyes. He coughed and then went on, [57] "When someone says, 'I have faith in the grace of the holy dove without works,' they live in a dream world, as if the Kingdom of God exists only in ourselves. [58] Work! Only the Breath of God at work opens the gate to paradise on earth. [59] Anyone who turns his back on the plight of his neighbor or carries griefs of vengeance, that man lives not in everlasting light, but shifting shadows. [60] You are of a wasted and useless generation. Your breath is that of a corpse.

61 "If your circumstances allow you to give only a little, give what you can. Every drop fortifies the river of salvation. [62] For we are all brothers and sisters to each other. And stronger together. [63] If you see your brother or sister clothed in rags and their daily portion of food does not fill their bellies, do not say to them, 'Blessed be you; may you find warmth and bounty,' and walk away. [64] What good have you done them? What good are you in this world? You will never live in Sovereignty.

65 "If you go about with the broken blade of vengeance and you honor a gold goat, what field in paradise do you till? You too are of an unregenerate nation. [66] To receive grace is to share it not only in words, but in deeds." Many in the congregation nodded their approval. [67] "You must do more than mouth holy words. You must take

holy action. ⁶⁸ To speak of generosity without the works of generosity is to stab Forgiveness and Charity in the back. ⁶⁹ If you do not provide for the needs of your brothers and sisters, if your forgiveness is a hollowed-out smile with nothing to support it, there is no Breath of God in you. You have gutted the holy dove.

70 "You may find days when your efforts lie futile like hyacinths bowed down in a terrible storm, and doubts run madly within you. Then rest in your faith. ⁷¹ I assure you, you are never alone. The breath of Yeshua, through the Holy Breath of God, lives within you. ⁷² The works of your brethren, even from a distance, reach out to you as the rays of the distant sun. Nothing separates us."

73 The fire within him burned his words rising as smoke from an offering. ⁷⁴ "Therefore I tell you, put your faith in your work and your work in your faith. ⁷⁵ The labors of saving grace exalt our existence. ⁷⁶ Worshipping a gold goat within you scatters bitter seeds. The poor are fed tares and chaff. Bounty is a feast spread out to nourish all. ⁷⁷ Forgiveness is the balm and myrrh that cleans wounds from sin. With Forgiveness all injuries heal wrapped in peace to make us whole. ⁷⁸ Like libanos, mercy and sharing purify our bodies. Together they make a paradise on Earth.

79 "Our community is for us to create." The face of Cephas glowed. The faces before him reflected like indomitable candles no wind could snuff out. ⁸⁰ "Works are the fruit of the holy dove. Our good deeds fortify and generate more works of generosity and forgiveness. ⁸¹ The stronger we are, the stronger the holy dove." The fingertips of Cephas pressed against his chest. ⁸² "Our breath needs to act to live. When our acts are of the Breath of God, we live in the Kingdom of God." ⁸³ His broad smile took them all in. Though small, this was a good congregation. Cephas felt a moment of delicious satisfaction.

Notes: 63:1 In Samaria, Simon of Gitta made a good living performing many acts of mystic magic. He became famous as Simon the Sorcerer. Philip the Evangelizer, a student accepted by the emissaries, visited and converted many in Samaria. To the words of Philip, the ears of Simon opened as if he were hearing for the first time. He accepted baptism. Discovering that many had been baptized but not filled with the Holy Breath, Cephas and Yohanan hurried to Samaria. They taught and imparted the Holy Breath by laying their hands on the faithful. With eyes stretched open with opportunity and carrying a pouch with an expansive mouth eager to swallow the jingle of coins, Simon offered Cephas thirty pieces of silver to give him the power to impart the Holy Breath with his hands. Cephas cast him out as a sinner of simony. **63:3** Magus is the singular of Magi. The Magi are Zoroastrian priests. **63:6** What Simon Magus preached became known as Gnosticism. Miryam, Phillip, Toma, Judah Iscariot, and others are credited as authors of gospels deemed to be Gnostic works. A majority of bishops voted to exclude them from the New Testament at the Council of Nicaea for a few reasons. The canonical gospels of Matthew, Mark, Luke, and John proclaim Yeshua manifested the Kingdom of God on earth. The Gnostic writings concern themselves not with this earth, but with returning to the spiritual world. The canonical gospels connect Yeshua to the traditions and history of David's kingdom while the gnostic works portray him as completely separate from them. Perhaps the best reason for excluding these works was that Gnostic means "secret knowledge." Their books were intended to impart wisdom to a chosen few as opposed to the canonical gospels advocating an open message for all to find grace. **63:28** For Cephas to betray his rabbi would be damning enough; to do so three times–a magical number representing wholeness–and to a servant woman, a social subordinate both as a servant and a woman, would have completely destroyed his reputation to any who believed the rumor.

64 Cephas spent the next two years in the marketplace by the Jewish quarter, or speaking to groups in homes, or welcoming new arrivals to Rome. ² Rome, the center of The Internal Sea, cosmopolitan Rome, a strange home for an old emissary to labor in, harvesting for the Kingdom of God in a new Israel. ³ The task proved to be endless, since many tongues of Rome wagged many different ways to carry many people down many erroneous paths.

4 Cephas worked tirelessly against a mischievous wave throwing thousands of misled worshipers, like starfish onto a beach. ⁵ Running hither and thither, he tossed wayward sinners back into the waters of redemption. ⁶ For every three he saved, laughing snarls of waves hurled seven more wayward Nazarenes onto the shore. Cephas ate and slept in snatches.

7 Had Rome not burned, perhaps the accomplishments of Cephas would have immortalized him with his fellow Yahwehists in Jerusalem. ⁸ Nero, though popular, proved incapable of fiddling away the whispering suspicions that he had started the Great Fire. ⁹ As public opinion raged against him, the Most Honorable Caesar pointed to the Christians, and Roman mobs gleefully followed his fishy allegation. ¹⁰ This was the first time Romans persecuted those "haughty cannibals," but many more opportunities were to follow.

11 With a shrug and a grin, the soldiers granted Cephas his request to be crucified upside down. On a crux decussata they fastened his ankles and wrists near the Colosseum along the Via Sacra, lined with other crucified Christians. ¹² On the first day, many people stopped to enjoy the spectacle of suffering. After the third day, the crucified blended into the scenery. ¹³ People returned to their daily habit of walking up and down the Via Sacra to go where they wanted to go and do what they needed to do. ¹⁴ By the end of a week, birds held a feast. They could not eat fast enough; rotting corpses needed to be disposed of.

15 When the soldiers fastened Cephas to his cross, he viewed with no regret the path that led to setting him on his head. Though trembling like a dog threatened to overwhelm him, the burning brands of his faith chased

the demon away. [16] Fastened to his cross, did his mind wander to his rabbi, to his fellow emissaries? Did he contemplate their lives together? Did he know how his brother and the others fared?

17 Certainly Cephas knew of Jacob, the younger of the two "sons of thunder," the first emissary to be martyred twenty years ago. Twenty years. [18] His execution happened in part due to his fiery temper. Jacob lost his head in an argument with Herod Agrippa. [19] It is uncertain whether he won the argument. Agrippa, however, made certain that a sharp blade finished the discussion and the Emissary Jacob.

20 What tidings about the other emissaries pulsed with the throbbing blood in the head of Chephas? How often did they communicate with one another? [21] Philip left Jerusalem, returned to Phrygia, and zealously spread the word of Our Spirit. With Christianity outlawed, he made little headway except among the poor. [22] When he finally managed to reach upper society by converting the wife of the proconsul of Hierapolis, his success cost Philip his head.

23 Having preached a great deal in Syria, Toma spent the last two decades of his life in India, where he converted many people. [24] Success, of course, creates attention that can produce adverse consequences. Royalty beckoned and took him to their bosom. [25] King Misdeus, following the conversions of his wife, Queen Tertia, his son, Juzanes, his sister-in-law, Princess Mygdonia, and her friend Markia, ordered four soldiers to lead Toma to a nearby hill outside of the city and demonstrate his displeasure at the tips of their spears.

26 When the emissaries scattered from Jerusalem to spread the word of Yeshua and our dove, Simon the Zealot twice ventured across Mare Bretannicum to Britain. [27] He hoped a smaller community of Jewish Roman soldiers, slaves, and traders might form into the Nazarene Community Yeshua had al-

ways longed for. ²⁸ Radiating from Britain, the Kingdom of God might still be realized in Israel.

29 Pomponia Graecina, wife of Aulus Plautius, governor of Britain, heard of Simon the Zealot and, out of curiosity, summoned him. ³⁰ A spark in his speeches captivated her. His words rolled over her like warm soothing oil. ³¹ Back in Rome several years after leaving Britain, she and her friend Poppaea Sabina faced charges of "foreign superstition." Both were acquitted. ³² It is believed Simon the Zealot died naturally and quietly in Edessa in northern Greece.

33 It was said from ear to ear, many years after learning from Yeshua on Mount Tabor, that Judah Thaddaeus proved his devotion before meeting his end at the sharp edge of an ax. ³⁴ Remarkably, Andreas preached all the way into Scythia and Byzantium. He too supposedly found his martyrdom on a crux decussata in Greece. ³⁵ All that is truly known about Jacob the Just is that the sturdy arms of Jewish orthodoxy almost certainly stoned him for preaching the New Way in Jerusalem.

36 Whether Cephas knew of his fellow emissaries from rambling rumors or reliable sources–or knew at all–is impossible to tell. For most of Yeshua's students, history swallowed them up among nameless multitudes. ³⁷ Their lives can be found, as if on a busy beach after everyone is gone, their steps lost indistinguishably among the crowded bustle of trampled sand. ³⁸ Yet the breath moving their beliefs, still revels in the tides of Our Spirit.

39 In a delirium Cephas saw Saul being led to his execution. Saul ran to Cephas, knelt down beside him, and held his head up with a gentle hand. ⁴⁰ Each peering into the eyes of the other, their dreams collided. "How could you," Cephas scolded. ⁴¹ "You stole our dream, the Kingdom of God, the vision of Yeshua, our rabbi. How could you? How…?" The words of Cephas choked in his throat as he scoured the face of Saul.

42 Paulus answered, "I followed your way, and it led only to a wall too steep to climb and too thick to penetrate. What could I do, Cephas? What else could I do? 43 I made the dream bigger. Instead of Jews and Israel, it is anyone with faith and the entire world." 44 Cephas spoke with words carrying swords, "Our God is not a God for anyone! There is a covenant!" 45 "A covenant fulfilled by faith," Paulus calmly retorted. Pointing with his eyes at the bodies hanging from crosses, "Look, Cephas, see all the Christians! Listen! That is not the wind! Hear their groans." 46 Cephas turned his head to the left and to his right. His head filled with the sound of suffering. The words of Paulus sank into him like a sword. 47 "How many have foreskins, Cephas, and how many are circumcised?" He paused, "You know the answer." Nodding, Paulus said again with feet firmly on the ground, "You know the answer. 48 I do not beg for your forgiveness, Cephas; I ask for your understanding." Pointing with his right finger, he declared, "They deserve it!"

49 Locking his eyes onto the eyes of Cephas, Paulus continued "Now no matter how many of us they murder, the Breath of God will pass from generation to generation through the body and blood of Yeshua. 50 One day through the bounty and mercy of the holy dove, Yeshua will return and establish the Kingdom of God. 51 In the name of our master who died and with his resurrection showed us the way to eternal life, is there no room for all the faithful in the Kingdom of God?"

52 The face and hand of Paulus disappeared. The head of Cephas dropped. He looked up at the hanging bodies surrounded by the smoldering ruins of Rome. Their moaning and cries filled his spirit, Our Spirit. 53 For the first time, hanging several crosses away from him, he noticed Chloe, her back whipped raw, the front of her body facing the cross. 54 Cephas raised his head and hoarsely blessed those struggling on their crosses. Dropping his

head he forgave the bustling feet on the busy pavement. [55] Cephas extended the grace of Our Spirit to everyone until he had no voice left. [56] On soaring wings our dove grew and diminished with possibilities at the death of each Christian. [57] Would they, as exemplars of Our Spirit, inspire others to follow the New Way? Or would their faith be marginalized–or even face extinction–as has been the fate of so many other religions?

Notes: 64:2 The Romans called the Mediterranean Sea, the "Internal Sea" or "Mare Nostrum," Our Sea. **64:8** The Great Fire, occurring in the tenth year of Nero's reign of almost fourteen years, destroyed two-thirds of Rome. Long before the slaughter of Christians, Tiberius tried to legalize their religion as a counterweight to querulous Judaism. The Senate, aghast at the eating and drinking of the body and blood of Yeshua along with Christian unwillingness to make sacrifices to Augustus as a God, refused to countenance the legitimacy of their worship. Succeeding Caesars ignored the Christians until Nero. For the next 250 years, the Gentile worshipers of Yahweh, through Yeshua, remained oppressed and suffered martyrdom as occasions warranted. Yet their resilience and compassion laid seeds that bore fruit as more and more Gentiles joined them. Finally, the Emperor Constantine declared Christianity the official religion of the Roman Empire. It did not take long for the tables to shift, much to the wagging of Our Spirit's head, and Christians persecuted Pagans, heretics, and eventually Jews. **64:11** A crux decussata is shaped like an X. **64:18** By this time the kingdom of Herod Agrippa, once again called the Kingdom of Judea) extended over an area as large as that ruled by his grandfather, Herod the Great. It was his son and daughter, Herod Agrippa II and Bernice, who dealt with Paulus in Caesarea over his defiling the Temple. Bernice had an affair with Titus, the Roman general who destroyed Jerusalem and later ascended to be the tenth Most Notable Caesar. To become emperor, he needed to separate from Bernice because the Romans did not accept a foreigner as a suitable wife for a Caesar. Notably, Vesuvius erupted during his reign. Unable to prevent Zealots from starting a rebellion, Agrippa II, who succeeded his father, fought alongside Titus. The First Jewish-Roman War ended with the destruction of Herod's Temple and the mass suicide of Jews at Masada. **64:20** There is little documentation of the emissaries' lives. The earliest account, the Acts of the Apostles, was likely written 50 years after the crucifixion. **64:31** Poppaea Sabina married at the age of fourteen. This marriage produced one child and ended in divorce. Sometime later, Nero executed her ex-husband. She next married Otho, a close friend of Nero's. While she was carrying Nero's child, the emperor forced Otho to divorce her. The baby, Claudia, lived only a few months. (Nero divorced and later executed his barren wife–who was also his stepsister–in order to marry Poppaea.) Sent to govern a remote province, Otho joined Galba's insurrection against Nero. Nero committed suicide. Galba became emperor but was quickly assassinated. Otho then became emperor. In the western provinces the soldiers of Vitellius declared him emperor. After a bloody battle, Otho's forces retreated. Reinforced, his army wanted to continue the fight but Otho told them, "It is better for one to die for many, than the many for one." Retiring to his tent, Imperator Marcus Otho Caesar Augustus stabbed himself in the heart. Three years before Nero's suicide, Poppaea, noted for her patronage of Judaism, died from complications of her third pregnancy. **64:32** Several hundred years after the missions of Simon the Zealot, Christianity took root in Britain thanks to missionaries like St. Augustine. **64:39** As a Roman citizen, the self-appointed Emissary Paulus could not be crucified. Most likely he was beheaded. **64:53** Crucifying a woman was rare. No doubt the outrage over the fire and Chloe's significant position in the church resulted in her crucifixion. Had she stayed in the East with Barnabas, she would have avoided this persecution. Left to his own devices, Barnabas returned to baptizing only converted Jews. Today there are 300,000 Messianic Jews. Everyone, except themselves, considers them a Christian sect.

65 Judah Iscariot tended his field. He had bought it with several pieces of silver. Turning his head from the living, he occupied himself with death. ² Judah gathered the dead poor, discarded as if they were broken pots. Washing and purifying their bodies, the former emissary sowed them, with grace, in his field. [3] Their bereft kin wept their gratitude to him. Their tears offered up all they could afford. Judah wept with them.

4 On a day when the sun lay light on the earth like the fingers of a carpenter stroking wood being worked on, Judah, preparing a plot for burial, was startled by the appearance of Yeshua. [5] In each hand Yeshua held a ripped half of the Temple curtain. With the halves as wings, Yeshua circled many times, smiling on the field of Judah before landing near him. [6] Judah reached out. Yeshua turned to blood and dissolved with the wind. The wind turned and blew a great gust into the face of Judah. [7] The warm blast carried the breath of the words both he and Yeshua whispered simultaneously into the ear of the other after Judah kissed him: "Be strong." Judah sat down and wept.

8 Over and over a dream occupied his nights and harried portions of his day. Sometimes, while eating, the dream hit him and stopped the mouthing of his meal cold. [9] In his dream Judah lay in the ground under a persea tree in a cradle of roots with his arms crossed. Eyes excitedly open, he stared through the trunk into limbs stretching into, instead of leaves, an expansive cloud of stars– the greatness of boundless Sovereignty. [10] In the midst of Elyon, the seventh of the seven heavens, God shines as three shades while the three shades blend as one from within and without, a splendor wrapped in mysteries. [11] The stars of the persea tree wafted as shoots of smoke where the light of God spun as a seed that took root and transformed into the Tree of Life. Three as one, one as three thrived as the tree of existence. [12] One light branching from the tree, *ra*, fundamentally composes all that exists–all the properties of space and tree from atoms to flesh of wood, leaf, and fruit. [13] Gleaming with identity, *ka* uniquely stamps each star and ter-

restrial body, every individual singularity of the tree. [14] Idea or tribal identity, *ba,* penetrates as a force illuminating and radiating from within and without. [15] Three lights in one, one light in three transcend in harmony or trample in discord as land and sea and space and all life.

16 Among the limbs of swaying fruit radiating starshine, Judah observed many wafting phantoms. Richly colored willful ignorance crushed wood, leaf, and fruit it coiled around while filling its fangs with venom. Nuzzling against flesh, a ram drooled in a cushioned corner. [17] A trembling dog shivered in every shadow. Wrath as a bull stomped to and fro and up and down, or hunted as a sharp-toothed wolf. A spectrum of hope stretched from limb to limb. [18] The excitement of death, twiddling thoughts, sat in cold isolation. All smiles and with tail fanned open, the cry of a strutting peacock echoed against the horizon. A voiceless raven sat on an abandoned branch bathing wounded wings with bitter water. [19] In velvety colors our graceful dove flew from branch to branch.

20 Judah held a star in one hand and a planet in the other as different but the same fruit. He crushed them. Their pulp squished between his clenched fingers. The star then dried like a dead leaf, crumpled and shattered like thin glass in the palm of his hand. [21] The mash and shards glowed. His hands turned into balls of fire. [22] Judah stretched out his arms and beacons of light sparkled, emanating grace. The light grew up his arms, consumed his body, and adhered to the tree as drops of rain.

23 Three lights as one, one light as three meld and shine distinctly and center creation everywhere. The tree of existence, of God, of *ra, ka,* and *ba* drops leaf and fruit. They scatter. [24] God is the air, the land, and the sea. All creatures are God. Whatever exists is God. All light shines as God. Every shadow hides with God.

25 Under the persea tree Judah closed his eyes and swallowed the Sover-

eignty as Sovereignty devoured him. A breath crowned the head of the tree and whispered, [26] "Butcher of life, from where do you come? Oh conqueror of earth and time, where are you going?" [27] The *ka* of Judah stood up and answered, "With dust of *ra* I issue. With the breath of *ba* I ramble. What intended to destroy me is at rest. What turns me about is no longer a part of me. [28] My ambition precedes me and rots in my grave. My pain is no longer a plank in my sight. [29] From God I was released into God. Eon holds me. This world no longer carries any meaning for my flesh. [30] From this day on, from every season forward I will reap my time in silence. My sustenance is *ra*. My *ka* rests. My *ba* moves with the breath of Yohanan and Yeshua and the holy dove."

31 All his days Judah withered and thrived in the spell of his dream. He lived daily as if his life was a fresh breeze. [32] There are those who say an accident while working his field ripped open his bowels. Others clap their hands and say he hung himself from a tree chattering with demon tongues. Rumor whispers he slipped off to Egypt never to be heard from again. [33] Wherever and whatever his last day, certainly, when he died, more than a few of the poor gathered to wash and purify the body of Judah to be interred in his field of broken pots.

Notes: 65:11 The persea tree is in the avocado family. The tree, sacred to the ancient Egyptians, was called ished, the "tree of life." After Alexander the Great conquered Egypt and the Greek Ptolemies ruled the country, they named the tree after one of their great heroes, Perseus. Chief among his adventurous deeds was the slaying of Medusa.

66

After many emissaries scattered over the world, a small group gathered in the village of Bethany near Jerusalem, under the roof of the father of Rachel. There the sister of Yeshua stood, Miryam Magdalene by her side, in the midst of women and children. [2]

With the eyes of a turtle peeping out from its shell, Miryamla looked at the faces staring up at her. ³ A baby began to fuss in the cradled arms of her mother. A little mouth wailed until breast milk satisfied gnawing hunger. ⁴ "Do you, do you know…about my brother, Yit…Yeshua?" She stammered but then continued more firmly, "How he wore out sandal after sandal to reclaim his life by redeeming others?" ⁵ She inhaled. When Miryamla spoke again, a tongue of fire danced on her words. "And how he sacrificed his life to show us how to live in the Kingdom of God?

6 "Though cradled by my mother and raised by my kind father, still he defied their love for him. Troublesome demons settled on him early and often. ⁷ When our cousin, Yohanan the Baptist, washed sins away in the River Jordan, he roused the blessed dove of forgiveness. ⁸ How many people did Yohanan inflame with the Breath of God?" Miryamla swept the room with her question before settling her eyes on Rachel. "Many. Many people," she paused, "and Yeshua was one of them too.

9 "My brother then worked the Holy Breath as no other did. He taught the grace of forgiveness and sharing. And with that power he wrested demons from the sick. ¹⁰ The lame walked. The mute spoke. The dead rose to live again. Yeshua pulled us up from fouled wells to reveal the Kingdom of God reigns inside us." ¹¹ Miryamla softly beat her closed hands against her chest, "It is here! All we have to do is live it; dwell in it as Yohanan and my brother did. ¹² When we live in the Breath of God, we become one with the Holy Breath." ¹³ She paused and felt searching eyes watching her. "We are the Holy Breath."

14 Miryamla pointed to a wall with her finger, "They cut off the head of Yohanan." ¹⁵ "They hung," she swallowed and composed herself, "Yeshua from a cross." Once she released those terrible words, Miryamla continued with the urgency of a bird, long in pregnancy, building a

nest, [16] "Still they could not kill their breath because their breath was one with the Breath of God." [17] "They cannot stop us. They can kill our bodies. They cannot kill the Holy Breath within us."

18 Miryam paused and enhaled as if fetching water from a deep well to quench a parched thirst. "When my brother Yeshua died, I hated him for what he did to my family, what he did to me. [19] My mother wanders around the house. She picks at her meals. [20] My father works and works and works; the wood absorbs his sweat and tears. When he finishes his day, he can barely hold a cup. [21] My grief cut me, and the hurt bled into my every breath. Living within death, I worked my loom, but nothing came out right.

22 Then I heard from others, Yeshua appeared to them. I could not believe my ears. [23] When he told them, among other things, that his step would always be by their side, I fell to my knees. I wailed through the night. I grieved through my days. [24] The pain of loss gutted me like a miscarriage." Why did he have to die? Why did he not come back to me or anyone in our family? Why did he utterly abandon us?

25 "I died the day Yeshua died. And yet I lived. [26] Like bread dough my breath lay folded over and beaten again and again. A dough too dry to pull together, I crumbled and lay helpless. [27] Alive and yet dead, I did not know what to do with myself. Alive but numb, I lived in a world that did not wholly exist. [28] In a veil of grief I turned away from friends and family. It was as if I lived in my tomb, a shadow world where a sharp-toothed wolf, with hungry red eyes and foul breath, ravaged me.

29 "I ate little, slept on stormy waves, until one night the breath of my brother visited me. He came to me not as a shade, but as himself as he lived." [30] Her words opened wide the eyes of the people in the packed room leaning towards her. "He showed me his wounds, still open and bloody. [31] Taking off his crown of thorns, he

placed it on my head. I shrieked and he laughed. ³² In his teasing voice he asked, 'Why do you wear thorns on your head?' ³³ I then realized I wore not his crown of thorns, but my own. A crown of biting anger I made and placed on my head. ³⁴ Not until I found the strength to forgive him," Miryamla paused, "and to forgive myself," faces opened kindly toward her, "did the grace of the holy dove remove the sharp nail of grief from my eye.

35 "I saw my brother within the heavenly light. I embraced him, and I too stood within the light ³⁶ He lifted off the crown of thorns from my head. Threw it on the ground. It shattered. ³⁷ His life, his sacrifice showed me how to cast out the demons that tortured me. ³⁸ I no longer walked through the valley with the ground trembling by the pounding hooves of snorting bulls. Now my brother walked with me. ³⁹ Now I rejoice in us. I feel my cousin beside me. I feel my brother beside me. I feel all of us as one breath and I am raised up.

40 "Sisters, I am here to praise living under the wings of the blessed dove. Join me; stand in the waters of redemption with Yohanan; work the fields of plenty with Yeshua; be as one with the light of the world. ⁴¹ When I hear the wind moan at night, I know it is the Breath of God carrying the lives of those beaten by rods of Shemyaza. ⁴² The many demons live off our breath. They possess us to work their evil. ⁴³ When greed dazzles your eyes like a gold goat, and hate feeds on you like a sharp-toothed wolf, you are dead inside. Through us demons live. ⁴⁴ And the greatest death is to be poisoned by a vicious snake of mindless ignorance. When you purposely turn your back to the Breath of God, when you shut your eyes to eternal light, you commit a great sin and live among the dead.

45 "Our bounty, no matter how meager or great, can be shared, our hate buried and left behind. ⁴⁶ A vicious snake wraps like a serpent around our rainbow. Its

venom sickens our prayers. [47] The will of the serpent crucified Yeshua. It may crucify us. [48] Only by living with the breath of Yeshua will the heavenly light shine. They can never extinguish our great light. [49] The Holy Breath began with the first word of God in creating the heavens and earth. So the Holy Breath lives in all things.

50 Accordingly, the Holy Breath in sun and rain nurtures fields to grow wheat. So also the Holy Breath in flowers gives to the bee to make honey. [51] So we, living within the Holy Breath, must sustain each other to live in the Kingdom of God. You are my sisters. [52] We are one family in the Breath of God. We must live, must care for each other as one family."

53 The words of Miryamla hummed around the room. Those attending to her words grew strong. She gathered them like seashells, treasures of humanity that had been trampled on a beach. [54] Smiling with eyes glazed with grace, Miryamla opened her arms, arms limned with Our Spirit. She embraced all within and beyond the reach of outstretched fingers. [55] Miryam Magdalene silently smiled like the warmth of a sunrise. Rachel clasped her hands to her breast and swayed. Others stood and lifted their hands. [56] Each person rose as a candle; a new vision danced like a stubborn flame refusing to be blown out.

57 The Holy Breath, Our Spirit, invigorated with many lives past and present shining from the wilderness, illuminates dense thickets of weeds and many colorful gardens of splendor.

Our Spirit

0
Our Spirit began before words existed.
We commenced when elements first bonded,
creating a fast fellowship, spiraling,
generating fire and, hurling through ages,

swirling matter in bursts of light. Gathered
rubble spun into planets; moisture swarmed;
beneficent heat grew microbe cultures.
Cellular colonies teemed to transform
into bodies starved with nettles of needs.
We endure to sustain community:
seek and crawl through wilderness of harsh truths;
navigate suspicious seas; bridge absurd
and grisly chasms. In a torn and smashed world,
we absolve and provide for union with grace.

i a
All too well in dazzle of a dreamy
day, demonic demonstrations spiral
loose; skilled whirlwinds of defilement will snatch
you up and spin your life out of control.

A time may come when your days no longer
fill with foolish filth and desecration.
When foul winds of error stand at ease, which
way walks from wreckage of your world? Will you
give up false idols; surrender to work
waves of boundless charity and goodwill?

i b
When your virtuous hold chokes delinquent
necks, when color hangs crazed in your mind's eye,
your blood-soaked hands pollutes the air you breathe;
when hunger-wail of a child no longer
touches you and your hoard of wealth piles on
gold gouged from decay of teeth, your haughty
whirlwind of vile righteousness will catch you.

Which way remains from havoc you wrought? Will
you smash cruel idols; submit to working
ways of endless largesse and forgiveness?

i c
our breathing exalts with our spirit's breath.
solar winds blowing moist air carry us.
infinite fundaments of motion spin
our bound and endless lives. what'll we become?

where are we going? myths of destiny
wink at our destination; for it's not
the end, savor the way: learning is all.
we evolve as sentient float, driven drift
prone to bend in twists and spirals a way
prevailing with primal waves of light, works
twined with eternal giving and mercy.

Appendix

Final Note: There are well over two dozen Protestant and more than a dozen authorized Catholic translations of the Bible into English. Several are of excellent quality considering literary style and literal faith to the original Greek, Aramaic, and Hebrew texts. Two translations have been recently updated: in 2021 New Revised Standard Version (NRSVue) and in 2020 the New American Standard Bible (NASB2020). Bible Gateway is a superb and free online resource for many translations.

The first two English translations, however, did not fare well for the translators. A linguist and Bible scholar, William Tyndale, while visiting Antwerp to see a friend who betrayed him, was tried as a heretic in 1536 for translating the Bible without the blessing of the Church. His guilt a foregone conclusion, Tyndale was executed at a stake by strangulation and his corpse set on fire. The stench of burnt flesh and smoke rose in the crisp autumn air. Four years after Tyndale's execution, King Henry the VIII, as the head of the Anglican Church of England established in 1534, approved four more translations based on his work. Here is John 1.1 from the Tyndale Bible: "In the beginnynge was the worde and the worde was with God: and the worde was God."

John Wycliff, a Catholic priest and theological professor at the University of Oxford, oversaw the first English translation of the Bible. This led to the Lollard reform movement that rejected many teachings of the Catholic Church. In 1408, a synod decreed in the Constitutions of Oxford that all unlicensed translations of the Bible and their proliferation outside the clergy were dangerous fallacies. Any unauthorized translator would be charged with the crime of heresy. The Council of Constance in 1415 declared Wycliff a heretic, ordered his body exhumed (He died in 1384.) and his translations burned. In 1428 the remains of Wycliff were finally raised and consumed in fire, his ashes flung to scatter in the Swift River. Here is an example from an edition of the Wycliff Bible, Genesis 1.3 "And God seide, Liȝt be maad; and liȝt was maad."

The first known depiction of Yeshua, "Alexandro worshiping his God," is a satirical piece of graffiti denigrating Alexandro for his Christianity. Yeshua, on a cross, has the head of a donkey. In ancient Rome donkeys were symbols of service and humility. They were also sacred to Vesta, the virgin Goddess of family, home, and hearth. It was the braying of a donkey that woke and saved her from being raped. None-the-less, a servile and humble God would have struck many Roman minds as preposterous. This picture, converted to black and white, taken from Wikimedia Commons, is of an etching in plaster on a wall in Rome made sometime in the first century.

The earliest known drawing that venerates Yeshua, depicts him healing the paralytic in Kfar Nahum. This is from the third century in a baptistry in an abandoned church in Syria–note Yeshua's short hair, clean shaven face, and Roman attire. This, converted to black and white, is a cropped picture of the drawing currently hanging in the Yale University Art Gallery.

A rendering of Herod's Temple, cropped and converted to black & white, taken from Wikimedia Commons.

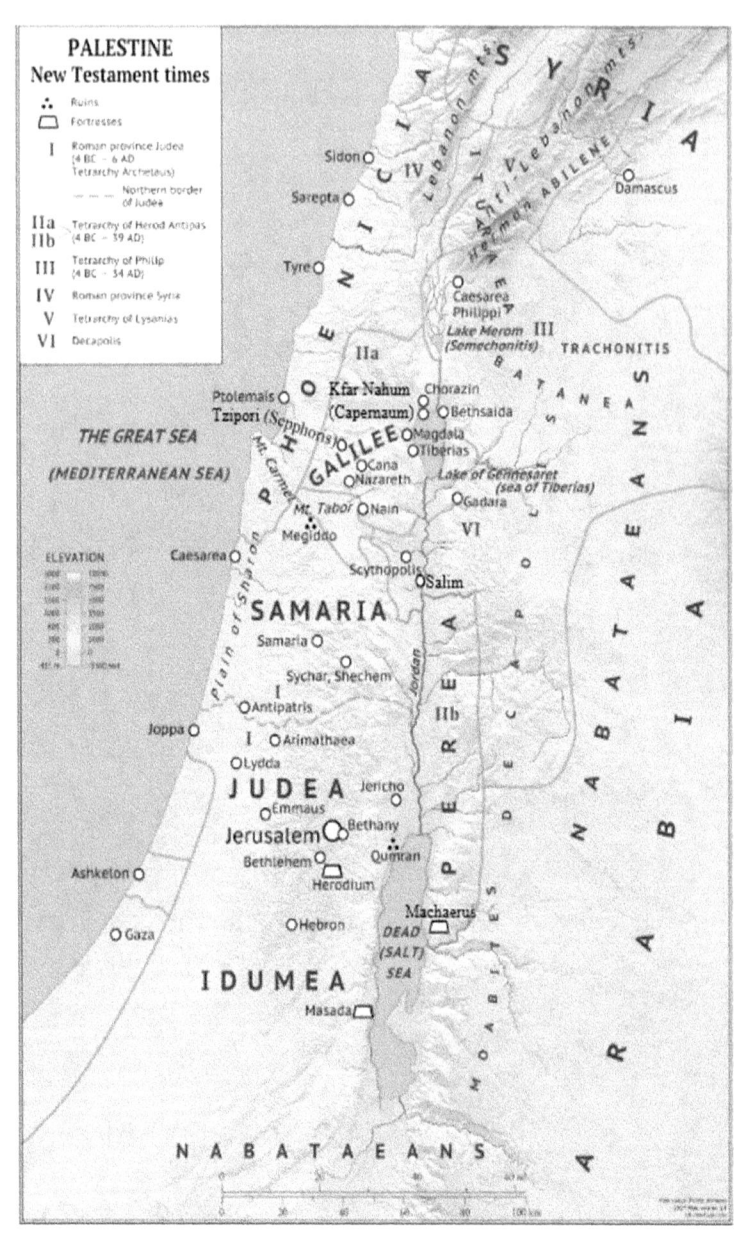

Converted to black & white and altered, this map was taken from churchmaps.info

Por favor (an author's plea)

If *The Book of Yeshua* was a gratifying & gladsome experience for you, please rate and write a couple of sentences about it on the following platforms: Amazon, Goodreads, LibraryThing, Book Riot. It is perfectly acceptable to copy and paste your review from one platform to another. Please also share your thoughts on any social media you are on.

With great appreciation,

Randy

www.ingramcontent.com/pod-product-compliance
Lightning Source LLC
LaVergne TN
LVHW010159070526
838199LV00062B/4415